G000123318

Collection

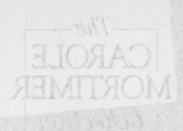

LADY SURRENDER

LADY SURRENDER

BY
CAROLE MORTIMER

MILLS & BOON LIMITED
Eton House, 18–24 Paradise Road
Richmond, Surrey TW9 1SR

First published in Great Britain 1985 by Mills & Boon Limited

© Carole Mortimer 1985

Australian copyright 1985 Philippine copyright 1985 Reprinted 1985 This edition 1991

ISBN 0 263 77556 9

Set in Monophoto Plantin 11 on 11 pt. 19-9110-44822

Made and printed in Great Britain

For John,
Matthew and Joshua

CHAPTER ONE

CHARLY barely had time to click back the lock on the apartment door before it was pushed forcibly open, knocking her off-balance as she grabbed at the towel she had quickly draped about herself when the doorbell rang seconds ago, having to get out of the shower to answer it.

The man who had pushed his way in towered over her five foot frame, but there was still challenge in her wide grey eyes as she looked up at him, successfully hiding her nervousness at this intrusion. 'I don't know who you are——'

'No,' he acknowledged harshly. 'But I know who you are!' His aggressive accent was definitely American.

'Obviously,' she drawled. 'If you're after money or jewellery I think I should tell you I don't have any here.'

His green-eyed gaze raked over her contemptuously. 'Women like you only have one jewel, lady, and even that gets tarnished after a while.'

Charly gasped at the crude insult, all nervousness fading. 'If you want to take what valuables there are then do so and leave,' she instructed haughtily.

His mouth twisted. 'You're pretty free with what doesn't belong to you, aren't you?' he scorned derisively. 'But then you have no idea of morality, do you?'

'I beg your pardon!' She raised light brown

7

brows indignantly, their indistinctive colour
making it difficult to tell whether the hair
beneath the second towel she had draped around
her wet hair was blonde, brunette, or auburn, or
a mixture of all three.

'I'm not the one you should be apologising
to——'

'Are you some sort of political fanatic?' Charly
frowned suspiciously.

'Hell, no!'

'Then what do you want? If it's me, I ought to
tell you I've been taught self-defence.'

'Lady, I wouldn't care if you were a judo and
Kung Fu expert rolled into one,' he dismissed
harshly. 'I'm not about to let a five foot nothing
woman defeat me in achieving what I came here
to do!'

As he must have stood about six foot four, was
deeply muscled beneath the pale green shirt and
leather jacket, his legs lean and strong beneath
black trousers, and her self-defence classes had
been nowhere near as expert as judo or Kung Fu,
he could be right! But she wasn't about to let him
know that. 'My husband is in the bedroom,' she
told him firmly, hoping the classical lie in a
situation like this sounded more convincing to
him than it did to her.

The green eyes became contemptuous. 'You
don't have a husband of your own, only someone
else's—and I happen to know he's out of town!'

Charly gave an irritated frown. 'Are you sure you
have the right apartment?' Maybe they could laugh
together about this once he realised his mistake—
but she doubted it. This man was beyond a joke,
and the situation wasn't at all funny!

In other circumstances she might even have thought him attractive. He had a certain rakish appearance, casually styled black hair, a reckless light in those deep green eyes, his mouth firmly sculptured, his jaw square, his lean body obviously kept in physical health, although the cynicism in his expression wasn't quite as attractive, or the derision for her he didn't try to hide behind politeness.

'This is Matt Parker's apartment, isn't it?' he rasped.

'Yes,' she frowned.

'And you are Charly, aren't you?'

She stiffened. 'Only my friends are allowed to call me that.'

He gave her a contemptuous look. 'And I'm sure there are a lot of them, honey—all male!'

She drew in an angry breath. 'I don't know if you mean to be insulting——'

'Oh, I do,' he drawled. 'Believe me, I do!'

'You don't know the first thing about me——'

'I know the *only* thing I want to know about you,' he scoffed. 'Matt must have been insane to get mixed up with a woman like you.' He looked at her critically. 'Admittedly, you're beautiful——'

'Thank you!' she said with sarcasm.

'In an earthy sort of way.' His gaze lingered on the pert fullness of her breasts and the generous curve of her hips. 'But you certainly don't look worth throwing away eight years of marriage, a lovely wife, and two kids for!' he added scathingly.

'I'm sure you're right——'

'You bet I am. And when Matt gets back from

this damned trip he's going to thank me for finishing things between you—after I've killed him,' he muttered grimly. 'I did enough bailing out for him at university; I don't expect to still have to do it!'

Charly was more puzzled than ever. 'You were at university with Matt?'

'Yes. Now when Molly gets here I want you to——'

'Matt's wife is coming here?' She frowned her confusion. 'Whatever for?'

'Don't act dumb,' he scowled. 'Or maybe you are,' he derided. 'A mistress doesn't usually answer the telephone in her lover's apartment and speak to his wife! Unless you're trying to break them up?' he grated. 'You don't fancy being the next Mrs Matt Parker, do you?' he scorned. 'Believe me, it will never happen. Matt may be infatuated with you at the moment, but he'll listen to me when I tell him you're nothing but a mercenary little tramp.'

Charly had a feeling much like it must be to be run over by a steam-roller! 'I'm sure he will,' she answered dazedly.

He nodded, as if there were no doubting the fact. 'In the meantime we have to convince Molly that she's all wrong about the two of you.'

'And just how do you propose to do that?' she asked dryly.

'With the only language women like you understand—money,' he told her derisively.

Charly stiffened, resentment in every bone of her body. 'Is that so?' she drawled.

He nodded, his expression contemptuous. 'And a little acting on your part too—but I'm sure that won't be difficult for you either,' he dismissed with disgust.

In other circumstances she would have put this man firmly in his place, and friend of Matt's or not, it would not have been this apartment! But at the moment she was too bemused—certainly not *amused*!—by the assumption he seemed to have made about her and Matt. She was even more interested in hearing how he intended dealing with the situation.

'Go on,' she invited.

'I've told Molly that you're my girlfriend.' The man looked at her with dislike.

Charly returned that dislike—with interest. 'Couldn't you have thought of something better than *that*?'

'In the thinking time I had, *no*,' he glared at her. 'I got in to the country yesterday——'

'I guessed you weren't English,' she scorned.

'Not gentlemanly enough for you, hmm?' he derided. 'Well I don't know where you got that plummy accent from,' he dismissed harshly, 'but I can assure you I don't think of you as a lady either!'

Insulting man! Her parents had paid a small fortune for her to acquire this 'plummy accent'. And she didn't think it was 'plummy' at all, just correct English. Ignorant lout!

'You were telling me about this marvellous plan you had devised to convince Molly that Matt and I aren't lovers,' she prompted in a bored voice. 'And perhaps it would be better if you introduced yourself.'

Green eyes glittered dangerously. 'The name is

Aaron Grantley. And I'd advise you not to irritate me, lady; I'm angry enough already!'

The threat passed unheeded. Aaron Grantley! She had had no idea what he looked like and so hadn't recognised him, although he was much more well-known in his native America. But she had heard of him, knew that when it came to business there was none better, that the man had amassed a fortune and a hotel empire in America using his business acumen, that he was now interested in advancing into England. Charly hadn't realised he was in the country. Perhaps she ought to put an end to this right now, before——

'Women like you are a dime a dozen,' he told her coldly. 'Damn parasites, living off the vulnerability of married men——'

'Mr Grantley——'

'Believe me, the thought of having to pretend to be your lover makes my skin crawl,' he added disgustedly. 'You would have to get me so damned drunk I wouldn't know what I was doing before I could make love to you!' he bit out insultingly. 'But I'm sure there are lots of men who aren't averse to paying for your services, one way or another.'

Charly was very pale by the time he had finished, all idea of denying a relationship with Matt completely forgotten. Even if she were the sort of woman this man thought she was he had no right to talk to her in this way. People who knew her well would have recognised and understood the anger in silver eyes that were usually a calm grey, and they would have very wisely not pushed her any further.

'I believe you mentioned something about money yourself,' she prompted hardly.

The firmly sculptured mouth twisted derisively. 'I didn't think you would have missed that.'

She gave a haughty inclination of her head. 'I never ignore the mention of money, Mr Grantley.'

He nodded. 'I already guessed that,' he drawled. 'I'm prepared to pay you well to pretend to be my girlfriend while Molly is here.'

'How much?'

'I see the thought of money puts colour in your cheeks,' he scorned harshly.

If there were any colour in her cheeks it was anger at this man. How dare he come here making assumptions, throwing out accusations and insults! She might regret her silence later, but for the moment she relished the time she would tell this man how wrong he was.

'I said how much, Mr Grantley?' she repeated coldly.

He gave a disgusted snort. 'I bet Matt has never seen you like this; I'm sure you're always sweet and lovable with him!'

Charly looked at him steadily. 'I have no reason not to be,' she stated truthfully.

'I suppose he bought you those little rocks.' Aaron Grantley glared at the diamond studs in her earlobes.

'Actually, no,' she told him smoothly.

'Then some other poor besotted idiot did,' he accused disgustedly.

James had never been poor, and certainly not a besotted idiot, she thought bitterly. 'What sort of

payment did you have in mind, Mr Grantley?'
she asked him hardly.

'How about a bracelet to match the earrings?'

Her brows rose; whatever this man was he
wasn't miserly! 'Your friendship with Matt must
be a very close one,' she frowned.

'Not close enough, obviously.' His gaze raked
over her contemptuously. 'He certainly didn't tell
me about you.' He made the statement an insult.

Charly shrugged. 'Probably because he knew
you would disapprove.'

'Any real friend would,' he rasped. 'The
damned fool is married!'

'Are you married?' She didn't remember ever
hearing about any marriage, but it was always a
possibility.

His mouth twisted. 'My marital state is none of
your business!'

'I just thought, with Molly being a friend, you
might find—this—awkward, if you have a wife
too.'

Aaron Grantley sighed. 'I don't have a wife, a
live-in girlfriend, or indeed any serious relationship at the moment. Which is just as well
with Matt in this mess,' he ground out.

She nodded. 'You had better tell me exactly
what you've told Molly about us.'

'Not a lot,' he grated forcefully. 'How could I
when I knew nothing about you? Matt had
mentioned to me that this apartment wouldn't be
available for my stay because he was letting
Charly stay here for a while; I assumed it was one
of his colleagues from the hospital that he lets use
it when it isn't convenient for them to travel out
of town to their homes. He also told Molly that

someone was using the apartment before he left yesterday but he didn't say who, and like me she assumed it was one of his colleagues from the hospital. Then she realised Matt had left an address book here that she needed, and telephoned to see if this colleague could send it on to her. You answered the telephone,' he accused.

Charly vaguely remembered the hastily ended conversation with a woman caller earlier, the other woman ringing off once she was told Charly wasn't the doctor on duty at the hospital that evening. Charly hadn't thought anything of it at the time, now she realised that must have been Molly.

'The poor woman is worried out of her mind,' Aaron Grantley told her harshly. 'She's left the kids with her mother and is driving up here immediately.'

Charly frowned. 'And where do you come in to it, besides being Matt's friend?'

'Molly telephoned me after talking to you, to invite me down to dinner tomorrow, and also to ask me if I knew anything about you—casually. Too casually,' he added pointedly.

'You're having dinner with Matt's wife while he's away?' she taunted.

His mouth tightened formidably. 'He'll be back tomorrow afternoon; don't credit everyone else with your alley-cat morals!'

She drew in an angry breath. 'If you're so damned pure why does Molly believe you're capable of keeping a woman at your best friend's apartment?' she accused coldly.

'Doesn't the fact that she's driving up here anyway tell you that she doesn't believe it?' His eyes glittered. 'She knows damn well I would do anything to protect Matt, and that includes lying for him. So you had better give the performance of your life, lady!'

'How do you know I don't work at the hospital?' she frowned. 'They have allowed women to enter professions for some years now, you know,' she added scornfully.

'Molly knows the names of the people Matt lets stay here, and none of them are called Charly! Besides,' he looked at her derisively, 'you don't look as if you have the brains to do more than entertain a man!'

A chauvinist as well as everything else! 'I'm not surprised you don't have a woman in your life at the moment, Mr Grantley,' she bit out coldly. 'In fact, I'm surprised you've *ever* had one with your opinion of us!'

'How do you think I came by this opinion?' he scorned.

She looked him over coolly. 'By choosing the wrong sort of woman, obviously. But they were probably the only sort *you* could get! Certainly no intelligent woman would want to be involved with such a male chauvinist.'

'Pig,' he finished derisively. 'That is the colloquialism of today, isn't it?' he drawled at her questioning look.

'Male chauvinistic pig,' she tested the statement for sound. 'Yes, I believe that applies to you quite nicely.'

'And we both know my opinion of you,' he rasped. 'So my acting had better be good too!'

'Just when are you expecting Molly to arrive?'

'It takes just over an hour from the house, so

any time now, I would think,' he scowled. 'So you had better get yourself dressed.'

'Wouldn't it look more convincing if I stayed as I am?' she mocked.

Cold green eyes looked her over critically. 'Get dressed,' he instructed abruptly. 'There's no reason for us to look as if we've just been to bed together.'

'Heaven forbid it should look as if you had actually made love to me!' Her eyes flashed.

'How old are you?' he rasped.

'Twenty-six,' she was surprised into answering the question. 'What does that have to do with anything?'

His mouth twisted. 'I would have thought that by now you would have been used to the knocks.'

Her expression became unreadable. 'I am,' she answered abruptly. 'I just don't expect insults from a man I don't even know—and who certainly doesn't know me,' she added hardly.

'What I do know I don't like,' he bit out. 'But you had better tell me a little about yourself so that this act at least stands a chance of succeeding.'

'My name is Charly—Allenby, I'm unmarried, and as I've already told you, I'm twenty-six.'

Aaron Grantley frowned darkly. 'That's all?'

'The prisoner is only required to give name, rank, and number,' she drawled derisively.

'Stop being so damned blasé,' he rasped grimly. 'I'm trying to save the marriage of my two dearest friends—and you're being paid to help me!'

'Maybe if you didn't make assumptions——'

'The next thing I know you'll be claiming that

your being here is perfectly innocent,' he scorned.

'It is. Look, why would Matt tell you or his wife I were here if I were his mistress?'

'He told Molly because he didn't want her to come here and find you in residence, and he told me for the same reason. Charly, go and get some clothes on,' he said wearily. 'You're just wasting time.'

She had never met anyone like him, even James hadn't been this arrogant! 'If you'll just let me explain——'

'I don't want to hear all the details,' he snapped, settling himself down in an armchair. 'After tonight I don't even want to see you again.'

She sighed. 'I don't suppose it's of any interest to you that I was going out this evening?'

'None at all,' he confirmed flatly. 'And remember, as far as you're concerned Molly is merely coming here to collect an address book; don't embarrass her by letting her know you're aware of the real reason.'

She left the room after giving him an indignant glare. Living with James' arrogance had been frustrating enough, accepting a far deeper arrogance from a complete stranger was unacceptable to her.

But he wasn't a *complete* stranger. She had heard all too much of Aaron Grantley in the business world during recent weeks, his latest business venture even intruding into her life. And now the man himself had come bursting into her life with the same intrusive determination to get what he wanted. Well he was going to get far more than he had bargained for from her tonight!

She was putting the finishing touches to her hair when she heard the doorbell ring, turning off the dryer to hear the murmur of voices in the lounge, a breathless female one, and Aaron Grantley's softer soothing one. She hoped his acting ability was as good as he seemed confident it was, because he was going to need it during the next few seconds!

The couple in the lounge weren't initially aware of her presence, and she took the opportunity to watch Molly unobserved. She was a tall, pretty woman, about Charly's own age, with short black hair, darkly lashed blue eyes, talking worriedly to Aaron Grantley. They both seemed to become aware of Charly's presence at the same moment, turning simultaneously.

It was lucky for Aaron Grantley that the other woman did turn to look at her too, because his mouth literally fell open as he gazed at Charly in dazed surprise. She had been well aware of the impact she would make, had dressed with just that idea in mind. The black and gold dress was Japanese in style, high-necked, short-sleeved, completely figure-hugging, her legs long and shapely beneath its knee length, her gold sandals adding to her height with three-inch heels. Her hair was a straight golden swathe to her waist, her make-up dark and dramatic, far heavier than she normally wore it. Aaron Grantley could now see exactly why a man, married or otherwise, could lose his head over her!

'I hope I wasn't too long, darling.' She swayed gracefully into the room, putting her arms about his neck to kiss him lingeringly on the mouth as he stood perfectly still, rigid with shock. 'And you must be Molly.' She turned to the other woman, smiling warmly. 'Matt has told me so much about you.'

Molly looked taken aback. 'I—He has?'

'Oh yes. And your two adorable children. It was so kind of him to let me use his apartment like this.' She glared hardly at Aaron Grantley before moving out of his arms. 'Did you find your address book?' she smiled at the other woman once again.

'Er—yes.' Molly looked uncomfortable.

'Oh good,' she nodded. 'I hope it doesn't inconvenience you that I'm staying here; the fire just about gutted my lounge, although the decorators hope to be finished soon. Shall we sit down?' she invited smoothly.

Molly plopped down on to the sofa while Charly sank down more gracefully, the length of the slit up the skirt of her dress revealing most of her thigh as she crossed one knee over the other.

'Fire?' Molly prompted.

'Mm,' Charly nodded, turning curiously to Aaron Grantley as he stood across the room still staring at her. 'Darling, why don't you sit down,' her voice lowered throatily. 'I'm sure Molly doesn't have to rush off.'

'I—I think I'll have a drink first,' he spoke decisively. 'Ladies?' he added abruptly, as if he had just remembered his manners.

They both declined, and Charly turned to Molly as she guessed the other woman was still waiting for an answer to her question. 'I detest smoking at the best of times,' she confided, having to choke back a laugh as she saw the gold cigarette case Aaron Grantley had been reaching for drop back unopened into the breast-pocket of the pale green shirt. 'But now I refuse to have it anywhere near me,' she added firmly, all humour gone. 'A guest at my apartment the other evening forgot about a cigarette she had been smoking and it fell beneath the coffee-table. It smouldered there until I'd gone to bed and then the carpet caught fire.'

'Oh how awful,' Molly was genuinely disturbed. 'Were you hurt?'

'I inhaled a lot of smoke before a neighbour broke down the door,' she revealed abruptly, very aware of how intently Aaron Grantley was listening now. 'They kept me in hospital for observation but I was fine.'

Molly looked accusingly at Aaron Grantley. 'You didn't tell me any of this.'

'Actually, I didn't tell him,' Charly explained truthfully. 'I knew he wouldn't have liked my having the dinner party while he wasn't here; he can be so jealous,' she confided indulgently, studiously avoiding his furious gaze.

'Aaron can?' Molly looked stunned.

'Oh yes,' Charly nodded. 'Besides, there was nothing he could do in America.'

'Then Matt should have told me about it,' Molly muttered uncomfortably.

'It only happened at the weekend,' Charly excused. 'And now that Aaron is here I can forget all about it,' she added mockingly, looking up at him challengingly.

Molly shook her head. 'The two of you seem so close, and yet Aaron hasn't breathed a word about you to us.'

'Aaron's not used to our relationship himself

yet,' she confided. 'I'm afraid he's still a little wary of the speed with which we fell in love.'

Molly's eyes widened at this information. 'Are the two of you engaged?' she gasped.

'I——'

'Aaron is a little too old for an engagement,' Charly dismissed lightly, meeting his furious gaze innocently. 'So we've just decided to get married.' She kept her face straight as Aaron almost choked on his whisky, his face going red with anger.

'When?' Molly squeaked.

'Well we haven't actually decided on a date yet, but——'

'But you can be sure you and Matt will be the first to know when we do decide on one,' Aaron put in forcefully. 'I thought that was going to remain our secret for a while?' he added gratingly to Charly.

She raised innocent brows. 'Surely not from such good friends as Molly and Matt?'

'From anybody.' He sounded as if he were spitting nails!

'Well, you didn't tell me that, darling,' she drawled, relaxing back in her chair, her grey eyes meeting his calmly. 'I'm sorry if I've ruined your surprise.'

He looked as if that 'surprise' might have pushed him to breaking point, although somehow he maintained his control. 'It doesn't matter,' he dismissed abruptly.

'I'm so glad you told me.' Molly smiled, all doubts obviously laid to rest with this announcement. 'Matt is going to be pleased too.' She turned to Charly. 'I invited Aaron down to dinner tomorrow evening before I realised how seriously involved the two of you are; please come too, Charly.'

'Fine,' Aaron Grantley accepted abruptly. 'We'll look forward to it, won't we, honey?'

He was getting his revenge now! 'Yes,' she agreed curtly. 'We will.'

'Good.' Molly seemed relieved that the meeting had turned out so differently from what she had been expecting.

'Would you like some coffee before you leave?' Charly offered warmly, liking the other woman and her courage to want to fight for her husband if she had to.

'That would be nice, thank you,' Molly nodded acceptance.

'I'll help you, Charly,' Aaron Grantley put in hardly, following her from the room, swinging her round to face him once they reached the privacy of the kitchen. 'What game do you think you're playing?' he demanded furiously.

She glared up at him, shaking off his hand on her arm. 'I'm not playing at all, Mr Grantley,' she snapped. 'Your manners since you arrived here this evening have been highly insulting, to say the least. You prejudged Matt and I——'

'Molly may have fallen for that fire and smoke inhalation story, Miss Allenby,' he ground out, 'but don't expect me to be as gullible!'

'What would it take to convince you?' she demanded angrily. 'Third degree burns?'

His mouth twisted. 'I already know there aren't any; I've seen sixty per cent of you, remember?'

'You're right, Mr Grantley,' she told him

flatly. 'There are no burns.' She couldn't tell this man of the way she woke in the night, her body bathed in perspiration as she imagined that choking smoke filled her bedroom once more and she couldn't get out.

It had only been the quick action of her neighbour that had saved her from death. She had taken a sleeping tablet as usual before she went to bed that night, hadn't been aware of any danger until Jeff Pearce dragged her through the smoke-filled apartment to safety.

'I know that,' Aaron Grantley scorned. 'But it was a good story. Molly certainly believed it. It's this idea of marriage between us that you've given Molly that I don't like,' he scowled, the green eyes dark.

Charly looked up at him unblinkingly. 'I thought it was a nice touch,' she drawled.

'You realise you've put us both in an awkward position?' he rasped.

'Us?' she raised her brows, shaking her head. 'I've put *you* in an awkward position; I have no intention of going to Matt's for dinner tomorrow. You'll have to make my excuses to them.'

He gave her a contemptuous look. 'You're right; I doubt Matt has the nerve to carry out an evening with his wife *and* his mistress.'

Charly gave him a pitying look. 'I'm sure you would have more bravado,' she scorned. 'Now shouldn't you go and keep your guest company; the coffee is almost ready.'

He nodded impatiently. 'But no more wise-cracks about us getting married,' he warned.

'Or?' she drawled.

'Wait and see.' He gave a humourless smile,

challenge in the narrowed green eyes. 'You look like a woman who would like surprises,' he taunted before rejoining Molly in the lounge.

There hadn't been many surprises in her life, even fewer of them pleasant ones, while the shocks she had received in recent years had been even less pleasant. It seemed, from Aaron Grantley's viewpoint at least, that the outer shell had faired far better than the inner Charly; he certainly didn't believe there had been a fire in her apartment. He would be even more sceptical about the rest of her life!

Molly was very relaxed as she drank her coffee, her mind obviously at rest now about her husband's involvement with Charly. For all that she disliked Aaron Grantley Charly was glad they had managed to do that; it had been the only reason she had agreed to go along with Aaron Grantley's plan. No woman should have to go through the torture of believing her husband had another woman when it wasn't true; it was hard enough to bear when it was true!

'You will let us know when you decide about the wedding, won't you?' Molly prompted eagerly. 'I know Matt wouldn't want to miss the great event; for years he's been saying he doubted Aaron would ever marry,' the other woman teasingly explained to Charly. 'I'm sure he has no idea how serious your relationship is.'

'It came as a surprise to us all,' Aaron Grantley drawled derisively.

'Oh yes.' Charly put her hand in the crook of his arm, leaning into him as they sat on the sofa together. 'But now that I've managed to get a commitment from him I'm going to hang on to him.' She looked at him challengingly as she felt him stiffen.

'There's no rush,' he muttered, giving her a fierce glare.

'Neither of us is getting any younger, Aaron,' she lightly mocked.

'Thirty-five isn't old,' he grated.

'It is for a first marriage,' she drawled. 'Not so long ago people would have thought there was something wrong with you,' she added tauntingly.

His hand covered hers as it rested on his arm, crushing down on her fingers in a gesture that, to an observer, must look loving. 'We both know how wrong that assumption would be about me,' he ground out between clenched teeth, his eyes blazing with anger. 'Don't we?' His hand was even more painful on her fingers.

'Well, of course we do, darling,' she gave him a coy smile, triumph in her eyes that she had managed to unnerve him once again. 'I was merely pointing out that we shouldn't delay the wedding too much longer.'

His mouth tightened ominously. 'I don't believe in rushing into these things.'

She gave a light laugh. 'We wouldn't be rushing into anything. I don't——' her next taunt was cut off by angrily firm lips descending roughly on to hers, the brief contact of Aaron Grantley's mouth showing her just how furious he was. It was the first time she had known such intimacy from a man since——

'I think it's time I left,' Molly gently teased, standing up. 'I hope you didn't mind my collecting the address book.' Once again she avoided Charly's gaze. 'I—I'll see you both tomorrow.'

'I——'

'Yes, we'll be there,' Aaron cut in firmly, not wanting to give her the chance to say anything that might be even more damning, standing up to join Molly at the door. 'Tell Matt I'll call him tomorrow.'

'So will I,' Charly put in determinedly, making no effort to join them as Aaron saw the other woman to the lift.

She was standing in front of the window trying to decide how she felt about that kiss when she sensed he had come back into the room. She didn't actually have a lot to compare his kiss with, certainly hadn't been expecting it, or he could have been deeply embarrassed by her violent recoil from the caress. She finally decided she didn't *know* how she felt about the kiss.

'You will not call Matt tomorrow or at any other time,' Aaron ground out icily.

She straightened her shoulders, her expression cold as she turned to face him. 'I won't?' she drawled.

'No,' he rasped. 'You've had your fun here tonight, but now it's over. I want you to pack your things and move out of here right now.'

'And where would I go?'

'Find some other fool to support you in the life to which you've become accustomed,' he scorned. 'I really don't care where you go—just do it.'

She shrugged. 'Matt isn't going to be too pleased about this.'

Aaron Grantley scowled. 'Matt will soon realise what an idiot he's been!'

'You think so?' she frowned thoughtfully.

'I know so,' he said contemptuously.

'You probably know him better than I do,' she nodded consideringly. 'But I have no intention of moving out of here tonight.'

'Now look, lady——'

'Will you stop calling me "lady" in that contemptuous tone,' she snapped coldly. 'We both know you consider me to be the opposite!'

He looked at her with narrowed eyes, his lashes a sooty black against the green depths. 'With that damned haughty manner of yours you could find yourself an earl or something, why pick on Matt?'

'He's a very eminent doctor——'

'But hardly jet-set material.'

Her mouth twisted scornfully. 'I'm not interested in the so-called jet-set,' she dismissed. 'I like my men intelligent as well as interesting; Matt is both of those things,' she added pointedly.

'Implying I'm not?'

Her brows rose coolly. 'I thought the idea was for me not to find you attractive?' she mocked.

He drew in a ragged breath. 'It is!'

She looked at him with derision. 'And I can assure you I don't.'

'I'll make your excuses to Molly and Matt tomorrow,' he ground out. 'You just make sure you're gone from here before Matt comes up to town again.'

'And if I'm not?'

'You don't have the diamond bracelet yet, Charly,' he reminded harshly. 'Something Matt, for all his ability as a doctor, isn't able to buy for you.'

'rich bitch' Aaron Grantley had accused her of being? It was true that her parents were already very rich by the time she was born, and she, a late addition to their lives, had wanted for nothing. It was also true that James had been extremely rich when she married him. But whoever had quipped 'money can't buy you happiness' had known what he was talking about! She was richer now than her parents or James had ever been, had made even more of a success of the company since she took over, but her parents were gone, and so was James. And she certainly wasn't happy.

She picked up the receiver on the second ring, having been lost in thought as she stared out of the window. 'Yes, Sarah?' she prompted briskly.

'Mr Anderson is on line one,' her secretary informed her lightly.

For a moment she had forgotten her request for Sarah to call him. 'Put him through,' she instructed softly.

'Charly, now lovely to hear from you.' The man who had been her father's lawyer before hers, greeted her cheerfully. 'I was going to call you myself later.'

'Ian,' she returned abruptly, able to visualise the senior partner of Anderson, Anderson, and McCloed in his book-lined office, the decor comfortable to say the least, not at all musty and dusty the way most people imagined a lawyer's office to be. Ian was another advocate of her father's rule, his offices were the epitome of elegance and comfort. 'I'm not sure you'll still be pleased to hear from me at the end of this conversation,' she added ruefully.

'Oh?' he prompted guardedly.

Charly smiled; Ian had a lawyer's usual reserve, despite knowing her for years. And this time perhaps he had reason to have; she was very displeased about the turn her negotiations for Shevton House had taken. 'Aaron Grantley knows the identity of his competitor in the Shevton House deal,' she came straight to the point.

'Are you sure?' The frown could be heard in his tone of voice.

'I spoke to the man myself yesterday,' she revealed with a sigh. 'Or rather, *he* spoke to me,' she amended ruefully, remembering the conversation—vividly. No one had ever made the assumption before—erroneous or otherwise—that she was any man's mistress, not even James'. 'He left me in no doubt that he was well aware I was the other party interested in the deal. I told you I wanted my involvement kept strictly private,' she reminded hardly, having been completely shaken the evening before when Aaron Grantley had so casually mentioned her interest in a deal she had considered not to be public knowledge. Years of hiding her true feelings had enabled her to hide her shock, but nevertheless it had greatly disturbed her.

'I've done exactly as you instructed, Charly,' Ian sounded concerned. 'You don't suppose Shevton himself would have——'

'He would have if he knew I was behind the second offer he received—did he?'

'Well, I may have mentioned——'

'Ian, I told you not to reveal my identity,' she cut in angrily.

'I know,' he soothed. 'But the man was proving

difficult, and I thought he would keep the information to himself. He wanted to make sure the house that's been in his family for centuries wasn't going to be knocked down and the estate built on. I had to tell him who you were to convince him you didn't have anything like that in mind, that's why I was going to call you later. I had no idea Grantley would actually confront you with the offer. I also have to tell you Shevton leans more towards you, he doesn't particularly want the place to be turned into a hotel.'

'You told him my plans for the house?' she demanded sharply.

'Of course not,' Ian denied. 'But he knows the way you do business.'

Charly sighed. 'He now also knows who the two bidders are and can play one off against the other.'

'I had to stall him in a hurry,' Ian defended. 'Otherwise he would have let the deal go directly to Grantley; he wasn't much in favour of letting it go to an anonymous party for mysterious reasons.'

'Very well, Ian, I can see you didn't have any choice,' she accepted heavily. 'But I'm not happy about the situation.'

'I can understand that,' he acknowledged ruefully. 'But I knew this was one deal you wouldn't want to lose, and I couldn't contact you last night when I called your apartment.'

'I've been staying at a friend's,' she explained in a preoccupied voice.

'I'm really sorry about all this, I had no idea Shevton would tell Grantley who you were.'

'It's done now,' she dismissed abruptly. 'Keep

me informed on your progress—or lack of it,' she added flatly, knowing they were in for a long haul.

'I will. And, Charly, I really am sorry,' he sighed.

'No harm done,' she assured him with more confidence than she felt. Richard Shevton would have had to have been told of her identity eventually, she knew that, just as she couldn't dictate what he did with that information. He must be more of a businessman than she had realised, she decided. The congenial owner of Shevton House and its surrounding thousand acres didn't come over as being shrewd when it came to business, but Charly knew better than anyone how deceptive appearances could be.

'Sarah.' She looked up with a smile as her secretary came in answer to her call. 'I have a feeling a Mr Aaron Grantley will either be telephoning or coming here in person some time today; I want you to make sure he knows I'm unavailable,' she frowned. She had no doubt that when Matt told the other man *she* was Rocharlle Hart he would demand an explanation from her. She would have given him one last night if he had given her the opportunity to do so. Now she didn't feel that she owed him anything, after all he was the one who had jumped to conclusions.

'Yes, Mrs Hart,' Sarah looked puzzled by the request.

Charly gave a rueful smile. 'He's been making a nuisance of himself.' That wasn't exactly a lie, he was a nuisance, and she also knew Sarah would be even more determined to keep Aaron Grantley at bay if she thought he was one of the

numerous men who believed it would be nice to
marry her money. She had met a lot of them the
last year.

'I'll make sure he doesn't bother you,' Sarah
told her firmly.

She didn't normally need help to deter the sort
of man she had implied Aaron Grantley to be,
had been brought up as Rocharlle Allenby, had cut
her adult teeth on fortune-hunters. One of the
pluses in becoming James's wife was that he had
been even richer than she. But of course he had
wanted something from her far more important
to him than money, and marrying her had
instantly given him that.

By late afternoon she had begun to think she
had been wrong about Aaron Grantley's next
move; there had been no contact from him. Then
just after four she heard raised voices in the outer
office. Aaron Grantley didn't sound as if he were
accepting Sarah's claim that she wasn't available.
Charly thought of going to the younger woman's
rescue, but that would only make a liar out of
Sarah. It would also make *her* look ridiculous.
She realised now she should never have given
Sarah that instruction, should have known Aaron
Grantley wasn't the sort of man to be fobbed off
with such an excuse.

She stood up slowly as her office door was
flung open, the man himself standing there, very
dark and attractive in an iron-grey pin-striped
suit. His eyes narrowed on her, and Charly tried
to see herself as he must see her, the long golden
hair confined in a neat pleat at the back of her
head, the black business suit and white blouse
with its bow-neckline smart rather than feminine.

She looked completely different from the woman he had met the previous evening.

'I'm sorry, Mrs Hart.' Sarah glared at Aaron Grantley. 'He just pushed past me,' she muttered indignantly.

'It's all right, Sarah,' she soothed. 'I'll deal with Mr Grantley myself,' she added hardly.

The green eyes glittered vengefully. 'I know we argued last night, sweetheart,' he murmured huskily, crossing the room to her side, 'but I don't think that's any reason to be so formal.' He put his arm about her waist to pull her close to the hardness of his body. 'After all, we are engaged to be married,' he said challengingly, his head bending down to hers.

Charly only had tome to register Sarah's gasp of surprise before coolly firm lips claimed hers, his arms about her, one of his hands pressed to the back of her head, preventing her moving away. He kissed her with deliberate thoroughness, savouring the taste of her lips, the probing of his tongue only withdrawn as Charly's small white teeth bit down sharply on the tender flesh.

'Vixen!' he grated before turning to Sarah with a totally charming smile. 'A lovers' quarrel,' he drawled.

Sarah looked totally disconcerted, and Charly couldn't blame her!

'Mr Grantley——'

'Sweetheart, do stop calling me that.' His eyes promised retribution if she didn't! 'And do let this young lady leave so that we don't embarrass her any further with our disagreement.'

Charly gave him a furious look before turning

to her secretary. 'Thank you, Sarah.' She gave a rueful smile. 'I can handle this now.'

'Can you?' Aaron Grantley challenged softly after Sarah had left them, the younger woman still frowning her confusion.

'Yes,' she snapped, moving pointedly away from him. 'I gather you've spoken to Matt.'

'Graphically,' he drawled.

'I'm sure,' her mouth twisted. 'So now you know I'm the "rich bitch" who is trying to ruin your bid for Shevton House.'

He grinned, looking about the room appreciatively 'Mrs Hart apparently likes to surround herself with luxury,' he derided.

'Mrs Hart *earned* this luxury,' she told him tightly, taking the bronze sculpture of a horse out of his hand and placing it back on her desk-top.

'That isn't what I heard,' he mocked, stretching his long length out in one of the armchairs, watching her through narrowed lids. 'You took over when your husband died. Which brings me to the point of why you lied about your name yesterday,' he added sharply.

'I didn't lie.' Her eyes flashed silver. 'My name is Allenby.'

'Was,' Aaron Grantley corrected abruptly. 'Before you married the son of your father's business partner seven years ago. Maybe you did *earn* this company after all,' he derided. 'The marriage was certainly a convenient one.' He raised mocking brows.

'I don't have to explain myself to you——'

'I doubt Rocharlle Hart ever explains herself to anyone. How did you ever get a name like Rocharlle, anyway?' he taunted.

'My parents.'

'That's obvious,' he dismissed mockingly. 'But it isn't what I meant.'

'Rowena and Charles,' she explained impatiently. 'When they were told I was to be an only child they named me after both of them.'

'It would have been easier to call you Charlotte after your father,' Aaron Grantley derided.

It would have been a lot less embarrassing too; her unusual first name had been a talking point all her life. 'You didn't come here to talk about my name——'

'In part I did,' his voice hardened. 'Why didn't you tell me last night who you were?'

'For the same reason you came here today and acted as if our engagement were a reality; which incidentally I want you to correct before you leave—I was angry,' she bit out. 'Matt innocently told you I was staying at his apartment, and then because you were told it was a woman and not a man as you had supposed you assumed I had to be his mistress.'

He shrugged broad shoulders, perfectly relaxed. 'I'm still not sure that isn't true.'

Charly gasped. 'I thought you said you had spoken to Matt?'

'I have,' he nodded. 'But like you, he doesn't feel he has to explain himself. He's mad as hell at both Molly and me for jumping to conclusions,' he added ruefully.

'He's told Molly the truth?'

'Not exactly,' Aaron Grantley derided. 'Apparently she's a little emotional at the moment, and he seems to think we've complicated the situation by pretending to be engaged, believes that if he told her the truth now Molly would think he had something to hide.'

Charly sighed. 'I'm inclined to agree with him.'

'I'm willing to accept that,' Aaron Grantley nodded. 'Although Molly's emotional state seems a little convenient to me.'

She gave him a disparaging look. 'Are you always this suspicious?'

'Only when I find a beautiful woman staying at my best friend's apartment,' he drawled.

'I hope to be moving out at the end of the week,' Charly snapped.

'To go where?'

'My own home, of course,' she told him impatiently.

'Ah yes, the one that's been damaged by fire.'

'Mr Grantley, I don't care for your tone——'

'And I don't care for this whole charade,' he rasped, his eyes bright with anger. 'Especially now that I know the woman I'm engaged to is also the woman who's interfering in my property deal.'

'There are some that would say you have that the wrong way around, Mr Grantley,' she returned coldly.

'Aaron,' he instructed tensely. 'Shevton was on the point of accepting my offer when you came along with a better one,' he scowled.

'And you counter-offered.'

'And so did you,' he ground out. 'How high are you prepared to go?'

'I don't believe that is any of your business,' she snapped indignantly.

'What the hell does Hartall Industries want

with a house like that and a thousand acres?' His eyes were narrowed.

Hartall Industries didn't want them at all; the offer to buy was a purely personal one. But obviously Aaron Grantley wasn't aware of that, at least.

'I suppose you plan to turn it in to yet another hotel?' she scorned.

His mouth tightened. 'You have to see that it would be ideal.'

'It could have other uses,' she dismissed.

'Don't tell me, as a health-farm for all your over-indulged friends,' he derided. 'Or perhaps as a clinic where they can go to "dry out",' he added contemptuously. 'I hear that's very fashionable nowadays.'

'I don't have any friends that need to "dry out",' Charly snapped at his condescension. 'Just as it's none of your business what I do with Shevton House once I've bought it.'

'*If* you buy it,' he corrected gratingly. 'Which you won't,' he said confidently.

'I wouldn't put money on it,' she warned him softly, her grey gaze calm and confident.

'It's perfect for what I want,' he announced arrogantly. 'The building itself, and its location in that little cove is ideal too. You aren't thinking of going in to the hotel business yourself, are you?' he mocked.

'No,' she dismissed with a derisive laugh. 'I've stayed at several of your hotels in the past, Mr— Aaron, and I don't think I could compete.' His hotels offered the sort of first-class accommodation James had always insisted on when they travelled abroad. 'I'm sure Shevton House would make a very good hotel, I just happen to have other plans for it.'

'Shevton isn't likely to sell to either of us now until he gets top dollar,' Aaron grimaced.

She shrugged. 'We both know it's worth it.'

Green eyes narrowed thoughtfully. 'You must want it very badly.'

'Yes,' she confirmed flatly.

He continued to look at her steadily for several seconds, then he shrugged. 'May the best man— person, win.'

Her mouth twisted. 'Oh, I will,' she assured him.

Aaron looked amused. 'That might be difficult, as I intend Shevton House to be mine.'

'We'll see,' she said enigmatically.

'You weren't in for your delivery this morning, so I brought this with me.' He drew out a jewellery box from his pocket, holding it out to her.

'You must realise now that I don't want—or need—the bracelet and necklace,' she told him stiffly.

'It did occur to me,' he drawled. 'So I took them back and got you this instead.'

Charly took the velvet box uncertainly, flicking open the lid. Inside was a gold charm bracelet, but it was the charms attached to it that made her smile, tiny animals all made in minute detail. 'It's beautiful,' she smiled up at Aaron, frowning as she saw the last charm. 'But what's this?' she held up the miniature engagement and wedding rings, the emerald in the former obviously genuine.

'Obligatory, I'm afraid,' he grimaced. 'Window dressing for Molly tonight.'

Charly looked up at him slowly. 'I thought we had agreed we would make my excuses?'

'Hm,' he sighed. 'I'm afraid, as Matt pointed out to me, it would look a bit odd, to Molly, if we broke off our engagement so quickly. Which is why I also purchased this,' he took a ring-box out of his other pocket.

'Oh no,' Charly put her hands behind her back, staring with horror at the finger-sized replica of the emerald ring on the charm bracelet, the emerald the size of a penny. 'I'm not wearing that,' she shook her head.

'I know we told Molly we weren't bothering with an engagement, but——'

'I am not wearing it.' She repressed a shiver of revulsion as she imagined the gold shackle around her finger. 'I'm allergic to rings,' she told him breathlessly.

'To the gold, you mean?' he frowned.

'No—to wearing them!' This time she couldn't hold back the shudder. 'They're a licence to imprison.'

His brows rose. 'So the marriage wasn't so convenient after all,' he drawled.

She looked at him sharply. 'I don't wish to talk about my marriage.'

'There seems to be quite a few things you refuse to talk about,' Aaron taunted.

'Have I tried to pry into your private life?' Her eyes shone silver. 'Have I asked even one question?'

'You asked if I were married,' he reminded.

She sighed. 'In the circumstances I would have

thought you would be as averse to the thought of my wearing your ring as I am,' she derided.

'But I know it's only temporary.'

'It's also unnecessary. Thank you, but no thank you,' she said firmly. 'And are you absolutely sure you can't get me out of dinner this evening?' she frowned. 'I'd really rather not go.'

'Matt seemed to think it was necessary.' He pocketed the ring-box.

She chewed on her inner lip. 'Very well then—if I have no choice.'

'My ego has taken a severe beating since I met you,' Aaron drawled dryly.

'I don't think it's going to do it much harm,' Charly derided.

'You aren't exactly lacking in self-confidence yourself, you know,' he pointed out softly.

Perhaps if he had met her a year ago he would have thought differently. Six years of marriage to a man as strong-willed as James had stripped her of most of the poise and confidence that had been imbued in to her at the finishing-school she had attended in Switzerland. When a man was as assured and arrogant as James had been something had to give in a marriage, and for the sake of peace it had always been Charly. It would never happen to her again, she was her own woman now, and intended to remain that way.

'I'm Rocharlle Allenby-Hart, remember?' she drawled. 'With the gold spoon in my mouth.'

He looked at her thoughtfully. 'Maybe that gold becomes a little heavy to carry at times,' he murmured.

She wasn't sure if he meant literally or

figuratively—whichever one he was right! 'I can live with it,' she mocked.

'Who couldn't?' he derided. 'And if Matt isn't the man in your life then who is?'

She avoided his probing eyes. 'There isn't one. My husband has only been dead a year,' she defended—and then mentally chastised herself for doing so; she had given up justifying her actions after James died. 'Now if you'll excuse me,' she added briskly, 'I have work to do . . .'

'Buying country houses being part of it,' he mocked.

'Yes,' she acknowledged challengingly.

'We'll see,' Aaron murmured.

She could see the return of challenge in his own eyes, and knew that he was enjoying himself. James had enjoyed challenges too, an easy conquest held no interest for him. But she hadn't known that until it was too late, until she found him in her cousin's arms, Jocelyn treating him in the same casual way James regarded Charly. And how James had loved it. And how he had loved Jocelyn too. But when she had asked him for a divorce he hadn't wanted Jocelyn enough to give up the one thing he did want from his marriage to Charly. And then when he had decided *he* wanted a divorce he had once again used the one threat against her guaranteed to make her agree to anything he wanted.

'Where have you gone to?'

She focused her attention on Aaron Grantley with effort, having forgotten his presence as she thought of that last conversation with James that had ended in tragedy. 'Nowhere, Mr Grantley.'

She moved to sit behind her desk. 'For a moment you reminded me of someone,' she added as he seemed to expect more.

His eyes narrowed. 'They seemed unhappy thoughts.'

'They were,' she acknowledged bluntly.

'I realise we got off to a bad start last night——'

'We didn't get off to a start at all,' she corrected abruptly. 'You threw out a lot of groundless accusations, bullied me into acting like your girlfriend——'

'No one bullied you into anything,' Aaron cut in. 'I don't think anyone ever could—What did you say?' he frowned as she muttered something under her breath.

She straightened her shoulders. 'I said they could try,' she spoke loud enough for him to hear this time.

He shrugged dismissively. 'You wanted to put Molly's mind at rest,' he stated firmly.

'Matt adores her,' she said flatly.

'He wouldn't be the first man in love with his wife to be attracted to another woman,' Aaron spoke hardly.

'What time are we expected for dinner this evening?' she ignored the question in his tone.

'Eight o'clock.'

She nodded. 'I'll drive myself down,' she told him briskly. 'I expect to be working late.'

'I'll call for you.'

'I'd prefer to drive myself,' she said determinedly.

'Independent, huh?' he derided.

'Absolutely.' Cold grey eyes met his amused gaze.

'James Hart must have been a bastard,' he said with narrowed eyes.

'He was a very charming and well-liked man,' she stated flatly.

'But hell to live with, I bet.'

Hell exactly described what it had been like to live with James. 'I was married to him for six years,' she taunted. 'So it can't have been all that bad.'

'Bad enough,' Aaron said dryly. 'You have Matt's home address?'

'Yes.' She met his gaze challengingly, daring him to make something of that fact.

He nodded. 'Try not to be late; it might be awkward trying to explain the non-appearance of my "fiancée".'

As she had been the one to actually announce their engagement to Molly she had to go! 'I'll be there,' she assured him.

'Looking a little more like you know what love is, I hope,' he mocked.

She drew in a ragged breath. 'I believe, of the two of us, I am in a better position to have known the emotion than you are!' she scorned harshly. She certainly knew what love *wasn't*!

'If you mean I've never been in love with a woman then that's true. But I do know what love is; my home life as a child was a very happy one. My parents always showed their love for me and each other.'

'It wasn't so different in my home,' she told him hardly.

'I take it your own child hasn't fared as well,' Aaron drawled.

Charly stiffened, her face paling. 'I don't have

a child,' she said between numbed lips.

He frowned. 'But I thought——'

'Whoever your informant was, Mr Grantley, they are out of date,' Charly looked at him coldly, the trembling of her hands hidden beneath the desk. 'My daughter was in the car with James when he crashed. She died too.'

'I didn't know . . .'

She didn't talk to anyone of the agonisingly slow loss of her daughter, of the hatred she had for James because of that even though he, too, was dead and unable to defend himself. There *was* no defence for what he had done!

'I had no idea,' Aaron Grantley sounded concerned. 'Charly, I——'

'I don't need your sympathy,' she snapped, her mouth tight. 'Sympathy can't bring back Stephanie.'

'Or your husband,' he put in softly.

'I'm sure it must be obvious that I don't want James back,' she rasped.

'I did get that impression, yes,' he confirmed dryly. 'What did the poor guy do to you?'

'He married me, Mr Grantley.' She stood up, her eyes cold.

'I see,' he frowned.

'I doubt it,' she derided. 'Now if you wouldn't mind, I have an appointment in a few minutes . . .' It was a lie, but she didn't want to talk any more just now, this man was getting to the vulnerability of her private grief without even seeming to try.

He shrugged. 'I have to be somewhere else myself,' he nodded. 'But I'll expect to see you tonight, wearing the bracelet as I can't persuade you to wear the ring.'

'Take the ring back where you bought it, Mr
Grantley,' she advised dryly. 'And get your
money back.'

'You really are allergic, huh?'

'They make me nauseous!'

'You're going to make some lucky man a good
mistress one day,' he mused.

Her eyes flashed deeply silver. 'It's only men's
illusion that women are subservient to them, *we*
know that we actually aren't. Some man might
make me a good lover,' she said with distaste,
unable to envisage the day that she ever took a
lover.

'Don't you think that's taking your independence too far? No, probably not,' he grimaced.
'Not for Rocharlle Allenby-Hart.'

'It doesn't matter who I am,' she dismissed.
'I'm just a woman——'

'A very bitter one,' he put in softly. 'You're too
young to let one bad experience sour you.'

'Age has nothing to do with it,' she scorned.
'And it wasn't an experience, Mr Grantley,' she
added hardly. 'It was a marriage. At least, I
thought it was.'

He looked as if he wanted to say more, then he
shrugged dismissively. 'I'll see you tonight.'

Charly was still standing tensely in front of the
window when Sarah entered her office a few
minutes later. She turned to face the younger
woman, her features schooled into their usual
calm.

'Are you really going to marry Mr Grantley?'
Sarah was too stunned to be politely silent about
the man who had just left.

Charly gave a rueful smile. 'Didn't you

recognise a ruse to get in to see me without an appointment?' she said lightly, having decided this was the only way to treat Aaron Grantley's vengeful statement, having no intention of acting a part at work too.

'But——' the other woman looked confused. 'Is that all it was?'

'Of course,' Charly smiled, meeting her secretary's gaze steadily. She would not find herself intimidated by Aaron Grantley in any aspect of her business life!

'Oh.' Sarah looked disappointed.

Charly laughed softly. 'He's much too bossy for me,' she teased.

'But gorgeous, don't you think?' her secretary said eagerly.

She grimaced. 'Very,' she admitted. 'If he calls or turns up like that again perhaps you had better just let him in,' she said dryly. 'I don't think we need a repeat of today's scene.'

Sarah looked disappointed. 'So you really aren't going to marry him?'

She shook her head. 'I'm not going to marry anyone, I'm leaving that to you.' Her secretary was marrying her long-time boyfriend in a couple of months.

Sarah nodded, turning to leave. 'By the way, I like your bracelet. It's new, isn't it?' she teased knowingly.

Charly couldn't prevent the colour that brightened her cheeks. 'Yes, it's new,' she confirmed abruptly, wishing she had never entered into this deceit with Aaron Grantley.

But she knew better than anyone how painful it was to believe your husband had another woman, how the bitterness and uncertainty eroded away at love and finally left only bitterness. She had never met Matt's wife Molly before, but he had spoken of her often, always with deep love, and she hadn't liked to think his kind gesture of letting her use his apartment while her own was being redecorated would result in a serious misunderstanding between him and his wife. Jocelyn had once made her very aware of the fact that her involvement with James wasn't quite so innocent.

At eighteen Charly had suddenly found herself without parents, half owner of the Hartall empire, with not a clue how to cope with the sudden responsibility. James' parents, Will and Glenda, had been on a weekend trip with her own parents to Scotland, their plane going down on the return journey, all four passengers and the crew killed. If it hadn't been for James' support during the next few months she didn't know how she would have got through. Ten years her senior, he had been involved in the running of Hartall Industries for some years, taking over the reins of complete control with no trouble at all.

With the difference in their ages Charly hadn't socially had a lot to do with the son of her father's partner, but during the next few months she came to rely on him totally, for the running of the company and also for her mental salvation, the two of them spending most of their evenings together. When she had begun to fall in love with him she didn't know, but suddenly it was a fact, her contentment complete when James asked her to marry him. Of course he had used words like love and forever in his proposal, what he should have said were gain and convenience! In her youthfully trusting innocence she had entrusted the running of Hartall Industries to James. Ian Anderson had advised her against such a move, but she had laughed off his caution. After all, James was her husband, and she trusted him implicitly.

For two years she had lived in ignorant bliss, had given birth to Stephanie during their first year of marriage, giving almost all her attention to the beautiful baby that was her daughter. When she first heard the rumours of James' mistress she had dismissed them as malicious gossip; she and James were ecstatically happy together. But the rumours persisted, and she finally asked James about it. He had flown into a temper, saying it was her fault, that she gave all her attention to the baby and ignored him and his needs. The fact that he did have another woman was blow enough, that it was her fault affected her badly. She began to put James first in everything, to give her love and attention to Stephanie only when they were alone during the day, virtually ignoring the confused baby when James was at home. That hadn't satisfied him either, he accused her of suffocating him with her love, and within a few weeks there was yet another woman. And then another. And then another . . .

During the following years she lost count of the amount of women that passed briefly through James' life, for the most part ignoring their existence, her confidence in herself completely undermined, leaning more heavily on James than ever in her effort to hold on to their marriage. Stephanie thought her father was wonderful, and by the time she got past the baby stage he was taking quite an interest in her too. Just seeing them together was enough to show Charly that none of the other women really meant anything to James.

On their fifth wedding anniversary they had given a family party, James' absence when it came time for them to receive her uncle's good luck toast causing her to stumble across James in the arms of his latest mistress. She had heard noises from their bedroom, had guessed James must be in there, the smile freezing on her lips as she walked in on the partly undressed couple, James glaring at her furiously, Jocelyn giving a self-satisfied smile. Charly had hastily backed out of the room, too shocked to even speak.

She had returned downstairs to the party as if nothing had happened, too numbed to even think just yet, but knowing she couldn't cause a scene with all these people in the house. James and Jocelyn had rejoined the party several minutes later, her stricken gaze meeting James' bored one as her uncle finally made his toast to them.

She avoided being near either Jocelyn or James the rest of the evening, almost at breaking point by the time they had seen the last guest depart, her tension causing her to tremble uncontrollably.

James poured himself a drink, facing her across the lounge. 'I suppose you want to talk now,' he drawled.

'How could you?' she accused. 'For years I've ignored your affairs, but I won't allow this relationship with Jocelyn to continue.'

Blue eyes glazed over with an icy chill. '*You*

won't allow?' he repeated softly. 'Since when have I asked your permission to do anything?'

He had never spoken to her in quite this contemptuous way before, and Charly could only stare at him, waiting for the next blow to fall. As she knew it must.

'I married you for one reason and one reason only,' he told her in a coldly cruel voice. 'To have complete control over Hartall Industries——'

'James . . .?' she gasped her disbelief.

'Which you so kindly gave me,' he taunted, drinking some of his whisky. 'I've allowed you to stay my wife the last five years, don't force me to choose between you and Jocelyn; you would lose,' he scorned.

Charly dropped down dazedly into one of the armchairs. 'You—You've never loved me?'

'I've never been interested in small, childish blondes,' he dismissed harshly. 'You're satisfying enough in bed but out of it you have the intelligence of a schoolgirl!'

She wanted to point out to him that when they had married she had only recently stopped being a schoolgirl, that instead of growing and maturing in her marriage she had remained youthfully insecure, unsure of her husband and their life together. But once again she remained silent.

'I want Jocelyn in my life,' he told her softly. 'And I'll have her for as long as I want her.'

This time Charly did speak. 'In that case I want a divorce,' she stated flatly.

'No,' he derided.

'You can't stop me——'

'Stephanie . . .?'

Charly paled, looked at him sharply. 'What about her?'

'If you divorce me you will take your half of the company with you,' he bit out hardly. 'And I can't allow that. If you insist on divorce, Charly, I'll fight you for custody of Stephanie.'

'You would lose,' she gasped.

'Would I?' he mocked. 'Whatever else I've been I've also been a good father to Stephanie, not even you can dispute that. I love her. And the courts are more inclined to listen to the wishes of a father nowadays when it comes to giving custody of children.'

'If you love her as you say you do then you won't put her through that.' Charly shook her head.

'Oh, I love her,' he confirmed grimly. 'But I want Hartall Industries more!'

'And Jocelyn,' she said dully.

'And Jocelyn,' he nodded challengingly.

Charly had stood up with all the dignity she possessed. 'Even though there will be no divorce our marriage is still at an end,' she announced coldly, taking the first painful step towards emotional independence, knowing James had never loved her killing what little affection had remained for him from that first heady love. 'I will never again share the bedroom with you that you were in earlier with Jocelyn; I shall be sleeping in the spare room from now on.'

'Please yourself,' he shrugged dismissively. 'It won't be any great loss.'

She was past feeling pain at that moment, but once the numbness of the situation wore off she became sensitive to every cutting and derogatory remark James made. The next year was unbearable, James not even trying to hide his affair with Jocelyn now, often escorting the other woman to parties that would normally be attended by his wife. For Stephanie's sake Charly had borne the humiliation, feeling only relief when James himself had told her he now wanted the divorce, and in return for giving her custody of Stephanie he wanted complete control of Hartall Industries. She had had to refuse, Hartall Industries was Stephanie's inheritance. James had driven off with Stephanie in his car after telling her she would never see her daughter again.

It had been James she had never seen again, Stephanie's injuries in the accident so severe that she lay in a coma for the next two months before finally dying.

That had completed Charly's maturity, and she had promised herself that no man would ever hurt her like that again. She had thrown all her energies into making Hartall Industries more successful than it had ever been, and she had succeeded more than her wildest dreams. She certainly wasn't going to let another arrogantly assured man beat her in what she considered a very important property deal.

She picked up the telephone on her desk. 'Sarah? Get me Ian Anderson,' she instructed curtly.

CHAPTER THREE

SHE enjoyed the lengthy drive to Berkshire, rarely found the time or occasion to get out of London nowadays. She envied Matt his beautiful country home, appreciating why he found it nicer to live here even though it meant, with his duties at the hospital, he occasionally had to stay the night at his apartment in town. Surely knowing he had the secluded house and lovely family to come home to more than made up for that.

She had little difficulty finding the house, parking her Porsche next to the bottle green sports model Jaguar already in the driveway, guessing who that belonged to. The man seemed to have a thing about the colour green. She had to admit that the green of his eyes was—Was what? She wasn't going to fall for a good-looking charmer a second time. She wasn't going to fall for any man!

'Charly!' Matt met her at the door, a tall distinguished looking man, his blond hair showing signs of greying, his eyes a warm brown. 'Oh, love, I can't tell you how sorry I am about this mess.' He helped her off with her coat, handing it to the butler before dismissing him. 'I never dreamt when I offered you the use of the apartment that it would come to this,' he frowned.

'It's all right.' She put her hand comfortingly on his arm. 'I should have realised at the time that it was a bad idea. Once I realised the conclusion Molly had come to I was glad to help. Although maybe I just complicated things even more,' she grimaced.

'I thought so,' he agreed consideringly. 'But not since talking to Molly. She's a little emotional at the moment, this third pregnancy is——'

'You're having another child? How wonderful!' She was genuinely excited for them.

'I think so,' he sighed. 'But Molly feels it's too soon after Tommy; he's only just a year old, you know. In the circumstances I think you and Aaron did the right thing; Molly has enough to cope with at the moment without doubt between us.'

Charly frowned her concern. 'Is there anything I can do to help?'

He put his hand over hers. 'You've already done enough,' he said gratefully. 'Without you——'

'I think your wife is feeling neglected, Matt.' Aaron Grantley told him with forced cheerfulness as he joined them, turning narrowed eyes on Charly. 'Ah, my charming fiancée,' he drawled mockingly.

'Aaron——'

'Charly and I understand each other,' the other man assured him harshly. 'Molly,' he prompted.

To say this man looked devastatingly attractive in an evening suit was an understatement; he looked magnificent, wide shoulders, tapered waist and thighs. His skin looked very tanned against the whiteness of his shirt, his eyes glittering like twin emeralds. It was the anger in his eyes that brought Charly to her senses, challenge in her gaze.

'That was a touching scene I just interrupted,' he drawled insultingly.

'Wasn't it?' she returned sweetly, not prepared to justify her liking for Matt to this man.

'I thought I told you to stay away from him,' Aaron grated.

She shook her head. 'You told Charly Allenby, not Rocharlle Hart.'

'Don't play games with me,' he warned softly.

'Games?' She raised her brows. 'I don't know what you mean, Mr Grantley.'

'You know,' he rasped.

Charly sighed. 'As usual you're mistaken about the situation,' she snapped. 'Molly's pregnant, did you know?'

His gaze became wary. 'They just told me.'

'That's the emotional state Matt told you about; he's frightened she might lose the baby.'

'Which is why he's got himself involved with you, I suppose,' Aaron scorned. 'Try again, Mrs Hart.'

'I don't have to,' she shrugged. 'My conscience is clear, and that's all I care about. You can take your opinion of me and——' She broke off as Aaron roughly pulled her into his arms and began to kiss her. He didn't even try to make it pleasant for her, kissing her contemptuously, his mouth savaging hers.

'Whoops! Sorry,' Molly told them teasingly.

Charly was released as soon as the other woman returned to the lounge, breathing hard. 'You didn't have to be so rough!' She touched her bruised lips, her lipgloss completely gone, her eyes a dark stormy grey.

Aaron shrugged non-committally. 'You were being indiscreet.'

'I was telling you exactly what I think of you,' she corrected, marching over to the hall mirror to check her appearance; she looked a mess. Her hair had escaped in loose tendrils from the neat pleat at the back of her head, her cheeks were flushed, and her mouth was pink and moist from his rough handling. The silky sheath of her black dress still looked as good, but she definitely needed tidying. She opened her bag to find her brush.

'Don't bother.' Aaron took hold of her arm to drag her towards the lounge. 'You look as if you've just been kissed.'

'I feel as if I've been savaged!' she glared at him.

'I'm sorry about that,' he sighed. 'But I heard Molly coming, and you didn't exactly sound loverlike,' he derided.

'I sounded angry—which I am,' she snapped. 'I wouldn't do to Molly what you're accusing me of doing; I like her.'

'She likes you too,' he nodded grimly. 'But that's only because she doesn't really know you.'

Charly stiffened. 'Other women's husbands hold no attraction for me.'

He shrugged. 'Maybe Matt forgot to mention he was married until it was too late.'

Her fingers curled about her handbag, only just resisting the impulse to swing her arm and smack him around the face with it. 'Your erroneous opinion of Matt is only superceded by your opinion of me!'

Aaron's mouth twisted. 'Let's just say I'm beginning to realise what your attraction could

be,' he drawled, his gaze lingering appreciatively
on the creamy softness of her breasts exposed by
the low neckline of her dress.

She gave him a look of intense dislike. 'Remarks
like that only emphasize your *lack* of attraction!'

His mouth quirked, the green eyes warm with
enjoyment of this encounter. 'I bet you're a hell-
cat in bed.'

She gasped her outrage at this casually made
statement. 'You'll never know that!' she bit out
angrily.

'I wouldn't be too sure of that,' he mocked.
'You're beginning to interest me.'

Her eyes flashed, her body stiff with indignation. 'And I couldn't be *less* interested in you!'

'I have been known to change a woman's
mind,' he taunted.

'Not mine.' Charly shook her head. 'Now shall
we join Matt and Molly?'

She was aware of him behind her as they
entered the lounge, a little startled when his arm
came possessively about her waist, although the
smile remained on her lips. 'I hope we haven't
kept you waiting,' she greeted smoothly.

'Not at all.' The other woman looked very
attractive in a midnight blue dress, although
Charly doubted the slender style would fit her for
much longer. 'Dinner is only just ready.'

'Congratulations,' Charly told her warmly.
'Matt told me your good news.'

Molly gave a rueful smile. 'I only found out for
certain myself today. In fact, that was why I
needed that old address book from the apartment,'
she explained awkwardly. 'I needed the number
of my gynaecologist.'

'If I'd realised we were celebrating tonight I would have brought champagne,' Aaron said regretfully.

'I'm not allowed to drink alcohol now anyway,' Molly grimaced. 'Even the small glass I am allowed when I'm pregnant makes me sick.'

The pregnancy had obviously come as something of a shock to Molly, it was there in her voice, and Charly was more relieved than ever that she had helped put this woman's mind at rest about Matt and herself. Her own pregnancy seven years ago had been a surprise too, and at nineteen she had found it difficult to cope with the changes in her body. Molly had obviously been through those changes twice before, but as she had probably only just regained her figure after giving birth to one-year-old Tommy she must feel a little anger mixed in with her excitement about the thought of being pregnant again. In the circumstances it was understandable.

'Never mind, love,' Aaron sympathised. 'You only have seven months to go.'

Charly could see it had been the wrong thing to say even as Molly's eyes took on a hunted look.

'I can't cope with it,' Molly suddenly cried. 'It's too much!' She turned and ran from the room.

Charly turned on Aaron. 'You have the sensitivity of a moron!' she snapped, throwing her handbag down in a chair at go after Molly.

'What did I say?' He looked dazed by the scene such a casual remark seemed to have made.

Matt shrugged. 'Pregnancy tends to make a

woman act a bit strange,' he grimaced. 'It's all those hormones going haywire!'

Charly whirled back to face them. 'While the two of you are standing here musing over the quaint little ways of women when they're pregnant perhaps you would like to consider the fact that although seven months may not sound very long to you it is in fact over *half a year!*' She glared at them as she now held their attention. 'You both have your pleasure for half an hour or so, but it's the woman who for the next nine months feels sick, tired, blows up like a balloon, is kicked under the ribcage whenever she tries to get any rest, and on top of all that she has to cope with teasing idiots like you two!' She was breathing hard in her agitation. 'If men were the ones who had to go through all that the birthrate would go down to a dangerous low!'

'When you put it like that . . .' Aaron mocked.

'I do,' she snapped. 'Now I am going to try and calm Molly, I would advise the two of you to try and straighten up your act while I'm gone. You *are* some sort of comedy team, aren't you?' she derided hardly.

'Vicious,' Aaron murmured admiringly.

'I never knew you had a temper, Charly,' Matt said in awe.

Green eyes mocked Charly. 'I have a feeling there's quite a lot you don't know about her, Matt,' he drawled.

Grey clashed with green. 'There's quite a lot you both don't know about me,' she bit out before leaving the room.

She found the other woman upstairs in her

bedroom, deep sobs wracking her body as she lay across her bed.

'I'm sorry,' she choked as she saw Charly, trying to mop up the tears with a tissue. 'You must think I'm awful reacting this way.'

'Not at all,' she assured her softly, sitting on the side of the bed to hand Molly another tissue. 'It isn't easy being pregnant.'

Molly sniffed, the tears ceasing. 'Do you have children? Matt told me you've been married before.'

'No,' she answered regretfully. 'My daughter died——'

'Oh I'm so sorry,' Molly was instantly contrite. 'You must think from the way I've been acting, that I don't want this baby. It isn't that——'

'You just haven't had time to get over your son's birth yet,' she acknowledged ruefully. 'It's supposed to get easier, but I'm not sure it does,' she smiled.

'Tommy wasn't a good baby,' Molly grimaced, sitting up. 'He used to cry a lot, and he didn't really have much of an interest in food. And he's only just started going through the night. Matt's been marvellous——'

'But?' Charly prompted indulgently.

'But he's a doctor,' Molly sighed. 'He's used to going into a ward, seeing his patient, issuing instructions, and then expecting them to be carried out while he goes on to see another patient.'

'And he did the same with you and Tommy,' she said knowingly.

'Sometimes,' Molly nodded. 'It isn't that I

don't want the baby, I just—I'm not sure I can cope with another one just now.'

'Are you sure it isn't just that you're tired?' Charly suggested gently. 'It's hard work bringing up children.'

'Lucy should almost be at school by the time this one is born,' the other woman said heavily. 'But she's so independent anyway, two children both under two is a different matter altogether.'

'It could be fun,' Charly smiled. 'I'm not saying it will be easy, but they should amuse each other to a certain extent, and once the new baby gets over the very young stage it can go on the floor and play with Tommy. I'm sure that at the moment you seem to be constantly telling Lucy she isn't big enough to pick Tommy up?'

'Why . . . yes,' Molly nodded slowly.

'Tommy and the new baby would soon be more or less the same size so you wouldn't have that problem with them. I'm sure it will be hard work, but it could also have its compensations,' she encouraged.

Molly gave a shaky smile. 'You could be right,' she gave a wan smile. 'Matt and Aaron are going to think I'm so stupid,' she grimaced, standing up to repair her make-up. 'Especially for a doctor's wife!'

'I don't think so.' She smiled as she remembered the two men's faces as she left the lounge. 'Not after what I said to them.'

Molly gave her a questioning look. 'What did you say to them?'

'Enough to make them think a little harder next time before speaking,' she mocked.

Molly tidied her hair. 'I'm so happy for you and Aaron; you seem so happy together.'

Her mouth tightened. 'Yes.'

'I—I have a confession to make.' The other woman turned to her. 'Last night, when I came to the apartment, it wasn't just for the address book, I—I thought you were Matt's girlfriend,' she admitted in a self-conscious rush.

Charly kept her expression bland with effort. 'But Matt's married,' she frowned.

'Yes, but I—I knew you were staying at the apartment, and I—I thought——'

'That Matt and I were lovers,' she laughed dismissively, the other woman's admission totally unexpected and taking her slightly off-guard. 'I can't see Aaron liking that, can you?' she teased.

Molly grimaced. 'I have to admit, I didn't like the idea much either!'

'I'm sure you didn't,' she laughed softly. 'Now shall we rejoin the men before they start dinner without us? I don't suppose——'

'Oh, what a beautiful bracelet!' Molly exclaimed, looking at the charm bracelet Charly wore. 'Oh it's lovely,' she admired as she looked at it closely. 'And I see Aaron did buy you a ring after all,' she teased as she saw the two gold ring charms.

'Yes,' Charly answered abruptly.

'I'm so glad he's going to marry you, Charly,' Molly looked at her warmly. 'I'm sure we're going to be good friends.'

'I'm sure we are too,' she agreed with genuine warmth, glad the other woman had been diverted from the subject of the bracelet. She almost hadn't worn it, despite—or *in* spite?—of Aaron's request, but at the last moment decided it was a nice touch.

'Would you like to look in on the children with me?' Molly asked shyly. 'That is, if you——'

'I love children,' Charly assured her, guessing that Stephanie's death was the reason for Molly's sudden hesitation. 'And I'd like to see Lucy and Tommy.'

The little girl was exactly like her mother, dark-haired and pretty, while Tommy was most like Matt, his blond hair in curls, his face still chubby with baby fat, his lashes fanned out across his baby cheeks as he lay asleep in his cot.

'They're adorable,' Charly told the other woman softly as they went downstairs together.

'Yes, they are,' Molly agreed ruefully. 'I feel better about this baby already.'

'I'm glad to hear it, darling,' Matt put his arm about his wife's shoulders as they entered the lounge. 'I was worried about you,' he admitted softly.

'I was being silly,' she snuggled against him. 'Just think, Tommy will have a playmate now.'

Matt looked over his wife's head and gave Charly a grateful smile. 'And Lucy can mother both of them,' he agreed indulgently.

Charly walked at Aaron's side as they went through to the adjoining room to have dinner, studiously avoiding his gaze.

'That was very nice of you,' he murmured so that only she could hear.

'I can be nice when I like the person involved,' she returned huskily, not looking at him.

He chuckled appreciatively. 'God, I bet you're dynamite in bed!'

She turned to him furiously. 'Keep your opinions to yourself!' she snapped.

He shook his head mockingly. 'All that energy wasted on just talking!'

'How would you like to sit down to dinner without your "fiancée"?' she threatened.

'You won't leave.'

'Try me.'

Aaron sighed. 'I was only making conversation.'

'You were being personal!'

'I'm your fiancé——'

Now she did turn to look at him. 'Don't let this bogus engagement make you think you have any rights over me,' she warned harshly. 'Physically, or in any other way. Because if you push me too far I won't hesitate to let you go through this alone.'

'You wouldn't do that,' he claimed confidently. 'You wouldn't hurt Molly in that way.'

No, she couldn't do it, especially now that Molly had admitted believing Matt to be Charly's lover. But the look she gave Aaron Grantley wasn't in the least defeated. 'I'm Rocharlle Hart, remember, "without wants or needs, with only a quest for power". You think someone like that would care who got hurt if events didn't suit me?' she challenged.

He looked at her steadily. 'I think *you* would,' he said slowly.

Her mouth twisted. 'You won't know until you push me too far—and I really wouldn't advise it.'

His look was admiring. 'You've acquired quite a business reputation since you took over from your husband last year; I can see why.'

'Thank you,' she accepted it as the compliment it was, sitting down as he held out her chair for her.

'Matt and I had a talk while you ladies were upstairs,' he spoke loud enough for the other couple to hear too now.

Charly was suddenly wary, not liking the gleam of satisfaction in his eyes. 'Yes?'

'He and Molly haven't been able to get away since Tommy was born, and now that Molly's expecting number three I suggested maybe they would like to go away together for a few days,' he still spoke lightly.

'It sounds like a good idea.' But she still frowned, watching him warily.

'Alone,' he added with slow emphasis, holding her gaze challengingly.

'Yes?' she prompted again, still not sure what point he was trying to make.

'It sounds wonderful, Aaron,' Molly put in lightly. 'But there's only my parents to take care of the children, and while I don't mind leaving the children with them for a day or evening I really feel a few days would be too much for them. They aren't getting any younger, and Tommy is a bit of a handful. It was a nice idea, though,' she sighed at the lost opportunity.

'I wasn't suggesting your parents have the children, Molly.' Aaron still looked at Charly. 'I thought Charly and I could come here and take care of them for you. After all, they know me, and they would soon get used to Charly.'

Molly turned uncertainly to Charly. 'You really wouldn't mind?'

Bastard, Charly's furious gaze transmitted the message to Aaron, knowing he had received the message as his mouth quirked triumphantly. 'No, of course not,' she assured the other woman, avoiding Aaron Grantley's gaze now. 'I'm sure Aaron is excellent at changing nappies,' she added vengefully.

Matt gave a scornful laugh. 'He doesn't know one end of a baby from the other!'

Aaron scowled at him. 'I know a damn sight more than you did when Lucy was born!'

'Not much more,' Molly laughed. 'I sincerely hope you won't let him loose on Tommy, Charly.'

'I think it would be a good idea.' Charly ate her soup with an air of feigned innocence, once again ignoring Aaron's furious gaze. 'It will be good practise for him for when he becomes a father. I'll supervise them to make sure he doesn't do anything drastic with Tommy, Molly, but I do think he should have complete charge of the baby that weekend.' She looked at him challengingly.

His mouth was tight. 'It isn't very likely I'll ever have to take care of a baby.'

'Oh but there might be occasions when you will, Aaron,' Molly put in seriously. 'Matt tells me Charly is an important lady in the world of business; you would have to take your turn in taking care of the children.'

He scowled. 'I'd hire a nanny.'

Charly shook her head. 'I don't believe in them.'

'Then we won't have any children,' he glared.

'I had a feeling that might be your answer,' she said triumphantly, sipping at her wine.

He gave her an impatient look. 'Are we looking after the children next weekend or not?'

'We are,' she nodded, her mouth curved into a smile. 'With an emphasis on the "we".'

'I think we could have an enjoyable break just watching Aaron trying to cope with Tommy,' Matt mocked. 'In a boardroom he's lethal, but he might not have the same success in a nursery.'

'Tommy likes me,' he claimed indignantly.

'You're his favourite uncle,' Matt nodded. 'But he *dislikes* going to bed at night.'

'All kids dislike that,' Aaron shrugged it off as being unimportant.

'But Tommy *really* dislikes it,' his friend taunted. 'To the point where——'

'Don't tell him any more,' Molly pleaded. 'Or he might change his mind about the offer.'

'He won't,' Charly put in firmly. 'Is next weekend okay for you?' she asked the other couple.

A situation Aaron had created to put her at a disadvantage had been neatly turned on him, and she couldn't help feeling satisfied that she had managed to do so. He had been enjoying himself at her expense; she found it infinitely enjoyable that the roles had been reversed!

'Are you really sure you don't mind?' Molly still hesitated about accepting their offer.

'Not at all,' Charly answered smoothly. 'This is a beautiful house, the children look adorable; I'm sure I'll enjoy myself.' The look she shot Aaron told him it would be mainly at his expense.

He turned to Molly. 'We'll only be needing the one bedroom,' he told her. 'Unless you think it would be better for the children if we slept apart?'

The colour came and went in Charly's cheeks in rapid succession, her mouth tight. Aaron had certainly wreaked his vengeance with interest!

'Of course not,' Molly dismissed. 'They're both too young to ask questions.'

'Oh good,' he smiled his satisfaction. 'We haven't liked to be together at the apartment because it seemed as if we were taking advantage of you.'

'We don't mind if Aaron moves in, do we, darling?' Molly shook her head.

Matt looked at Aaron with narrowed eyes. 'I think that's for Charly to say,' he said tightly.

She cleared her throat awkwardly. 'I'm sure Aaron and I can come to some sort of agreement,' she nodded. 'Thank you,' she added abruptly.

Aaron looked at her with amused green eyes. For every verbal and mental battle that she managed to win over this man he paid her back two-fold! That bit about them sharing a bedroom here next weekend had stunned her, the idea of him moving into the apartment with her was unthinkable.

'Don't let Aaron get to you,' Matt advised as she prepared to leave later that evening, Aaron and Molly still in the lounge. 'He's enjoying himself, that's all.'

'Don't worry,' she assured him. 'He doesn't bother me at all.'

'I can try to put off next weekend if you would like me to?' he frowned.

'I wouldn't hear of it.' She shook her head firmly. 'Please don't worry about Aaron, I can handle him.'

'I'll make sure there are two bedrooms ready for you.' Matt said grimly.

'Even if there were only the one we wouldn't

be sharing it,' she told him hardly. 'Aaron would be sleeping on the sofa in the lounge.'

'He can be very persuasive.'

'I'm not interested,' she dismissed.

Matt frowned at the determination in her voice. 'Most women find him very attractive.'

'I'm not denying his attraction, just stating that he doesn't appeal to me.'

'Sure?'

'Very!'

He shrugged wide shoulders. 'As long as this situation isn't bothering you?'

'It isn't.' She shook her head. 'Look, I'm going down to the house tomorrow, why don't you come with me?' she suggested eagerly. 'I'd really like you to see it, to know your opinion of it before I buy it.'

'Charly, I told you——'

'I know,' she soothed. 'And I understand how you feel, but it's something I want to do.'

'I can't let you——'

'It isn't a question of letting me do anything, Matt.' She put her hand on his arm. 'It's something I really need to do.'

He nodded. 'When do you intend going to the house?'

'In the afternoon,' she told him. 'Please come with me,' she encouraged.

'I'll see if I can get away,' he nodded slowly. 'Although I'm not promising anything,' he warned.

'It's enough that you'll try.' Her eyes glowed. 'I'm sure you'll find it's completely suitable.'

'It's convenient anyway,' he grimaced. 'Only a short drive from here.'

'That's one of the reasons I liked it,' she

nodded. 'This way you could still have the best of both worlds.'

'It's time we were going, Charly.' Aaron cut in with rasping tension, Molly behind him.

Charly looked at him steadily. 'I've been waiting for you,' she told him calmly.

His hard green eyes questioned the validity of that fact before he turned to kiss Molly on the cheek. 'Thank you for a lovely evening,' he smiled affectionately. 'If I were you I would make this husband of yours take you shopping for some new clothes for your weekend away.' He looked challengingly at Charly after this last statement, and she frowned her puzzlement. 'Tomorrow,' he added pointedly.

He had overheard part of her conversation with Matt! And from his manner now she could only presume he had come to his own conclusions. She smiled ruefully, her head going back proudly as Aaron's eyes hardened angrily.

'Matt doesn't like to go shopping,' Molly dismissed with a laugh.

'Then perhaps Charly would like to go with you,' he suggested harshly.

'I can't tomorrow, I'm afraid,' she refused softly. 'But I'd love to go with you some other day,' she agreed.

'I'll call you,' Molly nodded eagerly.

'How can you do it?' Aaron demanded impatiently once they were out on the driveway.

'Do what?' She looked up at him innocently.

He glanced over to where Matt and Molly stood together near the front door waiting to wave their goodbyes. 'We can't talk here,' he muttered. 'I'll meet you at the apartment.'

'I'd rather you didn't.'

'Why, is Matt going to suddenly discover there's an emergency at the hospital?' he derided harshly.

'No!' She looked at him defiantly.

His eyes glittered in the darkness. 'Then I'm not asking you if I can come to the apartment; I'm telling you!'

She shrugged. 'In that case I suppose I'll see you later.' She came to an abrupt halt as he grabbed her arm. 'What is it?' she asked impatiently.

'We ought to say good night in the appropriate manner,' he told her roughly.

'It isn't good night,' she pointed out calmly, not at all cowed by his manner.

'Nevertheless, we do have an audience,' he ground out, bending his head to claim her mouth.

But instead of the anger she had been expecting she found only deep sensuality in Aaron's kiss, the slow drugging exploration of her mouth affecting her in spite of herself, her hands about his waist as he curved her body up into his, Charly made aware of every hard plane of his thighs and chest.

Aaron raised his head, his eyes narrowed. 'You're very responsive,' he accused.

She was glad of the darkness to cover her blushes. 'We have an audience, remember,' she said sharply.

He gave her a scornful look. 'Are you hoping to make Matt jealous?' he rasped softly.

She pulled away from him, her gaze contemptuous. 'He's well aware of the fact that I despise you, Mr Grantley,' she dismissed harshly. 'Just as he's aware that your kisses are forced on me.'

His mouth tightened. 'I'll see you back at the apartment.' He turned on his heel and got into the Jaguar, accelerating out of the driveway with a brief wave of his hand to Matt and Molly.

Charly took a little longer to get into her own car, slightly dazed by her reaction to a man she had just claimed to despise.

'Is everything all right?' Matt had joined her beside her car without her being aware of it.

'Yes, of course.' She shook off her feeling of unease, smiling brightly. ''Night, Molly,' she called out to the other woman. 'Good night, Matt,' she turned back to him reassuringly. 'And please don't worry about me.'

'We can end this any time you want to, you know.' He frowned his concern.

'I told you, I can handle the situation and Mr Aaron Grantley!'

But as she drove home she couldn't help wondering if Aaron Grantley weren't more than a match for her, both physically and mentally.

She wasn't in the least surprised when she reached the apartment first, more familiar with the roads than Aaron was likely to be, living in America as he did most of the time. Consequently she was in the lounge enjoying a relaxing drink when the doorbell rang, bracing her shoulders determinedly as she went to answer it.

'I stopped off for some cigarettes,' Aaron explained his lateness as he walked past her into the apartment.

'Please do come in,' she told him with sarcasm as she followed him through to the lounge. 'And

I thought I had made it clear that I don't like anyone smoking near me,' she reminded hardly as he flicked on a gold lighter beneath the cigarette in his mouth, smoke instantly filling the room.

'I need a cigarette,' he rasped unrelentingly.

Charly could feel herself begin to pale as the consequences of someone else 'needing a cigarette' began to wash over her, reliving the nightmare of being dragged through her smoke-filled apartment. 'Would it help if I said please,' she asked faintly.

Puzzlement flickered in deep green eyes before it was quickly replaced with impatience. 'No.'

She moved to the windows, opening one wide despite the cold night air that instantly blew into the room.

'Don't carry this charade into the farcical,' Aaron advised hardly. 'You're just making yourself look ridiculous.'

Anger flared in the depths of silver-grey eyes as she turned back to face him. 'I'd like to show you something that's really ridiculous!' she bit out furiously, marching over to the door and throwing it open. 'Well don't just stand there.' She turned on him. 'Come and see something *really* ridiculous!'

'Charly——'

'What's the matter, Aaron?' Her eyes glittered silver. 'Afraid *you* might be made to look ridiculous for once?'

His mouth was tight as he joined her at the door. 'Where are we going at this time of night?'

'Not far,' she revealed flatly, leading the way over to the lift, her hands becoming clammy as she pressed the button for the top floor, her body tense as it made its smooth ascent.

'Charly, where are we going?' Aaron demanded again tersely.

'This way.' She stepped out of the lift on to the top level of the building, taking him to the door of one of the three luxury apartments on this floor, unlocking the door, pushing it open and stepping back to allow Aaron to precede her inside.

He frowned. 'What the——'

'Go in,' she urged harshly.

He gave her a glittering look before entering the apartment, looking about uninterestedly before turning back to her. 'I don't——'

'Through there.' She nodded towards the door to his right, hanging back herself as he pushed open the door with barely concealed impatience, coming to an abrupt halt just inside the room, the smell of new paint very strong.

For a moment he just stood in stunned silence, then he turned to her with blazing eyes. 'Your bedroom is where?' he demanded gruffly.

'Through the back of this room,' she replied shakily, her own curiosity getting the better of her as she looked into what had once been her comfortably furnished lounge.

The room was empty except for a couple of ladders and some pots of paint, the elegant blue carpet that had once graced the floors taken out along with all the other things that had been burnt in the fire. Some of the wallpaper had been stripped off the walls but the rest of it remained, burnt and scorched, hanging down damply in places where the fire had been put out, the ceiling having black smoke marks streaked across it where the flames had licked against it.

Aaron strode across the room to fling open the door to her bedroom, no sign of the fire in there that had almost taken her life. He closed the door again softly, looking down at the cigarette in his hand before closing his fingers around it and crushing it to ashes.

'Aaron, no——!'

He looked up at her with dark eyes. 'Let's get out of here,' he rasped, grasping her arm to drag her outside and back down to Matt's apartment, closing the door firmly behind them.

'Did you burn your hand just now?' She frowned at him dazedly, stunned by his action.

'You almost died in there and yet you're worried about a little burn on my hand!' he snapped impatiently. 'When do you move back in?' His eyes were narrowed.

'The decorators optimistically claim the weekend,' she answered dully.

He nodded. 'Why don't you move to another apartment building altogether; the thought of going back there obviously disturbs you!'

'I'm surprised you noticed!' she snapped.

'You would be more than surprised if you knew my thoughts most of the time,' he said grimly.

Her mouth tightened. 'I'm moving back to that apartment because it happens to be my home.'

'And what about the house you intend buying so that you can be near Matt?' he accused.

She had thought he was annoyed earlier because she was meeting Matt tomorrow, it seemed it was more than that. 'What house?' she frowned.

'The one that's "completely suitable" and

"convenient", and not too far from the house Matt shares with Molly so that he can continue to have the "best of both worlds".' He revealed just how much of her conversation with Matt he had overheard—and misunderstood.

'You don't understand——'

'You're wrong, I *do* understand,' he scorned. 'Only too well. You dislike marriage and the commitment of such a relationship so much that it doesn't bother you in the least that the man you want is a married man. You don't even want him to give up that marriage, are quite content to keep your independence and him as well. I suppose the intention is for Matt to spend his time between the two households.'

'You know Matt, he's your best friend, do you think he would agree to that?' she dismissed scornfully.

'He seemd to be trying to fight his attraction for you—without much success,' Aaron rasped. 'He's meeting you there tomorrow, isn't he?'

'Aaron——'

'*Isn't he?*' he demanded she answer him.

Her eyes flashed. 'I'm not going to be brow-beaten into admitting something that isn't true.'

'But you are meeting Matt tomorrow?' he prompted softly.

'Yes. But——'

'At a house you're purchasing so that you can be together?'

'No!'

'I heard you, Charly,' he sighed. 'And I don't want you meeting him there tomorrow or any other time.'

'Do you really think this is any of your business?' she demanded impatiently.

He nodded. 'It has been since Molly first telephoned me. What do you think this would do to her if she ever found out the truth?'

'I know exactly what it would do to her,' she said bitterly. 'Which is why I agreed to this false engagement to you. But it's all a lie, and this latest idea you have that I intend to set up a little love-nest that Matt can fly to whenever he has a spare moment is ridiculous!' She glared at him. 'I thought I had made it clear that I will never be any man's convenience.'

'Again,' Aaron put in softly.

She gave him a sharp look. 'I beg your pardon?'

'From your attitude towards men and marriage I can only assume I was wrong about your marriage to James Hart being convenient for you, that it was *he* who found the marriage convenient. I take it there was another woman involved?'

'Several,' she acknowledged hardly.

'One of them perhaps serious enough to want to keep him,' Aaron guessed shrewdly.

She nodded. 'Which is why I don't want Molly to get the wrong idea about Matt and me.'

'Because you have no intention of keeping him!' Aaron derided scornfully.

'There is nothing between Matt and me except friendship,' she insisted impatiently.

'Then why was it his apartment you moved into after the fire?'

'Because he only uses the apartment occasionally,' she explained exasperatedly. 'And because he offered.'

'You must have been pretty good friends for him to have made the offer.'

'We knew each other, yes,' she confirmed guardedly, not willing to go into the reasons of their meeting with this man.

'Before or since your widowhood?' Aaron derided.

'Since,' she snapped. 'Look, I'm not on trial here, and I don't have to answer any more of your impertinent questions. It's late, and quite frankly, I have had enough for one day.'

'You're asking me to leave?'

'*Telling* would be a better description.' She looked at him unflinchingly.

He shook his head, his gaze admiring. 'Small chubby blondes may not be in fashion,' he drawled. 'But one small chubby blonde interests me.'

'You can take your interest and——'

'Now, now, Charly.' He took her in his arms, one hand beneath her chin as he lifted her face up to his, taking his time about kissing her. 'Remember, you're a lady,' he taunted. 'A *real* lady.'

His kiss contained all the sensuality of the one they had shared earlier—and more. He coaxed and teased and tempted, until she stood on tiptoe to deepen the caress, groaning low in her throat as his tongue dipped enticingly into her mouth, slowly withdrawing before thrusting inside once again.

His eyes were dark as he looked down at her. 'I have a feeling,' he murmured, 'that you and I are going to be lovers one day.'

She recoiled from the statement, her eyes wide. 'No!'

His mouth twisted as he thrust his hands into his trouser pockets. 'I'm no more thrilled with the idea than you are,' he bit out. 'But I know it's going to happen.'

'Not if it isn't what either of us wants,' she told him determinedly.

'Sometimes we have no control over these things,' he shrugged. 'And maybe if it does happen Matt will see what a fool he's making of himself over you,' he added thoughtfully.

Charly gave him a scornful look. 'I'm surprised you didn't make love to me for that reason alone!'

His eyes narrowed. 'Maybe I would have done if I'd thought of it. But I know it's going to happen anyway.'

Long after he had left Charly sat alone in the lounge with the lights off. Aaron Grantley threatened to destroy the very existence she had made for herself the last year.

CHAPTER FOUR

SHE watched Matt's face as they looked around the house, seeing the excitement in his eyes that he was trying so hard to contain. The house was perfect, she had known it was the moment she first saw it!

'These old places always need a lot of work doing to them,' he murmured. 'The mere fact that there's no heating is going to cause tremendous problems——'

'I've already had the place surveyed and all the estimates for the work that needs doing,' she cut in firmly. 'It's well within the budget I estimated would be necessary.'

He sighed heavily. 'It's a tremendous opportunity, Charly, and don't think I'm not grateful——'

'But?' she prompted softly, sensing the refusal in his voice.

His blue eyes deepened compassionately. 'But I can't accept such a generous gift. I didn't save Stephanie——'

'You tried.' She put her hand on his arm. 'That's all anyone could have asked of you.'

She and Matt had first met just over a year ago across the bed of her unconscious daughter, Matt the one to tell her Stephanie had received serious head injuries, that even if she did regain consciousness she might never recover completely, but if by some miracle she did recover it would be a long, slow process, months spent in hospital.

Charly had seen a lot of Matt during the next two months as he often spent an hour or so with her during the long night hours she sat with her daughter, a bed having been made up for her in the same room as Stephanie. They had talked of everything during those times, had become firm friends, and it had been during that time that Charly had decided she would give this man the hospital he needed to be able to specialise in patients like Stephanie. Not even her daughter's death had changed her mind about that.

Shevton House did need a lot of work and alterations to make it into the relaxed and welcoming atmosphere Matt wanted to work with these long-term patients, but the extensive grounds and secluded cove made it ideal for the therapy activities he had in mind. She knew Matt was aware of that too.

'I can't accept this, Charly,' he told her again stubbornly. 'I was only doing my job.'

'And I want you to continue doing it,' she insisted. 'With the best equipment available.'

'It would cost you millions.' He shook his head.

Charly gave a sad smile. 'I have millions, and no one to spend them on. I'll buy the house even without your agreement,' she added stubbornly. 'I'm sure *someone* would like to use the facilities I intend providing.'

He looked around the beautiful old house that could be made functional as well as comfortable. 'I haven't even discussed it with Molly yet,' he murmured.

'Then do so,' she urged, sensing he was weakening, 'Tell her next weekend while you're away.'

He frowned, indecision still in his face. 'It's a big step to take,' he grimaced. 'Working for a hospital is one thing, going out on my own is something else.'

'When we talked you told me this was your dream in life,' she reminded.

Matt gave a rueful shrug. 'Having a dream and then having you buy it for me are two different things.'

Charly turned angrily to face him. 'In other words it was all just talk, you didn't really want——'

'No, that isn't true,' he shook his head emphatically. 'Dare I say "this is so sudden, Mrs Hart"?' he derided.

Her mouth quirked. 'No, you daren't.'

'Because it isn't,' he acknowledged. 'But I have to admit I didn't think you would come through with your offer.'

Charly frowned at this admission. 'But I said I would.'

'I know,' he sighed. 'But people tend to—I won't say forget, because that wouldn't be true,' Matt frowned. 'But once a patient has left my care, or—or died,' he added regretfully, 'then relatives tend to want to put out of their minds anyone and anything that reminds them of that time.'

She nodded. 'It was a traumatic time, but I promised you the hospital, and I'm going to make sure you get it. I know you weren't able to save Stephanie, but that wasn't your fault,' she told him earnestly. 'And with the facilities I want to provide for you here you'll be able to run one of the best hospitals for injuries of that kind possibly in the world.'

'Staffing it would definitely be no problem,' Matt acknowledged ruefully.

She looked up at him with anxious grey eyes. 'Then you will seriously consider accepting it as a gift?'

He grimaced. 'I'd be a fool to turn it down.'

'I think so, yes,' she confirmed mockingly.

He laughed softly. 'But as most people who know me would tell you, I have been known to be a fool on occasions,' he said dryly.

'And this time?'

'I really don't know, Charly,' he told her truthfully. 'It's a wonderful opportunity, but I do have to talk it over with Molly first, see how it will affect her. You saw what she was like last night, I have to know she could cope with it before I accepted your offer,' he frowned. 'I know that must sound ungrateful——'

'Not at all,' she assured him warmly. 'It sounds exactly like one half of a happy marriage *should* react. It's good to hear.'

'How is the situation with Aaron going?' he asked casually—too casually!

She stiffened. 'He's bossy, overbearing, totally impossible to reason with——'

'And he's very attracted to you,' Matt finished dryly.

She gave him a sharp look, her eyes narrowed. 'He told you?'

'He didn't have to,' his friend derided. 'I've known him long enough to recognise the signs.'

'You mean he's often attracted to women who can't stand him!' Charly scorned.

Matt laughed softly. 'Usually you can't keep the woman away from him.'

'I can see how quite a lot of them would want to do him physical harm!'

'That wasn't quite what I meant,' he chuckled.

'Matt.' She looked at him sternly. 'I hope you don't intend matchmaking between Aaron and me——'

'Good heavens, no,' he dismissed. 'Aaron never has any trouble doing his own attracting.'

'He's out of luck this time,' she scowled.

'He can be quite good fun to be with if you let him,' Matt told her softly.

'I'm not letting him,' she stated firmly. 'Not with me.'

'Hm,' Matt considered. 'Obstinacy on the part of the woman has been known to make him more determined.'

'And giving in to him isn't part of my plans,' she drawled. 'I'd rather be obstinate. And in the meantime I would prefer it if you didn't mention anything about this house or the hospital to him.'

'Why?' Matt was obviously puzzled by the request.

'Because I——I have a competitor for the sale of this house.' She avoided his probing gaze. 'And the less people that know about the deal the better.'

'Aaron can be the soul of discretion.'

Her mouth twisted. 'I have yet to witness that! He still doesn't believe I only moved into your apartment because of the fire in mine, and he's also implied I married James to get control of Hartall Industries,' she recalled hardly.

'Aaron can be a lot of things,' Matt muttered, 'but I've never known him to be this much of an idiot before!'

She gave a derisive smile. 'He seems to have a blind spot where I'm concerned, prefers to believe the worst.'

'He wouldn't if you explained it all to him——'

'No,' she stated firmly. 'Let him go on thinking what he likes about me. I do not want any publicity about my part in the acquisition of this property,' she told him determinedly. 'The press would take delight in splashing a story like this across the front pages of their newspapers. I can almost see the headlines now,' she said bitterly. ' "Allenby-Hart Heiress Buys Hospital for her Dead Daughter's Doctor". I couldn't bear that, Matt,' she shuddered with loathing.

'But it's the truth,' he put in gently.

'Not the way they would write it,' she grimaced. 'I've been the subject of publicity too many times not to know how the press would deal with that information. They could take it two ways, either making it into something sickeningly sentimental, or imply so much into our relationship that no matter how we both denied it, or how much she loves you, Molly would have to wonder if there weren't some truth to the story. The acquisition of this house is to be a private deal, and as soon as possible I will be deeding it over to you. Hopefully no one will ever need to know I was involved,' she dismissed.

'I had thought of calling it the Stephanie Hart Hospital.' Matt looked at her anxiously.

Charly swallowed hard, blinking back the tears. 'I—I'm grateful for the sentiment,' she spoke huskily, 'but I'd rather you didn't.'

'No, perhaps not,' he agreed heavily. 'But I'm sure Aaron would respect the confidence.'

And she was equally sure that if Aaron Grantley knew the reason she was buying Shevton House, that she intended giving it to Matt for his hospital, that he would completely misinterpret the gesture, as he had misinterpreted everything else about the two of them. He did indeed seem to have a blind spot where she was concerned!

'I'd prefer that you didn't tell him,' Charly said with quiet forcefulness. 'Not until something definite has been decided, at least.'

'I can understand that,' Matt nodded. 'And I will talk to Molly about it next weekend.'

She gave an inclination of her head. 'I would be grateful if you would; I really do need an answer as soon as possible.'

She was already confident of what Matt's answer would be, knew Molly was the sort of wife who encouraged her husband's advancement in his career. She was also well aware of what Aaron Grantley would think of her buying Shevton House for Matt; he would think she was trying to buy the other man!

The decorators had finished by the Thursday evening, as they had promised they would, the carpet and new furniture delivered and put in on the Friday, and all that she had to do now was move her things back upstairs. And that was something she was reluctant to do.

She was grateful for the ringing of the doorbell shortly after seven to interrupt her packing, although once she had identified her caller as Aaron Grantley she wasn't quite as pleased.

His gaze raked critically over the clinging

denims and fitted blue cashmere sweater she wore, her hair braided down her spine to keep it out of the way as she worked. She met his gaze challengingly.

'Now you *look* like Charly Allenby,' he finally drawled.

She blinked. 'I beg your pardon?'

'The first night I met you you looked like Matt's mistress, Charly, the next day at your office you were every inch Rocharlle Allenby-Hart,' he recalled dryly. 'That evening too. Now you look like Charly Allenby, a beautiful woman just relaxing at home.' His eyes were dark with appreciation.

She gave him the same slow perusal he had given her, liking the way his own denims fitted snugly to his lean hips and long legs, a tan leather jacket worn over a fitted green shirt. He hardly looked like the board-room barracuda he was either!

'You don't look so bad yourself,' she drawled mockingly.

'Hey, I meant it as a compliment,' he frowned.

'So did I,' she returned straight-faced.

He grimaced ruefully. 'Now I know what it feels like to be "looked over".'

She nodded. 'Not very nice, is it?'

Aaron shrugged. 'Depends who's doing the "looking over", I suppose,' he taunted.

Charly decided that it was time she put an end to this conversation, that it was actually bordering on *flirtatious*. 'What are you doing here?' she demanded to know. 'We aren't due to meet again until next weekend.' She looked at him questioningly. 'Are we? You haven't made any other arrangements for us of which I'm unaware, have you?' Her voice hardened.

His answer was to walk past her and into the apartment, frowning as he saw the boxes she had been packing, his eyes narrowed as he looked back at Charly. 'Going somewhere?'

'Obviously,' she drawled.

'Surely there's legal procedures to go through before you can actually move in?' Aaron rasped.

She frowned her puzzlement. 'Legal procedures?' she repeated. 'If you're talking about the insurance people, they've already been in.' She shook her head in bewilderment.

'Insurance . . .? Charly, where are you going with all this stuff?' he asked slowly.

'Upstairs,' she supplied dazedly. 'Where did you——' Her brow cleared as she realised what he meant. 'Yes, Aaron, there are legal procedures you have to go through before you can buy and move into a house,' she derided.

'Well?'

'Well what?' she taunted.

'Charly, don't play games with me,' he scowled. 'If I hadn't had to go back to the States on business I would have been to see you earlier to find out if Matt approves of the house you picked out for the two of you!'

Charly looked at him with a steady grey gaze. 'He's still thinking about it,' she returned softly.

'Hell, Charly,' Aaron bit out impatiently, 'Matt's a nice guy, but——'

'I think so,' she nodded calmly.

'He's married!' Aaron reminded forcefully.

'I've found that most of the nice ones are,' she returned coolly.

'Charly——'

'*Aaron*! I'm really not in the mood to be lectured by someone who had a much-publicised affair with a senator's wife!' She looked at him challengingly, having made it her business to find out a little bit more about *him* since they last met.

He had the grace to look uncomfortable. 'I didn't have an affair with her,' he denied impatiently. 'I was involved in helping her husband's campaign, and the media made a lot of noise about the fact that I accompanied her to an official dinner when her husband was ill one night.'

Charly gave him a mocking look. 'Isn't it terrible how the most innocent of incidents can be misconstrued?'

He sighed. 'It *was* innocent, Charly.'

'Of course it was,' she humoured him, her eyes wide as he looked at her sharply.

'I can see we aren't going to get anywhere with this conversation,' he dismissed tersely. 'Could I just *ask* you to reconsider before buying a house to be near Matt?' He obviously had to force himself to make it into a request. 'Molly would be sure to realise what was going on eventually.'

Her mouth tightened. 'It's going to be Matt's decision on whether or not I buy the house.'

'No man in his right mind would turn down the opportunity to have you marked private property.'

She shied away from the intensity of his gaze. 'I remember an occasion when you told me the thought of having to make love to me made your skin crawl, and that you would have to be drunk to attempt it!'

He winced as she reminded him of that

conversation. 'I think I may have been a little hasty——'

'I don't,' she cut in briskly. 'And *no* man will ever mark me his "private property!" Now instead of standing there looking useless perhaps you would like to help me take some of these things upstairs?' She considered the idea a brainwave; she didn't particularly want Aaron here, but she dreaded going up to her apartment alone even more.

'You're moving back up to your apartment tonight?' Aaron frowned.

She nodded, putting several more things into boxes; it was amazing how much she had accumulated down here the last week. 'Normally, I would have asked Matt to help me——'

'But as he's having dinner with his in-laws tonight I'll have to do!'

She had had no idea what Matt was doing this evening, but obviously this man was keeping a check on the times they could be together. 'Yes,' she mocked.

He gave her a resentful glare. 'I'm not used to being thought of as a substitute!'

She smiled. 'It must be another terrible blow for your already shattered ego!'

'I doubt if I have one left,' he muttered, picking up two of the boxes. 'Are you coming up with me or do you trust me not to go through your personal things the moment I'm out of your sight?'

She looked at him with steady grey eyes. 'I trust you,' she told him softly.

'That's something at least.' He took the key to her apartment as she held it out to him.

'Just put them in the bedroom,' she requested. 'I'll follow with some more things.'

No matter how annoying she found his behaviour the majority of the time she was grateful for his presence while she reacquainted herself to living in her own apartment again, accepting his help in unpacking the boxes, finding the silence between them strangely companionable.

'That didn't take long,' she thanked him once the last box had been emptied. 'Would you like a cup of coffee?' she offered, still reluctant to be alone up here.

Aaron nodded, having discarded his jacket to fully reveal his muscled arms and chest beneath the green shirt. 'Do you have an apple or something I could eat too?' he requested hopefully.

Her brows rose. 'You haven't had dinner?'

'I came straight to see you once I'd showered and changed,' he shrugged. 'There wasn't time to eat too.'

'And you didn't think you would be staying this long,' she acknowledged ruefully.

'You don't usually make me this welcome,' he agreed dryly.

'You aren't exactly welcome now either.' Her eyes flashed silver. 'But I think you've earnt some dinner.'

'Charly——'

'I won't be long.' She strode into the kitchen without a backward glance, sure he had guessed the reason she had wanted him here tonight.

She didn't need anyone, had deliberately made herself self-sufficient the last year, and she didn't appreciate Aaron pointing out her weakness tonight.

'A sandwich will do,' Aaron murmured from the kitchen doorway as she perused the contents of her fridge.

She turned to face him. 'I haven't had dinner either,' she snapped.

'In that case I'll have whatever you're having.' He wisely left her to it.

She cooked as she did most things, quietly and efficiently, Aaron hidden behind her newspaper when she swept through to lay the table. He lowered it slightly as he heard her moving about the room, the newspaper rustling back into place as she looked at him.

'I don't throw things,' she mocked, standing with her hands on her hips.

The newspaper was slowly lowered again, green eyes dark with amusement. 'Sure?'

'Yes,' she laughed softly. 'You'll find some wine in that cupboard over there.' She pointed across the room.

'You're giving me wine too?' he taunted, folding the newspaper neatly before putting it back in the rack. 'What did I do to deserve that?' He stood up to open the wine cupboard. 'Hm, what are we having for dinner?' He looked up at her from his crouching position on the floor.

'Beef.'

'Red wine, then,' he quirked mocking brows at her. 'Any preferences?'

'Any one will do,' she shrugged. 'I chose them all personally.'

'A woman that knows what she likes,' he murmured, studying the contents of the wine cupboard. 'How about if we forget about red wine and settle for champagne?' He held up a vintage year of Dom Perignon. 'We haven't celebrated our engagement yet.'

'Champagne will be fine, I like sparkling wines,' she said stiffly. 'But I don't think we have anything to celebrate.'

'Possibly not.' He stood up with the bottle of champagne in his hand.

'A bogus engagement to a man I barely know——'

'And have no wish to know,' he put in softly.

'And have no wish to know,' she repeated forcefully. 'Is no cause for celebration!'

'I agree,' Aaron nodded. 'So how would it be if we drank to *getting* to know each other?'

'I'd just like the wine to complement my meal,' she told him sharply. 'For no other reason.' She left to check on the food.

The spaghetti bolognese probably wasn't the beef Aaron had been expecting but it was well-prepared, quick to cook, filling and tasty—and he ate every morsel on his plate, the Italian way. Charly watched in amazement as he twirled the spaghetti neatly on to his fork before popping it neatly into his mouth.

'I have an Aunt Maria who taught me how to appreciate Italian food at an early age,' he explained.

She looked at the trimness of his waist and body. 'It doesn't show,' she mocked.

'Willpower,' he acknowledged. 'Every time I see a pizza or any other Italian dish I think how much exercise I would need to take to run off all the calories, and somehow the temptation isn't there any more.'

'And what reason did you give yourself for giving up smoking?' She patted delicately at the spot of sauce on her chin; unfortunately she didn't have the same expertise with the spaghetti as he did!

He sobered. 'Can't you guess?'

She had noticed he had not had a cigarette the whole evening.

Charly shrugged. 'It can't have been because you can no longer afford it!'

'Every time I even *think* about having a cigarette I remember this room as it was when you showed it to me last.' He looked about the newly decorated room. 'The fact that it was a cigarette that did that much damage scares the hell out of me!'

Her appetite had suddenly faded, and she sipped at her wine to hide her sudden feeling of panic. 'It was an accident,' she dismissed.

'It was damned carelessness,' he scowled. 'And when I thought about it I knew I wasn't always conscious of disposing of my own cigarettes properly.'

'You do it automatically.'

'Your friend didn't,' he reminded grimly. 'I wouldn't ever want to feel I'd been responsible for almost killing someone.'

'So you gave up, just like that?' she frowned, finding it incredible that the fire here should have had such an impact on him.

He grimaced self-derisively. 'I now chew a lot of mints.'

'You'll get fat,' she warned, doubting it was even a possibility; he seemed to be naturally slim.

'Probably,' he agreed ruefully. 'You know, your spaghetti's-a-lika-Aunta-Maria-usa-make.'

Charly laughed at his ham Italian accent. 'Thank you for the compliment.'

'But your method of eating it could do with a little working on,' he mocked as she once again ended up with sauce on her chin. 'Here, let me.' He took her napkin out of her hand, leaning forward—and instead of using the napkin his tongue moved in a silky caress across her chin.

Charly flinched back, glaring at him. 'I'll do it myself, thank you,' she snapped.

He shrugged, completely unperturbed by her anger. 'Then let me show you how to use your spoon and fork so that you at least stop dropping food down your chin.'

She eyed him suspiciously for several seconds, but she couldn't see anything wrong in the suggestion, nodding her agreement. She knew she had been wrong as he stood up to come around the back of her, his body pressed against hers as he showed her the correct way to twirl the spaghetti on to the fork.

He was too close, she could feel the heat of his body on her back, his aftershave spicy, his hands warm as they clasped hers. She didn't want this closeness, had shunned any contact with men the last year, knew she had been right to do so as heat spread through her body, her nipples hardening against the sensuous warmth of her sweater. It was so long since she had known this sexual awareness, if she had ever felt it this strongly before. She couldn't even remember reacting to James' close proximity like this, usually had to be coaxed into lovemaking. Aaron Grantley had merely touched her, and she was so aware of him the colour burnt in her cheeks, her nipples seeming to throb.

'You see,' Aaron murmured against her hair.

'See?' she repeated breathlessly. 'I don't—Oh yes,' she said nervously as he held up the spaghetti on the fork. 'Very nice. But I don't think I'm hungry any more.' She moved restlessly within the confines of his arms, her sexual tension rising. She had to get away from him!

'Charly . . .?' He frowned down at her as he sensed her panic.

She avoided his gaze. 'If you've had enough to eat I'll clear away——'

'Charly!' he groaned now.

Her breathing was ragged and uneven. 'Please. I have to clear away——'

'You aren't going anywhere.' Compelling green eyes held her gaze as he pulled her to her feet in front of him. 'Oh, Charly!' he groaned before his mouth claimed hers, their mouths open to each other, tongues entwining, breaths mingling, Aaron curving her body into his as he showed her how deeply he was aroused.

His hands moved restlessly over her body, each caress too fleeting to be enjoyed to the fullest, Charly beginning to moan her frustration, wanting those leanly sensitive hands on her.

'No!' she pleaded as his hand would have once again left her breast after only the merest of touches, pressing him into her heated flesh. 'Touch me,' she urged, her mouth returning to his.

His caresses warmed her, excited her, their mouths locked together moistly, Charly feeling

her sweater moved aside as Aaron probed
beneath its warmth, cupping beneath the full
weight of her breast, his thumb-tip moving lightly
over the turgid nipple. She had always been
highly sensitised there, and she pressed weakly
against him, begging for more.

Both hands were beneath her sweater now,
caressing rhythmically against her breasts, the
force of his thighs telling her of his own deep
need. She moved to touch him, hearing him gasp
with pleasure as her hand slipped beneath his
clothing to lovingly caress him.

'Oh, Lady. Lady!' he groaned as she continued
to touch him. 'What are you doing to me?'

Her hand began to move, leaving him in no
doubt what she was doing—if indeed he had ever
doubted it. It was as if years of restraint had
suddenly been lifted from her, and she wanted to
share with Aaron all the things she had been too
shy to do with James, wanted to explore the
depths of her own sensuality as well as his.

The deep pile carpet felt soft against her back,
Aaron's weight pressing her down into it; it was a
pleasure-pain that she welcomed, blocking out
the little voice at the back of her head that kept
telling her this was Aaron Grantley, the man who
had been nothing but a torment to her since the
moment she first met him. He was still a torment,
but in a much more pleasurable way.

'I knew you would look like this,' Aaron
groaned, her sweater discarded, her breasts firm,
the nipples darkly brown.

'Please don't stop,' she begged, feeling the
pressure building between her thighs.

'I don't intend to,' he promised, claiming her

lips once more while he caressed beneath her denims. 'You're so moist,' he groaned. 'So ready for me.' He raised his head to look down at her. 'Lady, I need to make love to you, will you let me?'

The way he called her 'Lady' now was so different from that first night, almost like a caress. 'I can't stop you,' she admitted raggedly.

'But will you *let* me?' he persisted.

'I——' she broke off in confusion as the telephone began to ring. Why did they always do that when you least wanted them to!

'Damn!' Aaron seemed no more pleased by the interruption than she was, looking down at her regretfully. 'By the time you've finished taking that call you're going to regret what just happened between us,' he realised ruefully.

She moistened her lips, reaction already setting in, although it wasn't regret for what had happened, it was confusion, need, and a little fear. No—a *lot* of fear!

'I'll get it,' Aaron sighed as the telephone continued to ring, pushing the bottom of his shirt back into his trousers as he crossed the room to pick up the receiver. 'No, Molly, this isn't Charly,' he drawled. 'But I can get her for you.'

Charly had stiffened into a sitting position as soon as the caller identified herself, pushing back the loose tendrils of her hair from her face after pulling on her sweater, her body still deeply aroused. And Aaron Grantley had been the man to excite her to a pitch that she had never known before, not even with James.

'Charly,' he prompted softly, holding out the receiver to her, his hand over the mouth-piece.

She stood up, awkwardly avoiding his gaze. 'Hello, Molly,' her voice was very gruff.

'I haven't interrupted anything, have I?' the other woman sounded concerned. 'I was calling our apartment most of the evening until Matt arrived home and told me you were moving back into your own place tonight, that's why this call is so late,' she apologised.

'What can I do for you?' she asked politely.

'You did say you wouldn't mind going shopping with me some time . . .' Molly sounded uncomfortable. 'Look, I've obviously called at a bad time——'

'You haven't,' she quickly assured her. 'When did you have in mind for the shopping?' She looked round as Aaron disappeared into the kitchen.

'Well my mother has offered to look after the children for me tomorrow, but——'

'Tomorrow sounds fine.' She could hear Aaron opening cupboards in the kitchen, wondering what on earth he was doing in there. 'Would it be easier for you to meet me here or in town?' she asked Molly.

'There, if you wouldn't mind?' Molly agreed eagerly. 'You're sure it's convenient?'

'Very sure.' Charly's brows rose as Aaron came in with a tray of coffee, nodding as he asked if she would like some; the last thing she had expected him to be doing was making coffee! 'About two o'clock, okay?'

'Lovely. I'll see you tomorrow, then,' Molly rang off.

Charly wished the other woman hadn't ended the conversation quite to abruptly, slowly replacing her own receiver. 'Thank you for the coffee.' She wearily sank down into the chair opposite Aaron, the two of them sitting in silence for several minutes.

'I know this is the part where you're supposed to protest at my seduction of you.' Aaron finally spoke, his eyes a dark slumbrous green, his dark hair tousled on to his forehead. 'But that wouldn't be true, would it?' he watched her intently.

She took a sip of her coffee, gasping as it burnt her top lip. 'Maybe *I* should be apologising for seducing you?' she suggested self-derisively, knowing she had been the aggressor in the encounter.

His mouth twisted. 'That wouldn't be true either.'

'Then what is true?' she asked sharply.

'That we want each other,' he shrugged. 'That we have a need of each other.'

'It isn't enough for—for what just happened,' she snapped.

'Surely it's better than that unhappy marriage you had with James Hart?' he demanded angrily. 'At least we genuinely want each other and wouldn't be making love out of duty!'

'I never made love with James out of duty!' Her eyes flashed warningly.

'Never?' he taunted softly.

'Never,' she insisted defiantly.

'Never once cried off with a non–existent headache?' Aaron mocked.

Embarrassment coloured her cheeks. 'It is possible to have a genuine headache,' she defended.

'Charly, we want each other,' he told her intensely. 'You can't stop the fact that sooner or later we are going to make love.'

She stood up. 'Thank you for helping me bring my things up here this evening.'

'End of conversation?' he derided.

She nodded. 'End of conversation.'

Aaron shrugged, standing up too. 'You didn't appear to me to be a woman who would hide from the truth when confronted with——'

'I'm not hiding from anything!' She handed him his jacket. 'I'm well aware of the fact that I'm attracted to you,' she snapped. 'I just don't intend doing anything about it.'

'Again,' he taunted.

Charly's mouth tightened. 'Tonight was unfortunate——'

'And your choice of word is *unfortunate*,' he ground out hardly, taking hold of her chin roughly. 'I'm going to keep working on you, Lady, until you have to give in.'

She turned her face away, only to have it wrenched back by his hand on her chin. 'Take your hands off me,' she ordered through gritted teeth, breathing heavily. 'And don't go away with the idea that today was a foretaste of what's to come; I have always been in control of my actions.' Until now, a little voice in her head mocked. A voice she ignored.

'Then you've slipped up badly tonight,' Aaron mocked. 'Because now that I've seen what it's like between us I'm not going to make do with anything less than all of you. You may think I don't have the choice, but I've never given up on anything I wanted as badly as I want you. Matt may be my best friend, but he's going to find himself ousted from your life so quickly he'll wonder if he was ever in it!'

'That much confidence is going to leave you looking rather stupid,' Charly scorned.

'You don't love Matt,' Aaron stated arrogantly.

Her mouth tightened. 'I like him better than any other man I know!'

'Including me.'

'Especially you!'

He looked at her mockingly. 'Don't worry, I'm not going to settle for any half-hearted emotion such as liking.' He leant forward and lightly kissed her forehead. 'I'm going to want a complete surrender.'

'You won't get it from me!' she spat the words.

He shrugged. 'I'll call for you late Friday afternoon. We won't need both cars, so you might as well drive down with me,' he told her firmly as she looked about to protest. 'Independence is fine in its right place, Charly, but I'd like a little more togetherness in future.'

'*You* would like?' she repeated indignantly, stepping back, anger her only defence when she was feeling so exposed emotionally. 'I really don't care what you would like or dislike,' she flared at him. 'Now would you please leave?'

'Of course I'll leave, you didn't think I was about to overstay my welcome, did you?' he taunted.

Her head went back. 'You did that the moment you arrived!'

'You didn't seem to think so at the time,' he drawled. 'In fact, you seemed quite pleased to see me.'

She blushed as she realised the truth of his words. 'And now I want you to leave.'

'I'm going,' he smiled. 'After all, we have all of next weekend together for me to look forward to.'

She closed the door behind him with more force than was strictly necessary, anger at herself making her angry with him. There had been men, a lot of men since James died, who had tried to induce desire where none existed; Aaron hadn't even tried, it had just been there for him. She had thought she disliked him, that his erroneous assumptions about her and Matt made her despise him. It hadn't been dislike she felt for him tonight.

And she could still feel that fear licking through her body, fear that her dependence on Aaron Grantley could be completely different from her emotional need of James at the beginning of their marriage. She wasn't sure which was worse, the emotional or physical need. Or which was going to hurt her the worst.

One thing she did know, her nervousness about sleeping in the apartment because of the fire had completely gone now, no longer imagining smoke and flames in the lounge, haunted by a much more vivid picture of her in Aaron's arms on the carpet as they made love!

And it was that memory that made her run to the peace and protection of her bedroom.

CHAPTER FIVE

'I KNEW there was a reason I didn't shop in London very often.' Molly collapsed into the chair opposite Charly in the restaurant, the two of them having ordered a reviving pot of tea.

Charly smiled. 'It is exhausting.' She had forgotten herself just *how* exhausting, rarely finding the time to brave the shops of London herself any more, not even for clothes, having her dressmaker send over a selection for her to choose from. But it had been a pleasant change to enjoy the relaxed company of another woman as they browsed through the clothes shops, Molly finding several new dresses.

They both smiled gratefully at the waiter as he brought their tea, Charly leaving it to Molly to pour.

'Now you really must tell me all about you and Aaron,' Molly invited avidly.

She couldn't say she was exactly surprised by the question, but that hadn't really helped her find any answers; she knew little or nothing about Aaron's likes and dislikes. 'What do you want to know?' She stirred the milk into her tea, her gaze evasive.

'Oh not much,' Molly shrugged ruefully. 'Just where you met? How long you've known each other? How long have you been in love?'

'Just a few facts, then?' Charly derided.

Molly laughed. 'Yes.'

She shrugged. 'We met at a party a couple of months ago.' She felt the generality was pretty safe. 'The last time Aaron was in England,' she added for effect.

'In August?' Molly frowned. 'But he was only in the country overnight.'

Charly laughed dismissively. Rule number one, she must remember not to enlarge on an already accepted answer! 'You're right, that visit was so fleeting I'd forgotten about it,' she nodded. 'I meant the time before that, of course.'

'June,' Molly nodded. 'He certainly kept quiet about you for a long time.'

'That was my fault, I'm afraid.' She really would have to find out more about Aaron Grantley before being caught in a conversation like this again! 'I'm a little cautious about relationships since my marriage.'

'Aaron explained about your husband dying; it must have been so sad for you,' Molly sympathised.

'Yes,' she answered abruptly.

'But now you and Aaron have found happiness together.' The other woman brightened. 'I can hardly wait for the wedding!'

'It is sure to be an event,' Charly agreed wryly.

'Aaron has asked Matt to be his best man.' Molly told her in a pleased voice.

Charly stiffened. 'He's what?' she gasped.

'Well it is a little premature yet, with no date having been set,' the other woman acknowledged. 'Aaron explained that,' she nodded. 'But he asked Matt anyway.'

'I see,' she bit out, wishing she did 'see'! Surely this was taking the pretence too far!

'I suppose it will be a church wedding?' Molly asked curiously. 'Aaron said you would both prefer it.'

Charly frowned. 'When did he say that?'

'He called over late yesterday afternoon to see the children on his way from viewing a property he's interested in buying, and he was still there when Matt got home. I would have thought he would have mentioned it when he came over last night.' She sounded surprised that he hadn't.

'It was late when he got there,' Charly hastily excused. 'And we had to move my things back upstairs; we didn't get a chance to talk about the wedding at all.' But she had an idea the property Aaron had been viewing yesterday afternoon had been Shevton House!

'Aaron is so much in love,' Molly said indulgently. 'He can't wait for the two of you to be married.'

'I'm looking forward to it myself,' she said through gritted teeth. 'But there are still a lot of the details to be worked out.'

'Where you're going to live for one thing,' Molly teased.

'That is a problem,' she agreed non-committally, not going to fall into that trap a second time.

'The country is nicer,' Molly nodded. 'But I realise London would be more convenient for you.'

That hadn't been exactly what she thought the problem might be in such a marriage, but as Molly seemed to be assuming she and Aaron would live in England she realised she had been right to be cautious; she had no way of knowing *what* Aaron had told the other woman.

'It is,' she nodded.

'It will be lovely having Aaron living closer; we see so little of him at the moment. Not that we'll expect to see much of either of you the first few months,' she teased. 'There's something about being just married.' She gave a whimsical smile. 'Matt and I lived together for a year before we got married, and yet even so it was a magical time after we were married. I think it's the total commitment that does it, the *knowing* that you want to be together.' She gave a rueful smile. 'It seems strange to think of myself as the student-nurse I was then. Especially now I'm expecting our third child.'

'How do you feel about that now you've had chance to get used to the idea?' Charly prompted gently.

'Still shocked, but resigned. And I don't mean that in a bad way,' she hastened to explain. 'It's just that the baby is a fact, so we have to accept it, and look forward to its birth. I'm getting quite excited actually,' she confided. 'Aaron told me the two of you would like three or four children yourselves.'

Now he had gone too far! It was all right talking about mythical engagements, even mythical weddings, but mythical *children* was just too much!

'I think wanting and actually having are two different things,' she evaded.

'Aaron will make a very good father,' Molly told her thoughtfully.

Surprisingly enough, she believed he would too! He would be firm but not strict, understanding rather than uninterested, teasing rather than overindulgent. But he would never father any children by her!

He could at least have warned her of his visit to Molly yesterday, and of the subsequent intimate revelations he appeared to have made about their imagined future together.

'He's marvellous with our two,' Molly added lightly. 'Are you really going to give him complete control of Tommy next weekend?' she teased.

'If you wouldn't mind?' she nodded.

'I don't mind,' Molly smiled. 'Men can be so complacent about coping with children. They spend a couple of hours with them on a Saturday and Sunday, and then can't understand why some days you're at screaming pitch after being with them all day.' She shook her head. 'I think I should let *you* in on the little secret I have for getting Tommy to sleep, though,' she said ruefully. 'Even Matt doesn't know what it is; he thinks I've performed a miracle when I get the little monkey to sleep in minutes when he's been trying all evening!'

Charly returned the other woman's smile. 'Aaron is convinced he'll succeed where you've failed.'

'Not without my secret he won't,' Molly said with certainty.

'Then by all means let me in on the secret,' she urged.

'It's simple really, you just sit in the rocker with him in your arms and gently sing "The Lullaby Song". Do you know the one I mean?'

She nodded stiffly. 'It used to be a favourite of Stephanie's. My daughter,' she explained abruptly.

Molly frowned. 'Then perhaps I ought to let Aaron in on the secret after all; it will be too painful for you.'

'Not at all,' she shook her head firmly. 'I'll enjoy holding and singing to a baby again. Besides,' she lightened the conversation, 'it won't hurt Aaron to suffer a little.'

'What's he done to upset you?' Molly giggled.

'Nothing. But he might consider bringing the number of children down from three or four to just one!'

Molly chuckled. 'Men have very short memories when it comes to the unpleasant things in life, such as irritable children.'

'Yes,' Charly agreed ruefully. 'Well, I suppose we ought to be making a move.' The pot of tea was empty, the sandwiches and cakes eaten. 'You have to get back, and I have a date this evening. With Aaron,' she added hastily.

'Who else?' Molly dismissed, motioning for the bill.

Who else, indeed! Bill Shaw was a business acquaintance who would like to be much more, and Charly had arranged to have dinner with him before she entered into this bogus engagement with Aaron. And she had no intention of cancelling dinner with the pleasant man Bill was because of that.

But before she went on her date with Bill she intended paying Aaron a visit at his hotel. There was really no need for him to complicate matters with a lot more lies, and she was going to tell him so before things went any further.

She insisted on paying for the tea before she and Molly went outside.

'Maybe we can do this again some time,' Molly suggested as she unlocked her parked car outside the apartment building. 'Once you and Aaron have settled down.'

She and Aaron would never settle down—at least, not together! 'I'd like that,' she nodded, waving to the other woman as she drove away.

Her smile faded as soon as the car drove out of sight. Damn Aaron Grantley! He had turned a pleasant afternoon's shopping into a fiasco, as she headed off one claim after another that he had made to Molly only yesterday afternoon!

She was still angry when she got into her car later that evening, unaware of how attractive she looked with the flush to her cheeks, her gown the same shimmering silver as her eyes, her hair plaited and coiled in a golden crown about her head. She looked regal as she parked the car in front of the hotel, leaving the key with the doorman, too angry to be aware of the admiring glances following her progress across the lobby to the reception desk.

'Tell Mr Grantley I'm on my way up,' she informed the male receptionist, surreptitiously watching the room number he dialed. 'Rocharlle Allenby-Hart,' she supplied as the man looked at her enquiringly. Aaron was in room seven-one-seven! 'Don't bother,' she instructed the man. 'I've decided I'd like to surprise him after all,' she gave him a friendly smile.

The man hastily put down the receiver as she turned and walked towards the lift. 'Miss Hart—er—Allenby-Hart!' he amended, following her.

She turned slowly, one brow raised in haughty enquiry. 'Yes?' she drawled arrogantly.

The man moistened his lips nervously. 'I really should inform Mr Grantley you're here before allowing you up.'

'Very well.' She gave a haughty inclination of her head. 'But you'll ruin the surprise.'

He looked even less confident. 'Surprise?'

Charly gave him a dazzling smile. 'Yes—surprise,' she drawled provocatively.

'Oh.' The man coloured with embarrassment. 'Er—Okay,' he beat a hasty retreat back to his desk.

Charly's mouth tightened once the lift doors had closed. Aaron Grantley was going to get a surprise, all right, but she wasn't sure it was one he would like!

Her foot tapped impatiently on the carpeted corridor as she waited for him to open the door to her knock, the three-inch heels on her sandals giving her legs a slender elegance. Only the slight widening of her eyes showed she was put off-guard as Aaron opened the door wearing only a towel draped about his hips, a second towel about his neck as he wiped the excess shaving-foam off his recently shaved chin.

He didn't look in the least surprised to see her, and Charly could only assume he had already identified his caller through the small peep-hole in the door. She wished she had thought to put her hand over it!

'Well can I come in?' she asked waspishly. 'Or do you always keep women standing outside your door like this?'

His mouth quirked as he stepped back to let her enter the comfortably luxurious suite. 'Not my bedroom door, anyway,' he drawled.

'I'm sure,' she derided coldy. 'I——' she broke

off as she saw the pretty redhead seated in the lounge for the first time, her brows rising questioningly as she turned back to Aaron.

'Charly, this is Erin Brody,' he introduced calmly, not in the least perturbed by her arrogance. 'Erin, this is Rocharlle Allenby-Hart. Charly to her friends,' he added with a grin. 'And as her fiancé I think I must qualify as that,' he said goadingly.

Her mouth tightened. 'Miss Brody,' she greeted abruptly.

'Nice to meet you,' the other woman nodded, smiling openly, American, like Aaron. 'I had no idea you were engaged, Aaron.' She looked at him curiously.

He shrugged, seeming not to care that he had just greeted his supposed fiancée wearing only a towel when he had been alone in the suite with another woman. 'Charly doesn't actually believe in engagements,' he dismissed. 'But we are getting married.'

'Congratulations,' the younger woman said warmly.

Aaron arched mocking brows at Charly's puzzled look. 'I think I forgot to mention that Erin is my secretary,' he drawled, triumphant humour in emerald eyes. 'That's all for tonight, Erin,' he told the younger woman. 'We'll continue in the morning.'

'Secretary?' Charly derided softly once Erin had taken her leave, the other woman, with her voluptuous figure, looking the least like a secretary that she had ever seen. 'At least James used to tell me they were business acquaintances!' she scorned.

Aaron shrugged. 'Erin *is* my secretary. I like to have beautiful women around me.'

'So did James.'

His face darkened at this second mention of her husband. 'Don't keep comparing me with a husband you obviously despised,' he rasped.

Her head went back proudly. 'Why not? You're very much alike.'

'I doubt that,' he bit out. '*I* would never have treated you in the way he obviously did.'

Charly's mouth twisted. 'So you're sticking to the story that Erin is *just* a secretary?'

'It isn't a story, and it happens to be the truth as far as I'm concerned. What she does with other men is none of my concern. She has a brother who plays professional football who would probably rearrange my face if I so much as looked at her suspiciously,' he grimaced.

Charly sighed. 'Don't try and make me laugh. I'm angry with you and I want to stay that way!'

He pulled a face. 'In that case I think I'd better go and put some clothes on before we continue this conversation; I have a feeling the argument you're spoiling for might go more in my favour if I looked a little more dignified!'

'By all means get dressed,' she invited impatiently, preferring not to have to look at his bare muscled chest any longer anyway. 'But don't be long, I have to leave in a few minutes.'

His eyes narrowed to hard slits. 'Am I to take that to mean you didn't get dressed up like that just to see me?'

'Of course I didn't,' she snapped, sitting down, crossing one silky covered leg over the other.

'Then who's it for?' His eyes were still narrowed.

'None of your damned business,' she bit out coldly.

His expression darkened. 'We'll continue this conversation when I get back!'

Charly slumped down in the chair slightly once he had gone into the bedroom, wishing she had a drink at that moment, knowing she would have had a cigarette if she didn't hate the damned things so much. Because for a moment, a very brief moment, jealousy such as she had never known before had wracked her body as she looked at Erin Brody in Aaron's suite with him!

Jealousy! She couldn't believe it, still felt devastated by the realisation that she had hated the thought of Aaron being with any other woman but her. She didn't even like the man, but after yesterday night she knew that she wanted him!

'Charly, I—Are you all right?' Aaron frowned as he came back into the room, and Charly realised she must have gone pale as she admitted to herself that her physical need of this man hadn't just been for last night.

'Of course I am,' she snapped a reply, glaring at him. 'I spent the afternoon with Molly listening to how Matt is going to be your best man, we're having a church wedding, and three or four children!'

'Ah,' he nodded understandingly. 'You're a little annoyed, right?'

'I'm a *lot* annoyed! Although *annoyed* doesn't really begin to describe how I feel about it!' she bit out, her anger at her attraction to him in spite of herself also contained in this exchange. 'You could at least have warned me!' she accused.

'I did mean to,' he assured her slowly. 'But somehow we got sidetracked last night.'

She avoided his gaze at the mention of last night. 'You shouldn't have told them those things in the first place!'

Aaron shrugged. 'It just seemed to come out so naturally. Molly was very pleased for us.'

'Well *I'm* not!' She glared up at him.

'Okay, I'll try and avoid conversations like that in future,' he dismissed, his eyes narrowing. 'Now you can tell me who you're meeting tonight?'

'A business acquaintance,' she dismissed.

'Dressed like that?' he scorned.

Her eyes flashed silver. 'There's nothing that says I can't look nice to meet a business acquaintance!'

'There is—*me*!' he bit out. 'I don't want you meeting another man looking like that.'

'Well that's just too bad, because there's nothing wrong with the way I look!'

'I'm well aware of that,' he rasped. 'Which is why I don't think you're going to any business meeting——'

'I didn't say I was,' she cut in coldly. 'Just that I know the man *through* business.'

'You aren't going!'

Her eyes flashed. 'I am!'

'You're supposed to be marrying me!' His mouth was tight.

She gave a scornful laugh, standing up. 'We both know that isn't true, so I'm at liberty to see who I please, when I please.'

'You didn't seem to feel the same way about Erin being here with me earlier,' he taunted.

She avoided his probing eyes. 'I couldn't care

less what women you see, but it might not have been me at the door,' she pointed out desperately, knowing she had hated the thought of him making love to the other woman.

'Is that the only reason you were so annoyed at seeing her here?' he mocked.

'Of course,' she snapped. 'You don't seriously think I *minded* for myself, do you?' she derided.

'I know damn well you did,' he mocked.

Her mouth firmed into a thin line. 'I think you were wrong the other day, Aaron, your ego is still very much intact—in fact, it's running wild! Now if you'll excuse me, I have a date.'

Aaron grasped her arm. 'Who is he?'

Her eyes flashed. 'None of your business!'

'Tell me, Charly,' he ordered in a softly threatening voice.

She hadn't seen him this angry since the first night when he arrived at Matt's apartment to accuse her of being his mistress. 'If you must know,' she began contemptuously.

'Oh I think I must,' he drawled mockingly.

'His name is William Shaw.'

'Of Shaw Electronics?'

She looked at him sharply. 'Do you know him?' That would be just her luck the way things were going lately!

To her relief Aaron shook his head. '*Of* him. So,' he released her, stepping back, 'does Matt know you see other men on the evenings you don't see him?' he bit out.

Her mouth twisted. 'Why don't you ask him?'

'Because I'm asking you,' he rasped.

She shrugged. 'I doubt if he knows about Bill,' she answered truthfully.

'Or vice versa,' Aaron derided.

'Bill wouldn't be interested in Matt,' she answered, again with complete honesty.

Aaron frowned. 'Don't you find your life a little—complicated, the way it is?'

She gave him a haughty look. 'I like my life exactly the way it is. Or rather, I *liked* it.'

'Before I came along to spoil it,' he guessed dryly.

'You're the only complication I can see,' she nodded, looking down at the slender gold watch on her wrist. 'I'm late,' she realised irritably.

'Why not call him and tell him you'll be there soon?' Aaron suggested mildly.

Charly eyed him suspiciously. 'What are you up to now?'

'Nothing.' He moved across the room to pour himself a drink. 'I just thought you might like to ring his home and explain that you'll be late.'

'He isn't at home.' She still frowned at Aaron's helpful about-face. 'We're meeting at the restaurant.'

He shrugged. 'Then call the restaurant.'

'Aaron——'

'If you don't want to, fine,' he dismissed. 'I was only trying to be helpful.'

'Why?'

'Because you're late for your date——'

'A date you were trying to stop me going on a few minutes ago!' she reminded hardly.

'I realised you're right, it's none of my business.' He met her stormy gaze with calm green eyes.

She was still wary of the reasons for his sudden change of attitude, but she made the call to the restaurant anyway, Bill coming on the line a couple of minutes later. She explained that a friend had dropped by unexpectedly and she had been delayed, avoiding Aaron's mocking gaze as she assured Bill she would be at the restaurant shortly.

'I have to leave now,' she told Aaron once she had rung off. 'Thanks for the use of the telephone.'

'Any time,' he nodded.

'And I really would appreciate it if you didn't embellish our relationship to Molly any further.'

'Fine,' he nodded again.

'Aaron, what are you up to?' she snapped demandingly, hesitating in the act of leaving.

'Me?'

His look of a feigned innocence convinced her more than ever that he was up to something. 'Aaron——'

'You really should be going, Charly,' he suggested mildly. 'You did say fifteen minutes,' he reminded.

'Yes,' she still frowned suspiciously. 'I'll see you next weekend.'

'If not before,' he nodded.

She gave him a sharp look. 'And what do you mean by that?' she looked at him warily.

Aaron shrugged. 'Well there's always the possibility that I might need to see you before for some reason. But don't worry,' his voice hardened, 'I'll call you first.'

She stiffened. 'There's no need.'

His gaze was steady on her flushed face. 'I'll call first,' he stated flatly.

Charly knew he was implying he didn't want to

call at her apartment without her knowledge in case she had Matt there, taking her leave abruptly.

But she still wasn't convinced by his suddenly helpful mood, his air of innocence, a frown marring her brow all the way to the restaurant.

CHAPTER SIX

SHE didn't know why she was surprised to see Aaron enter the restaurant about fifteen minutes after she had, Erin Brody at his side. But she was. And her surprise must have shown in her face, Bill turning round to follow her line of vision.

'Do you know them?' He looked back at Charly.

She dragged her stunned gaze away as Aaron and Erin were seated at a table a short distance away from them. 'Yes,' she confirmed abruptly, furiously wondering how Aaron had known it was this particular restaurant she was meeting Bill at; she felt sure she hadn't mentioned the name of it during her telephone conversation with Bill earlier.

'Rocharlle?'

She looked up guiltily, knowing she had missed something Bill said. 'Sorry?'

'I asked if you would like them to join us?' he offered politely.

'No! Er—I'm sure they would rather be on their own,' she spoke more calmly, giving him a dazzling smile. 'As we would.'

Bill looked visibly taken aback by this intimate warmth. As well he might! He had been trying to persuade her for months to go out to dinner with him, and even when she had finally agreed it had been with some reluctance. No wonder he was surprised by her flirtatious manner now. She had a feeling he was going to be a lot more surprised by her behaviour before the evening was finished, Aaron's arrogance in following her here bringing out a rebellious streak in her. Because he had followed her, the coincidence of being here was just too great for it to be otherwise.

She felt herself stiffen as she saw Aaron getting to his feet and coming towards their table, keeping her eyes averted as she sensed him standing beside her.

'What a coincidence,' he said with obvious insincerity—at least, it was obvious to Charly, Bill seemed completely convinced by the act. 'I had no idea it was this restaurant you were going to, Charly.'

'Charly?' Bill was surprised by the nickname.

She shot Aaron an impatient look before turning to the other man. Until tonight Bill had remained purely a business acquaintance, and in business she always preferred the formality of being Rocharlle Allenby-Hart; who could take a woman called Charly seriously in business! 'Just a shortened version of my name,' she dismissed, doubtful if this man would ever be more than a 'business acquaintance'.

Aaron nodded, a wicked gleam in his eyes. 'Charly and I are old friends.'

Bill stiffened, a man in his early forties, silver gleaming in his thick dark hair, a look of cynicism to his handsome face. 'Oh?' he prompted warily.

'Very old friends,' Aaron antagonised.

'I believe Erin is feeling neglected,' Charly told him through stiff lips.

He turned to glance at the other woman, Erin giving a little wave of acknowledgement as she saw that glance. 'She looks happy enough to me,' he mocked. 'Actually I came over to see if you would care to join us?'

Charly's mouth tightened even more. 'I don't think so, thank you,' she glared at him warningly.

'Why not?' he asked bluntly.

Colour darkened her cheeks. 'Because I'm sure the two of you would rather be alone,' she snapped.

'Not particularly,' he shrugged. 'Besides, how *can* you be alone in a crowded restaurant?'

She gave an impatient sigh. 'Bill and I have business to discuss.'

'You can discuss it later,' Aaron told her arrogantly. 'Come on, Charly,' he encouraged throatily. 'It's been so long since we saw each other.'

She held on to her temper with effort at his deliberate goading of her. 'Bill?' she prompted abruptly.

He looked no more pleased, now he had heard the familiar way Aaron spoke to her, with the arrangement. 'I have no objections, but it would be an inconvenience for the management if we were to change tables now,' he added with relief.

'Not at all,' Aaron contradicted smoothly. 'In case you haven't noticed, Erin and I are at a table for four.'

Charly looked up at him accusingly, sure that fact hadn't come about as casually as Aaron was implying it had. 'In that case . . .' she muttered. 'Bill?'

'Of course.' He stood up, holding her chair back for her, the waiter carrying their cocktails to the other table.

Aaron made the introductions as they all sat down, Charly somehow finding herself seated between Erin and Aaron, giving Bill a helpless look as he looked less than pleased at being seated across the table from her.

It was an awkward meal for everyone except Aaron, who seemed unaffected by Charly's scowls, Bill's displeasure, and Erin's puzzlement, talking about everything and nothing, drawing Bill into a business discussion.

Charly could cheerfully have hit him, was furiously angry with both him and Bill by the time they reached the coffee stage of their meal, seriously considering walking out on them as she returned from the ladies' room.

'That would only embarrass Erin and Bill,' Aaron drawled.

She turned furiously to find him leaning against the wall in the entrance area. 'And whose fault would that be?' she demanded. 'You had no right following me here.'

'I didn't follow you,' he told her calmly.

'Then how did you know I would be at this restaurant?' she scorned.

'What makes you think I did know?' he enquired with a pained innocence.

'Because these sort of coincidences didn't happen to me until you came into my life!' she hissed, lowering her voice as some people entered the restaurant behind them.

'What a boring life you must have led until I came along,' Aaron drawled.

'How-did-you-know-which-restaurant-I-would-be-at?' she asked again with controlled violence.

He shrugged, bending his head guiltily. 'Okay, I'll confess——'

'And stop trying to look and act like a naughty boy caught out in a misdemeanour,' she snapped. 'It's ridiculous in a man of thirty-four.'

'Thirty-five,' he corrected.

'It's ridiculous in a grown man whatever his age.' Her eyes flashed.

Aaron grinned. 'But cute, huh?'

'It is not cute!'

'You know I'm beginning to think that something was left out of your expensive education,' he frowned.

'Oh yes?' she scorned.

'A sense of humour,' he taunted. 'It can help you through a lot of awkward occasions.'

'No doubt you've had great need of your *warped* sense of humour over the years!'

'Not nice,' he reproved. 'Okay,' he shrugged. 'I can see you definitely aren't amused. It was the telephone number that brought me here.'

She frowned. 'What telephone number?'

'This telephone number, of course.' His voice was edged with impatience.

She shook her head. 'I know for a fact that I didn't mention this telephone number.'

'I watched you dial. I have a good memory for numbers, and this was an easy one to remember. As soon as you left my suite I called here and made my own reservation, with a table for four, of course.'

'How enterprising of you,' she bit out, annoyed that he had used the same subterfuge she had when obtaining the number of his hotel room.

'I thought so,' he nodded.

'Well, now that you've had your little game could Bill and I leave?' she said with sarcasm.

'Bill and you, sure. But if you walk out of here alone—as you were thinking of doing just now— you'll only embarrass Bill and Erin. That is, unless they've already left,' he added softly.

Charly gave him a sharp look. 'What do you mean by that?'

'Haven't you noticed the way they've been looking at each other all evening? They're attracted to each other.'

She frowned, having noticed nothing. 'You're imagining things,' she scoffed.

'I'm not,' he shook his head confidently. 'Perhaps you were too interested in me to notice them.'

'I don't think so,' she drawled derisively.

'No, perhaps not,' he conceded dryly. 'But I know Erin well enough to realise when she likes a man, and Bill Shaw seems to return the interest. I hope you aren't too upset about it?' he taunted.

She bit her tongue to stop herself denying being in the least affected by Bill Shaw's interest in Erin or any other woman. Last night she had almost made love with this man; it was better for her defences if he continued to believe he was only one of many in her life instead of the only man to affect her in that way since the beginning of her marriage to James. She had enough complications in her life without Aaron Grantley knowing he was the first man she had been physically attracted to in years!

'Perhaps if you hadn't insisted on monopolising quite so much of my attention they wouldn't have found the time to become attracted to each other,' she said coldly.

Aaron's eyes widened. 'You *are* upset.'

She looked at him unflinchingly. 'What did you expect me to be?'

'You didn't seem that interested in him earlier,' he frowned.

'I'm not a very demonstrative person.' Her icy gaze dared him to dispute that claim. He didn't. And she didn't know if she was angry or relieved that he didn't! After last night he had to know she could be *very* demonstrative, but she didn't want him to talk about that time she had spent in his arms. And yet she didn't like the idea of him perhaps not realising how deeply she had been aroused. It was a no-win situation, and she impatiently dismissed it from her mind. 'But if you don't mind, we'll leave now.' It was a statement, not a request.

Bill gave her a curious look once they returned to the table, and she couldn't help wondering if her cheeks were as red as their heat implied they were.

'Sorry to be so long,' Aaron told the other couple cheerfully. 'Once Charly and I start talking about old times we forget the time.' He looked at her challengingly.

She didn't resume her seat back at the table. 'Bill, are you ready to leave now?' she asked tightly.

He looked startled by the request. 'It's early yet,' he frowned. 'Erin and I were just discussing going on somewhere to dance.'

Her mouth tightened. 'I'm not in the mood for dancing.'

'Neither am I,' Aaron said with satisfaction. 'So I'll go home with Charly and you can take Erin dancing,' he told the other man.

'Oh, I couldn't let you do that.' Bill shook his head. 'Rocharlle is here with me; I'll drive home with her.'

Although politely made the offer was none the less reluctant. 'I have my car and can take myself home, thank you,' she snapped, her eyes flashing silver, looking from Aaron to Bill and then back again. 'I'm not some simpleton who needs an escort home.'

'That isn't very nice, Charly.' Green eyes danced with fun at her anger, and she realised that by showing her anger at Bill as well as Aaron she had played into the latter's hands.

She turned to Bill with a warm smile. 'I really would like to go home now, I have a headache,' she told him softly. 'But please feel free to take Erin dancing,' her smile included the younger woman, 'I really don't need an escort for the short drive home.'

'I think I'll come with you anyway.' Aaron mocked the fact that he had been right about the other couple's attraction to each other.

Her eyes frosted over, her smile fading. 'I'd rather go alone.'

He shrugged. 'Okay, I'll see you at the apartment later.'

She felt herself pale even as she gasped, glancing worriedly at Bill. 'Don't be silly, Aaron,' she dismissed lightly, 'of course you won't be seeing me at my apartment later.' She gave the stunned Bill a reassuring smile.

'Sweetheart, this argument of ours is ridiculous,' he told her cajolingly, satisfaction gleaming in his eyes. 'I told you earlier that Erin is only my secretary.'

So he had persuaded the other woman to come along with him by telling her she had left in a jealous huff! She had wondered how he persuaded Erin to go along with his plan after telling her they were engaged.

'Earlier?' Bill looked even more puzzled. 'Rocharlle, I don't understand what's going on?'

She gave a defeated sigh. 'I'm sure Aaron will explain everything to you once I've left!' She turned and walked out of the room without a backward glance, although she sensed admiring green eyes following her every move.

Damn the man. He had completely ruined her evening with a pleasantly interesting man, and she hated to think what lies he was now telling Bill. She hadn't thought there would be such repercussions from her initial vengeful announcement to Molly only a week ago. By this time tomorrow, with Bill obviously told of the bogus engagement, the whole of the business-world would know about it!

'Slow down!' Aaron caught up with her just as she got out on to the pavement, holding on to her arm.

She shook off his hand. 'You deliberately made a fool of me in there!' she bit out through clenched teeth.

'I didn't need to,' he drawled. 'You managed that quite well on your own!'

'Why you——'

'Charly, you're so confused right now you don't know what you want,' he chided.

'I've always despised women who claim to be confused all the time!' she snapped.

'You aren't confused all the time,' he teased. 'Just right now. You don't know whether to be mad at me for following you to the restaurant, because I had Erin with me, or because I told Bill we're engaged.'

She looked at him fiercely. 'I'm mad at you for all those things. You made me look like a spitefully jealous child to Erin and a confused idiot to Bill. And I'm not used to being thought of as either!'

'Poor Charly.' He caressed the hair at her temple, his expression indulgent.

She flinched from his touch. 'I'm not "poor" anything——'

'Oh yes, you are,' he nodded regretfully. 'You've had to be strong since your husband and daughter died. It's time you let someone else take charge for a while.'

'You?' she scorned.

'Me,' he confirmed arrogantly.

Her mouth twisted. 'When James died I swore no one else would ever "take charge" of my life,' she told him coldly. 'No one else ever has.'

'Until now.'

She looked at him with narrowed assessing eyes. 'I'll admit you're making a nuisance of yourself, but that's all you are doing.'

Aaron sighed. 'Is Matt the only man that can get through to you?'

'At the moment, yes.' Matt posed no threat, offered only friendship, a friendship she greatly valued.

He shrugged acceptance of the situation. 'The

way you said that tells me that it won't always be that way. And I can be very persistent.'

'I know that,' she said dryly.

'Will you drive me to my hotel; Erin and I came in a taxi.'

She sighed. 'Very well. And after this I don't want to see you again until next Friday,' she warned. 'No more popping up to my apartment when you feel like it, and no more friendly confidences to Molly about our future life together. Is that agreed?'

'What do I get out of the deal?'

She smiled. 'A lift back to your hotel.'

Aaron frowned. 'That doesn't seem a very fair deal on my side.'

'It isn't,' she acknowledged smoothly.

'Then what makes you think I'll agree to it?' he derided mockingly.

'It's almost impossible to get a taxi here this time of night, and it's just starting to rain?'

Appreciation for her show of humour shone in his eyes. 'That was pure Charly Allenby,' he grinned. 'And you have yourself a deal.'

She turned to him frowningly as they hurried to her car. 'I wish you would get the idea out of your head that I'm two different personalities.' She unlocked the door, both of them hurrying inside the car, the rain falling heavier now. 'I'm just me, Charly Hart.'

'You have never been "just" anybody in your life,' he mocked. 'What did I tell you?' he added with satisfaction.

'What——?' She followed his line of vision, just in time to see Bill and Erin crossing the car park to his car a short distance away. 'Her brother won't mind about the owner of an electronics company?' she derided, manoeuvring her car out into the flow of slow traffic, visibility poor.

'I won't tell him if she doesn't,' Aaron dismissed. 'I'd offer to drive,' he murmured as the traffic slowed almost to a stop, the rain, with typical English weather unpredictability, turning to hail, 'but I don't want to run the risk of being called a chauvinistic pig again.'

She gave him a brief grin. 'Did I once call you that?' she mocked.

'You know you did,' he said dryly.

She shook her head. 'I only called you a male chauvinist, you added the pig. Why did you follow me tonight, Aaron?' she asked abruptly.

'The truth?'

'I never ask for anything less,' she bit out sharply.

'We have unfinished business,' he shrugged. 'I'm not about to let any other man collect on that.'

Her mouth tightened as she knew what business he was referring to!

'Tell me, Charly.' He turned completely in his seat to look at her. 'If Erin and I hadn't broken up your evening would you have slept with Bill Shaw tonight?'

'I don't have to answer that!' she snapped.

'You don't *have* to,' he agreed softly. 'But I'd like you to.'

'I've already told you Bill is a business acquaintance,' she dismissed.

'That doesn't answer my initial question,' he pointed out determinedly.

'The truth?' she delayed.

Aaron nodded, his gaze compelling. '*I* never ask for anything less either.'

She moistened her lips, knowing he was stubborn enough to just keep asking until he got the answer he demanded. 'No,' she answered abruptly.

His breath left his body in a relieved sigh. 'Thank you.' His hand rested lightly on her thigh, gently caressing.

The now familiar heat coursed through her body at his touch, and she stiffened resentfully. 'Aaron——'

'No, don't spoil it,' he interrupted, his fingertips on her lips.

'I don't want you——'

'Please,' he instructed gently, turning her to face him as she stopped the car outside the front of his hotel. 'Good night, Lady,' he kissed her gently, getting out of the car to stand on the steps watching her as she accelerated away.

CHAPTER SEVEN

'YOU have to see that it's worth it, Ian.' She looked at the middle-aged man for his opinion.

He continued to look around the old stone building. 'Shevton's demands still seem excessive to me,' he finally commented.

Richard Shevton was now asking a ridiculous price for his old family home, both Charly and Aaron still determined to own it. As her lawyer and adviser Ian had questioned her need for this particular house, and she had brought him down here today to show him just how suitable it was for Matt's purposes.

Charly liked Ian, had always respected his opinion in the past, but she knew about this he was wrong. 'Pay him,' she instructed.

He shrugged. 'If you say so. But Grantley seems to be as determined as you are.'

She knew all about Aaron's determination, wasn't she fictitiously engaged to him because of that same determination to stop Matt making a fool of himself over her! 'The price now asked must be going past the realms of viability for the hotel he has in mind,' she dismissed. 'He'll have to back down soon.'

Ian sighed. 'The price has gone past the realms of viability for you too!'

She gave him an encouraging smile. 'You know as well as I do that I can go a lot higher before it even begins to hurt me.'

'That isn't the point——'

'The point is, Ian,' she cut in firmly, 'that I want Shevton House.'

'Unfortunately, so do I.'

They both turned simultaneously to face Aaron, leaning against the thick stone doorway as he made the statement. He looked so arrogantly confident, so condescending, that Charly knew he had once again misunderstood her motives, that he suspected her relationship with Ian now. He suspected her relationship with every man she even spoke to! Although perhaps that wasn't so surprising after the initial assumption he and Molly had both made about her staying at Matt's apartment.

'Aaron,' she greeted abruptly as he strolled towards them.

'The agent for the house told me you were here,' he drawled, looking at Ian with narrowed eyes. 'I assumed you were alone.'

Her mouth tightened. 'It's amazing how assumptions can so often be wrong.'

Green eyes hardened as he picked up her double meaning. 'Not always,' he muttered, putting out his hand to Ian, slightly taller than the lawyer, his dark blue suit and shirt perfectly tailored. 'Charly seems to have forgotten her expensively bought manners,' he bit out. 'I'm Aaron Grantley,' he introduced himself.

Ian was visibly startled, meeting the other man's hand cautiously as he murmured his own name.

'Ian is my lawyer,' Charly supplied irritably as Aaron continued to look at them speculatively.

His expression didn't change. 'Really?'

'Yes,' she snapped as he didn't even try to hide

his scepticism. 'He's the man who has been doing my negotiating for this house.'

'There always seems to be a man involved somewhere,' Aaron drawled.

Ian frowned at the insult. 'Now look here——'

'It's all right, Ian.' She put her hand on his arm. 'Perhaps you wouldn't mind waiting for me outside?' she suggested gently.

He looked from her to Aaron, and then back again, obviously not liking what he read from the other man's expression.

'Please, Ian,' she persuaded. 'I shouldn't be long.'

'Very well,' he agreed. 'I'll go through and have another look at the kitchens.'

Charly watched him go, knowing he resented being asked to leave. But Aaron was spoiling for a fight, and she didn't want Ian involved in that.

She turned to Aaron with snapping eyes, ignoring the fact that her senses had leapt when she first saw him, not having seen him for the last two days. 'Did you have to be so rude?' she demanded coldly.

'Rude?' he scorned. 'I haven't even started! Every time I look around there's a different man holding on to your skirt!'

Her eyes frosted over. 'Ian was James' lawyer, my father's and Will Hart's before that!'

'So?'

'So I've known him almost since I was in the cradle!'

'The man is forty-five years old at the most,' Aaron derided.

'Forty-four,' she corrected abruptly. 'And you just embarrassed him.'

'A little sensitive about your relationship, is he?' Aaron scorned. 'Is he another married one?'

She drew in an angry gasp. 'You——'

'Is he?' he demanded roughly.

'Ian is married,' she nodded. 'He is also the nearest thing to a best friend I've ever had!'

'Besides Matt,' Aaron's mouth twisted. 'Best friends are usually of your own sex.'

'So I'm unusual,' Charly snapped.

'You certainly are,' Aaron scorned harshly. 'You have the bedroom habits of a rabbit—anyone and everyone!'

She knew she paled, could feel the colour drain out of her cheeks. 'I didn't have you!' she spat out.

'And aren't I glad about that now,' he nodded. 'I'm a little more discriminating about my bed-partners!'

Each word was designed to wound, and if she really were the woman Aaron believed her to be maybe they would have done. As it was his insults were almost laughable. Even James, an expert in the art of deliberately hurting her, would never have accused her of being a sexual athlete, had known of her aversion to all men once he had finished humiliating her.

'Actually, so am I,' she told him coldly. 'Which is why *you've* never been invited into my bed.'

'I would never ask to be!'

'Good!'

She knew they must look and sound ridiculous as they glared mulishly at each other, but she also knew they were both too stubborn to back down. And despite his painful denial of desiring her she knew that Aaron did still want her; it was there in the heat of his emerald gaze, and the pulse throbbing in his jaw. If they weren't both aware of Ian's presence somewhere in the house they could have lain down on this cold stone floor and made love to each other right now! She was beginning to wonder why she had ever said no to this man.

'I'd better go,' she said jerkily, disturbed by her own thoughts. 'Will you lock up or shall we?'

'I'll do it,' he rasped, his jaw tight.

She nodded, walking away, tired suddenly, weary of answering this man's accusations.

'Charly . . .?'

She stiffened, looking at him with icy eyes. 'My name is Mrs Allenby-Hart,' she stated flatly. 'Or Rocharlle if you prefer.'

His mouth firmed. 'I wish I understood you,' he muttered.

'Maybe if you stopped thinking every man I'm with is a lover you might,' she said heavily.

'But there are so many of them,' he shook his head.

'All explainable.'

'Matt?'

'A friend.'

'Shaw?'

'Not even that.'

'Anderson?'

'My lawyer and friend.'

Aaron shook his head. 'No woman has that many male friends.'

'I do,' she sighed. 'But you obviously don't believe that, so let's end this conversation before you say anything I'll regret hearing. I'm sure you wouldn't regret saying it!'

'Maybe I would,' he muttered. 'But it wouldn't make it any less the truth.'

She gave him a pitying look before leaving him to join Ian, the other man taking one look at her face and wisely not saying another word until they were well on their way back to London.

'So that was Aaron Grantley,' he finally murmured.

She gave a choked laugh, still a little shaken by the unexpected encounter. 'Yes.'

Ian glanced at her, the two of them having driven down in his car. 'Does he always make snap judgments like that?' he drawled knowingly.

She shrugged. 'How would I know?'

'I just thought you might.'

'Well I don't,' she snapped.

'Charly, if the man is bothering you——'

'He isn't,' she dismissed tersely, knowing she lied. Aaron bothered her more than any other man she had ever known. But she was still afraid, so very afraid, of trusting her emotions again.

'Does it make you feel safer, emotionally, if you buy a man's affection?'

Charly recoiled from the accusation as Aaron forced himself into her apartment as soon as she opened the door. His words hit her like a physical blow.

He faced her angrily across the lounge. 'Does it?'

She swallowed hard. 'I don't know what you mean.'

'Then let me help you understand,' Aaron scorned harshly. 'Matt's apartment.'

She looked more puzzled than ever. 'What

about it? You know why I was staying there.' It was only yesterday she had had her last argument with him at Shevton House; she couldn't imagine what she had done to merit this second attack.

His mouth twisted. 'I also know now why that apartment was the obvious choice.'

She stiffened, her hands twisting together. 'I told you——'

'You've told me one load of garbage after another. You own this building, don't you?' he accused scathingly, very dark and attractive in faded denims and a thick black sweater, the sleeves of the latter pushed up to his elbows, his arms tanned and covered in fine hair.

Her head went back challengingly. 'And what if I do? There's no law that says I can't own an apartment building!' she snapped.

'You can own as many apartment buildings as you damn well please,' he bit out furiously. 'It's the men you keep in them that bothers me!'

'What on earth do you mean?' she demanded indignantly.

'Matt lives in this apartment building.'

'He occasionally sleeps here,' she corrected haughtily. 'He doesn't live here. But there's nothing wrong in that.'

'No,' he acknowledged scornfully. 'If he legitimately rented the apartment there wouldn't be.'

She swallowed hard, moistening suddenly dry lips. 'Of course he rents the apartment. He——'

'He pays no rent, Charly,' Aaron put in softly, challengingly.

'That's nonsense——'

'I checked,' he slowly shook his head. 'Only

two people in the building don't pay rent, you and Matt.'

'That's ridiculous,' she blustered. 'Of course he——'

'Don't lie to me, Charly.' Steel edged his voice. 'I may come over as an easygoing sort of guy.' He ignored her snort of disbelief. 'But I grew up in the tough streets of New York, and I grew tough with them.' His eyes were cold. 'But one thing I've always despised is liars. You're a liar, Rocharlle Hart,' he told her harshly. 'Matt stays here when he can get out of going home free, gratis, for nothing——'

'I do know the meaning of the words,' she snapped resentfully, wishing she knew who had told him that piece of confidential information. But he would never tell her, and she knew she would never be able to find out any other way. 'I just don't happen to consider it any of your business how Matt lives here.'

Many a night after spending time with her as she sat at Stephanie's bedside Matt had slept on a cot-bed a friend kept for him. It had been far from an ideal arrangement, and the strain often showed. She had moved into this apartment herself so that her home was near the hospital, rarely leaving Stephanie's side, but when she did not wanting to be away too long. An apartment on a lower floor had become vacant and she had offered it to Matt. Of course he had refused it, but when she had pointed out that he could let other colleagues in the same position use it he had reluctantly agreed to accept the use of it. But neither of them had ever thought their motives would be so misunderstood!

'I'm making it my business,' Aaron rasped. 'Molly won't be fooled for ever, you know. She believes that several of the doctors got together to pay for the rent on this place. It would break her up if she knew Matt was no more than a bought and paid for lover!'

Charly shook her head. 'You don't know what you're talking about.'

'Believe me, I know,' he bit out disgustedly. 'So answer my question, do you feel safer if you buy affection?'

'Get out of here!' she gasped. 'And take your filthy thoughts with you!'

'Can't you face the truth of what you're doing? Or have you always been like this?' he frowned. 'Did you buy yourself a husband too?'

'No!'

'I think you did.' His eyes glittered. 'You dangled your father's partnership with Hart's father in front of his nose to get him to marry you.'

'You have it all wrong—as usual,' she told him shakily.

'The man was years older than you——'

'Then he was also more experienced,' she pointed out heatedly. 'Do you honestly think an eighteen-year-old could seduce an experienced man of twenty-eight?'

'*You* could!'

'Thank you for your confidence,' she said wearily. 'But you have that the wrong way around. My husband was constantly unfaithful——'

'I know all about Hart's affairs.'

She sighed. 'You've been doing your homework.'

Aaron's mouth twisted. 'I've always believed in knowing all that I could about my adversaries.'

She frowned. 'We aren't enemies.'

'Oh yes, we are,' he nodded hardly. 'Because you're so damned beautiful I lost sight of my reason for knowing you at all for a while,' he rasped. 'But it's all clear to me now.'

'I wish it were to me,' she said wearily.

'It will be,' his voice was softly threatening. 'You may be discreet in your affairs, but once you look deeper than the surface beauty it becomes obvious just how many men you know. It was probably the reason your husband turned to other women.'

'Now listen here——'

'To more lies?' he scorned. 'The rumour is that your husband and daughter were leaving you at the time of the accident; as you were obviously unfit to be any child's mother he should have done it years before!'

Dry sobs wracked her body as she struck out at him blindly, pounding at him with her fists, unaware of the time the tears began to cascade down her cheeks, just hitting him over and over again, calling him every foul name James had ever called her, and a few more that he hadn't.

'Charly, for God's sake!' Aaron sounded exasperated as he warded off her hands, clasping her wrists as she didn't stop striking out at him. 'You're damned hysterical,' he rasped.

'I always get this way when I'm accused of being an unfit mother!' She was breathing heavily, hatred for him in her eyes. How dare he say she was unfit to be Stephanie's mother when she had suffered numerous humiliations just to stay close to her daughter?

'Do you deny that your husband was taking your daughter from you when they crashed?'

'I'm not denying or admitting anything to you,' she told him icily. 'Get out of my home and never come back.'

Uncertainty flickered in his eyes. 'Charly——'

'Get out,' she said again flatly.

'Maybe if we talked——'

'I have nothing to say to you.' She turned her back on him, willing him to leave before she broke down completely, the trembling beginning as soon as she heard the door close behind him.

She moved blindly across the room to the telephone, dialling before she had time to think. 'Ian?' She sighed her relief as he answered on the third ring. 'I know it's late—Yes, I'm fine,' she lied, her whole body shaking in reaction now. 'I hope I haven't disturbed you? Good,' she nodded as he assured her she hadn't, 'Ian, I want the Shevton House deal sewn up by the weekend. I don't care what you have to pay to get it but I want it to be mine by Friday afternoon at the latest.'

She stared sightlessly at the wall after the call had ended. The house would be hers, she would give it to Matt after he had spoken to Molly over the weekend—and then she never wanted to see Aaron Grantley again!

CHAPTER EIGHT

'AND this is where I keep the tea and coffee.' Molly closed the last cupboard in the kitchen. 'I think I've shown you where everything is.' She looked around the room frowningly.

'Including the sink,' Charly teased, being given a conducted tour before the other couple left on their weekend away.

Aaron was in the lounge with Matt, and Charly had been studiously avoiding any verbal or physical contact with him since he had arrived shortly after her an hour ago, their original plan to drive down together ignored by her; she couldn't have stood to be alone with him all that time! She had also ignored his numerous calls to her office the last week, not interested if he wanted to apologise, and not wanting to listen if he just wanted to throw out more accusations. He had refrained from coming to see her in person.

'Yes, well——' Molly looked embarrassed. 'I've never been away like this before.'

'You'll enjoy it,' she assured the other woman. 'I know it's no good me telling you not to worry about the children,' she had already spent a pleasurable hour with the two youngsters, 'because you will anyway,' she gently chided. 'But I can assure you they will be fine with me.'

'Are you and Aaron okay?' Molly frowned her concern.

'Of course.' She feigned surprise at the question.

'You both seem a little—distant.' Molly still looked worried.

Charly smiled reassuringly. 'We've both had a difficult week,' she understated, having had trouble getting through the latter part of hers. Although Aaron didn't seem to have had the same trouble, had looked just as relaxed and confident as usual when he arrived. 'Don't worry, we'll soon relax,' she told the other woman.

'Matt and I can always go away for this weekend some other time if you and Aaron need to——'

'Molly, will you stop worrying and take that gorgeous husband of yours away from here,' she teased.

Molly wrinkled her nose. 'I've got to the stage where I don't want to go.'

'I know,' Charly acknowledged gently. 'But by this time tomorrow you'll wonder what all the fuss was about.'

'You think so?' Molly didn't look convinced.

'I know so.' She firmly turned the other woman and pushed her out of the room in the direction of the lounge. 'Matt, take this wife of yours away for a romantic weekend before she decides she would rather stay here and change nappies.'

'Well, when you put it like that . . .' Molly giggled, her arm about Matt's waist as he cuddled her to his side. 'I can't tell you how grateful we are to you.' She sobered. 'Maybe we can do the same for you one day?'

Charly's laugh was forced as she avoided looking at Aaron. 'Maybe,' she said non-committally.

She cuddled Tommy, and Aaron held Lucy aloft on his shoulders as they walked out to the car with the other couple.

'Now Tommy's spare nappies are in his cupboard upstairs, and if Lucy——'

'Molly, will you get in the car and just go,' Aaron drawled. 'Charly and I will cope.'

'Oh all right.' Molly glared at him as she got in the car and wound down the window. 'I'm only behaving like a mother, aren't I, Charly?'

'Yes.' She smiled to take the sharpness out of her reply, aware of green eyes on her. 'But I can assure you Tommy won't run around without a nappy, and Lucy won't go hungry.'

'She's such a finicky eater——'

'Molly, close the window and let's go.' Matt was ruefully impatient. 'Women!' he added indulgently.

'I'm only concerned——'

'Mummy, as soon as you've gone Aunt Charly is going to give us a bath,' Lucy told her mother primly.

Molly spluttered with laughter. 'Well that puts everything into perspective.' She kissed her daughter as Aaron held her up in front of the car window. 'Have a nice time, darling,' she choked before giving Tommy his kiss, waving at them out of the back window until the car disappeared out of sight.

'Okay,' Charly said briskly, seeing that now that their parents had actually gone the children weren't altogether sure they liked the idea, Tommy's bottom lip trembling precariously. 'Last one undressed and into the bath gets a sweet.' She took hold of Lucy's hand as Aaron put her down on the ground, running into the house and up the stairs to the bathroom with Tommy in her arms.

'You said the *last* one,' Lucy finally realised as she jumped naked into the warm water.

Charly laughed. 'So I did,' she teased.

'Then I must be the winner,' Aaron watched them from the open doorway as Tommy was gently placed in the bubble-topped water opposite his sister. He strolled further into the room. 'Do I get the sweet, Aunt Charly?'

She concentrated on washing the children. 'We all get one sweet after the bath,' she said flatly.

Lucy squinted up at him as Charly washed her silky hair. 'Are you really coming in the bath with us, Uncle Aaron?'

'Not this time,' he smiled. 'I might embarrass Aunt Charly.'

'Mummy and Daddy often get in the bath together,' the little girl told them candidly.

'Do they indeed?' Aaron said with mock seriousness, while Charly did her best to hold back a smile.

'They often get in with us too,' Lucy said with all the intensity of a five-year-old.

'How about it, Charly?' He quirked dark brows at her.

'No, thank you,' she refused primly, hearing how pompous she sounded but unable to do anything about it. She was going to find it difficult just being polite to Aaron this weekend, but she had been determined not to let Molly and Matt down. 'I bathed earlier,' she added stiltedly.

'Need any help here?' Aaron offered gently, seeming to sympathise with her awkwardness.

'No, thank you,' she refused again, still not looking at him.

'Then I'll go and see about getting dinner started.'

She turned sharply. 'I can get it!'

Green eyes held her gaze steadily, refusing to let her look away now that she had finally looked at him. 'We're in this together, Charly,' he told her softly. 'I wouldn't dream of letting you do all the work.'

'Don't you think I'm capable?' She couldn't help the sharpness of her tone, but luckily the children seemed too engrossed in the toys they had floating about on top of the water to take any notice of the adults' exchange.

'Charly——'

She turned away from the regret in his eyes. 'Molly left the food for dinner out in the kitchen. The steaks are ours,' she added dryly.

'With Tommy only having six teeth I would never have guessed,' Aaron derided.

She sighed. 'I'm sorry.'

'So am I. Charly, about the other night——'

She turned furious eyes on him. 'This is hardly the time or place to discuss it!'

'No,' he conceded heavily as Lucy looked up curiously. 'Later, then?'

'I don't think so.' She got Tommy out of the water, making him giggle as she dried him, ignoring the broodingly silent man across the room, aware of the exact moment he turned impatiently and went downstairs.

Whether it was the novelty of having Aaron and Charly in the house that made Lucy eat Charly didn't know, but the little girl ate quite a good meal. Aaron volunteered to put Tommy to bed while she took Lucy up, and although she offered to do it he insisted. Somehow the little joke she had intended playing on him concerning the baby no longer seemed appropriate and after settling Lucy down for the night, her well-worn teddy bear cuddled up against her, she went along the corridor to Tommy's bedroom. Surprisingly all was quiet inside.

The door was slightly ajar, and she pushed it open a little further, taking a few minutes to adjust her eyesight to the warm orange glow from the small night-light, making out a figure sitting in the rocking-chair in one corner, a blond head nestled against the darkness of Aaron's shirt. Aaron nodded as he stood up to put the baby in his cot; Charly hurried downstairs.

She was in the kitchen when she became aware that Aaron had joined her, the nervousness that she had been fighting all day creeping over her. 'Molly thought that was a secret,' she murmured, checking on the potatoes she had put on to cook.

'Singing Tommy to sleep?' He lounged against a cupboard. 'Matt found out about it a long time ago, but he didn't let Molly know he knew.'

'It would have ruined it for her,' Charly nodded.

'Yes. But Matt thought I ought to know about it.'

'I was just coming to tell you.'

'Charly, can't you even look at me?' he coaxed.

Her back stiffened. 'No,' she answered honestly.

'We can't go on like this,' Aaron sighed.

'No,' she acknowledged huskily.

'Charly——'

'I'm doing this for Molly and Matt.' She avoided his hands as he would have reached for her. 'There's nothing that says I have to enjoy it!'

'The children——'

'Will know no tension from me.' Her eyes were silver as she at last looked at him. 'I'm not as insensitive as you seem to think I am!'

'Charly, we have to talk about the other night,' he insisted firmly. 'Maybe we were a little hasty——'

'*I* wasn't the one that was hasty. And there was no maybe about it,' she told him coldly.

'After watching you with the kids tonight I think perhaps you're right,' he sighed wearily. '*I* was hasty. You obviously adore children and they adore you.'

She just looked at him, still too emotionally aroused by the accusations he had made concerning Stephanie, completely bewildered by the way she had totally lost control afterwards and beat at him with her fists; she had never done anything like that before, not even when she had first learnt of James' affairs.

'Charly, I'm sorry about what I said concerning your daughter.' He looked at her worriedly as she still didn't speak. 'Whatever your husband was doing with her that day I'm sure——'

'He was taking her away,' she revealed flatly. 'As you said he was.'

'I don't believe it—'

She gave a scornful laugh. 'Do you always react this way when told you were right?'

Aaron frowned. 'You weren't an unfit mother——'

'I didn't say I was,' she rasped. 'Just that James was taking Stephanie away from me.

'Why?'

'Dinner is ready,' she told him briskly.

'*Why*, Charly?' He grasped her arms, forcing her to look at him.

'He wanted a divorce.'

'And you wouldn't give him one?'

'No.'

'So he took your daughter away from you?'

She avoided his eyes. 'For good,' she said abruptly.

'I knew they both died in the accident but—Do you think he deliberately killed them both?' Aaron said disbelievingly.

She didn't correct the assumption he had made that Stephanie had died in the accident with James, those months of watching her daughter slowly die still too painful to talk about. 'I'm sure he didn't; he liked life too much for that.'

'Charly, will you talk to me?' Aaron requested softly. 'I have a feeling a lot of my other accusations could be explained away as easily,' he said self-derisively.

It would be so easy to talk to this man, to tell him everything, but her emotions were still bruised, her feelings for him still something she was frightened to acknowledge even to herself.

She looked at him coldly. 'I am not in the habit of explaining myself to anyone, and I'm certainly not going to start with you!'

He gave a pained wince. 'All right, Mrs Hart,' he drawled. 'I won't push you. But you—or Charly—will talk to me one day. And in the meantime I'm not going to jump to conclusions

any more. I'm not naturally a jealous person,' he
derided. 'It must be something you alone bring
out in me.'

Jealousy? To feel jealousy surely he had to
care? Did that mean she cared about him too; she
had felt jealousy until she knew who Erin was!

'Would you watch the steaks for a moment?'
she requested abruptly. 'I think I hear Lucy
calling.'

Aaron frowned. 'I didn't hear anything.'

Neither had she, but she couldn't stay in the
same room with him at this moment, was too
shaken by the realisation that she *did* love this
man!

But loving someone didn't solve any of the
problems that love caused. She had loved once
before, unhappily, and she had no reason to think
it would be any different with Aaron, didn't think
he was a better choice than James had been.

The trouble was she hadn't chosen to love
Aaron. If she had had a choice it would be not to
love any man ever again. She had known enough
pain in her life already, and she had no reason to
suppose loving Aaron would be any better than
loving James.

She watched Aaron warily once she returned
from seeing to a quite undisturbed Lucy, but he
seemed determined to be charming, talking to her
about his New York childhood, his happy
homelife with his happily married parents.

She liked listening to him, and hadn't realised
how late it was until he stood up stretching
tiredly.

'It's been a long week,' he sighed at her
questioning look.

'Please, go up to bed.' She stood up too. 'I'll just tidy our cups away.'

'Charly——'

She flinched as he touched her. 'I don't know what your plans were for tonight,' she rasped, 'but I hope they didn't include me.'

His mouth twisted. 'The trouble at the moment is that *all* of my plans include you,' he derided. 'Before I do anything I find myself asking "Will Charly like it?", "Will she approve?".'

The colour left her cheeks. 'I won't approve if you try to get me to go to bed with you.'

'I haven't said or done anything to imply I would do such a thing,' he chided.

'You haven't needed to!' she told him shakily. 'I can't, Aaron,' she choked.

'I know.' He touched her cheek gently. 'What woman could after the things I've said to you?'

'It isn't just that——'

'I do understand, Charly,' he assured her softly. 'Which is why I'm going up to bed now. Alone.'

She smiled her relief that he didn't try and force the matter, knowing that if he had she wouldn't have been able to resist.

'Which isn't to say I'm not going to kiss you good night,' he groaned, bending his head.

She was caught off-guard, her lips opening to his, her arms going slowly about his waist. It was a long drugging kiss of deep sensuality, and Charly felt herself sway slightly as he released her.

'Good night,' he said huskily, walking to the door. He turned before leaving. 'Congratulations on the Shevton House deal, by the way,' he told her admiringly.

She gave him a startled look as he strolled out of the room and up the stairs. Her acquisition of the property had been made final only that morning, but as the other interested party she felt sure Aaron had known about it almost immediately. And yet he had chosen not to mention it until now. Why now?

She followed him up the stairs, knocking on the door of the room Molly had told her had been made up for them, the room Matt had told her she could use further down the corridor. 'Aaron, I——' He had instructed her to enter after her knock, but she froze in the doorway; he must hold some sort of record for undressing, stark naked as he stood across the room from her, taking his time about picking up his brown robe and pulling it on. She swallowed hard, affected by the lithe beauty of his body in spite of herself. 'Why didn't you mention Shevton House earlier?' Her voice sounded slightly higher than it usually did.

He shrugged. 'There was nothing else to say about it; you got it.'

She looked at him warily. 'You aren't angry?'

'Business is business.' He shrugged again.

'Oh.' She frowned her consternation. 'Good night, then.'

'Good night,' he drawled.

Charly was still frowning as she reached her own room. The acquisition of Shevton House had seemed very important to him earlier in the week, that had been one of the reasons she had been determined to get a quick decision on the deal herself, and now Aaron acted as if he hadn't cared if he got it or not. Even loving him she didn't trust him.

CHAPTER NINE

SHE still didn't trust him the next day as he set out to be charming to both her and the children. He took them all shopping, then out to lunch, holding Tommy on his knee as he fed him the food he was able to eat.

Charly knew that to anyone looking at them they must look like a normal family out on a shopping trip. And the feeling filled her with disquiet. She didn't want a husband or a family again, and yet Aaron and the children made it seem possible.

'A good day, huh?' Aaron smiled as they sat down together for a few minutes after the children had been put to bed.

'You're very good with children,' she said non-committally.

'I love them,' he nodded.

'Lucy and Tommy are——'

'Not just Lucy and Tommy,' he shook his head. 'I love all kids.'

'Ah yes,' her mouth twisted. 'You told Molly we would have three or four!'

'And I intend to,' he nodded.

'Not with me,' she scoffed.

Aaron shrugged. 'With whoever I marry.'

'Don't you think you would have to discuss that with her first?' Charly bristled at his arrogance.

'Most women want children.'

'But most women would also like the choice about having them!'

'If I don't get married it won't really matter will it,' he dismissed.

She heartily disliked the thought of Aaron marrying or having any kind of permanent relationship with another woman. She had kept love out of her life for so long and now it was ripping her to pieces!

'How about you?' he eyed her curiously. 'Do you really not intend marrying again?'

'Maybe if the right man came along I might——' She broke off as she realised what she had said, shock widening her grey eyes.

'Charly—Damn,' Aaron scowled as the telephone began to ring. 'I bet it's Molly again to see if we've put the offspring to bed properly!' He reached for the receiver with a rueful shrug, Molly having telephoned four times this weekend already. 'Yes, Molly,' he raised his eyebrows at Charly, the two of them sharing a moment of laughter together.

Charly went into the kitchen to begin preparing their dinner while Aaron related all the details of the day to Molly. She kept herself busy, determinedly not dwelling on what she had said about marrying again. She almost had the meal ready by the time Aaron joined her ten minutes later.

'I'm sure not all mothers can be that concerned,' he grimaced.

She smiled. 'They are. I remember—' She broke off again in confusion. She never talked about her beloved daughter, the memories too painful!

'Yes?' Aaron prompted softly, his gaze compelling. 'Tell me about your daughter, Charly.'

'There's nothing to tell,' she said abruptly, carrying their dinner through to the dining-room, her appetite completely gone.

'She was part of you,' Aaron pursued relentlessly. 'There must be something to say.'

She swallowed hard, tears flooding her eyes. 'I—She was a lovely little girl,' she began again. 'She hadn't even begun to live.' Anger entered her voice, her body rigid with tension. 'That— that bastard——'

'James?'

'Yes,' she hissed, beyond thinking now, all the resentment and pain she had harboured towards James the last year released as the torrent of words flooded out. 'Give him Hartall Industries, he said,' she no longer even saw Aaron, locked in her own private hell, 'and he wouldn't fight to keep Stephanie. But I couldn't do that,' she told Aaron pleadingly. 'Hartall belonged to Stephanie, it was her inheritance. He wanted to divorce me and marry my cousin Jocelyn, but if they had had children Stephanie would have got nothing. I couldn't agree to disinheriting her,' she told Aaron again chokingly.

'So he took her.'

'Yes.' She shuddered as she remembered the horrific scene when James had taken Stephanie from her. 'He destroyed her because I wouldn't agree to what he wanted.'

'I thought you said it wasn't deliberate?'

'It wasn't,' she rasped. 'But he still killed her. She would never have been with him that day if he hadn't wanted to punish me.'

'Surely you would have got Stephanie if you had gone to court for her?' Aaron frowned.

'I was not an unfit mother——'

'I know that,' he soothed her. 'I know that, Charly,' he encouraged.

'I might have got custody of her,' she sighed. 'But then again I might not. James had always been a good father, and the courts always take that into consideration nowadays. But none of that really mattered, because James knew that I would never put it to the test, that I would give him everything just to get Stephanie back. I never had the chance,' she choked.

'Charly, it wasn't your fault,' Aaron told her softly.

She froze. 'What do you mean?' she rasped. 'Of course it wasn't my fault.'

'You blame yourself for what happened——'

'I do not!'

'And it's only natural that you feel partly responsible,' he continued remorselessly. 'You and James argued, he took Stephanie——'

'I do not blame myself——' She stopped as her voice broke emotionally, giving up all pretence as sobs wracked her slender body. 'God, yes I do!' she cried. 'I should have agreed to what he wanted, should have let him have Hartall, as long as he left Stephanie alone.' She spilled out the guilt that had been haunting her the last year, not questioning how Aaron knew of that guilt; he seemed to know things about her she wouldn't admit to herself!

'Charly, you have to stop blaming yourself,' he held her close against his chest, smoothing her hair with soothing motions.

'But I could have saved her!' she choked.

'You couldn't!' He crushed her to him. 'It was all an accident. James only meant to punish you a little by taking Stephanie, he didn't mean either of them to get killed. You *know* that!'

'Yes. But——'

'Honey, you can't go on giving yourself this punishment.' He looked down at her with gentle eyes. 'You can't continue to live behind that wall where you don't allow emotions to touch you. Charly, you have to allow *me* to touch you.'

She knew he didn't mean physically. 'No!' she recoiled.

'Lady, I understand why you've been acting the way you have, I even understand why you choose men like Matt and Anderson; neither of them are a threat to your real emotions. But *I'm* a threat, and I'm going to go on being one until you can accept that it's me you want.'

He still believed she was involved with Matt and Ian! He had guessed so much else about her, had even realised what no one else had—that she blamed herself for the accident that had taken Stephanie from her. And yet he still didn't realise that she had kept all men at a distance except him.

Before she could answer him there was a cry from upstairs. 'Tommy?' he frowned.

She shook her head, moving swiftly out of his arms. 'It's Lucy.' She ran up the stairs.

The little girl was sitting up in bed crying, seeming to cry even harder as Charly entered the room.

'Darling, what is it?' She cuddled the little girl to her, shooting a worried frown at Aaron as he stood in the doorway. 'Lucy?' she prompted gently.

'When are Mummy and Daddy coming home?' she sobbed.

'Soon,' she crooned, the novelty of having her parents away obviously having faded for Lucy.

'*When?*'

'Tomorrow. Lucy——'

'I want Mummy,' the little girl wailed.

'She'll be home tomorrow, darling,' Charly continued to hold her. 'I bet she'll bring you a present too.' She already knew Molly had bought the children a toy each.

Blue eyes widened, the tears ceasing although she continued to sob gently. 'You think so?'

'I'm sure of it,' she smiled warmly. 'Now what happened? Did you have a bad dream?'

'Yes,' the little girl mumbled into Charly's neck. 'Will you stay with me until I'm asleep?' she pleaded.

'Of course,' Charly assured her, looking ruefully at Aaron.

He nodded, quietly leaving the room before Lucy became aware of his presence.

She sat on the bed for over an hour, Lucy determined not to go back to sleep, forcing herself to stay awake every time she seemed in danger of drifting off to sleep. Charly sat with her patiently, had often done the same with Stephanie, leaving it ten more minutes or so even after she was sure Lucy had fallen asleep before leaving the room, not wanting to disturb the little girl.

Aaron was in the lounge when she got downstairs, a glass of whisky in his hand. 'All right now?'

'Yes.' She avoided his eyes. 'I'll go and clear away in the dining-room. Would you like me to make you something else?' Neither of them had eaten earlier!

'I've done it,' he told her abruptly. 'And I couldn't eat a thing.' He looked at her with dark eyes. 'You should have children of your own, Charly.'

'No——'

'*My* children,' he continued determinedly.

She paled, swallowing hard. 'You're talking of marriage?'

'Yes.' He looked at her steadily.

She moistened stiff lips. 'Are you asking me to marry you?'

'Yes.'

'Why?'

His mouth firmed. 'The usual reasons!'

'You would have to explain them to me,' she derided. 'My last marriage was made out of greed and convenience. And I don't mean mine,' she added hardly.

Aaron sighed. 'I only say those things because I resent every other man in your life, including your husband.'

'James used me, he didn't love me!'

'I'm learning that,' Aaron nodded. 'I'm slowly learning all the reasons why you're locked in behind your emotions. But I love you, Lady,' he told her intently. 'I love you and I want to marry you.'

Elation flared—and then died. 'You don't know me,' she stated flatly.

'I know more about you than you think,' he denied. 'I know that you love children, that you have compassion for other people, that you're loyal to your friends. I also know that when you feel like it you can throw all business caution out the window,' he taunted.

'If you're talking about Shevton House——'

'Oh I am,' he nodded. 'We both know you paid over the odds for what, to most people, would be a damned monstrosity.'

'Not to me,' she told him tightly.

'Or me,' he accepted. 'But its purchase became a personal vendetta as far as you were concerned, one you were determined to win.'

'And I have,' she challenged.

He shrugged. 'In part. You own the house—but you haven't got rid of me. That was the idea, wasn't it?'

She gave him a resentful glare. 'Don't be ridiculous——'

'Admit it, Charly, now that the weekend is almost over, the deal won, you hoped never to see me again.'

'I *won't* ever see you again,' she told him firmly.

'You'll see so much of me you'll wonder how you managed without me!'

Her mouth twisted. 'Trying to save me from myself and my impetuous ways?' she scorned.

He shook his head slowly. 'There's nothing impetuous about you.'

'You might be surprised,' she said bitterly. Loving this man was pure madness! And she *daren't* even begin to believe he loved her in return.

'Lady, surprise me,' he invited huskily.

She was tempted, her senses jumping at the

thought of being in this man's arms. And maybe if they could just have gone to bed together it would be worth it. But Aaron was asking for so much more from her, and if she gave it she was afraid he would guess how she felt about him.

He sighed. 'I wish that hesitation didn't mean no.'

'And if it didn't?' she said recklessly, the force of her need taking over from caution.

His gaze probed hers. 'I'd carry you off to bed right now.'

She swayed with the force of her desire for this man. 'It doesn't mean no, Aaron,' she groaned.

His eyes darkened questioningly until he read from her expression that she was past fighting him. He took a step forward, not quite touching her but close enough for her to feel the seduction of his masculine warmth. 'You're sure?' he murmured.

She gave a choked laugh. 'Never ask a woman if she's sure, especially a confused one like me! I'm not sure about anything any more, Aaron.' She fell into his arms. 'But I do know I want you to make love to me.'

'It's a start,' he groaned as he bent his head, his lips claiming hers.

Charly deliberately blocked all other thoughts but this moment from her mind, meeting the devouring passion of his kiss, returning the thrust of his tongue, purring deep in her throat as he loosened her hair to press his fingers into her scalp.

By mutual consent they turned and walked up the stairs together, Aaron slowly undressing her once they reached the bedroom, his gaze never leaving her as he stripped off his own clothes. He didn't touch her except with his magnetic green gaze, her nipples filling and hardening to peaks, a heated warmth between her thighs.

'I know this is the part where I'm supposed to throw you on the bed and make love to you until you're senseless,' he drawled. 'But I don't want to rush this.' He took her hand in his. 'And I have a yearning to see all that golden hair slicked down your body, to lick the droplets of water from your breasts, to——'

'If you're suggesting we take a shower together then let's do it.' Her breathing was constricted with desire.

He laughed softly as they stepped under the hot spray of water, beginning to slowly wash every inch of her body. Charly was trembling uncontrollably by the time he reached her torso, her whole body tingling for his caresses, meeting his mouth hungrily.

'Aaron . . .!' she moaned longingly, excitement burning in her veins. 'I want you!'

'I know, Lady,' he breathed ruefully. 'Let's get out of here.' He turned the water off abruptly, making no move to pick up any of the towels on the rails, their inner heat drying their bodies within minutes as they lay down on the bed together.

'You're beautiful, Lady.' He touched her body almost reverently.

'I've had a child.' She knew she had the marks of that pregnancy on her body.

'It only makes you more beautiful.' He moved to kiss the tiny silver marks on her stomach. 'Will you have my children?'

'Aaron, please——!' she groaned as he found and explored the most sensitive part of her body. 'Now isn't the time to discuss children.'

'Perhaps not,' he conceded as he moved back up her body to kiss her on the mouth. 'But we will talk about it tomorrow,' he promised.

As the fire spread through her body, their caresses fevered, tomorrow seemed a long way off.

Aaron caressed and touched her until she felt on the edge of insanity, moving restlessly beneath him as she felt the probe of his hard desire against her thighs, his hair-roughened skin an eroticism in itself as he denied her full possession.

She almost went over the edge of her desire as he gently opened her thighs to enter her, her tightness closing about him moistly, the slight initial discomfort soon forgotten as Aaron began to move slowly inside her.

He continued to move slowly even though she begged for release, her fingers digging into the taut skin of his back, her mouth meeting his hungrily as her head came up to meet his, groaning her satisfaction as he quickened his pace, thrusting deeper and deeper inside her as she arched up in spiralling completion, wave after wave of pleasure shuddering through her body, her gasped cries turning to ones of triumph.

Aaron held her as the tremors continued to shake her body, her starved lungs gasping for air, clinging to his shoulders as she buried her face against his throat.

'You haven't—You didn't——'

'I'm going to,' he assured her throatily. 'I had

to make it good for you first.'

As he slowly began to move inside her once again Charly knew a moment's surprise as she felt the heat rising within her once again, and then she gave herself up to the sensation of pleasing Aaron so that he couldn't hold back any more, going up in the clouds with him again herself.

They didn't speak afterwards as they lay with Charly's head on his shoulder, but there was no awkwardness between them as they drifted off to sleep together.

Charly was in the kitchen supervising the children's breakfast when Aaron put in an appearance the next morning, and she met his rueful smile shyly, having left him in bed still sleeping half an hour ago, not wanting to disturb him.

'Coffee?' he asked as he moved to the pot to pour some for himself.

'Not just now, thanks.' She turned back to feeding Tommy as he banged on the top of his high-chair impatiently. 'Tommy's hungry,' she derided, spooning more cereal into his waiting mouth.

'We're late,' Lucy put in disapprovingly.

Charly glanced at Aaron again as he leant against the cooker drinking his coffee. 'Yes, we are,' she murmured, unable to read anything from Aaron's expression. She needed his reassurance, but she realised that he was leaving the next move—if there were one!—up to her.

'You're even later than us.' Lucy looked at Aaron accusingly, obviously his sleeping in until ten o'clock not suiting her at all.

'I'm older than you are,' he excused, sitting

down at the table with them. 'How are you this morning, Charly?' he watched her intently.

'Is Aunt Charly ill?' Lucy looked up frowningly.

Aaron looked at her questioningly too, and she moistened her lips nervously as she realised he was giving her an opening for that 'move'. 'I was, Lucy,' she answered the child but looked at Aaron as she acknowledged that fact. 'But I think I'm getting better.'

Aaron seemed to visibly relax, his hand covering hers as it rested on the table. 'I hope so,' he said huskily.

She turned away awkwardly, covering her embarrassment by feeding Tommy. It was true, she had been ill, with a sickness of the heart. James had hurt her and humiliated her until she closed herself in from people. But loving Aaron had knocked down those barriers.

'We have to talk,' she told him as Lucy and Tommy dragged him out to the garden after breakfast.

'Tonight,' he promised as he was pulled out the door.

She was in love, as she had never loved James, and if Aaron were willing to take a risk on her she would do the same with him. Aaron had shown her in every way that he could that he loved her, even that hurtful jealousy. She had to put irrational uncertainties behind her, had to stop thinking of herself as unworthy of being loved just because James hadn't been able to love her. But she and Aaron also had a lot of things to talk about before they made any decisions about a future together.

*   *   *

Molly looked glowing as she stepped out of the car, laughing happily as Lucy and Tommy ran down the steps to greet them, bending down to hug them both before they ran over to their father.

'I think we'll have to go away more often.' Matt carried a child in each arm as he and Molly walked up the steps to the front door.

'Charly, it's wonderful, simply wonderful!' Molly hugged her, tears in her eyes. 'I don't know how we can ever thank you.'

'Hey, I had a hand in it too,' Aaron pretended indignation at being excluded.

Charly had stiffened at Molly's effusive thanks, and as the other woman looked puzzled by Aaron's statement she knew she had reason to be worried.

'You did?' Molly frowned at him. 'Matt?' she looked at her husband.

He slowly bent to put the children down, grimacing apologetically at the rigid-faced Charly. 'I think the two of you are talking at cross-purposes,' he murmured.

'We are? Oh.' Molly's brow cleared. 'Of course I'm very grateful to you for taking care of the children for us this weekend, Aaron,' she nodded. 'But I was talking about the house earlier. About Charly buying it to turn into a hospital.'

Charly looked anxiously at Aaron, cringing at the guarded look that came over his face.

'Oh yes?' he prompted non-committally.

Molly gave Charly another glowing smile. 'It's the most wonderful opportunity for Matt,' she said happily, looking at her husband proudly.

She forced herself to speak normally, although she was very aware of Aaron's narrow-eyed look. 'I take it you approve?' she teased the other woman.

'Of course,' Molly laughed dismissively, putting her hand in the crook of Matt's arm. 'It's what he's always wanted, but we would never have had the money for such a project,' she said regretfully.

'We were worried in case you couldn't cope, with the new baby coming along.' Still she avoided looking at Aaron.

'I'll cope,' Molly said determinedly. 'Isn't it marvellous, Aaron?'

Charly tensed as she waited for his response, her gaze fixed firmly on the carpet.

'Marvellous,' he finally agreed, moving forward to shake the other man's hand. 'Shevton House is very suitable for a hospital, and so convenient for you being only a short distance from here. This way you'll still be able to have the best of both worlds.'

Charly paled as he repeated everything she and Matt had said about the house when she had invited Matt to go down and look at it! But did he mean the praise as innocently as she and Matt had done, or did he still think she was trying to buy the affection of the other man?

CHAPTER TEN

'EXACTLY,' Molly agreed enthusiastically. 'Now let's all have a nice cup of tea and the children can open their presents.'

It wasn't until they were all seated in the lounge with their cups of tea, the children on the floor playing with their new toys, that Charly dared glance at Aaron again. What she saw frightened her. He looked cold and distant, his eyes hard, his mouth tight. He did believe she was still trying to buy Matt!

'I think it's time I left.' She stood up jerkily. 'I have a thousand things to do before going to work tomorrow,' she added lightly, wondering if she sounded as falsely bright as she felt.

'Oh, we thought you would both stay to dinner.' Molly looked disappointed.

'Not this time,' Charly refused regretfully—knowing there would never be another time.

'No, I'm afraid we have to be going,' Aaron stood up too.

Charly looked at him sharply—and then wished she hadn't. When she looked at him, seeing him as remote as that first evening they met, she knew she had lost him. 'There's no need for you to leave too—darling,' she added the endearment to take the sting out of her words, conscious of the fact that on Friday Molly had already believed things to be strained between them. Aaron could tell the other woman of the end of their relationship some other time! 'After all, we each have a car here.'

He met her gaze steadily. 'I have to leave now, anyway. I have some things to sort out in London myself.'

She paled slightly at the warning in his voice, turning away. 'I'll just go and get my case and bag.'

'I'll help you,' Matt offered before Aaron had the chance to do so.

She gave him a grateful smile. 'Thank you.'

Matt waited until they were in her bedroom before speaking. 'I'm sorry about that,' he grimaced.

'Don't be,' she dismissed reassuringly. 'If I were in Molly's position I wouldn't be able to stay quiet either.'

'I forgot to ask her not to say anything in front of anyone,' he admitted ruefully.

'I doubt if she would have thought that included Aaron anyway,' she derided.

Matt frowned. 'Have the two of you argued? You seem very on edge with each other.'

'Everything has gone very smoothly.' She picked up her bag to hide her flushed cheeks. 'And Shevton House is finally ours,' she told him with satisfaction as she followed him out of the room and down the stairs.

Excitement brightened his eyes. 'That's wonderful!'

She nodded. 'I'll call you towards the end of the week and make the necessary arrangements.'

'But not Friday,' Aaron put in softly, he and Molly standing in the hallway.

Charly swallowed hard, looking at him warily. 'Why not Friday?'

He didn't answer her, turning to look down at Molly. 'I forgot to mention it earlier, but Charly and I have decided on the date for our wedding.'

'Not—not *Friday*?' Molly sounded astounded.

'Why not?' he returned mildly.

'Well because—because——' She looked desperately at Charly. 'Tell him it isn't time enough to get ready for a church wedding!'

Charly had turned to ice at the mention of a wedding, knowing that Aaron had decided that now, more than ever, Matt needed saving from himself.

'We've decided to scrap the church idea,' Aaron told the other woman briskly, kissing her on the cheek before shaking Matt's hand. 'I can't wait any longer than Friday. Come on, honey.' He took a firm hold of Charly's arm and guided her towards the door.

She felt numb as they walked over to their cars, knowing that last night had meant nothing to Aaron after all.

'Aren't you going to say something?' he prompted gently as they reached her car. 'I realise I was high-handed in announcing we were getting married like that, but——'

'I understand your reason,' she told him woodenly.

He frowned. 'Then why can't you look at me?'

She did look at him then, the pain etched into her face. 'Trust is a fragile thing, Aaron, but last night I trusted you. It's a pity you can't do the same.'

'What are you talking about?' he shook his head.

She threw her case in the back of her car. 'I

would have thought by now you would have realised I have no designs on your friend,' she sighed.

'But I do realise that,' he told her unhesitatingly. 'I knew last night that you and Matt have never been lovers.'

'Then why——'

'Which one of them survived the crash, Charly?' he asked gently. 'It must have been Stephanie, you would never have felt this way if it were James.'

She was very pale. 'How did you know?' she asked in a hushed voice.

He shrugged. 'After Molly dropped her bombshell I tried to put two and two together without making my usual five. Was it Stephanie Matt tried to save?'

'Yes,' she confirmed chokingly.

He nodded. 'I'm going to follow you back to your apartment,' he told her firmly. 'Where we are going to clear up these misunderstandings once and for all. Then we are going to plan our wedding for Friday.'

Her eyes widened. 'You were serious about that?'

'Well, I did propose last night, and although I didn't actually receive a verbal reply I believe our actions afterwards were enough of an acceptance,' he mocked indulgently.

She blushed as she remembered the times in the night that they had turned to each other. 'Aaron——'

'Sweetheart, we can't talk here.' The gentle rebuke reminded her they were still standing in Molly and Matt's driveway. 'I'll follow you to your home. And please drive carefully,' he added tensely.

She knew how he felt, could feel herself on the edge of happiness, and was so afraid it was going to be taken from her. As it had so often in the past!

'Charly.' He touched her cheek lovingly. 'I'm going to be around for the next fifty or sixty years.'

She smiled tearfully at his ability to guess what was troubling her. 'Is that all?'

'Well I did once have a great-aunt that lived to one hundred and three. I suppose I could try and match that.'

'Please,' she smiled at him between her tears.

He put a hand either side of her face, cupping her cheeks. 'I love you, Charly Hart.'

'I—I——'

'You can do it, Charly,' he encouraged.

She smiled shakily. 'I love you, Aaron Grantley.'

He chuckled triumphantly. 'It will get easier with time.' He kissed her achingly. 'Drive carefully, but *fast*, hmm?' Desire gleamed in his eyes.

She drove badly and slowly, realising after she almost knocked one poor man off his bike that her concentration wasn't as good as it could have been, and that if she wanted them both to get back to London in one piece she had better calm down.

But she couldn't help the exhilaration she felt, sure that everything was going to work out.

As soon as her apartment door closed they fell into each others' arms, their mouths meeting hungrily, as if they had been parted for days and not minutes.

'Enough, woman.' Aaron finally put her away from him, his breathing ragged, his eyes dark. 'Stop trying to seduce me!'

She gave a splutter of laughter, questioning who had been seducing who!

'God, you're beautiful when you laugh.' His arms closed about her as he crushed her to him. 'I want you to laugh a lot when we're married,' he told her intently. 'I want you to be so happy you can't *stop* laughing!'

She clung to him, so happy *now* she didn't think she could be any happier.

'Now, we're going to talk.' He held her firmly away from him. '*I'll* talk,' he told her. 'You interrupt me if I go wrong. Okay?'

She was too full of emotion to want to talk now, and he knew it.

They sat down on the sofa together, Aaron's arm about her shoulders as he began to talk. 'After your parents died you were lonely and confused, James Hart took advantage of that loneliness and married you to gain full control of Hartall Industries.'

'I thought I loved him,' she admitted huskily.

'You mean he *wanted* you to think that,' Aaron corrected grimly. 'It wasn't a happy marriage——' He looked down at her questioningly as she made a murmur of protest. 'Correction, it did have one happy aspect,' he said gently. 'Stephanie. After years of indulging himself in fleeting affairs Hart decided he wanted to marry your cousin. But he didn't want to lose the company, not even a part of it, considered it

belonged to him now. And so he used the love he
knew you had for Stephanie to put pressure on
you to agree to his terms. We both know what
happened when you refused.' His arm tightened
about her. 'Stephanie was ill in hospital for a long
time——'

'Two months,' she confirmed heavily.

'You and Matt became friends during that
time,' he nodded. 'He was Stephanie's doctor,
wasn't he?'

She turned and buried her face in his chest.
'She never regained consciousness.'

'My poor love!' He crushed her to him. 'It was
because you saw how Matt cared, how much he
wanted Stephanie to live and get well, that you
decided to provide him with a hospital that
would specialise only in such patients. For
months you looked for the right building,
somewhere big enough to be a hospital, but
comfortable enough for those patients to regard it
as home while they recovered——'

'How did you know that?' she gasped.

'I know you, my darling,' he smiled. 'I also
know Matt's opinion of nursing such patients.
But once you found Shevton House you found
you had a rival for its purchase, an arrogant son-
of-a-bitch whose thoughts of you were usually in
the sewer!'

'Aaron——'

'I don't blame you for not wanting me to know
why you wanted Shevton House,' he assured her.
'Even loving you as I do, before last night I
would probably have suspected your motives.'

'I thought you did anyway,' she admitted
chokingly.

'I know you did,' he nodded. 'But after last night——'

'What was so special about last night?'

He looked down at her mockingly. 'You mean you don't know?'

Colour darkened her cheeks. 'Well of course I *know*. But——'

'Sweetheart, last night you gave yourself to me time and time again, exposed your inner emotions and needs, something I knew you would never do unless you loved me. Also, I made love to a woman who hadn't been made love to in a very long time—if ever. Oh, I know you slept with your husband, you had Stephanie, after all. But it wasn't what we had together last night.'

'No,' she acknowledged openly.

'Last night was love, for both of us. And so when Molly thanked you for giving Matt the chance to have his own hospital to specialise in I knew it had nothing to do with a close relationship between the two of you. For a while I was a little puzzled, but once I'd realised *which* house it was you were giving to Matt I worked it all out.' He grimaced. 'So much for my idea of it being a love-nest for the two of you! I have to admit I was a little put out at first that you hadn't trusted me with the truth, but once I thought about that some more I asked myself why the hell should you? Here was a woman who had been used and abused by one man, who had little reason to trust anyone, so why should she trust a man who does nothing but insult her!'

'I do trust you, Aaron.'

'Then it's about time I started earning that trust!'

'Darling, it wasn't your fault.' She touched his cheek lovingly. 'I could have cleared up many of our misunderstandings if I had cared to. But I didn't want to become involved again, so I deliberately let you think the worst of me. And then once I realised I loved you it seemed almost too late to put things right.'

'It will never be too late between us,' he told her forcefully. 'Although we are going to have to start confiding things to each other a bit more.'

'About Friday——'

'Yes?' He tensed.

She gave him a glowing smile. 'Can't we make it any sooner?'

'Lady!' His eyes darkened. 'As far as I'm concerned we've been married since last night.'

It was the way she felt too, knew that they had become two parts of a whole last night when they had given themselves to each other time and time again.

'Are you sure you won't mind having a working wife?' she asked tentatively.

'I wouldn't have it any other way,' he answered instantly.

She should have known that would be his answer. Aaron was a man who would never suppress or suffocate her, who would just love her for what she was.

'You were the one who said "now isn't the time to be talking about children",' Aaron reminded her anxiously.

Charly rested between the strong contractions, the two of them having arrived at the hospital just over three hours ago, she insisting on leaving it until the last minute before coming in.

It wouldn't be long now before their baby was born, and then Aaron would quickly forget all the worry he was feeling now. 'Darling—' she broke off as another contraction gripped her, squeezing his hand until his fingers looked bloodless, although he didn't make a move of protest, sharing her pain. The contraction had been even stronger this time, quicker too; it wouldn't be long now. 'I didn't mean for us not to think about them *at all*,' she teased.

Almost nine months after their wedding their first child was being born, and both of them were convinced it had been conceived that weekend at Molly and Matt's. Aaron had been actively involved in the preparations for the birth and afterwards since the beginning, but none of the classes they had attended together seemed to have prepared him for this moment.

She gasped as another contraction gripped her, knowing the birth was imminent as it went on and on, doing her best to help their child make its entrance into the world, feeling the exhilarating relief as the baby was born in a sudden rush of activity, the look on the doctor's face enough to tell her everything was all right with the baby.

'It's a boy, Charly,' Aaron choked as he stood up to look at his son. 'My God, it's a boy!'

She smiled through her exhaustion, sitting up enough with Aaron's help to look at her son for the first time. He was smoothly round, had a beautiful face, and a shock of golden hair.

'A healthy seven pounds four ounces,' the

nurse told her as she handed the blanket-wrapped baby to Charly.

She held the baby to her gently, slightly shaky still from the birth, awed by the perfection of her son. 'He's beautiful,' she said tearfully.

'Almost as beautiful as his mother.' Aaron's own cheeks were damp as she handed the baby to him. 'Daniel Aaron Matthew Grantley,' he murmured softly, the baby asleep in his arms. 'Quite a mouthful for such a little man.'

'He'll grow into it.' Charly smiled, moved by how deeply she loved this man and was loved in return by him, and how much they would both love their son. The nine months of their marriage had been happy ones—more than happy, *ecstatic*! She hadn't believed there could be such happiness. Daniel made everything perfect.

'Congratulations,' the doctor smiled. 'I'll see you again next year,' he teased before leaving.

'Like hell he will!' Aaron rasped.

Charly smiled tiredly. 'I thought you wanted three or four?'

'I've changed my mind.' He handed Daniel back to the nurse to be washed, holding Charly's hand. 'I had no idea what you would have to go through.' A frown marred his brow. 'Daniel is enough for me.'

'I don't believe in only children,' she teased.

'We'll borrow Lucy, Tommy, and Sara for weekends,' he answered instantly. 'They can keep Daniel company.'

'Coward,' she laughed softly.

His hand tightened on hers. 'How could you want to go through that again?'

'Quite easily,' she said ruefully.

'We'll talk about it once you're stronger,' he compromised.

'Just talk about it?' she teased.

'Nurse, are all new mothers as sexy as this?' He turned to the other woman, Daniel all snuggled down in the clear-sided crib.

She laughed. 'Only when they have husbands as handsome as you!'

Charly joined in the laughter as *he* was the one to look embarrassed. 'I love you, Aaron Grantley.'

'I love *you*, Charly Grantley. We finally got the name right,' he said with satisfaction.

She felt her lids begin to droop tiredly. 'Charly Grantley does sound rather nice.'

'I thought so,' he nodded smugly.

'Perfect . . .' She fell asleep, her *world* perfect at last.

LOVERS IN THE AFTERNOON

LOVERS IN THE AFTERNOON

BY
CAROLE MORTIMER

MILLS & BOON LIMITED
Eton House, 18–24 Paradise Road
Richmond, Surrey TW9 1SR

First published in Great Britain 1985 by Mills & Boon Limited

© Carole Mortimer 1985

Australian copyright 1985 Philippine copyright 1985 Reprinted 1985 This edition 1991

ISBN 0 263 77556 9

Set in Monophoto Plantin 11 on 11 pt. 19–9110–48970

Made and printed in Great Britain

For
John, Matthew
and Joshua

CHAPTER ONE

WHAT was this man *doing* in her bed!

Dear God, it wasn't even her bed but his, she remembered now. She had been introduced to him at his office only that afternoon, and five hours later here she was in his bed!

She looked down at the man sleeping so peacefully at her side, one strong arm flung back across the pillow as he lay on his back, dark hair silvered with grey, all of his body deeply tanned, from a holiday he had taken in Acapulco he had told her over dinner. And she was well aware of the beauty of all that body, had touched every inch of it, from the broad shoulders, muscled chest with its covering of brown-grey hair, taut flat waist, powerfully built thighs, down long supple legs. The black silk sheet was pushed back to his waist now to reveal the strength of his chest and arms, the thick dark hair disappearing in a vee past his navel and down.

Her gaze returned quickly to his face. It was a strong, powerful face even in sleep, a wide intelligent forehead, widely defined eyebrows, beneath the long-lashed lids were eyes of a piercing grey, a long straight nose, firm uncompromising mouth, and a jaw that was firm as he slept. He was one of the most attractive men she had ever seen, or was ever likely to see, and she had spent most of the evening here in this bed with him, the first man to make love to her since her separation from her husband eight months ago.

7

But why did it have to be Adam Faulkner, rich industrialist, sixteen years her senior at thirty-nine, and her most recent client with the interior designing company she worked for!

She had gone to work so innocently this morning, had got out of bed at her usual seven-thirty, fed the fish and cat, warned the cat not to eat the fish while she was out all day, got her usual breakfast of dry toast and black coffee, both of which she consumed on her way to the shower as she usually did, applied the light make-up to her heart-shaped face and ever-sparkling green eyes, styled her feathered red-brown hair into its usual mass of uncontrolled lengths to her shoulders before donning the tailored blue suit and lighter blue blouse that made her hair look more red than brown, the white camisole beneath the blouse clearly the only covering to her unconfined breasts.

She had gone down to the underground car-park to her delapidated VW, sworn at it for the usual ten minutes before it deigned to start. She had then emerged out into the usual helter-skelter of traffic that was London in the rush-hour, dodging the other seasoned drivers as she drove to her office at Stevenson Interiors, cursing the fact that she needed to take the car at all, but the reliable London underground system went nowhere near her flat or the office. Yes, it had been a pretty usual day up to that point in time.

Her breathless entrance on to the sixth floor that housed the employees of Stevenson Interiors, after being stuck in the lift for fifteen minutes was also usual; the lift broke down at least once a week, and Leonie was usually in it when it did. It would have been *unusual* if she weren't!

'The lift again?' Betty, the young, attractive receptionist, asked ruefully.

'Yes,' her sigh was resigned. 'One of these days I'm going to fool it and take the stairs.'

'All twelve flights?' Betty's eyes widened.

Leonie grimaced, running controlling fingers through her flyaway hair. 'That would be a little drastic, wouldn't it?' she conceded wryly.

Betty handed her her messages. 'In your state of physical *un*fitness it could be suicide!'

'Thanks!' She skimmed through the pieces of paper she had been given, dismissing all of them as unimportant before pushing them into her navy blue clutch-bag. 'What's on the agenda for today?' she looked at Betty with her usual open expression.

'The staff meeting at nine o'clock?'

'Nine——! Oh Lord,' Leonie groaned, already fifteen minutes late for the meeting David had warned all employees *not* to be late for. 'Maybe if I just crept into the back of the room . . .?' she said hopefully.

'David would notice you if you crept in on your hands and knees and stood hidden for the whole meeting,' Betty told her derisively.

The other woman was right, of course. David had picked her out for his individual attention from the moment he had employed her six months ago, and although she occasionally agreed to have dinner with him she made sure it was only occasionally, not wanting any serious involvement, even if David was one of the nicest men she had ever known. An unsuccessful marriage had a way of souring you to the idea of another permanent relationship. Besides, David had little patience with the way things just seemed to happen to her, believing she should be able to have some control over the accidents that just seemed to occur whenever she was around.

She remembered another man, her husband, who had also found these accidents irritating, and she didn't need that criticism in her life a second time. She could handle these 'incidents' left to her own devices, she didn't need some man, no matter how nice he was, constantly criticising her.

'I'll creep in anyway.' She narrowly missed walking into the pot-plant that seemed to be following her about the room. 'What do you feed this on?' She looked up at the huge tree-like plant in horror. 'It's taking over reception, if not the world!'

'A little love and conversation do seem to have done the trick,' Betty acknowledged proudly. 'Now shouldn't you be getting to the staff meeting?'

David's office was crowded to capacity as she squeezed into the back of the room, but nevertheless his reproachful gaze spotted her instantly, although he didn't falter in his flow of how well the company was doing, of how good new contracts were coming their way every day.

Leonie yawned boredly, wishing she had been stuck in the lift even longer than she had been, receiving another censorious glare from David as she did, plastering a look of interest on to her face that she had perfected during her marriage, while her thoughts wandered to the Harrison lounge she had just completed, as pleased with the result as the elderly couple had been. She always felt a sense of immense satisfaction whenever she completed a job, knew she was good at what she did, that she was at last a success at something. Although some people would have her believe differently.

'Leonie, did you hear me?'

She looked up with a start at David's impatiently spoken question, blushing guiltily as she realised she was the cynosure of all eyes. 'Er——'

'Steady,' Gary warned as he stood at her side, deftly catching the papers she had knocked off the top of the filing cabinet as she jumped guiltily, grateful to the man who had taken her under his experienced wing from the day she came to work here.

Her blush deepened at the sympathetic ripple of laughter that filled the room; everyone knew of her habit of knocking and walking into things. 'Of course I heard you, David,' she answered awkwardly, her gaze guilelessly innocent as she looked at him steadily.

'Then you don't mind staying for a few minutes after the others have gone back to their offices?' he took pity on her, knowing very well that she hadn't been listening to a word he said.

'Er—no, of course not,' she replaced the papers on the filing cabinet that Gary had caught for her, wondering what she was guilty of now, feeling like the disobedient child that had been asked to stay in after school. It couldn't be her lack of attention to what was being said that was at fault, she never did that anyway, and David knew it.

She moved to sit on the edge of his desk as the others filed out to go back to work. 'Good meeting, David,' she complimented brightly.

'And how would you know one way or the other?' he sighed, looking up at her, a tall loose-limbed man with wild blond hair that refused to be tamed despite being kept cut close to his head, the rest of his appearance neat to precision point. He was only twenty-eight, had built his interior designing business up from a two-room, three-man operation to the point where he had a dozen people working for him. And Leonie knew she was lucky to be one of them, that Stevenson Interiors was one of the most successful businesses in its field, and that it was all due to David's drive and initiative.

She grimaced. 'Would it help if I were to say I'm sorry?' she cajoled.

'You always are,' David said without rancour. 'I wanted to talk to you about Thompson Electronics.'

A frown marred her creamy brow. 'Has something gone wrong? I thought they were pleased with the work I did for them. I don't understand——'

'Calm down, Leonie,' he ordered impatiently at her impassioned outburst. 'They were pleased, they *are* pleased, which is why the new President of the company wants you to personally design the decor for his own office suite.'

'He does?' she gasped.

'Don't look so surprised,' David mocked. 'It was a good piece of work. Even I would never have thought of using that particular shade of pink—indeed any shade of pink, in a group of offices.'

'It was the brown that off-set the femininity of it. You see I had——'

'You don't have to convince me of anything, Leonie,' he drawled. 'Or them either. You just have to get yourself over there at four o'clock this afternoon to discuss the details.'

She was still relatively new at her job, and tried to make every design she did a work of art, something personal; she was more than pleased to know that someone else had seen and appreciated some of her completed work enough to ask for her personally. It was the first time it had happened.

'Mrs Carlson will be expecting you,' David continued. 'She phoned and made the appointment first thing this morning. And she'll introduce you to the President then.'

'Ronald Reagan?'

He gave a patiently humouring sigh. 'Where do you get your sense of humour from?'

She grinned at him. 'It's what keeps my world going.'

David frowned at the underlying seriousness beneath her words. Except for the friendly, and often loony façade she presented to everyone here, he knew little about the real Leonie Grant. Her employee's file said she had been married but was now separated from her husband, but she never spoke of the marriage or the man she had been married to, her openness often seeming to hide a wealth of pain and disillusionment.

But it never showed, and Leonie found as much humour in her clumsiness as everyone else did, able to laugh at herself and the things that happened to her.

His mouth quirked into a smile. 'I have to admit that when Mrs Carlson said the President would expect you at four o'clock the same thought crossed my mind!'

'Naughty, David,' she shook her head reprovingly, her eyes glowing deeply green.

For a moment they shared a smile of mutual humour, and then David shook his head ruefully. 'Try not to be late for the meeting,' he advised. 'From the way Mrs Carlson was acting he sounds pretty awesome.'

Leonie grimaced. 'Are you sure you want to

send me, I could walk in, trip over a matchstick, and end up sliding across his desk into his lap!'

'He asked for you specifically.' But David frowned as he mentally envisaged the scene she had just described. 'I'll take the risk,' he said without enthusiasm.

'Sure?'

'No,' he answered with complete honesty. 'But short of lying to the man I don't know what else I can do. Just try not to be late,' he warned again.

And she did try, she tried very hard, but it seemed the fates were against her from the start. She caught her tights on the door as she got into her VW, drove around for another ten minutes trying to find somewhere to park so she could buy some new ones, getting back to the car just in time to personally accept her parking ticket from the traffic warden, making a mad dash to find somewhere to change her tights, laddering that pair too in her haste, although it was high enough up her leg not to show. By this time she in no way resembled the coolly smart young woman who had left Stevenson Interiors in plenty of time to reach Thompson Electronics by four o'clock. It was already five to four, and she was hot and sticky from her exertions with the tights, her make-up needing some repair, her hair having lost its glowing bounce in the heat of the day. She was already going to be a few minutes late; taking time to refresh her make-up and brush her hair wasn't going to make that much difference now.

It was ten minutes past four when she entered the Thompson building, her slim briefcase in her hand, and except for the fact that she was late, looking like a self-contained young executive. Ten minutes wasn't so bad, she could blame that on the traffic. She certainly didn't intend going into the story of the ripped tights as her excuse, or the parking ticket either! It was——

Oh no, she just didn't believe this, it couldn't be happening to her! But she knew that it was as the smooth-running lift made a terrible grinding noise and shuddered to a halt somewhere between the eighth and ninth floors. She was stuck in a lift for the second time that day! And as usual she was alone. She was always alone when the damned things broke down, never had anyone to help calm the panic that she felt. This was a large lift, not like the one at Stevenson Interiors, but she would still rather be on the other side of those steel doors. Oh well, at least the floor was carpeted if she had to spend any amount of time here, so she could be comfortable. But it wasn't likely that she would be here for long, this was a big and busy building, someone was sure to realise sooner or later that one of the lifts was stuck between floors. And she hoped it was sooner!

She sank to the floor after pressing the emergency button, knowing from experience that people rarely took notice of that bell. God, what a day it had been, worse than her usual string of mishaps. If she didn't know better she would think——But no, she wouldn't even think about him. God, this was a hell of a place to start thinking of the disastrous effect her husband had had on her, his disapproval of almost everything she did making her more nervous, and consequently more klutzy, than ever.

She determinedly opened her briefcase, going through the fabric book she had brought with her, wondering what sort of colour scheme the President of the company would favour. She had thought of a few ideas, but basically she just wanted to hear what his tastes were.

She became so engrossed in matching paints and fabrics, the books strewn over the floor, that for some time she managed to forget she was marooned in a lift eight-and-a-half floors up. It was almost five-thirty when she heard the sound of banging from above, a voice that sounded strangely hollow calling down that the lift would be working shortly.

Leonie stood up, her legs stiff from where she had been sitting on the floor for over an hour, losing her balance as the lift began moving almost immediately, jerking for several feet before moving smoothly, Leonie flung about in the confined space, falling to the ground in a sprawled heap as it shuddered to a halt and the door miraculously creaked slowly open.

The first thing Leonie saw from her floor-level view was a pair of well-shod feet, the man's black shoes made of a soft leather, a meticulous crease down the centre of the grey trouser legs. Before she could raise her gaze any further Mrs Carlson was rushing into the lift to help her to her feet, the black shoes and grey-covered legs turning away.

'Bring her into my office as soon as you've helped her tidy up,' ordered a curt male voice.

Leonie turned sharply to look at the man as the other woman fussed around her, but all she saw was the back of the man's head as he entered a room at the end of the corridor.

'Have you been in here long?' The middle-aged woman helped her pick up her sample books from the floor, a tall capable woman who had been secretary to the last President of the company for over twenty years. Leonie had met her when she worked here last, and although the other woman tried to be distant and authoritative, her warm brown eyes belied the role.

Leonie liked the other woman, but she wasn't sure she liked anyone seeing her sprawled on the floor in that undignified way. 'An hour or so,' she dismissed distractedly, pushing the books into her briefcase, anxious to get out of the lift.

Stella Carlson followed her out into the corridor. 'In all the years I've worked here I've never known any of the lifts break down before,' she shook her head.

Leonie grimaced, brushing her skirt down. 'I have a strange effect on lifts.'

'Really?' the other woman frowned. 'Well as long as you're all right now . . .?'

'Fine,' she nodded dismissively. 'I'm too late for my meeting, so perhaps you could explain the reason for my delay to your boss and I could make another appointment for tomorrow?'

'Didn't you hear, you're to go in as soon as you feel able to.'

She thought of the man with the black shoes and grey trousers. '*That* was the new President of the company?' she dreaded the answer, although she knew what it was going to be.

'Yes,' Mrs Carlson confirmed.

Oh David, Leonie mentally groaned, I didn't trip and slide across his desk into his lap, but I did lie sprawled at his feet on the floor of a lift that *never* broke down! David would never understand, things like this just didn't happen to him. They didn't happen to *any* normal person!

'Now seems as good a time as any,' she said dully, knowing her dignity was past redemption. 'I'm sure I've delayed you long enough already.'

'Not at all,' the other woman assured her as

they walked side by side down the corridor.
'Things have been a little—hectic, here the last
few weeks.'

The new boss was obviously giving the
employees a shake-up, Leonie thought ruefully,
her humour leaving her as she realised she would
probably be in for the same treatment. After all,
if she hadn't been ten minutes late in the first
place she wouldn't have been in the lift when it
broke down. Or would she? As she had told Mrs
Carlson, she had a strange effect on lifts. She had
a strange effect on most inanimate objects, things
just seemed to happen to them whenever she was
around.

She smoothed her skirt down as Mrs Carlson
knocked on the office door, unaware of the fact
that her hair was sadly in need of brushing after
her fall, that the fullness of her mouth was bare of
lipgloss where she had chewed on her lips as she
looked through the sample books. Not that she
would have worried too much about it if she had
known; she couldn't possibly make a worse
impression than she had as she grovelled about
the lift floor!

Mrs Carlson opened the door after the terse
instruction from within for them to enter. 'Miss
Grant, sir,' she introduced quietly.

Leonie stared at the man seated behind the desk,
the man that belonged to the black shoes and grey
legs, the rest of the dark grey suit as impressive, the
waistcoat taut across his flat stomach, the tailored
material of the jacket stretched across widely
powerful shoulders, the white shirt beneath the
suit making his skin look very dark.

But it was his face that held her attention, a
harshly attractive face, his chin firm and square,
the sensuality of his mouth firmly controlled, his

nose long and straight, ice-grey eyes narrowed on
her beneath darkly jutting brows, silver threading
the darkness of his hair at his temples and over
his ears. Anyone who was in the least familiar
with the businessworld would recognise Adam
Faulkner from his photographs in the newspapers,
one of the most successful—and richest—men in
England today. He was also——

'Miss Grant,' he stood up in fluid movements,
the coldness instantly gone from his eyes, his
voice warm and friendly, his hand enveloping
hers in a grip that was pleasantly warm, not too
firm and not too loose; the exactly right
handshake for a businessman to instil confidence
in the person he was dealing with.

But why he should waste his time on such a
gesture with her was beyond her, she was——

'I hope your unfortunate delay in our lift hasn't
disturbed you too much,' he continued smoothly,
releasing her hand slowly, leaving the imprint of
his touch against her flesh.

Leonie was stunned at his obvious concern.
'I—I have that effect on lifts,' she mumbled the
same lame excuse she had given Mrs Carlson,
conscious of the other woman still standing in the
room with them.

Dark brows rose questioningly. 'That sort of
thing happens to you often?'

Colour heightened her cheeks. 'Yes,' she bit
out. 'Look, I don't think——'

'Don't worry, I'm not expecting you to
conduct our business meeting after your ordeal in
the lift,' he assured her. 'I suggest we make
another appointment for tomorrow,' he looked at
Mrs Carlson for confirmation. 'Some time in the
afternoon,' he instructed as she left the room to
consult his appointment book.

'Please, I——'

'Please sit down, Miss Grant,' Adam Faulkner instructed when he saw how pale she had become. 'Let me get you a drink. Would you like tea or coffee, or perhaps something stronger?' He pressed a button on his desk to reveal an extensive array of drinks in the cabinet situated behind Leonie.

Leonie just kept staring at him, too numb to even answer.

'Something stronger, I think,' he nodded derisively at her lack of response, striding across the room to pour her some whisky into a glass. 'Drink it down,' he instructed her firmly as she made no effort to take the glass from his lean fingers.

She took the glass, swallowing without tasting, reaction definitely setting in.

Adam Faulkner moved to sit on the edge of his desk in front of her, dangerously close, the warmth of his maleness seeming to reach out and engulf her. 'Terrible experience, getting caught in a stationary lift.' He took the empty glass from her unresisting fingers, seeming satisfied that she had drunk it as instructed. 'I've been caught in several myself in the past,' he added dryly. 'Although not lately.'

'It's my second time today,' Leonie mumbled dully, feeling the alcohol in her bloodsteam, remembering too late that she hadn't had any lunch, that the piece of dry toast she had eaten for breakfast wasn't enough to stop the effect the whisky was having on her. That was all she needed to complete her day, to be roaring drunk in front of this man! 'The one at work has always been unreliable,' she added in defence of her clumsiness in getting stuck in two lifts that had broken down.

'Maybe you have too much electricity in your body,' Adam Faulkner suggested softly. 'And it has an adverse effect on other electrical things.'

She looked up at him sharply, and then wished she hadn't as a wave of dizziness swept over her. She was going to get up out of this chair to make a dignified exit and fall flat on her face, just to *prove* what an idiot she was! If this man weren't already aware of that!

'Maybe,' she nodded, swallowing in an effort to clear her head, having a terrible urge to start giggling. In one part of her brain she could logically reason that she had little to giggle about, and in another she just wanted to start laughing and never stop. There was so much about this situation that was funny.

'Miss Grant?'

She frowned up at him. 'Why do you keep calling me that?'

He shrugged. 'It's your name, isn't it?'

'Leonie Grant, yes,' she nodded in exaggerated movements. 'I—Hic. I—Hic. Oh *no*,' she groaned her humiliation as her loud hiccups filled the room. She really was making a fool out of herself—more so than usual, if that were possible! She should never have got out of bed today, should have buried her head beneath the bedclothes and stayed there until fate decided to be kind to her again. If it ever did, she groaned as she hiccuped again.

'Maybe the whisky was a bad idea,' Adam said in amusement, going over to the bar to pour her a glass of water.

Leonie gave him a look that spoke volumes before swallowing the water, almost choking as a hiccup caught her mid-swallow, spitting water everywhere, including over one black leather shoe as Adam Faulkner's leg swung in front of her as he once again sat on the edge of his desk. 'Oh dear,' she began to mop at the shoe with a tissue from her bag, becoming even more agitated when several pieces of the tissue stuck to the wet surface.

She closed her eyes, wishing the scene would evaporate, that she would find it had all been a bad dream. But when she opened her eyes again the black shoe dotted with delicate yellow tissue was still there, and the man wearing the shoe was beginning to chuckle. Leonie looked up at him dazedly, liking the warmth in his eyes, the way they crinkled at the corners as he laughed, a dimple appearing in one lean cheek, his teeth very white and even against his tanned skin.

Mrs Carlson entered the room after the briefest knock, breaking the moment of intimacy. 'I've checked your appointment book, Mr Faulkner, and you're free at twelve o'clock or three o'clock.'

'Twelve o'clock, I think,' he still smiled. 'Then Miss Grant and I can go out to lunch afterwards.'

'Oh but I——'

'Book a table, would you?' He cut across Leonie's protest, smiling at his secretary, much to her obvious surprise. 'My usual place. And you may as well leave for the evening now, Miss Grant and I are just going to dinner.'

'Er—yes, Mr Faulkner.' The older woman gave Leonie a curious look, seeming to give a mental shrug before leaving the room.

'She's wondering why you could possibly want to take me to dinner,' Leonie sighed, wondering the same thing herself. But at least the suggestion had stopped her hiccups!

Adam stood up after dusting the tissue from his shoe. 'It's the least I can do after your ordeal in the lift.'

'But that was my fault——'

'Nonsense,' he humoured.

Leonie blinked at the determination in his face. 'Why should you want to take me out to dinner?'

'Miss Grant——'

'Will you stop calling me that!'

'Would you prefer Leonie?' he queried softly, locking his desk drawers and picking up his briefcase in preparation for leaving for the evening.

'Yes,' she snapped.

'Then you must call me Adam,' he invited huskily.

'I'm well aware of your name,' she bit out impatiently. The whisky may have gone to her head but she wasn't that drunk! And she had no idea why this man should want to take her out to dinner, they——

'Then please use it,' he urged, as his hand on her elbow brought her to her feet.

Leonie swayed slightly, falling against him, flinching away from the hard warmth of his body. 'Please, I don't want to go out to dinner,' she protested as he propelled her from the room at his side, the top floor of the building strangely in silence, Mrs Carlson having followed his instruction and left for the evening, the other employees having left some time ago.

Adam didn't release her arm. 'When did you last eat?' he asked pointedly as she swayed again.

'I had some toast for breakfast this morning. I need to diet,' she defended heatedly as the grey eyes looked her over disapprovingly.

'You're too thin,' he stated bluntly.

'I'm a size ten,' she told him proudly.

'Definitely too thin,' he repeated arrogantly. 'I

happen to be one of those men who prefers his woman to have some meat on her bones.'

His woman? *His* woman! Just who did he think he was? 'I happen to like being thin,' she told him irritably.

He arched dark brows. 'Do you also like starving to death?' he drawled.

It was her weakness for good food that had pushed her up to a size fourteen in the past, and she had no intention of giving in to that weakness again, not when it had taken so much effort to lose the excess weight. 'I'll survive,' she muttered.

'Will you be okay in the lift now that it's working properly?' Adam asked as the lift doors opened to them invitingly.

'I'll be fine,' she dismissed his concern. 'Although the way today is going so far it could break down on us again,' she said ruefully.

Adam smiled down at her as they were confined in the lift together. 'I can't think of anyone I would rather be stuck in the lift with,' he said throatily.

Leonie gave him a sharp look, expecting sarcasm but finding only warm invitation in the dark grey eyes. He was flirting with her, actually *flirting* with her!

'Pity,' he drawled as they arrived safely on the ground floor, stepping into the carpeted reception area, nodding to the man on night security, guiding Leonie to the parking area, opening the passenger door of the sporty BMW for her, the top to the pale blue car back in the heat of the day. He took her briefcase from her and threw it in the back with his own before climbing in next to her, starting the engine with a roar. 'Would you like the top up or down?' he enquired politely.

She touched her hair ruefully. 'I think it's beyond redemption, so down, please.'

Adam glanced at her as he drove the car towards the exit. 'You have beautiful hair.'

Leonie tensed at the unexpected compliment, her breath held in her throat.

'The style suits you,' he added softly.

The tension left her in a relieved sigh. 'Thank you.'

Conversation was virtually impossible as they drove to the restaurant, although the fresh air did clear Leonie's head somewhat, giving her time to wonder what she was doing on her way to dinner with this man. She should have been more assertive in her refusal, shouldn't have allowed herself to be manoeuvred in this way. And yet she knew she was curious, couldn't think what possible reason Adam had for wanting to take her out to dinner. And his tolerance with the mishaps that just seemed to happen to her was too good to last!

She had been to the restaurant before that he took her to, but it had been a year ago, and hopefully no one would remember that she was the woman who had tripped on her way back from powdering her nose and pushed some poor unfortunate diner's face into his dinner!

'Good evening, Mr Faulkner,' the maitre d' greeted warmly, his eyes widening warily as he saw his companion. 'Madam,' he greeted stiffly.

He remembered her! It had been over a year ago now, and this man still remembered her. He probably didn't have many people who came here and assaulted another diner for no reason!

'Do we have to eat here?' she demanded of Adam in desperation as they followed the other man to their table.

His brows rose. 'You don't like the restaurant? Or perhaps the French cuisine isn't to your liking?'

'I love it,' she sighed. 'I just don't feel— comfortable here, that's all,' she mumbled.

'Thanks, Henri,' Adam dismissed the other man, pulling out her chair for her himself. 'Just relax, Leonie.' His hands were warm on her shoulders as he leant forward to speak softly in her ear, his breath gently ruffling her hair.

She felt strangely bereft when he removed his hands and went to sit opposite her, their table in a quietly intimate part of the restaurant. As the waiter poured the wine that had been waiting for them, she could feel the tingling of danger along her spine, wary of this romantic setting, wary of this game Adam was playing with her.

'Adam——'

'Try the wine,' he urged huskily.

'When are we going to discuss the work on your office suite?' she asked determinedly.

'Tomorrow. Before lunch.'

'About lunch——'

'Don't worry, I'm sure you'll like the restaurant I've chosen for us,' he sipped his own wine. 'Please try it,' he encouraged throatily.

She sighed her impatience, ignoring the glass of wine. 'Why are you doing this?'

'This?' he prompted softly.

She shrugged. 'The charm, the restaurant, dinner, the wine. Why, Adam? And don't say to atone for the lift breaking down with me in it because I won't believe you.'

'You're right,' he nodded, perfectly relaxed as he leant back in his chair, dismissing the waiter as he arrived to take their order. 'I had this table

booked for us tonight before I even realised you
were stuck in the lift.'

'Why?'

'Don't you usually go out for business meals
with your prospective clients?'

'Of course,' she sighed. 'But it's usually lunch,
and so far we haven't discussed any business.'

'We will,' he promised. 'Tomorrow.'

'Why not now?'

He shrugged at the determination in her face.
'Maybe after we've eaten,' he compromised.

This time he didn't wave the waiter away when
he came to take their order, and with the arrival
of their first and consequent courses there wasn't
a lot of time for conversation. And by the time
they got to the coffee stage of their meal Leonie
had to admit that she didn't give a damn if they
ever discussed business, feeling numb from the
head down, the wine one of her favourites, her
glass constantly refilled as soon as she had taken a
few sips, the food as delicious as she remembered,
forgetting her diet for this one night.

'You look like a well-fed cat,' Adam eyed her
appreciatively.

'I feel like a *very* relaxed one, if you know what
I mean,' she smiled happily.

He grinned. 'I know exactly what you mean.'

He was so handsome, so ruggedly good
looking, that he made her senses spin. Or was
that the wine? No, she was sure it was him. And
he had been so patient with her when she
knocked a glass of wine all over the table, had
dismissed the anxious waiter to mop up the
surplus liquid himself, had got down on the floor
and helped her pick up the contents of her
handbag when she accidentally opened it up the
wrong way and it all fell out, had even chuckled a

little when she knocked the waiter's arm and ended up with a potato in her lap. Yes, he had been very charming.

'Shall we go?' he suggested throatily as she smiled dreamily at him.

'Why not?' She stood up, narrowly avoiding another table as she turned too suddenly. 'I never go back to the same place twice if I can avoid it,' she assured him happily.

'It must be difficult finding new restaurants,' he smiled, a smile that oozed sensuality.

'I rarely eat out,' she dismissed. 'It's safer that way, for other diners, I mean,' she explained as they went outside, surprised to see it was already dark, a glance at her watch telling her it was almost ten o'clock. They had been in the restaurant hours!

His mouth quirked. 'I noticed you have a tendency to—well, to——'

'Drop things, knock things, bump into things,' she finished obligingly. 'My husband found it very irritating,' she added challengingly.

'Really?' Adam sounded non-committal.

'Yes. He—Where are we going?' she frowned as she realised they were in a part of London she didn't know very well, the exclusive residential area.

'My apartment.'

Leonie blinked as they entered the underground car-park. 'You live here?' she frowned.

'Since my separation,' he nodded, coming round to open her door for her.

Things were happening too fast, much too fast she realised as they entered the spacious apartment, barely having time to notice its elegant comfort before Adam swept her into his arms, his eyes glittering darkly with desire.

'I've wanted to do this ever since the lift doors opened and I saw you grovelling about on the floor,' he announced raggedly before his mouth claimed hers.

She wanted to ask him what he found so romantic about a woman making a fool of herself, but the magic of his kiss put all other thoughts from her mind, drawing her into him with the sensuous movement of his mouth, his arms beneath the jacket of her suit, his hands warm through the thin material of her blouse and camisole, his thighs hardening against her as his hands moved down to cup her buttocks and pull her into him.

The effects of the brandy and wine miraculously disappeared to be replaced by something equally as heady, sexual pleasure. She had heard all the old clichés about women who were no longer married, had scorned the idea of falling into that sexual trap herself knowing how little pleasure she had found in her marriage bed, and yet she knew that she wanted Adam. And he wanted her, there could be no doubting that.

Her lips parted beneath the assault of his tongue, knowing it was merely a facsimile of the lovemaking they really wanted, Leonie feeling filled and possessed by that moist warmth, drawing him deeper into her as she returned the attack.

Adam's breathing was ragged as he pulled away to kiss her throat, peeling the jacket expertly from her shoulders, throwing it to one side, beginning to release the buttons to her blouse, his hands sure in their movements, although they trembled slightly with anticipation.

It was this slight crack in his supreme self-confidence that encouraged Leonie to do some undressing of her own, his own jacket joining hers on the floor, his waistcoat quickly following, her fingers hesitating at the buttons of his shirt.

'Please,' he encouraged achingly.

Her own hands shook as she revealed the muscled smoothness of his chest, the dark hair there silvered with grey. He was beautiful without the trappings of the successful business-man, wearing only tailored trousers now, his arousal barely contained.

'Leonie!' His mouth captured hers again as she caressed his bared chest, moving fiercely against her, pulling her into him as the tip of her tongue tentatively caressed his lips.

They left a trail of clothes to the bedroom, both naked by the time they lay down together on the bed still kissing, Adam's hands at her breasts making her gasp with pleasure, the nipples hardening and aching, asking for the tug of his mouth. They didn't have to wait long.

Leonie didn't stop to question her complete lack of inhibitions, inhibitions that had made her marriage such an agony, only knowing that this man, with his gentle caresses, held the key to her sensuality in his hands.

Adam kissed every inch of her body, found pleasure in the secret places no other man had ever known, making her tremble uncontrollably as his tongue rasped the length of her spine to her nape, quivers of excitement making her arch back into him as he homed in on the sensitive flesh there.

She lost all lucidity as Adam's caresses brought her again and again to the edge of a fulfilment she had never known, as he always pulled her back from the edge before she could reach the pinnacle she craved, her movements beneath him becoming more and more desperate as he refused to let her escape him even for a second.

'Please, Adam. Please!' Her eyes were wild as she looked up at him.

'*You* take me,' he encouraged raggedly, his eyes black with desire.

'What——?' But she understood what he meant even as he pulled her above him, going to him eagerly, gasping as he lowered her on to him, filling her in every way possible before bringing her mouth down to his.

It was so right that it should be this way, that he should allow her the freedom to be the one to choose their pleasure, a pleasure she had never known during her marriage.

She was heady with delight, kissing the dampness of his salt-tasting shoulders and throat, quivering her own satisfaction as he groaned at the invasion of her tongue, feeling his movements quicken beneath her as he could hold back no longer, the hardness of him stroking her own desire until she felt the explosion begin in the depths of her being, beginning to shake as the warm aching pleasure ripped through her whole body in a climactic holocaust.

'My beautiful Leonie,' Adam gasped as he reached the summit of his own pleasure, exploding in a warmth of warm moistness. 'I knew it could be this way between us!'

And it hadn't stopped there, their strength and desire returning within minutes, their second lovemaking even more intense than the first, the pleasure seeming never-ending.

Leonie looked again at the face of the man who slept beside her, wondering what on earth she had done. Oh God, what had she done!

He stirred slightly as she moved from beneath

the curve of his arm, her movements stilling until she realised he was still sleeping. She blushed as she found her clothes scattered in a disorganised path from the bedroom to the lounge; she had never been so carried away by passion before. She hastily began to dress.

'What do you think you're doing?'

She balked only slightly in the movement of pulling the camisole over her head. 'What does it look like I'm doing?' she said sourly; at least he had had the decency to put on a brown towelling robe before following her from the bedroom!

'Isn't it usual to spend the whole night in circumstances like these?' he drawled, his dark hair still tousled, his jaw in need of a shave now. 'I didn't expect you to go sneaking off while I was asleep!'

'I wasn't sneaking off,' she told him resentfully. 'And there's nothing *usual* about these circumstances!' She tucked her blouse into the waistband of her skirt.

'I want you to stay the night.'

She shot him an angry glare, resentful that he could look so at ease, his hands thrust casually into the pockets of his robe, his stance relaxed. 'Why?'

His mouth twisted. 'I'm sure I've just shown you two very good reasons why.'

'Sex!'

'And what's wrong with that?' He arched dark brows.

'Nothing, you know I enjoyed it,' she snapped, knowing it would be useless to deny it, brushing her hair with angry movements, whether at Adam or herself she wasn't sure.

'So stay,' he encouraged softly.

'I can't, Adam,' she sighed impatiently. 'I

don't know what game you've been playing with me this evening——'

'A game you were quite happy to go along with,' he reminded gently.

She shook her head in self-condemnation. 'It seemed the easy way out at the time, so much easier for me to be Leonie Grant and you to be Adam Faulkner,' she said shakily.

He shrugged broad shoulders. 'Why not, that's who we are.'

'Because until our divorce becomes final I'm still officially Leonie Faulkner, your wife, and you're my husband!'

'And now I'm your lover,' he gave a slow smile of satisfaction. 'It was your idea, Leonie, you're the one that said we shouldn't have married each other but just have been lovers. And after tonight that's exactly what we're going to be!'

CHAPTER TWO

SHE vividly remembered shouting those words at Adam before she had walked out on him and their marriage eight months ago, remembered everything about her disaster of a marriage to this man. And she didn't intend becoming involved with him again in *any way*.

She was fully dressed now, straightening the collar of her jacket. 'Tonight was a mistake——'

'I have another name for it,' Adam drawled.

Her eyes flashed her resentment. 'I'm well aware of the fact that you planned what happened——'

'Don't pretend you didn't want it, too,' he warned her softly.

She blushed at the truth of that; from the moment she had seen him seated across the desk from her at the Thompson building her senses had become alive with wanting him. And the fact that he had acted as if it were the first time they had ever met had added to the excitement. But she had a feeling, knowing Adam as she did, a much less charming and relaxed Adam, that he had realised exactly what effect his behaviour was having on her, that it had been effected to get the response from her she had refused to give him during their marriage.

'It was certainly better than anything we ever shared during our marriage,' she snapped waspishly, waiting for the angry explosion she had come to expect from him when they discussed the failure of the physical side of their marriage.

'I agree.' Once again he disconcerted her; he had been doing it all evening, from the time she had discovered that her estranged husband was the new President of Thompson Electronics, during dinner when he had had such patience with her 'accidents', to the infinite care and gentleness he had shown her during their lovemaking. 'You were right,' he continued lightly. 'We're much better as lovers than as husband and wife.'

'We are not lovers!' She looked around desperately for her handbag so that she might get out of here. 'I've left my handbag in the restaurant,' she finally groaned in realisation. 'And that damned man——'

'Henri,' Adam put in softly, his mouth quirked with amusement.

'He already thinks I'm some sort of escapee from a lunatic asylum.' She hadn't missed his covert glances in her direction during the evening. 'I just can't go back there,' she shuddered.

'You don't have to——'

'And I don't need any of your high-handed interference either,' she cut in rudely. 'Why should one more visit to that place bother me!' she told herself defiantly.

'Because it does,' Adam soothed. 'And there's no need to torture yourself with the thought of having to do it; your handbag is in my car.'

Her eyes widened. 'Are you sure?'

'Very,' he replied with satisfaction. 'You were so eager to get up here that you left it next to your seat.'

'I was not eager to get up here,' she defended indignantly.

'Maybe I should rephrase that,' he said

thoughtfully. '*I* was so eager to get you up here that I didn't give you chance to think of such mundane things as a handbag. Better?' he quirked dark brows in amusement.

It was that amusement that confused her; there had been little to laugh about during their marriage, Adam always so grim. But no one knew the deviousness of his mind as well as she did, and she wasn't fooled by this charm for a moment.

'What are you up to, Adam?' she demanded impatiently. 'Why are you doing this?'

He strolled across the room to her side, his movements gracefully masculine, as they always were. 'I want a lover, Leonie,' he told her softly, only inches away from her as he stood with his hands thrust into the pockets of his robe. 'I want *you*.'

She shook her head. 'You had me for a year, and it was a disaster,' she recalled bitterly.

Adam nodded in acknowledgment of that fact. 'Nevertheless, I want you.'

'You've only just got rid of me!' she reminded desperately.

'Of the marriage, not you, Leonie.'

'It's the same thing!'

'No,' he smiled gently. 'We both found the marriage stifling, the sort of relationship I'm suggesting——'

'With me as your mistress!' she scorned.

'Lover,' he insisted. 'We would be lovers.'

'No!'

'Why not?' his eyes had narrowed, although he remained outwardly relaxed.

'I don't want a lover!'

His mouth quirked. 'You just proved, very effectively, that you do.'

Colour heightened her cheeks. 'That was sex——'

'The best sex we ever had, admit it,' he encouraged.

She drew in a ragged breath. 'Yes.'

'And as I said before, what's wrong with that?'

She sighed her exasperation. 'You just don't understand——'

'I understand perfectly,' he cut in soothingly. 'This has all come as a bit of a shock to you——'

'That has to be the understatement of the decade!'

Adam chuckled, at once looking younger. 'Poor Leonie,' he smiled. 'What's shocking you the most, the fact that we found such pleasure in bed together for the first time, or the fact that I want it to continue?'

She couldn't deny that she was surprised at the amount of pleasure she had known with Adam tonight, a pleasure she had known beyond all doubt that he felt too, his responses open and complete. Their sex-life during their marriage, as with everything else during that year, had been a disaster. Adam had been so experienced that in her innocence she had felt inadequate, and she had resented the way he had tried to control her body, her responses automatic and emotionless, refusing to be dominated by him. But the lovemaking they had shared tonight hadn't been restricted by any of that resentment, had been uninhibited. But that Adam should want such a relationship to continue she couldn't accept, not when the breakdown of the marriage and subsequent separation had been such a traumatic experience for her. They simply couldn't pretend they were two people they weren't.

'The first shocks me,' she replied coolly. 'The

second surprises me. Do you honestly not remember what it was like between us, the bitterness, the pain of knowing we were all wrong for each other from the start?'

'As a married couple, not as lovers,' he insisted forcefully.

'Have you forgotten what *that* was like between us?'

'Didn't this evening prove that it doesn't have to be that way?' he reasoned.

'I'm still the same person, Adam,' she told him with a sigh. 'I'm still sixteen years younger than you are, with the same inexperience—no matter what happened here tonight,' she added pointedly. 'I'm still the same klutzy person I was when we were married——'

'That's a new name for it,' he laughed softly.

'I read it in a book somewhere,' she dismissed impatiently. 'It seemed to suit me perfectly.'

'It does,' he nodded, still smiling, his eyes a warm grey, crinkled at the corners.

'Don't you remember how angry all those "incidents" used to make you!'

'You're right, I was intolerant——'

'You're missing my point, Adam,' she said frustratedly. 'It would take a saint to put up with all the things that happen to me in one day—and that's one thing I know you aren't!'

'Have I been angry tonight at all?'

'That was only *one* night,' she sighed her impatience. 'It would drive you insane—it *did* drive you insane, on a regular basis.'

'Haven't you heard, lovers are more tolerant?'

'Adam!'

'Leonie?'

She glowered at him. 'You aren't listening to a word I've been saying.'

'Of course I am,' he placated. 'You're young and klutzy.' He smiled. 'I really like that word, it describes you exactly.' He sobered. 'As a husband I was rigid and intolerant, lousy at making love to you. As a lover I will be generous and understanding—and very good in bed.'

'In your experience,' she snapped waspishly.

He raised dark brows. 'You sound jealous, Leonie.'

She felt the heat in her cheeks. 'I most certainly am not!'

'It's all right if you are.' His arms came about her as he moulded her body to his. 'From a wife it would sound shrewish, from a lover it sounds possessive. I like that,' he stated with satisfaction.

That wasn't all he liked from the feel of his body pressed so intimately against hers, aroused for the third time tonight. Leonie couldn't pretend not to be shocked by this evidence of his renewed desire; their sex life had deteriorated so badly at the end of their marriage that it was an effort for them to make love once a week; Adam had never wanted her *three* times in one night before!

'Adam, please stop this.' She pulled agitatedly away from him as her own body quivered in reaction to his. 'You've had your fun——'

'It was mutual,' he drawled confidently.

'Not that sort of fun!' she snapped. 'God, I can't believe this is really you proposing this preposterous arrangement! Have you thought of the consequences of your actions?'

'I already know you're on the pill to regulate your periods.' He dismissed the idea of pregnancy.

'Not those consequences!' It was embarrassing how intimately this man knew the workings, and malfunctions, of her body! 'We both have families, Adam, have you thought of their reactions to the relationship you're suggesting?'

'My father and your sister.' The amused glow to his eyes left for the first time that evening. 'I'm thirty-nine and you're twenty-three, do you really think either of us needs their permission?' he ground out.

'Your father hates me.' She deliberately didn't mention her sister's feelings towards Adam, although she was sure they were both aware of those feelings; it had been one of the reasons their marriage had proved such a failure.

'My father doesn't understand you,' Adam corrected gravely.

'There's nothing to understand,' she dismissed scornfully. 'I am what you see. A little more accident-prone around you and your father, but otherwise I'm an open book.'

'Then a few of the pages must have got stuck together, because I never felt that I knew you completely either!' He gave a deep sigh. 'I don't intend to argue about the past with you now, Leonie.'

'Lovers don't argue?' she mocked.

His mouth quirked. 'Only when they know it will take them back to bed to make up.' He took her back in his arms, his mouth claiming hers.

Her lips parted of their own volition, allowing access to the thrust of his tongue, trembling as desire claimed her, clinging to the broad width of his shoulders as she swayed weakly against him.

'Stay tonight, Leonie,' he urged against the creamy warmth of her throat.

She was tempted, God how she was tempted. But she couldn't do it. It had taken her eight months to put herself back together after the devastation of loving this man; she couldn't leave herself open to that sort of pain again.

'No, Adam.' She pushed away from him, breathing hard, knowing by his own ragged breathing that he was as aroused as she was. 'There's something else lovers can do,' she told him tautly. 'They can end the relationship at any time; I'm ending it.' She turned on her heel.

'Where are you going?' Adam asked softly.

'Home!' She didn't even turn.

'How?' his gentle question halted her. 'Your car is still at Thompson Electronics, your keys to the car are in your handbag, your money, too, in case you were thinking of taking a taxi home, and your bag is in *my* car downstairs,' he reminded softly.

She had done it again! 'So much for my grand exit,' she said dully as she turned around.

His smile was sympathetic. 'It really was very good.'

'Don't humour me, Adam,' she snapped.

'Lovers——'

'We are not lovers!' she bit out between clenched teeth. 'And we never will be. Now if you'll give me your car keys for a few minutes I'll go down and get my bag.'

'No.'

'You can't keep me here by force, Adam!' There was an edge of desperation to her voice.

'I don't intend to,' he soothed. 'I'm going to get dressed and drive you home.'

'My car——'

'Will be locked into the car park by this time of night,' he pointed out.

She looked at her wrist-watch; it was after midnight! 'If you will just let me get my bag I can get a taxi home.'

Adam shook his head. 'I can't let you do that this late at night.'

'That doesn't sound possessive, Adam, it sounds autocratic,' she taunted him.

He smiled. 'It's concern for your welfare,' he mocked. 'Lovers are like that,' he told her softly before going back into the bedroom.

Leonie stared after him frustratedly; she should have known that today was going to end as disastrously as it had begun. She should also have known Adam would have something to do with it, had felt a premonition of his presence while waiting to be rescued from the lift, her clumsiness always more pronounced whenever he was around.

She had been too stunned, too conscious of Mrs Carlson's presence, to do any other than follow Adam's lead of it being their first meeting when the other woman introduced them in his office. And once she recovered from the shock of seeing him again after all this time she was too intrigued by his behaviour to do any other than go along with the pretence. And as she had admitted to him, it was easier too. But the pleasant atmosphere of their evening together had seduced her into doing something she would rather forget, something that she wouldn't allow to be repeated, her reaction to Adam totally unexpected, given their history together.

Her breath caught in her throat as Adam returned to the room, the business suit replaced with a fitted black shirt and black cords. Adam *never* dressed this casually!

'Changing your image, Adam?' she taunted to hide her reaction to him.

'Like it?' he smiled, not fooled by her attitude for a minute.

She more than liked it, she wanted him again! It was ridiculous when she had been married to this man for a year, when they had been separated for over eight months, to feel the same instantaneous flood of emotion towards him as she had when she first met him almost two years ago. And yet looking at him now she did feel it, her mouth dry, her palms damp.

'You look very handsome,' she told him primly. 'Now could we please leave?'

'Certainly.' He picked up his car keys.

'Lovers are obliging too, are they?' She couldn't resist taunting as she preceded him out of the apartment and into the lift.

'Any time,' he said suggestively, his body pressed up against the back of hers. 'Just say the word,' he encouraged throatily.

She frowned her irritation, moving gratefully away from him as they walked over to the car, their footsteps sounding loud in the black stillness of the night. Adam proved to be right about her bag, it lay on the floor of the car as he opened the door for her to get in.

'You can pick your car up tomorrow,' Adam suggested during the drive to her home, the car roof up now in the cool of the night.

'Tomorrow?' she frowned.

'When you come for our meeting,' he nodded.

Her eyes widened. 'You don't seriously expect me to still come to that?'

He glanced at her, his brows raised. 'Of course.'

'But I—Wasn't that just a set-up?' she frowned.

'I wanted to see you again,' he acknowledged. 'And it seemed a good way to arrange it in view of the way *you've* felt about seeing me again, but I do also want my office decorated.'

'Not by me,' she shook her head determinedly, quivering at the thought of having to see this man on a day to day basis in connection with her work.

'By you,' he said firmly.

'No!'

'Yes,' he insisted softly. 'I really was impressed by your work on the lower floor.'

'Adam——'

'Yes, Leonie?'

She drew her breath in sharply at his tolerant tone. 'I am not going to work for you,' she told him stubbornly.

'Yes, you are,' he nodded confidently.

'You can't force me!'

'I wouldn't even attempt it,' he assured her mildly. 'But I think you might find it a little awkward explaining to your boss, David isn't it, the reason you won't work for me.'

'You wouldn't make me do that?' she groaned.

Adam shrugged. 'I don't see what else you can do.'

'But David has plenty of other designers, much more capable ones than me!'

'I don't want them,' he stated calmly. 'I want you.'

'Please don't involve my career in this, Adam,' she pleaded desperately.

'All I want is my office decorated, is that too much to ask?'

His innocence infuriated her! 'You aren't just asking *anyone* to do it, I was your *wife!*'

His expression softened into a reminiscent smile. 'I'm not likely to forget that.'

'But I've been trying to!' She was twisted round in her seat as she tried to reason with him. 'I've put my life back together, made the career for myself that I gave up when I married you. I am not about to let you jeopardise that.'

'But I don't want to.' He shrugged broad shoulders.

'You're forcing me into a situation I don't want. You deliberately sought me out for this job, didn't you,' she accused.

He nodded. 'I bought the company because I knew you had worked there once.'

'You—you did *what*?' she gasped.

'Well, I had to have a valid reason for seeing you, I knew you would flatly refuse to go anywhere where you knew I would be.' He shrugged. 'So I bought Thompson Electronics.'

It was an example of the arrogance she had always associated with him in the past; if he wanted something then he went out and bought it. He had once bought her with that same wealth and self-confidence that had blinded her to how wrong they were for each other.

'Then you wasted your money,' she told him tautly. 'Because nothing would induce me to work for you.'

'I didn't waste my money, the company is a very profitable one,' he announced calmly. 'And I don't intend to induce you into doing anything; surely you're adult enough that you could design something for my office suite without letting personalities enter into it?' he raised dark brows.

'It isn't a question of that,' she said stiffly. 'I just don't want to work for you. Wasn't one member of my family enough for you?' she added disgustedly.

'You mean Liz?'

'Who else?' she scorned.

'Liz was the best personal assistant I ever had.' She had been a little too 'personal' as far as

Leonie was concerned! They had met because of her sister's relationship with Adam, and they had parted for the same reason. 'Look, I'll talk to David tomorrow,' she told him tautly. 'I'm sure he'll be only too glad to send someone else over to work with you.'

'I don't want anyone else,' Adam said flatly. 'I wondered about you and him for a while, you know,' he added softly.

She looked over at him with startled eyes. 'David and I?'

'Mm,' he nodded.

Her mouth tightened resentfully. 'And what stopped you wondering?' she snapped.

He shrugged. 'Your dates were too occasional for them to be anything more than placating the boss who has designs on you,' he dismissed.

Leonie's eyes widened. 'You've been having me watched!' she realised disbelievingly.

'You are my wife——'

'Was,' she corrected tightly. 'We're legally separated, and once the appropriate time has elapsed our divorce will be finalised.'

'I was just seeing if we couldn't speed up the proceedings,' he explained.

Leonie blinked at him for several timeless minutes, unable to believe what she was hearing. 'Are you trying to say you were after evidence of adultery against me?' she said with disbelief.

Adam shrugged. 'I thought you might feel more comfortable about our new arrangement if we were already divorced. I knew that I couldn't wait three years for you.'

'I'm sorry I couldn't oblige!' Somehow the knowledge that he had done such a thing hurt her unbearably. God knows she had enough evidence of adultery against *him*! But she had chosen not to subject any of them to the embarrassing ordeal of revealing their personal lives in public. Knowing that Adam had considered doing it to her made her angry.

'Maybe I should have had *you* followed,' she glared at him.

'Oh, I've been living very quietly since you left me,' he dismissed.

'Quietly doesn't necessarily mean alone,' she snapped.

'In this case it does.'

And she knew the reason for that; Liz had continued to stay with her husband Nick. 'Look, we're getting away from the subject,' Leonie sighed. 'You'll have to have someone else do your work for you.'

'No.'

'Adam, I will not be bullied by you into doing something I don't want to do.'

He held up his hand defensively. 'Have I tried to bully you? Did I bully you into anything tonight?' he added throatily.

Her mouth tightened. Tonight had been incredible, there was no denying that, and plenty of women would be only too agreeable to the sort of non-committal relationship Adam was now offering her. But not her. She had made a fool of herself over this man once, she wasn't going to do it again.

'Admit it was everything you thought it could be,' he encouraged softly. 'No complications of marriage, other people, just you and me making beautiful love together.'

Just talking about the experience made her body tingle. 'But it couldn't stay that way indefinitely,' she reasoned impatiently. 'Sooner or later one of us would expect more——'

'Not me,' Adam assured her with finality. 'I've tried being married to you; it didn't work out.'

She swallowed down the pain his casual admission of their year together caused. It *hadn't* worked out, she would be the first to admit that, but to hear Adam talk so casually about the commitment they had made caused a constriction in her chest, as if someone had physically struck her.

'You?'

'Sorry?' she frowned as she realised she had missed what he had said next.

'You wouldn't want more either,' he shook his head. 'After all, you were the one that ended the marriage in the first place.'

'Someone had to make that decision,' she bit out abruptly.

'Oh don't worry, I'm glad that you did.' He shrugged. 'I'm just not husband material.'

She hadn't thought about that at the time, although perhaps she ought to have done, Adam was already thirty-seven, had had several serious relationships, and even more that weren't serious, and before meeting her he had shown no inclination to marry any of those women, had enjoyed his freedom to the full. It was difficult enough for any man of thirty-seven to suddenly accept the changes marriage made to his life, to a man like Adam, who could have his pick of women no matter what his marital status, it was impossible. And she hadn't known about Liz then either.

'You think you would do better as a lover?' she derided.

'Haven't I?' he quirked dark brows.

She put a hand up to her aching temples. 'It's

late,' she sighed. 'And I'm too tired for this conversation right now.'

'There's no rush.' He turned to smile at her after stopping his car outside the old three-storey Victorian building that housed her flat. 'Are you going to invite me in?'

'Harvey wouldn't like it,' she shook her head.

There was a sudden tension about him. 'Harvey?'

He had been amused at her expense all evening, and now she couldn't resist a little amusement herself. 'Dick wouldn't be too pleased either.'

Adam frowned. 'I didn't know you were sharing your flat with two men.'

'Didn't your private investigator tell you that?'

'No,' he ground out. 'He—What are you laughing at?' he questioned suspiciously when she couldn't contain her humour any longer.

'Harvey's my cat,' she explained between giggles.

'And Dick?'

'Moby Dick.'

'You have a *whale* in there?'

Fresh laughter convulsed her. 'A goldfish,' she finally managed to choke out. 'But I thought the name might deter Harvey from eating him; so far it's worked.'

Adam shook his head tolerantly. 'Klutzy, insane, *adorable* woman,' he groaned as he pulled her over to his side of the car before fiercely claiming her mouth. 'Life has been so dull since you left me,' he rested his forehead on hers as he held her easily in his arms.

'Even a steady diet of caviar can get boring after a while; and I'm *nothing* like caviar!'

'You never, ever bored me; I never knew what you were going to do next!' he smiled.

'That isn't practical for a wealthy industrialist's wife. And I wouldn't stay hidden out of sight as a lover either,' she told him before he could point out that he wanted a lover not a wife. 'Not that I'm considering becoming one,' she added hastily as she realised it sounded as if she were.

'You *are* one.' His quick kisses on her mouth stopped her protest. 'Sweet dreams, Leonie,' he finally released her. 'I'll see you tomorrow.'

She didn't argue the point with him; so far it didn't seem to have got her anywhere. He would find out soon enough that if he really did want his office decorated that someone else would be in charge of it.

'Good night, Ad—Ouch!' She groaned as her hair seemed to be caught on the button of his shirt. 'Adam, help me!' she pleaded, tears of pain in her eyes.

'Sit still, woman,' he instructed with patient amusement, his lean fingers working deftly to free her hair. 'There you go,' he released the last strand, his eyes gleaming with laughter. 'I've heard of giving your lover a lock of your hair, but this is ridiculous!'

'You're the one that's ridiculous,' she snapped, getting out of the car, her exit foiled somewhat as she had difficulty unlocking the door. Her cheeks were red with embarrassment as she turned to speak to him through the open window. 'Good night, Adam. Thank you for tonight, it was an interesting experience.'

His smile didn't even waver at the coldness in her voice. 'One of many,' he promised huskily.

Her mouth tightened before she turned on her heel and walked over to the huge front door that was the entrance for all the tenants of the building. She was aware that the BMW hadn't moved away from the side of the pavement, of Adam watching her, congratulating herself on reaching the door without mishap when the keys fell out of her hand straight into the empty milk bottle standing out on the doorstep waiting for collection in the morning.

For a moment she just looked down at her keys inside the bottle in disbelief. Someone ought to lock *her* up for her own safety and throw away the key!

'Are you all right?'

She turned reluctantly to acknowledge Adam's concern at her delay in entering the building. 'Fine,' she answered brightly as he now stood outside the car, leaning on the roof to look over at her.

How could she nonchalantly pick up a milk bottle and start shaking the daylights out of it! But how could she get in to the building if she didn't? God, she felt so *stupid*.

'Leonie, are you sure you're all right?' Adam sounded puzzled as she still hesitated.

'Yes, of course,' she answered waspishly, trying to unobtrusively pick up the bottle, the keys inside rattling loudly in the still of the night as she tried to furtively shake them loose.

'What on earth are you doing?'

She was so startled by his sudden appearance at her side, having been so intent on her keys in the bottle that she had been unaware of his approach, that she dropped the bottle. Adam caught it deftly before it could hit the ground, looking down at the keys inside.

'Isn't this a strange place to hide keys?' he frowned as he tipped the bottle up and was rewarded by them falling smoothly into the palm of his hand.

Leonie snatched them from his hand. 'I wasn't hiding them,' she snapped. 'I dropped them.'

'Ah.'

Her eyes blazed deeply green as she turned on him. 'What do you mean "ah"?' she challenged. '"Ah, I should have guessed"? Or, "ah, that such an unfortunate occurrence should have happened to me"?'

'Ah, that such an unfortunate occurrence should have happened to you, of course,' he said tongue-in-cheek.

Her movements were agitated as she unlocked the door. 'I wonder why I have difficulty believing you,' she muttered.

'Darling, calm down.' He took her in his arms once more. 'I really don't mind these little accidents that happen whenever you're around,' he soothed.

'I don't remember your saying that the time I caught the bodice of my gown on your father's tie-pin and it took you half an hour to separate us!' She strained away from him, but his superior strength wouldn't allow her to move far, his thighs pressed intimately against hers.

'Dad was the one that was so annoyed, not me,' he reminded with amusement. 'Look at it this way, Leonie, at least he was a captive audience for that half an hour; you always did say he didn't listen to you!'

She looked up at him in surprise; she had never heard him talk about his father so disparagingly before. 'He used to look straight through me,' she said slowly.

'Well he didn't that evening!'

'That gown cost a fortune, and it was ruined,' she reminded him.

'It was worth it just to see the expression on

Dad's face. Every time I thought about the incident afterwards I burst out laughing,' he was grinning even now.

'You never told me that,' she accused. 'I thought I had embarrassed you once again.'

He sobered at the admission. 'You've never embarrassed me, Leonie,' he shook his head. 'You never could.'

She was more puzzled than ever now, some of that emotion showing on her face as Adam let her go this time when she moved out of his arms. 'I have to go in; Harvey hasn't had any supper yet,' she told him in a preoccupied voice.

'You'll have to introduce me to him some time,' Adam straightened. 'I've always liked cats.'

'I didn't know that,' she frowned.

'Maybe you don't know as much about me as you thought you did.'

She was beginning to realise that, she thought as she slowly went up the stairs to her second-floor flat. She would never have dreamt Adam could behave as light-heartedly as he had this evening, that he could laugh at himself as well as his father, that he could find her mishaps so amusing. She had been married to him for over a year, and he was still an enigma to her.

Harvey was sitting on the window-ledge outside when she entered her flat, coming in through the small open window as soon as he saw her, miaowing plaintively.

'All right, all right,' she cut off his reprimand mid-stream. 'You aren't the only one that can spend a night out on the tiles, you know,' she told him as she opened a tin of food for his supper, groaning as she realised what she had said. 'Oh, Harvey, what am I going to do?' She bent down to pick up the bundle of ginger and white fur, burying her face in his side. 'Tonight was so perfect,' she told him achingly.

The cat gave a loud screetch of indignation before jumping to the ground.

'All right,' she snapped at his lack of sympathy. 'I can see you're more interested in your stomach than in my problems.' She put his plate down on the floor, the cat immediately pouncing on it. 'I know you catch mice outside so you can stop acting as if you're starving to death,' she told him crossly, suddenly rolling her eyes heavenwards. 'God, I'm having a serious conversation with the cat now!' She sat down dejectedly in one of the armchairs, oblivious to the passing of time as, his appetite appeased, Harvey jumped up into her lap and instantly fell into a purring sleep, Leonie absently tickling behind his ears as he did so.

Her first meeting with Adam had been totally unexpected. She knew of him of course, her sister Liz having been his Personal Assistant for the last year, but he wasn't at all what she had expected of the wealthy industrialist.

Liz and Nick had been away on holiday for two weeks, still had a week to go, and Leonie was house-sitting for them when Adam paid his surprise visit. The sisters had been close in those days, Liz the senior by eight years, having been like a second mother to Leonie since their parents death three years earlier.

Leonie had opened the door in all innocence that evening, had fallen in love the moment she looked up into that harshly beautiful face, the grey eyes warm, strangely luminous with the black circle around the iris. She hadn't heard a word he said as he spoke to her, having to ask him to repeat himself. He had wondered if Liz were at home even though it were her holiday, had needed to talk to her. Leonie had invited him in as she explained that Liz and Nick had gone away on what they called a 'second honeymoon'.

She had been shy with him, had wished she were wearing something a little more glamorous than an old dress that did little to improve her already plump proportions, her long hair in need of brushing. And then she had cursed herself for the fool that she was, from what little Liz had told her about this man's love-life he was hardly likely to be attracted to a cuddly redhead who barely reached his shoulders no matter what she was wearing!

But Adam had seemed reluctant to leave that evening, even though he knew Liz wasn't there, the two of them talking for hours, until Leonie suddenly realised it was after twelve and she had to go to work in the morning. She had been speechless when Adam asked her out to dinner the next evening.

There had been a week of dinners together, of talking into the early hours of the morning, and each time Leonie saw him she fell a little more in love. Although Adam gave away little of his own feelings, treating her more like an amusing child as he guided her through one mishap after another.

The night before Liz and Nick were due to return home was a magical one, Adam taking her to the ballet, something she loved but could only rarely afford to attend, taking her back to the house he shared with his father. It had been after eleven when they arrived, but even so the lights were on all over the house, the butler greeting them at the door, a maid bringing them a tray of coffee and sandwiches. Leonie had been so nervous she promptly knocked over the plate of sandwiches.

But even that had seemed unimportant as Adam dismissed the incident after helping her put them back on the plate, his eyes almost black as he followed her down on to the rug in front of the fire, his mouth fiercely claiming hers. It was the first time he had done more than give her a polite brush of his lips on hers at the end of an evening, and after her initial surprise at how fierce he was with her she opened her arms and her heart to him.

He could have taken her right then and there on the rug and she wouldn't have cared. But he didn't, his breathing ragged as he pulled away from her.

'Marry me, Leonie,' he had groaned. 'Marry me!'

'Yes,' she gasped her acceptance, on fire for him.

'Soon,' he urged.

'As soon as you want me,' she promised eagerly.

When her sister and Nick returned the next day she told them she and Adam were getting married the following Saturday. Liz had been stunned, and Leonie had thought it was because Liz was surprised at her young sister managing to capture such a handsome and sophisticated man. That was what she had *thought* it was, she should have probed deeper!

Adam had taken over her life from the moment he put the engagement ring on her finger that evening, a huge emerald that he said matched the colour of her eyes. She had been happy with his decision that she give up her job, wanting to be with him whenever he could get home from the empire that consumed such a lot of his time, knowing her career would make that difficult.

She had even agreed to live in the apartment Adam had always occupied at the top of his father's elegant London home. She had agreed to anything Adam asked of her.

Within two weeks of meeting him she found herself married to a man she barely knew and who she was soon convinced didn't know her. Her wedding night was a fiasco, with her acting the frightened virgin that she was despite Adam's understanding gentleness with her. The pain had been incredible, too much to bear, until finally they had to stop. Leonie had huddled miserably on her side of the bed while Adam slept. The next night had proved as disastrous, and the night after that, until the fourth night Adam didn't even attempt to touch her. She came home from their honeymoon still a virgin, too embarrassed to discuss her problems with anyone. Adam had had no such qualms, making an appointment for her to see a gynaecologist and ordering her to attend when she protested. The doctor had taken away all the embarrassment of her problem, had explained that it was something that occasionally happened, and within a short time the problem had been alleviated.

But the damage had been done, and she resisted all Adam's efforts to get her to join in his passion, until finally he lost all patience with her one night, pinning her to the bed as he held her arms at her sides, ignoring her cries for him to stop as he brought her to the peak of ecstasy. After that night he always made sure she had pleasure too, but he always had to fight her first, to break down the barriers of resistance that she had built up against him. In the end he became tired of the fight, hardly ever touching her even though they shared a bed every night.

She tried to make up for her inadequacies in bed by being the perfect wife in other ways, but Charles Faulkner made no secret of his contempt for the young girl his son had made his wife, and she didn't even have Liz to turn to for support, feeling too embarrassed to discuss the failure of her marriage even with her sister.

Her tendency to clumsiness became more pronounced as the months dragged on, so much so that she became nervous of leaving the apartment and going downstairs for fear of earning the derision of Adam's father. It was enough of an ordeal that she had to sit down to dinner with the elderly man every night, usually managing to knock something over. She and Adam had intended eating their meals in their own apartment, but after a week of burnt offerings Adam had decided his digestion couldn't take any more and suggested they go downstairs and join his father for their evening meal. She had been hurt, especially as she was usually such a good cook, but for the sake of peace—and Adam's digestion—she had agreed. It was just another brick falling out of the already crumbling foundations of her marriage.

Adam began to stay late at the office, working he said. They also stopped going out, a way of stopping her embarrassing him in front of his friends, she felt sure. But it just left her more and more to her thoughts of what had gone wrong between them. It was easier to try and find something that had gone *right*. The answer was nothing!

But she decided she wouldn't be a nagging wife, would make the most of the life they had together. Much to the disgust of her father-in-law she had offered to organise the decorating and refurbishing of the house; his reply to that was to call in the most well-known interior designing company in London. Next she tried to take an interest in Adam's work; that was met with blank dismissal. After only a year of marriage she was bored, and she was sure—when she wasn't attempting to break one of the family heirlooms or tipping wine over someone—boring! The marriage had been a mistake, and she knew that even if Adam didn't. She had finally had enough after a solid month of not seeing Adam any other time than when he fell into bed beside her, deciding to go to his office and confront him with the fact that she couldn't go on like this any longer.

She had wondered why Adam's secretary tried to stop her going in to his office, especially after telling her he only had Liz in with him. What she had seen and heard had told her exactly why Adam wasn't even trying to make a success of their marriage, and why her sister had been so stunned that he was marrying her at all!

Adam had tried to reason with her when he followed her home, but she had required only one answer to one question; had he been sleeping with Liz just before they met. His answer made her leave him immediately, telling him that he should never have married her, that if he had only wanted a replacement for her sister that an affair would have been a much better idea—and much less complicated to them all. For that was what she was sure she had learnt when she came upon them unwittingly, Liz in Adam's arms, that their decision to end their affair and for Liz to attempt a reconciliation with Nick, had been a failure. And now they were both trapped in marriages they didn't want. But Liz was expecting Nick's child, couldn't leave him now, and Adam was stuck with her young and klutzy sister.

He hadn't been stuck with her for long, although Liz was still married to Nick, their daughter Emma three months old now. And Adam was proposing that they, Leonie and he, had the affair she had once told him they would be better having!

CHAPTER THREE

'BUT, David,' she protested the next morning. 'I told you how badly everything went.'

He shrugged off her argument. 'Faulkner couldn't apologise enough about your ordeal in the lift. I didn't like to tell him you made a habit of it!'

She had arrived at work this morning all set to tell David how disastrously her appointment with the new President of Thompson Electronics had gone, sure that when he heard all the details that he would be only too glad to put someone else on that job, only to find Adam had already been on the telephone to David this morning, taking all the blame on his own shoulders!

Her pleas with David had been to no avail; he was adamant she work for Adam. And she was just as adamant that she wouldn't, had sworn when she left Adam that she wouldn't take anything from him ever again, and that included this boost to her fledgeling career. 'David, I don't want to work with him,' she told him flatly.

His eyes narrowed. 'Why not?'

She had no intention of telling David that Adam was her estranged husband. Much as she liked the other man, she knew how ambitious he was, and having the wife of Adam Faulkner working for him could give his company the boost into élite London society that he had been looking for.

'I—I don't like him,' she frowned as she knew that was no longer true either. When she had left

Adam eight months ago she had never wanted to see him again, had hated him for his behaviour with her married sister. But last night, the pleasure they had finally shared, giving and taking from each other rather than Adam having to force her response, had changed all that. She couldn't hate a man who had given her that sexual freedom.

Some of the remembered sensuality must have shown in her face. 'Did he make a pass at you?' David frowned.

A pass! Adam had never made a *pass* at a woman in his life! He was much too controlled for that. 'No, he didn't do that,' she answered tautly.

David looked relieved to hear it. 'Then where's your problem?'

'I've just told you, I don't want to work for him!'

'But he sounded very charming on the telephone.'

She grimaced, well aware of how charming Adam could be when he wanted something. He had once wanted her so badly in his bed that he had married her; how ironic that the one thing he had wanted from her had been so disastrous. 'Anyone can be charming for the few minutes of a telephone call,' she dismissed.

'Then he wasn't charming to you yesterday when you did eventually meet?' David probed.

'Yes, he was,' she sighed. 'Very charming.' Colour heightened her cheeks as she remembered just *how* charming he had been later that evening.

'Then why don't you want to work for him?' David repeated again in exasperation. 'I can tell you, he was very impressed with you.'

'I made such a fool of myself,' she said desperately. 'I feel embarrassed.'

David shrugged. 'You always make a fool of yourself sooner or later.'

'Thanks!'

He grimaced. 'But you do,' he reasoned. 'I've never known you to get through a day yet without something going wrong; and it's usually your own fault!'

'That's what I like, a little sympathy and understanding,' she glared at him.

He smiled at her anger. 'Trouble just seems to follow you around. Look, I'll tell you what I'll do, I'll call Faulkner's secretary and tell her I'll be joining the two of you for lunch. If I can see any reason, any reason at all, why you shouldn't work for him I'll put someone else on to it. All right?'

It was the best she was going to get, she could see that. And surely she could make Adam drop the tolerant charm for the few minutes it would take David to realise he would be better sending Gary or Sheila on this job, if only for the sake of his company's reputation.

'I'll drive over with you,' she nodded agreement, feeling a little happier.

David frowned. 'What's happened to the VW, has it broken down again?'

'It's still at Thompson Electronics,' she told him awkwardly. 'Mr Faulkner insisted on driving me home after my ordeal in the lift,' she invented.

David smiled. 'He doesn't know you very well if he thinks a little thing like that will shake you up!'

She gave him an exasperated look. 'Actually, I did some work while I was waiting.'

'See,' he laughed.

She went back to her own desk, her nerves becoming more and more frayed as twelve o'clock neared. Then just as she was tidying her desk in preparation for joining David a deliveryman arrived from a nearby florists. The single long-stemmed red rose took her by surprise, the bold black script on the accompanying card telling her that Adam had in no way changed his mind about where their relationship was going. 'For an interesting experience—one of many', the card read. She crumpled the cryptic message in the palm of her hand, would have done the same with the rose if David hadn't arrived at her office at that moment.

'A new admirer?' He raised blond brows as she thrust the rose into a sadly inadequate glass and pushed it to the far corner of her desk.

She shook her head. 'Another apology from Mr Faulkner.' There was no point in lying about the sender; knowing Adam he would ask if it had arrived!

'Nice gesture.' David helped her on with the fitted jacket to her brown suit, the pale green blouse she wore beneath alleviating its sombre colouring.

'A pity he didn't feel generous enough to send the other eleven,' she said with uncharacteristic waspishness.

David's brows rose. 'I'm sure he—Watch out!' he had time to call out as the sleeve of her jacket caught the perfection of the single red bud, overbalancing the too-short glass, smashing the latter on the floor, the rose crushed among the heavy glass.

Leonie looked down at the ruined perfection with tears in her eyes, instantly regretting what she had done. For the first time in her life she had committed a deliberately destructive act, had knocked against the flower on purpose, not wanting that reminder of Adam facing her when she got back.

'Careful!' David warned as she bent to pick up the crushed flower, sighing his impatience with her as a large jagged sliver of glass stuck straight into the palm of her hand.

Leonie gasped, automatically pulling out the piece of glass, the blood that instantly flowed from the wound the same colour as the rose she still held. She knelt and watched as it continued to bleed.

'You're dripping blood all over the carpet,' David snapped impatiently, taking out a handkerchief to wrap it about her hand, pulling her to her feet. 'We had better get you cleaned up before we go anywhere.' He led her into his office, the First Aid box kept there.

He took the rose she still clutched and threw it in the bin, concentrating on washing her hand and applying a bandage as the small but deep wound continued to bleed.

Leonie felt sick, and not because of the pain in her hand but because of her deliberate destruction of such innocent beauty. It wasn't in her to deliberately hurt anything. Even when she had discovered how Liz and Adam had deceived her she hadn't wanted revenge or retribution, had felt sorry for her trapped sister, although Adam seemed to be continuing with his life as if it had never happened.

'Are you all right?' David frowned at how pale she had become. 'Maybe we should cancel this meeting with Faulkner, you look as if you should go home and rest.'

She shook her head determinedly, not intending to delay this confrontation any longer than was necessary; she had already spent one sleepless night, she didn't intend having any more because of Adam Faulkner. 'I'll be fine,' she insisted, flexing her hand under the bandage; it was a bit sore, but workable.

'Sure?' David still looked concerned.

'Yes,' she smiled brightly, standing up. 'Shouldn't we leave now, Mr Faulkner is going to think unpunctuality is normal for us.'

'For you it is,' David mocked as they went down to his car, a white Cortina that he drove with the usual reserve he had to the rest of life.

The cut on her hand was only a throbbing ache by the time they reached Thompson Electronics, the bandage showing no sign of heavy bleeding.

Mrs Carlson greeted them with a smile, instantly informing Adam of their arrival, ushering them straight in to his office.

'Sorry we're late,' David greeted the other man, their handshakes firm. 'I'm afraid a little— accident, delayed us.'

Leonie hung back behind David, feeling uncomfortable about seeing Adam again. The flesh and blood masculinity of him was much worse than she had imagined after the passion they had shared the previous evening, the royal blue three-piece suit and lighter blue shirt he wore making him look devastatingly attractive, his eyes more blue than grey.

His gaze moved surely past David to her flushed face. 'What did Miss Grant do this time?' he drawled.

Leonie's blush deepened as David grinned. 'A collision with a glass, I'm afraid,' he explained.

'The rose you sent me was in it,' she put in

quickly, challenge in her eyes as she realised he wasn't about to reveal their marital status to David either. 'It had to be put in the bin, I'm afraid,' she added with satisfaction.

For timeless seconds Adam held her gaze, transmitting a message that made the colour burn in her cheeks. 'The rose can easily be replaced,' he finally said softly. 'There's only one Leonie Grant.'

'Thank God for that,' David said thankfully, missing the undercurrent of tension between them, taking the conversation at face value.

Leonie was perfectly aware of the double meaning to Adam's words, her mouth firming frustratedly as she longed to knock that smile off his lips.

'We may as well talk over lunch,' Adam decided arrogantly. 'If that's all right with you?' he consulted the younger man as an afterthought.

'Fine,' David agreed eagerly, seeing nothing wrong in this man taking charge of the meeting.

It was embarrassing how easily David had been taken in by Adam's charm, Leonie thought angrily. He was supposed to be romantically interested in her himself, and yet he seemed to find nothing wrong with the way Adam's fingers closed possessively over her arm as they left the office together, seemed not to notice when Adam moved his thumb erotically against her inner arm.

'What have you done to your hand?' Adam frowned as he noticed the bandage for the first time, his fingers entwining with hers as he lifted her hand for closer inspection.

'She cut herself with a piece of the broken glass.' It was left to David to answer for her, her breath catching in her throat at the intimacies

Adam was taking with her hand in full view of the other man.

Adam's gaze bored into hers. 'Have you seen a doctor?'

She swallowed hard, shaking her head to clear the spell he was casting over her. 'Only David,' she dismissed lightly, putting her other hand into the crook of the other man's arm. 'But he knows how to take care of me,' she added pointedly.

Dark brows met over suddenly icy grey eyes. 'Indeed? You have some experience in taking care of Miss Grant, Mr Stevenson?' the question was put innocently enough, but Leonie could feel the tension in the hand that still gripped hers.

'A little.' Once again David was innocent of the innuendo behind Adam's words. 'I took her to the hospital when she got high using glue in her office one afternoon, and another time when she stuck her letter-opener in her leg.'

Adam's eyes twinkled with suppressed humour as Leonie's ploy to imply intimacy between David and herself failed miserably. 'I wondered how you had acquired that scar,' he said throatily.

Leonie blushed as she remembered the way his caressing fingers had explored the half-inch scar above her knee, how they had explored the whole of her body, pulling out of his grasp to move closer to David. 'He's always rescuing this Damsel in Distress,' she gave David a warm smile. 'I don't know what I'd do without him.'

David looked pleased by her encouragement, having received little enough of it the last six months.

'We'll take my car,' Adam decided abruptly, striding over to the BMW. 'You don't mind if Miss Grant sits in the front next to me, do you,

Stevenson, she gets car sick in the back,' he said smoothly.

David looked surprised. 'I didn't know that.'

Neither did she! But short of calling Adam a liar, and possibly alienating him as a client for David she couldn't very well say so, getting ungraciously into the car next to Adam while David sat in the back. She almost gasped out loud when Adam took advantage of their relative privacy in the front of the car to guide her hand on to his thigh, keeping it there with his own hand when she would instantly have pulled away.

His leg felt firm and warm through the material of his trousers, and she could feel the heat rising in her cheeks as both of them acted as if the intimacy weren't taking place, Adam coolly conversing with the unsuspecting David.

By the time they arrived at the restaurant Leonie's nerves were in shreds, her senses in turmoil as she fought against the desire Adam had deliberately instigated. His gaze was silently mocking as he helped her out of the car, although she flushed as she saw his body wasn't quite as controlled, looking away quickly from the evidence of his arousal, her cheeks burning as they entered the restaurant.

She could see David was impressed by the other man, and the restaurant he had chosen, as they studied the menus. She was going to have to do something, and fast, if she wanted David to take her off this job.

'So,' Adam sat back after they had ordered their meal. 'Is there some problem with Miss Grant coming to work for me?'

David looked disconcerted by the other man's bluntness. 'Problem?' he delayed.

Adam shrugged. 'Does the owner of Stevenson

Interiors usually go to a routine business meeting with his employees?'

'Er—Well—No,' David answered awkwardly. 'But Leonie is rather new at her job. Not that she isn't good at it,' he put in hastily. 'She is. But she—we, wondered if you wouldn't rather have someone more experienced.'

'Just how much experience does Miss Grant have?' Adam asked softly, his hand somehow locating her knee beneath the table, his fingers caressing.

Leonie's mouth tightened at the—to her—unsubtle double-meaning behind the question. 'Not enough for you, I'm sure,' she bit out, drawing in a pained breath as his fingers tightened in rebuke.

'I'm sure you'll satisfy me,' he told her blandly.

'And I'm equally sure I won't,' she grated.

'I'm not a demanding man, Miss Grant,' he drawled. 'I simply know what I like.'

So did she after last night, having explored the hard planes of his body then more thoroughly than ever before, Adam encouraging her to do so, to both their delight.

'I like what you've done for me already,' he continued softly. 'I'd like it to continue.'

Her mouth thinned. 'I don't think I can—work, for you, Mr Faulkner.'

'Leonie!' David gasped. 'What Leonie means is that she does have a couple of other little jobs that need her attention,' he quickly invented. 'And anyway, this conversation might be academic.'

Adam looked at him. 'And why should it be that?'

David gave a nervous laugh at the other man's

quiet intensity. 'Well *I* know we're the best, but I'm sure you'll have other quotes in for the work, and——'

'No other quotes,' Adam told him arrogantly. 'I want Miss Grant to do this for me.'

David flushed with pleasure, and Leonie could understand why. Interior designing was a competitive business, and they lost as many prospective jobs as they won, other companies often undercutting them. If only Adam only had work on his mind!

'In that case,' he beamed, 'I can get someone else to clear up Leonie's odd loose ends.'

'I would appreciate it,' Adam drawled. 'I need Miss Grant right away.'

And he wasn't lying either! His hand had captured hers as she tried to pry his fingers from her knees, guiding it to the throbbing hardness of his thighs. She flinched away from him as if he had burnt her, glaring at him furiously for this subterfuge.

'And, of course, if her work proves as satisfactory this time as last I would consider using her when I have my apartment refurbished,' he added challengingly.

'It's a brand new apartment!' She almost groaned out loud as she realised she had revealed to a shocked David that she had been to the other man's home. 'Mr Faulkner insisted on taking me home to give me a drink to steady my nerves last night before driving me to my flat,' she quickly explained.

'Leonie has a habit of walking into one catastrophe after another,' David smiled.

'I've noticed,' Adam said dryly. 'I feel that my apartment lacks the homely touch at the moment, I'm sure Miss Grant could help me create that.'

She was so angry with him at this moment that if he didn't stop baiting her in this way she was going to pick up his soup and tip it over his head! But maybe if she could show David how Adam kept flirting with her he would realise she couldn't possibly work for the other man; the cold treatment certainly hadn't worked!

'I'm sure there must be a woman in your life who could do a much better job of that than I,' she suggested throatily.

His eyes widened questioningly, and then he smiled knowingly. 'I always think this sort of thing is better accomplished by someone who knows what they're doing.'

She blushed as he turned the innuendo back on her. 'I'm sure you're just being modest, Mr Faulkner,' her voice was husky.

'On the contrary, since my wife left my life has been lacking in a woman's—touch.'

She glared at him in silent rage. And if he really expected her to believe there had been no woman for him since their separation he was insane! Liz might be out of his reach at the moment, but there were plenty of other women who weren't, and God knows he had found little enough satisfaction during their brief marriage.

'How about you, Stevenson,' Adam turned to the other man. 'Does your life have that special woman's touch?'

'I'm not married,' David answered in all innocence, receiving a frustrated glare from Leonie at his candid reply.

'Neither am I—now,' the other man told him in amusement. 'But one doesn't have to be married to have a special woman in one's life.'

David glanced awkwardly at Leonie. 'I suppose not,' he muttered.

'Just as one can have a special woman in one's life even if one *is* married,' Leonie put in with sweet sarcasm, looking challengingly at Adam as his expression remained bland.

'Leonie!' David was shocked at the turn the conversation had taken.

She gave him a scornful look. 'We're all adults here, David,' she bit out. 'And the sanctity of marriage does seem to have lost its meaning to some people. Don't you agree, Adam?' she added hardly.

He shrugged, completely relaxed. 'Divorce has been made too easy,' came his reply.

'Easy?' she repeated disbelievingly. 'You'll excuse me if I disagree!' She glared at him, remembering that she had only been able to be legally separated from him without actually revealing the reason she could no longer live with him, had to wait two years to be free of him.

He gave an acknowledging inclination of his head. 'It seems to me that at the first sign of trouble in a marriage now one of the partners runs to the nearest lawyer rather than trying to work the problem out with the logical person, their spouse.'

If Leonie could have spoken immediately after that arrogant statement she would have told him exactly what he could do with his theory. As it was, by the time she had overcome her rage enough to be able to talk she had also controlled the impulse, conscious of David even if Adam wasn't. 'You believe that's what your wife did, hm?' she prompted hardly.

'Oh no,' he denied easily. 'My wife was perfectly right to leave me, I was lousy husband material.'

Having expected a completely different answer

Leonie was once again left speechless. Adam certainly knew how to disconcert her. And he knew it, damn him.

David coughed uncomfortably, obviously finding the conversation embarrassing.

'You'll have to excuse us,' Adam turned to him with a smile. 'Both being statistics in marriage failure I'm afraid Leonie and I got carried away comparing notes. We'll have this conversation some other time, Leonie,' there was a promise in his voice. 'I'm sure you must have been a much better wife than I ever was a husband.'

Had she been? She doubted it. She had been too young and unsophisticated to cope with the trauma of her honeymoon, had made no effort to bridge the gulf that had arisen between them because of it, had found the physical act between them embarrassing. Then why had last night been so different? Could Adam be right, the lack of a commitment between them made it all so much more uncomplicated, easier to relax and enjoy what they did have?

She looked up to find silver-grey eyes on her, realising he was still waiting for an answer. 'No,' she sighed. 'I don't think I could have been.'

His gaze held hers for long timeless moments before he turned to signal for the bill, breaking the mood, his hand finally leaving her knee as they all stood up to leave.

'So when do you think Miss Grant will be able to start work for me?' he asked David on the drive back to his office, the other man once again in the back of the car, although this time both Adam's hands remained on the steering-wheel; and why shouldn't they, he had no further reason to torment her, he had won. She was going to work for him.

'Monday,' David answered firmly, ignoring Leonie's dismayed expression. 'Is that suitable for you?'

'Very,' Adam nodded, his mouth quirking triumphantly at Leonie.

She glared back at him. 'You will, of course, have to move out of your office once the work begins,' she told him tightly.

'I understand that. But you will be supervising the operation personally, won't you?'

'It's the usual practice,' she conceded grudgingly, knowing that she had to give in, that she had to subject herself to several weeks of working for Adam. But working for him was all she intended doing. If he expected anything else from the arrangement he was going to be disappointed!

'You nearly lost us that contract!'

She had been expecting the rebuke from David ever since they had parted from Adam half an hour ago, but he had remained silent as they went down to the car park to their respective vehicles, had waited until they reached the privacy of his office before turning on her angrily.

'All that talk about not being good enough to do the work,' David continued furiously. 'The man will think I employ amateurs!'

'David——'

'And I could have sunk through the floor when you started talking about the sanctity of marriage. The man's private life is none of our business, Leonie,' he told her disgustedly.

'I——'

'And just how long did you stay at his apartment last night?' he added with a frown.

All colour left her face. 'I—What do you mean?' she forced casualness into her voice.

'The two of you seem pretty familiar with each other's private lives. I've been seeing you for the last six months and yet in one evening that man seems to know more about you than I do!' he accused.

He had given her the perfect opening for her to tell him that Adam was her estranged husband, and yet she couldn't take it. It was much too late for that. The time to tell him had been this morning, before she and Adam acted like strangers for a second time, before David would be made to feel too foolish by the knowledge. He would never forgive her if he was told the truth now.

'I knew you were separated from your husband,' David continued forcefully. 'But I had no idea you were actually divorcing him.'

She shrugged. 'It's the usual conclusion to that sort of mistake.'

'But don't you see, I didn't know,' he said heatedly. 'And yet you told Faulkner after knowing him only a few hours!'

'I—er—Maybe the fact that he's separated too gave us a mutual interest in the subject,' she invented.

'How mutual?' David asked suspiciously.

She sighed. 'Did I seem as if I wanted to see him again, even professionally?'

'No,' he acknowledged slowly. 'But that wasn't just because you're embarrassed about yesterday.'

She stood up, moving restlessly about the room, wondering what explanation she could give David that would sound plausible. 'I think we have a clash of temperaments,' she spoke softly.

'In what way?'

'In every way I can think of,' she snapped. 'I despise everything about the man!'

'Leonie!'

She sighed at her unwarranted vehemence. 'He's a rich playboy who buys and sells everything that he wants and then doesn't want, including women,' she said more calmly. 'I despise that type of man.'

'Are you sure he didn't make a pass at you?' David frowned, still not understanding.

'Yes,' she bit out.

'Disappointed that he didn't?' David sounded puzzled.

Her mouth twisted. 'I don't think that question even deserves an answer,' she dismissed disgustedly. 'Look, I know the type of man he is, David, because—because I was married to one,' she admitted gruffly.

His expression softened at the admission. 'I'm sorry, Leonie,' he said gently. 'I had no idea. If you really think you can't work with the man . . .'

'And how would you explain the change to him after assuring him I was definitely available?' she mocked.

'I could always tell him you broke your neck!'

'Now *that* I'm sure he would believe!' she returned David's smile. 'But I won't have you jeopardise the contract in that way. I'm just being silly, of course I can handle Adam Faulkner!'

There was another cellophane-wrapped box from the same florist laying on her desk when she returned to her office, and she opened it with shaking fingers, this single red rose made out of the finest silk, so delicate it looked as if it had just been cut from the garden. The card read '*This* rose won't be crushed—and neither will I.' Again it was unsigned, but Leonie knew the sender, only too well.

'An admirer?' Gary grinned at her from the doorway.

She sighed. 'You could say that.'

Gary sauntered into the room, a few inches taller than her, with sandy hair and light blue eyes. The two of them had been friends since she first came to work for Stevenson Interiors. He touched the rose. 'He has good taste,' he murmured, looking at her and not the flower.

Ordinarily she wouldn't have minded his teasing, was always refusing the invitations he made her, both of them knowing that he had been happily married for the last five years. But today she wasn't in the mood for his lighthearted flirting. 'It's been a long day,' she said abruptly, turning back to her work.

With a shrug Gary left her to it. Leonie sighed, angry with Adam for upsetting her so much that she had been rude to a man who, although a flirt, had always been kind to her. She stood up to go and apologise to him.

CHAPTER FOUR

'FOILED you, didn't we?' she looked triumphantly at Harvey as he sniffed the silk rose in puzzlement, sitting on the dining-table to eye what looked like a delicious-tasting flower but wasn't. 'You won't be able to chew this one beyond recognition,' she crowed, as with a disgusted tilt of his nose Harvey jumped down on to the floor.

She had brought the rose home with her, too impressed by its beauty to throw it away as she had the last one. And much to her delight she had found that Harvey, who usually demolished any flowers she brought into the house, had no interest in the delicate bloom.

'Out you go,' she opened the window for him. 'No, I'm not going out on the tiles again tonight myself,' she told him as he hung back reluctantly, obviously not intending going anywhere if he was going to be left on his own for hours again. 'Once was enough,' she muttered as she left the window open for him.

She stared broodingly at the rose as she tried to reconcile herself to working for Adam as from Monday. The second—indestructible—rose, had been a warning that he was still intent on having an affair with her. Why couldn't he—She looked up sharply as the doorbell rang, instantly knowing who it was. David was her only, rare, visitor here, and he had gone away for the weekend.

'Adam,' she greeted resignedly as she was proved correct.

'Leonie,' he returned lightly. 'Am I interrupting anything?' he arched dark brows.

'Yes.'

'Oh good,' he walked past her into the room beyond, his denims fitted tautly to his thighs and legs, his black sweat-shirt doing nothing to hide the bulge of muscle in his arms and chest. He looked about the empty flat, his gaze returning to hers. 'I thought you said I was interrupting something?'

'You are,' she closed the door forcefully before joining him. 'My privacy!'

He grinned, thrusting his hands into the back pockets of his denims. 'Nothing is private between us,' he dismissed, looking about him appreciatively.

Leonie tried to see the flat through his eyes, knowing the soft peach and cream decor, and the low-backed furniture and fluffy carpets, wouldn't be to everyone's liking. But it was to hers, was all her own work, and she didn't welcome any comments Adam might care to make.

His gaze returned to hers. 'I think Dad should have let you decorate and refurnish the house, after all,' he drawled. 'Maybe then it wouldn't look and feel like a mausoleum!'

'You agreed with the suggestion when he said he wanted to bring in professionals!' she was stung into accusing.

He shrugged broad shoulders. 'It was his house. But I didn't come here to discuss the past,' he frowned.

'Then why are you here?' she demanded resentfully.

'To take you out.'

She flushed. 'It's usual to ask first,' she snapped.

He shook his head, smiling. 'I knew what your answer would be if I did that.'

'I'm sure you did,' she bit out.

'You'll enjoy yourself,' he promised encouragingly.

She blushed. 'I'm sure I won't!'

Adam chuckled softly. 'Are they very naughty thoughts, Leonie?' he mocked.

'Let's leave my thoughts, naughty or otherwise, out of this,' she said sharply. 'I have no desire to go anywhere with you.'

'Oh yes you do,' he contradicted huskily. 'And maybe later on I just might take you there. But right now I have it in mind to take you skating.'

'Skating!'

'Mm,' he nodded.

She frowned. 'What sort of skating?'

'Well, hopefully, the sort where we manage to stay upright,' he grinned. 'Although I have no objection if you get the urge to fall on me!'

'Adam, have you been drinking?' she looked at him suspiciously.

He shook his head. 'I'm simply acting like a——'

'Lover,' she completed resignedly.

'Exactly. Lovers take their lovers out on mad escapades like this all the time.'

'Who told you that?' she derided.

'I read it somewhere,' he said with suppressed humour.

'You still haven't told me what sort of skating it will be,' Leonie frowned.

'Roller-skating.'

'But I can't roller-skate!'

'Can you ice-skate?'

'No.' Her sense of humour couldn't be repressed any further, not resisting as Adam

pushed her in the direction of the hall to get her
jacket. 'Can you?'

'Roller or ice?' he quirked dark brows.

'Either!'

'No,' he informed her happily. 'But just think
of the fun we'll have trying!'

And they did have fun, Leonie couldn't ever
remember laughing so much in one evening in
her life before, let alone with the man who had
always seemed so rigidly correct to her. Her
tendency to be clumsy wasn't so noticeable with
everyone else falling over too, in fact she had
almost mastered the sport by the end of the
evening while Adam still landed in an undignified
heap on his bottom most of the time, and that for
a man who had always seemed *so* dignified!

This new irrepressible Adam was impossible to
resist, laughing at himself and her in a way she
would never have thought he could. If this
evening was an example of his indulgence as a
lover she didn't know how she was going to
continue to say no.

'I'm coming in,' he told her when they reached
her flat, his expression suddenly serious.

'Adam——'

'I want to look at your hand.'

The statement startled her; it wasn't what she
had been expecting at all. 'My hand?' she
repeated incredulously.

'Well I'd like to take a look at all of you,' he
told her huskily. 'But I think we'll start with the
hand. Did you think I wouldn't notice the
discomfort it's given you tonight?' he chided as
they entered her home.

She had hoped that he hadn't, but she should
have known better; Adam noticed everything!
Her hand had been aching most of the afternoon

but she had put that down to the healing process. The increased pain she had been suffering the last couple of hours seemed to indicate it was more than that, her falls at the rink only aggravating it.

She took off her jacket, holding out her hand for Adam's inspection.

'You may as well sit down,' he shrugged out of his own casual jacket. 'I'm not going for a while yet.' He came down on his haunches in front of her, compellingly attractive.

He was very gentle with her as he peeled off the bandage, removing the gauze dressing to reveal a very red and angry-looking cut. Leonie grimaced as he unbuttoned the cuff of her blouse to show that the redness extended in a line up her arm.

'It's infected,' he mumbled, looking up at her. 'You'll have to go to hospital for treatment, I'm afraid.'

'Couldn't it wait until morning?'

'It could,' he acknowledged softly. 'But why suffer all night when you could get some relief now from the pain I'm sure you must be feeling?'

His logic always made sense, and he was right, the pain was bad; she doubted she would be able to sleep tonight without something to dull the pain.

'I'll just put a fresh bandage on it and then we'll go,' Adam stood up decisively as he sensed her consent. 'Do you have a medicine cabinet?'

'In the bathroom,' she pointed to the appropriate door. 'With my penchant for accidents I'd be insane to be without one,' she added self-derisively.

Adam grinned. 'I know you can't be feeling too bad when you still have your sense of humour. It was one of the things I always liked about you.'

One of the only things, Leonie thought ruefully as he went into the bathroom. The statement had reminded her of exactly who they were, of the fact that they were in the process of divorcing each other; she had been in danger of forgetting that fact with Adam being so boyishly charming.

He was still in the bathroom when the telephone began ringing. God, she had forgotten it was Friday night, hadn't realised it was already eleven-thirty!

'Yes?' she grabbed up the receiver, not in the least surprised when she recognised the caller's voice, giving a mental groan as Adam came out of the bathroom, frowning when he saw she was on the telephone. 'Oh yes?' Leonie answered her caller faintly. 'How interesting. Look, I'm sorry,' she cut in hastily as Adam approached. 'But I can't talk just now.' She slammed the receiver down, smiling brightly at Adam.

He frowned down at her. 'Who on earth telephones at this time of night?' he asked slowly.

She shrugged. 'I remember you did a couple of times during the two weeks before we were married.'

'That was different,' he dismissed.

'Why was it?'

'Because if I couldn't be in bed with you then I wanted to at least talk to you while you were in bed,' he told her absently, his thoughts obviously still on the call she had just taken.

'Maybe my caller felt the same way,' her voice was shrill at the irony of that statement.

'Is he the one that owns the man's razor in the bathroom?'

Her mouth tightened. '*I'm* the one who owns the man's razor in the bathroom,' she bit out resentfully. 'For some reason they happen to be cheaper and easier to find than the so-called women's razors are. And please don't ask why I need a razor,' she glared at him.

His mouth quirked. 'I won't.'

'Then let me say I don't appreciate your prying into my bathroom cabinet. The medicine chest is next to it,' she snapped.

'And the scissors were conspicuous in their absence,' he pointed out softly.

She remembered now, she had used them to cut a broken fingernail, and must have put them back in the wrong cabinet. 'Well I don't see that it's any business of yours even if the razor *had* belonged to a man,' she told him huffily.

Adam shrugged. 'I'm a very possessive lover.'

'You aren't——'

'Just as I expect you to be,' he continued softly, his gaze compelling.

'Being possessive didn't do me much good while I was your wife,' she reminded waspishly.

He shrugged. 'I've already admitted what a lousy husband I was.'

'And assured me you're a fantastic lover!' she derided harshly.

'And very possessive,' he nodded, his eyes narrowed. 'Which means I want to know who would call you this time of night?'

She had hoped to divert him off the subject, she should have realised he wasn't a man to be diverted. 'A friend,' she dismissed. 'I—They work nights,' she added desperately.

Adam frowned. 'Is that supposed to explain why they would call at eleven-thirty at night?'

'It goes on the company's telephone bill?' she suggested with a grimace for her inadequacy at lying.

'Not good enough, Leonie,' he shook his head. 'I want to know——' he broke off as the telephone began to ring again, picking up the receiver before Leonie had a chance to do so.

Leonie paled, knowing that the person on the other end of the line wouldn't realise from Adam's silence that it wasn't her he was talking to. She could guess what Adam's reaction was going to be.

'That's very interesting,' he suddenly ground out fiercely. 'Now let me tell you what I'd like to do to you——' his teeth snapped together as the caller obviously rang off, slamming his own receiver down with suppressed violence. 'How long has this been going on?' he demanded to know.

She pulled a face, knowing she couldn't evade answering him. 'Ever since I moved in here.'

'And how long is that?'

She shrugged. 'Six months or so.'

Adam's mouth compressed into a thin line. 'And is he always so—so——'

'Obscene?' she finished with a grimace. 'I think that's how those sort of calls got their name!'

She knew exactly what Adam would have heard when he picked up the telephone, had heard the same revolting filth only minutes earlier. The first time she had received such a call she had felt so sick she was almost physically ill, had felt so threatened she had moved into a hotel for the night. The second time she had been angry, so angry she called the police. They sent someone round to talk to her, but in the end all they could advise was that she change her telephone number. But the calls had still continued. She still felt sick at the disgusting things he said to her each week, but she no longer felt threatened, was sure after all this time that whoever he was he preferred to violate her over the telephone, that he wouldn't actually come to her home and carry out the things he threatened.

'Have you done anything about it?' Adam grated, the nerve pulsing in his jaw telling of his anger.

Leonie sighed. 'I've changed my telephone number twice, but it's made no difference.'

Adam frowned. 'He got your new number both times?'

She nodded. 'Even though they're unlisted.'

'How often does he call?' Adam's eyes were narrowed.

'Every Friday night at eleven-thirty,' she sighed. 'There's nothing we can do, Adam, and as long as he stays on the other end of that telephone I can cope with it. Actually, he's getting a little boring now,' she grimaced. 'His fantasy seems to be stuck in a groove.'

'I heard,' Adam rasped.

'Interesting idea, isn't it,' she dismissed with bravado. 'I've told him I think we could do ourselves a mischief, but he——'

'Leonie!' Adam cautioned tightly. 'Can't you take anything seriously?'

'I thought you always liked my sense of humour!'

'Not about something like this,' he said grimly, his hands thrust into his denims pockets. 'The man's a damned fruit-cake, how can you make jokes about it!'

'How?' her voice cracked emotionally. 'I'll tell you how! Because every Friday night I live in dread of those calls, and every Friday night at eleven-thirty he calls without fail. In a way it's a relief when he does call, at least then I can relax for another week. You see, I have a theory,' her voice was shrill. 'That while he continues to call he won't actually come here.'

'You think he knows where you live?' Adam frowned.

'I would say it's a logical assumption,' she nodded. 'If he can get my telephone number three times he can certainly get my address!'

'Then you can't stay here,' Adam decided arrogantly.

'Oh but I can,' she told him. 'I thought about moving, but don't you see,' she reasoned at his furious expression, 'I'm as safe here as I can be anywhere. This man obviously has the means at his fingertips to find out anything he wants to know about me. If I move he'll know that too, so why go through the bother of it?' She shrugged.

'Then you can't stay here alone,' Adam told her grimly.

'Are you offering your services as bodyguard, Adam?' she mocked.

'And if I were?'

She shook her head. 'I don't need, or want, a live-in lover.'

'Have you been to the police about this?'

'There's nothing they can do. The man doesn't threaten me, he just talks dirty!'

'He *talks* about violating you!'

'And do you realise how many obscene telephone calls are received and reported each year? I can tell you that it's thousands,' she said wearily. 'The police don't have enough people to follow up on all of them. They asked me all the usual questions, did I know of anyone who would want to do this to me, did I recognise his voice? I don't, and I didn't! It's all I can do to stop myself being sick when he calls. Now can we drop the subject, hm?' she said brittlely.

His mouth tightened. 'I think you should move from here,' he stated stubbornly, his jaw rigid.

'There's just no point to that,' she sighed. 'And except for his telephone calls, which will probably continue wherever I live, I like it here. No, Adam, I'm not moving,' she told him firmly. 'And one of these days he's going to get tired of calling me.'

'And what do you think will happen then?'

'Hopefully he'll leave me alone,' she shrugged.

'Hopefully!' Adam repeated raggedly. 'What if he decides to come here and act out his fantasy?'

She shivered as he put into words what she had tried not even to think about. 'The percentage of those that actually carry out the things they talk about is very low,' she dismissed.

'You could be one of the victims of that percentage! God, Leonie,' he groaned, taking her into his arms as she began to tremble. 'I don't mean to frighten you, but I can't bear the thought of some maniac wanting to hurt you.'

Her face was buried against his chest, and for a few minutes she allowed herself the luxury of leaning against his strength, of feeling protected. Then she moved back to smile at him brightly. 'Maybe the fact that you answered the telephone tonight will frighten him off,' she suggested derisively. 'I'm sure he didn't get the same satisfaction whispering those things in your ear!'

'No,' Adam agreed grimly, shaking off his worry with effort. 'Let's hope you're right. Now we had better get you to the hospital—What the hell was that?' he jumped nervously as there was a noise at the window.

Leonie laughed softly. 'It's only Harvey

wanting to come in.' She moved to open the window for the ginger and white tabby-cat to come inside.

Adam looked at him with relief. 'After that call my imagination is running riot!' he admitted ruefully, bending down on his haunches to stroke the cat's sleek fur as Harvey strolled over to inspect him.

'Stroking a cat is supposed to be good for the heart and blood pressure,' Leonie mocked him.

Adam glanced up at her. 'I can think of another redhead I would rather stroke!'

Leonie gave a rueful laugh. 'I think I walked right into that one!'

'You did,' he straightened. 'Any offers?'

She shook her head. 'I think one lecher per household is enough—and judging by the amount of females that wait outside for Harvey every night he's it!'

Adam laughed softly, his tension momentarily forgotten. 'Bit of a ladies' man, is he?'

'You could say that,' she grimaced. 'I certainly get the impression the cat population in the area could be on the increase in the next few months!'

'Is he going to need anything before we leave?'

She shook her head. 'He's already been fed, he's just home to rest after his exhausting evening out.' She moved across the room to check the wire mesh on top of the goldfish bowl that stood on the sideboard.

'So this is Moby,' Adam stood at her side watching the fish as it swam into the weeds at the bottom of the bowl.

'I think he snubs his nose at Harvey sometimes,' she smiled. 'A sort of "Hah, hah, you can't get me!" look.'

Adam chuckled, helping her on with her jacket,

careful of her aching hand and arm. 'This household is like you; crazy!'

'I like it,' she shrugged.

'So do I,' he said throatily. 'Leonie——' He stepped back as she winced. 'Is your hand getting worse?'

'It's—painful,' she conceded. But not half as painful as the casual way he kept taking her into his arms! He had been doing it all evening, first at the skating-rink, when he took every opportunity he could to touch her, and now, when the situation was much more precarious, her bedroom all too close.

Somewhere during the evening she had lost sight of the fact that they were adversaries, not lovers. After his disgusting behaviour at lunch today she shouldn't even have been talking to him, let alone have agreed to go out with him. Admittedly, with Adam in this irrepressible mood it was a little difficult to remain angry with him, but she shouldn't have actually enjoyed herself! The same problem still applied to any relationship between Adam and herself; Adam's feeling for her unattainable sister still standing between them.

'Shall we go?' she said sharply. 'It's very late, and I have to go out in the morning.'

'Where?'

She looked at him coolly as they went downstairs together. 'I always visit Liz and Nick on Saturday mornings,' she informed him distantly. 'Nick would think it a little strange if I didn't make the effort to visit my niece.'

'And Liz?'

'I'm sure you're well aware of the reason that I find it difficult to be with my sister,' she bit out, coming to a halt as they got outside. 'Thanks for a nice evening, Adam,' she dismissed. 'Even if I didn't quite manage to skate properly.'

'I'm coming to the hospital with you.'

'I'm not a child,' she snapped at his arrogance. 'I'm quite capable of taking myself to the hospital.'

'And driving yourself there?' he reasoned softly. 'With only one hand?'

She blushed at the truth of that. Unlike his own car hers wasn't automatic; she definitely needed two capable hands for driving, and she certainly couldn't use her injured one. 'I can get a taxi,' she insisted.

'As I told you yesterday, not at this time of night you won't. Especially now that I know there's some sex-pervert with his eye on you,' he added grimly.

God, had it only been yesterday that she and this man had shared so much passion! It seemed as if he had never been out of her life, as if they hadn't been separated for eight months, although she knew this was a different Adam from the one she just couldn't live with any more. This Adam had the power of seduction, a power he wasn't averse to using whenever she proved difficult; which was most of the time!

He took complete charge when they reached the hospital, declared himself her husband as he stood at her side and watched as they cleaned her wound, gave her tablets to fight the infection, and others to kill the pain.

Like this he was more like the Adam she had first fallen in love with, and as they left the hospital together she decided to make it plain to him exactly where they stood in this relationship he had decided he wanted with her. 'I accepted your offer to drive me to the hospital, but that's all I accepted,' she told him abruptly.

'Why, what do you mean?' he asked with feigned innocence as he opened the car door for her, quickly joining her as he got in behind the wheel.

'I mean you are not spending the night with me,' she looked at him with steady green eyes.

'Did I ask if I could?'

'Adam,' she sighed. 'I may not live with you any more but I do know that you aren't a man that asks; you take.'

His expression sobered. 'I took because you wouldn't give freely,' he rasped.

'And I wouldn't give freely because the more I gave the more you took!'

'I wanted to make love to my wife, I don't consider that a bad thing. Most wives complain their husband doesn't pay enough attention to them in bed!'

'The sexual act didn't hold the same pleasure for me as it did for you,' she snapped.

'But that's no longer the case, is it,' he reasoned calmly. 'Last night you demanded as well as gave.'

She blushed at the mention of her wanton responses the night before. 'Last night I wanted you too,' she admitted. 'Wanted to know if I could respond to you.'

'And you did.'

'Yes.'

'Then there's no problem, is there,' Adam dismissed.

'Yes, there's a problem,' she told him angrily. 'The problem is *you*, Adam. I can't deny that last night was a success, but I don't want to repeat it. I don't want to work for you, I don't want to be with you.'

'Too bad, the contract is already signed. And

as for being with me, you enjoyed yourself tonight, didn't you?'

She had, she couldn't deny the fun they had had together. 'But it wasn't you, Adam,' she protested impatiently. 'You're the man who owns an empire——'

'Several companies,' he corrected softly.

'It doesn't matter how many,' she sighed. 'You're rich, successful, sophisticated. You aren't really the man that took me roller-skating tonight.'

'Then who was he?' Adam asked her quietly, not expecting an answer.

And Leonie couldn't give him one. The man she had been with tonight, been to bed with last night, was a man she could like all too much. And she didn't want to like him, knew that if she ever came to truly like Adam rather than just have fallen in love with him that she would be lost.

'I'll see you at nine-thirty on Monday morning,' he told her as they parted at her door. 'You're sure you're going to be all right on your own?'

'My hand is fine now——'

'I wasn't thinking of your hand,' he said grimly.

'The telephone calls?' she realised, shaking her head. 'He only ever calls that once, at eleven-thirty on a Friday night.'

And it wasn't until she lay in bed that night, Harvey curled up against her side, that she realised that for the first time since the calls began she hadn't even thought about or dreaded tonight's call, that she had been so fascinated by Adam that she had forgotten all about it!

CHAPTER FIVE

LIZ was as beautiful as ever. No, more beautiful. Since Emma had been born three months ago Liz had possessed an inner glow of beauty that far outshone her obvious physical beauty. Her blonde hair was styled attractively close to her head, kept shorter now for convenience sake, having little time to fuss over her appearance now that she had a baby to care for. Her widely spaced hazel eyes were often more green than brown, glowing with the happiness she felt in her new role, her mouth curved into a perpetual smile, her figure having returned to its previous sylph-like elegance, although she wore little that emphasised that fact, her clothes loose and comfortable rather than fashionably styled as they used to be.

Yes, to an outsider Liz looked the perfect wife and mother, ecstatically happy in both those roles. And if Leonie hadn't seen her four-month pregnant sister in Adam's arms she may even have been fooled into believing that image herself.

But she had seen Liz in Adam's arms, had heard her sobbing about when they had been together. Adam had looked up and seen Leonie's stricken face as she watched them from the doorway, but he hadn't come after her straight away, had continued to hold Liz as she cried. In that moment Leonie had realised what a fool she had been, what fools they had all been to think that any marriage other than with the person you loved could possibly work out.

When Adam returned to the house over an hour later her suitcases were already packed, and she was waiting for the taxi to arrive that would take her to a hotel until she could decide what to do with her life now that her marriage was over, the Porsche Adam had given her when they returned from their honeymoon parked outside the house, the keys left on the dressing-table for Adam to pick up, all of the clothes he had given her still hanging in the wardrobe. She wanted nothing he had given her.

He had tried to reason with her, to explain what she had seen, but she had only one question she wanted answered; had he slept with Liz. The guilt on his face had been answer enough. Not that she could altogether blame him for that, Liz was a very beautiful woman, what she couldn't forgive was the fact that he had involved her in their triangle of misery.

She may have left Adam but Liz remained with Nick, both of them adoring the beautiful child they had created between them. But Leonie couldn't help wondering how long that would last, when Liz would decide she had shared Emma with Nick long enough and went back to Adam. Worst of all she wondered how Nick would react to knowing that his wife no longer loved him, that she had stayed with him only because she was expecting his baby. Nick adored Liz, had been in their lives ever since Leonie could remember, his love for Liz evident in everything that he did.

Leonie watched him now as he played on the floor with Emma, the little baby gurgling up at him, her huge green eyes glowing. Nick wasn't a handsome man, but he was strong, in body as well as mind. Having just passed his fortieth birthday he still remained remarkably fit, his blond hair peppered with silver giving him a distinguished air. He had lived next to them since their parents died, had been ecstatic when Liz accepted his proposal.

Leonie loved him like a brother, wished there were something she could do to prevent the pain and disillusionment he would feel when Liz tired of playing house and decided to leave him. But he was happy now, deserved that happiness after the long wait he had had for Liz; why end that happiness prematurely?

'You'll stay for lunch, won't you, Leonie?' Nick looked up to smile.

'Er—no, I don't think so,' she refused, finding even this two-hour duty visit per week a strain.

He grinned, straightening, Emma in his arms. 'I can assure you that Liz's cooking has improved since she's been home full time,' he mocked.

'Just for that, Nick Foster, I may decide not to cook your Sunday lunch tomorrow,' Liz pretended to be offended, but she couldn't help smiling.

'You wouldn't do that to a starving man,' he protested.

Liz grimaced at him. 'You look as if you're starving,' she looked pointedly at his muscular physique.

Leonie's heart ached at the way Liz was able to banter and share her life with a man she no longer loved; *she* certainly hadn't been able to do the same once she knew the truth about Adam and Liz.

'Your mummy is implying I'm putting on weight,' Nick spoke to his daughter of his indignation at the suggestion.

'She isn't implying anything,' Liz laughed

softly, taking the baby from him. 'She would tell you if you were. I can't have you running to seed after only a few years of marriage.' She began to feed Emma.

There was nothing more natural than a woman with a baby at her breast, and yet the sight of Liz and Emma together in that way twisted a knife in Leonie's heart. She had suggested to Adam that they have a baby, had hoped it might help draw them closer together, to give her the confidence in herself as a woman that she so sadly lacked with the failure of the physical relationship. But Adam had turned down the idea, had told her children didn't fit into his plans for some time to come. No doubt Liz's child would be a different matter!

She wondered if Liz would feel quite so content if she knew that Adam was trying to have an affair with her. Why didn't Liz just go to him now and save them all a lot of heartache! She stood up jerkily, unable to take any more. 'I really do have to go now.'

Liz frowned. 'But you've only just arrived.'

'I—My hand is aching,' she didn't exactly lie, her hand did ache, despite the pain-killers she had been taking to ease that.

'How did you do it?' Liz looked concerned.

She shrugged. 'Just another of my little "accidents",' she dismissed.

Nick gave her a teasing smile. 'I'm glad you've never come to me for insurance, it would be embarrassing having to turn down my sister-in-law as too much of a risk!'

She returned his smile. 'I don't think I could have afforded the premium anyway on my record!'

'You never used to be quite as bad as this.'

Her smile became brittle at her sister's observation. 'No,' she acknowledged tightly.

'I remember Adam always used to have the effect of making you worse,' Nick mused.

'Have you seen anything of him?'

How casually her sister made her interest sound! She had no idea if Liz saw Adam at all, rarely discussed anything personal with her sister, least of all Adam. But she assumed that they would meet occasionally, despite Liz's act of the devoted wife. 'I saw him yesterday as a matter of fact,' she replied lightly. 'He's looking very well.'

'He always does,' Liz observed affectionately. 'Have the two of you—resolved your differences?'

The look she gave her sister was scathing to say the least. 'We never will,' she said dully, knowing Liz must know that above all people. 'Our marriage is over.'

'I'm sorry, I assumed because you met yesterday . . .?'

'I'm going to be working for Adam for a few weeks, nothing more than that,' she dismissed.

Hazel eyes widened. 'Adam has hired you to work for him?'

'Yes,' she bit out. 'I may not be any good as a wife but I'm a damned good interior designer.'

Liz looked taken aback by her bitterness. 'I'm sure you are, it just seems an—odd, arrangement.'

Not half as odd as the other arrangement Adam was suggesting! She shrugged. 'Adam isn't a man that cares how things look. And I have little say in the matter, David decides who will do what.'

'How is David?' Nick asked interestedly.

'Very well.' Some of the tension left her at this

more neutral subject, looking gratefully at Nick, knowing by the compassion she could see in his deep blue eyes that he understood she would rather not talk about Adam. She had brought David here to dinner one evening, had found him the exact buffer she needed to help her get through an evening with Liz, and the other couple had liked him immensely.

'You see rather a lot of him, don't you,' Liz said conversationally.

Leonie at once stiffened resentfully. 'I work for him,' she reminded abruptly.

'I meant socially, silly,' her sister chided.

She looked at Liz with suspicion. What was Liz up to now, trying to absolve her conscience by making sure Leonie had a man in her life when she went to Adam? She was over her own shock and humiliation, needing no man in her life, it was Nick who was going to be devastated.

'I see him occasionally,' she dismissed. 'Very occasionally. Do you see anything of Adam?' she challenged.

Was it her imagination or did Liz suddenly become very engrossed in feeding Emma?

'Occasionally,' Liz replied distractedly, seeing to the baby.

'He came to dinner last week, as it happens,' Nick put in lightly. 'Strange, he didn't mention that he intended seeing you.'

'He meant it to be a surprise,' her voice was sharp. 'And it was definitely that.'

'It must have been,' Liz nodded.

Her mouth firmed. 'I really do have to be going,' she told them determinedly. 'I'll see you again next week.'

It was Nick who walked her to the door, Liz still busy with Emma. Leonie was just relieved at being able to leave, dreaded these duty visits, sure that both she and Liz were aware of the reason they could no longer get on even on a polite social level.

Somehow knowing she was to see Adam first thing Monday morning made the weekend pass all too quickly. But at least he didn't pay her any surprise visits during those two days; she had half expected that he would, had felt a sense of anti-climax when he didn't.

Her hand was a lot better by Monday morning, the red line of infection having faded up her arm, the wound feeling more comfortable, so much so that she felt able to leave off the sling she had been instructed to wear over the weekend.

'Damn, who can that be?' she muttered as the doorbell rang as she was brushing her teeth, grabbing up her silky robe to pull it on over her lacy bra and panties.

Adam eyed her mockingly. 'Either that's toothpaste, or you're foaming at the mouth.'

Colour flooded her cheeks as she belatedly remembered to remove the toothpaste from her mouth with the towel in her hand. She had just been so stunned to see him; it was only eight-thirty in the morning. 'What are you doing here?' she said ungraciously.

He shrugged, strolling past her into the flat. 'You need a lift to work, I'm here to provide it.'

Leonie followed him in to the lounge, scowling as Harvey lingered long enough on his way out to rub against Adam's trouser-covered leg, leaving ginger hairs on the dark brown material. 'I can drive myself to work,' she snapped.

He frowned as she freely used her right hand to prove her point. 'You're supposed to rest that.'

'I did. I have,' she added impatiently. 'It's

better now. Or perhaps you don't take my word for it and would like to inspect it yourself?' she challenged.

'I can see from here that it's in working order again,' he said dryly, making himself comfortable in one of her armchairs. 'Did you have a good weekend?'

'Did you?' she returned.

'Very good,' he nodded. 'Did you visit Liz?'

Her mouth tightened. 'Yes.'

'How is she?'

'Don't you know?'

'If I did, would I be asking?' he reasoned mildly.

'Probably,' she scorned. 'After all, you have to keep up appearances. It's Nick I feel sorry for, he just has no idea does he?' she added disgustedly.

'Leonie, you don't know what you're talking about, so just drop it, hm,' he was still pleasantly polite.

'I know you were having an affair with my sister when we were married——'

'You know I went to bed with her, it isn't the same thing.' Steel had entered his voice.

She gave a disbelieving laugh. 'Of course it's the same thing!'

'No,' he shook his head, his eyes narrowed. 'And one day you're going to want to hear the truth. In the meantime I'd like to concentrate on our affair.'

'I——'

'What did you have for breakfast this morning?'

The question took her by surprise. 'Toast and coffee,' she answered automatically.

'Dry toast and black coffee?' he guessed, standing up. 'The more sophisticated hair-style is an improvement, Leonie, but the loss of weight isn't,' he told her as he went through to the kitchen.

Leonie followed him. 'What do you think you're doing?' she demanded as he took butter, milk and eggs out of the refrigerator.

'Getting our breakfast,' he answered dismissively.

'Haven't you eaten?'

He shook his head. 'I thought I'd wait and eat with you.'

'But I told you, I've already eaten.'

'Rubbish,' he decided, beating the milk into the eggs. 'Go and finish dressing and then come and eat.'

'Adam——'

His gaze was steady. 'I prefer you as you were before you dieted.'

'So you intend fattening me up,' she protested.

'That's the idea,' he nodded. 'I should hurry and dress, Leonie, the eggs will be ready in a few minutes.'

'I'll be late for work!'

'I'm your first appointment, and I don't mind if you're late,' he dismissed with a smile. 'Now off you go,' he gave her bottom a playful tap.

Leonie gave him an indignant glare before leaving the room. How dare he ignore her all weekend and then calmly turn up here again this morning and attempt to take over her life once again!

Her movements quieted as she wondered whether she were more angry at being ignored the last two days or at the fact that Adam was taking command of her life. The answer made her wince.

'Very nice. Very professional,' Adam compli-

mented when she rejoined him in the kitchen.
'Now take off the jacket and put it over that chair
with mine; I'd like to eat breakfast with a lover,
not a businesswoman.'

He had effectively robbed her of her line of
defence! She had donned the formal oatmeal-
coloured suit and brown blouse in an effort to
remain distant from the situation he was trying to
create. But he had discarded his own jacket and
waistcoat, looking ruggedly attractive. With her
own jacket removed they looked like any other
couple having breakfast together before leaving
for work.

'That's better.' Adam divided the scrambled
eggs on to two plates, putting them on the table
with the rack of toast and pot of coffee. He
poured a cup of the latter for both of them as he
sat down opposite her, adding milk and sugar to
Leonie's.

'No——'

'You know you love milk and sugar in your
coffee,' he stubbornly added another teaspoonful
of the latter.

'But it doesn't love me,' she grimaced. 'Adam,
I can't eat that,' she protested as he liberally
buttered a slice of toast for her.

'Then I'll feed you,' he told her throatily,
holding the toast temptingly in front of her
mouth.

'Something else lovers do?' she rasped irritably.

'All the time,' he grinned.

The toast looked so delicious after the strict
diet she had kept herself on the last few months.
She closed her eyes so as not to be tempted,
although the smell tormented her. 'I've only just
given away all my size fourteen clothes to
charity,' she pleaded raggedly.

'So I'll buy you some new ones,' he dismissed.

Her lids flew open at the arrogant statement. 'You most certainly will not!'

'Independent as well as fiery,' Adam smiled at her. 'Eat, Leonie.' The smile didn't leave his face but his tone was firm.

With an irritated glare in his direction she took a bite out of the slice of toast, savouring every morsel; it seemed so long since she had allowed herself the luxury of butter, only keeping it in the refrigerator for guests. But after tasting the toast oozing with butter it was all too easy to eat the fluffy eggs and drink the sweet syrupy coffee.

She frowned as Adam ate his own eggs. 'Why didn't she provide you with breakfast?' she mocked.

'She?'

'The woman you spent the weekend with.'

'Ah, that she,' he nodded, lifting one of her hands to lace her fingers with his. 'I spent the weekend in business meetings, Leonie,' he told her reproachfully.

'That's a new name for it!' She glared at him as he refused to release her hand.

He smiled his appreciation of her humour. 'Would it bother you if I had spent the weekend with another woman?'

'Would it bother you if I had spent the weekend with another man?'

'Like a knife being twisted inside me,' he answered without hesitation.

Leonie gasped, meeting his steady gaze. 'Did you really spend the weekend working?' she asked uncertainly.

'Yes.'

'Why?'

'So that I had time to spare this week to concentrate on my reluctant lover,' he teased.

'And did you spend the weekend alone?'

'My personal assistant——'

'Ah.'

'Jeremy,' he finished pointedly. 'Accompanied me.'

'I see,' she chewed on her bottom lip. 'I spent the weekend alone too.'

'I know,' he nodded, standing up to clear away the debris from their meal before shrugging back into his waistcoat and jacket.

Leonie glared at him. 'If you're still having me followed——'

'I'm not.' He held out her own jacket for her.

She shoved her arms into the sleeves, turning to frown at him angrily. 'Then how did you know I spent the weekend alone?'

He grinned. 'Harvey told me.'

'Adam!' she warned tightly.

He bundled her out of the door. 'The only man you've been seeing since we separated is David Stevenson, and he mentioned at lunch on Friday that he was going away this weekend.'

'Oh.' She looked at him resentfully as they emerged out into the street, the BMW parked behind her orange, and rusty, VW. The difference in their cars seemed to echo the difference in themselves, Adam a man of caviar and fresh salmon, Leonie fish and chips and McDonalds. 'I'll meet you at your office,' she told him abruptly.

'Leonie?' he probed her sudden withdrawal even from arguing with him, frowning heavily.

'We're already late, Adam,' she sighed wearily. 'And my car isn't the most reliable of machines.' She unlocked the door.

'Is that yours?' excitement tinged Adam's voice as he walked over to the VW, touching one fender almost reverently. 'I used to have one exactly like it. I kept it until it just about disintegrated on me,' he chuckled reminiscently. 'You're lucky to have found one in such good condition.'

'Adam, the car is ten years old! And when did you ever have an old jalopy like this?' she scorned.

'When I was at college. Dad wanted me to buy something more prestigious,' he recalled dryly. 'But I'd worked in a bar in the evenings to buy my VW, I wasn't giving it up for anyone.'

He knew exactly how she felt about this rusty old car! He had given her the Porsche during their marriage, and there could be no doubting that it was a fantastic car, but even though she moaned and groaned about the unreliability of the VW she wouldn't exchange it for the Porsche at any price, had worked hard to buy this car for herself. And Adam knew how she felt. Why couldn't he do something, *anything*, so that she could dislike him once more!

'I'll meet you at your office,' she repeated lightly, climbing into her car.

With a shrug of his broad shoulders Adam strolled back to the BMW, sitting inside the car as he waited for life to spark in her engine. As usual the VW played up, and Leonie was hot with embarrassment by the time the engine roared into life, instantly stalling it and having to start the process all over again.

Mrs Carlson's brows rose questioningly as they entered the top-floor suite together, and Leonie blushed at what the other woman must be thinking about them; she had last seen them going to lunch together on Friday. She felt sure the secretary imagined they had spent the weekend together!

'Mr Spencer is waiting for you in your office,' she informed Adam coolly, obviously disapproving of the relationship between her boss and an employee, albeit an indirect employee.

'Thanks, Stella,' Adam dismissed. 'Could you bring in coffee for three?' he requested arrogantly as he ushered Leonie into his office.

A young man stood up at their entrance, his smile warm and friendly as he looked at Adam, cooling slightly as his gaze passed to Leonie, looking her over critically.

Leonie did some 'looking over' herself! The slightly overlong blond hair was deliberately styled that way, she felt sure, the face too good looking to be called handsome, his body slender, wearing the cream suit and brown shirt well, his hands long and thin, the nails kept short—and manicured.

Adam met her questioning gaze with suppressed humour. 'Leonie, this is Jeremy Spencer, my Personal Assistant,' he introduced softly. 'Jeremy, this is Leonie Grant, the young lady who is going to transform these offices into something approaching comfort.'

Leonie was aware of his amused gaze on them as she and Jeremy continued to eye each other critically.

'Miss Grant,' Jeremy Spencer made no attempt to shake hands with her. 'I hope you won't attempt to change the decor too much, I think this is exactly Adam already.'

She looked around the austere room, knowing that it needed light, that perhaps it would have suited the man she had been married to, but not the Adam she now knew, not the Adam that was her lover. 'It is very—masculine,' she agreed.

Jeremy Spencer turned back to Adam. 'I brought these contracts in for you to sign.'

Leonie was ignored by both men during the next few minutes as they discussed the contract that had obviously been decided upon during the weekend, unable to resist making a comparison between them as they bent over the desk. Jeremy Spencer didn't attract her at all!

He nodded to her abruptly when it came time for him to leave, and Leonie had trouble holding in her laughter until the door had closed behind him. 'Really, Adam,' she finally spluttered with laughter. 'What on earth made you employ *him*?'

Adam shrugged dismissively. 'He's harmless. Now come over here, we haven't had our morning kiss yet,' he invited huskily.

'Were we supposed to have one?' she delayed mockingly.

'But of course.' He strolled over to her, his arms about her waist as he moulded her body to his. 'After a weekend apart we shouldn't be able to keep our hands off each other!'

'Then how have we managed to?' she taunted.

'After the way you greeted me this morning I was afraid to touch you until I'd fed you!'

'You aren't afraid of anything,' she scorned. 'You never have been.'

'I'm afraid that if you don't kiss me I'm going to burn up with wanting you,' he groaned.

Her breath caught in her throat, her head tilted back to receive his kiss, her lips parting beneath his, her arms moving about his waist beneath his jacket. He felt warm and solid, his smooth jaw smelling faintly of limes.

'Adam, I forgot—Oh.' An astounded Jeremy Spencer stood in the doorway, staring at them in disbelief.

'Yes, Jeremy, what is it?' Adam's voice was

terse as he kept Leonie in his arms, the evidence of his arousal pressed against her.

'I—er—I forgot to get your signature on these letters.' Jeremy ignored Leonie as he placed the letters on the desk for Adam. 'I had no idea I was interrupting—something,' he added.

Adam eyed him warningly. 'Nothing that can't be continued after you've gone,' he dismissed. 'I'll sign the letters later,' he drawled as the younger man made a hasty departure.

'You've shocked him,' Leonie reproved.

Adam scowled. 'That's nothing to what he just did to me!'

She laughed softly at his obvious discomfort. 'You'll get over it.'

'Maybe—for a while,' he added warningly. 'But it will only be a delay, Leonie, not a reprieve.'

She blushed at the promise behind the words. 'Isn't it time we got down to business, I do have other clients besides you, you know.'

'None that can't wait,' he announced raggedly. 'I have no intention of discussing anything until I've received a proper good-morning kiss, with a certain amount of feeling.'

'That's blackmail,' she protested.

Adam grinned. 'Terrible, isn't it?' He didn't sound in the least repentant.

'Both lovers have the same physical power,' she warned as she moved into his arms, she the one to initiate the kiss this time, moving her mouth erotically against his, feeling the accelerated thud of his heart beneath her hand, moving sensuously against him as he groaned low in his throat, squirming away from him as he would have caressed her breasts. 'Good morning, Adam,' she greeted throatily.

He let out a ragged breath. 'That was with a "certain amount of feeling" all right,' he said ruefully.

She smiled. 'I thought so.'

His eyes narrowed. 'Enjoyed it, did you?'

She was well aware of how aroused he was. 'Immensely,' she nodded.

'Hm,' he muttered. 'Let's get down to the business of choosing the decor for this office.'

Leonie worked happily at his side for the remainder of the morning, a satisfied smile to her lips for the whole of the hour it took him to put his desire from his mind—and body; meeting his scowls with a bright smile.

The decisions made about colours and fabrics she had to get back to her office and begin the ordering and arranging, the part Leonie liked the best—apart from the finished result, of course.

'Lunch, I think,' Adam stood up decisively as she packed away her sample books.

She frowned. 'I hope I haven't delayed you.' It was after one o'clock.

'I meant lunch for both of us,' he pulled on his jacket. 'Together,' he added pointedly.

'Oh I don't usually bother with lunch——'

'I'm fattening you up, remember.' He closed her briefcase and picked it up, taking hold of her arm with the other hand.

'I'm still full up from breakfast,' she protested as he marched her out to the lift, blushing as she realised Mrs Carlson had heard her protest. 'Now she must have completely the wrong idea about us,' she muttered crossly as they went downstairs.

'The right idea,' he corrected with a smile.

'My car,' she protested as he led her to the BMW.

'You can come back for it.'

'I haven't forgotten what happened the last time I intended doing that,' she glowered at him.

His only answer was a mocking smile. Leonie seethed all the way to the restaurant, resentful of his high-handedness, feeling as if all decisions were taken from her whenever she was in his company. She had found her independence the last eight months, she didn't need him taking over her life a second time. He——

'Come on, dreamer,' he chided, the car parked, Adam having opened the car door for her and now waiting for her to join him.

She got out resentfully. 'I wasn't dreaming, I—— Adam, this isn't a restaurant.' She looked up at the tall building that was almost a national monument.

'No, it's a hotel,' he acknowledged, guiding her into the plush foyer.

'But they won't serve us here,' she whispered fiercely.

'Of course they will,' he dismissed.

'No——'

'Have you ever heard of room-service?' he taunted as he led the way over to the reception.

'Room——? Adam!' She came to a shocked halt.

He turned to look down at her with mocking eyes. 'I've booked us a room for the afternoon,' he announced calmly.

CHAPTER SIX

'YOU'VE done *what*?' she gasped disbelievingly, staring up at him in horror-struck fascination.

'I've booked us into this hotel for the afternoon,' he repeated softly.

Leonie looked about them self-consciously, sure that everyone must know they were here for an afternoon of illicit sex; no one appeared to be taking any undue notice of them. 'Adam, you can't be serious,' she muttered.

'I am. Very.'

'But I—We—I thought only married people sneaked off to hotels for the afternoon!'

'We are married.'

'I mean people who aren't married to *each other*,' she glared up at him frustratedly. 'Surely you have your apartment for this type of thing?'

'I don't know what you mean by "this type of thing",' he said softly. 'But I have my apartment to live in,' he corrected reprovingly.

'But you took me there last time,' she said desperately as she noticed one of the receptionists eyeing them curiously, sure they must look very conspicuous as she argued with Adam.

'But isn't this more exciting?' he teased.

It was exciting, there was no denying that. She felt deliciously wicked, could feel the heat in her veins at the thought of spending the afternoon in bed with Adam. But they couldn't just disappear for the afternoon, they both had responsibilities. 'Adam, I have to get back to work, and so do you,' she protested.

He shook his head. 'I told you, I intend concentrating on my reluctant lover; I cancelled all my appointments for this afternoon so that I could spend the time with you. I also told Stevenson I would need you all day. He agreed.'

'Oh, Adam, you didn't,' she groaned, sure David would be curious as to why Adam should need her for the whole day when they were only discussing colour and fabrics.

'It's the truth,' Adam told her huskily. 'And that need is getting out of control,' he added pointedly.

Heat coloured her cheeks at his verbal seduction of the senses. 'I feel embarrassed even being here,' she muttered self-consciously.

'Come on, Mrs Smith,' he chuckled as he took her hand firmly in his and strode the short distance to the desk. 'Or would you prefer to be Mrs Brown?' he paused with his pen over the registration card.

'I'd rather leave,' she groaned uncomfortably.

He shook his head, filling in the form before handing it to the waiting receptionist.

'Good afternoon, Mr Faulkner,' the beautiful young receptionist greeted after glancing at the card. 'The "Bridal Suite" has been prepared as per your instructions,' she continued warmly. 'And if you should need anything else please don't hesitate to call.' She held out a key to him.

'I won't,' he nodded curtly, taking the key, not glancing at Leonie as she would have pulled away at the other woman's mention of the Bridal Suite.

'Do you have any luggage?' the receptionist asked as they turned away.

'It's following on later,' Adam told her smoothly. 'A mix-up at the airport.'

'Oh, how annoying for you,' the young woman sympathised.

'Very,' Adam smiled. 'Come along, darling,' he urged Leonie as she stood numbly at his side. 'I know you would like to lie down after the exhausting day we've had.'

'Adam, how could you?' she demanded as soon as the lift doors closed smoothly behind them, breaking out of the numbed surprise that had possessed her. She couldn't believe this was happening to her!

'With a telephone call,' he deliberately mis-understood her.

'I meant how could you pretend to that woman that we've just got married,' she accused. 'What are you going to tell her when our luggage doesn't arrive and we leave in a few hours?'

Adam unlocked the door marked Bridal Suite, pushing the door open for her to enter. 'I could always tell her you left me,' he said softly.

Leonie was too engrossed in the beauty of the suite to detect the rasping edge of truth to his words. Vases of flowers filled every available surface, the olde-worlde decor adding to the feeling of this all being a dream.

'Oh, Adam, it's beautiful,' she told him breathlessly.

'You haven't seen the best part yet,' he assured her, pulling her towards the bedroom.

'Adam, I know what a bedroom looks like,' she blushed at his eagerness to occupy the wide double bed.

'Not just the bedroom,' he mocked, throwing open the adjoining door.

The room was as big as the lounge in the flat, two walls completely covered in mirrors, a huge sunken bath dominating the room. But it wasn't that that held her attention. 'Cham-pagne,' she was already intoxicated without it! 'Isn't that a little decadent in a bathroom, Adam?' she teased.

'Very,' he confirmed with satisfaction, bending down to turn on the water to the bath.

'Champagne next to the bath is hardly in keeping with the modesty of a newly married couple,' she said dryly, wondering what the hotel management had thought of these 'instructions' of Adam's. 'I—Oh, Adam,' her cry of surprise was a mixture of despair and choked emotion. 'It's a jacuzzi.' She watched as the depth of the water foamed and whirled at the flick of a switch.

Adam sat back on his haunches to watch her reaction. 'I think I must have telephoned almost every hotel in London trying to find a Bridal Suite that had a jacuzzi; most of them thought the "sweet young things" wouldn't have progressed to sharing a bath just yet!'

'A telephone call' he had said was all it took to arrange this magical afternoon, and yet he had now revealed it had taken a lot of planning, planning she was sure he hadn't consigned to the easily shockable Mrs Carlson. 'Why, Adam?' her voice was a husky rasp.

'Well I suppose they thought the bride and groom would be a little shy with each other to start with——'

'Not that, Adam,' she spoke quietly. 'Why have you done all this?' She hadn't realised at first, had been too fascinated by the idea of an afternoon in bed with Adam to notice the similarities to their failure of a honeymoon. Admittedly they hadn't stayed in a hotel then, but Adam's house in the Bahamas had also been filled with flowers at their arrival, a bottle of champagne cooling in the bedroom, a jacuzzi in the adjoining bathroom.

That night she *had* been embarrassed at the idea of sharing a bath with Adam, her inhibitions making her shy about revealing her body to him so blatantly. Adam didn't have an inhibited bone in his body, had walked about naked almost from the time of their arrival, teasing her when she wouldn't join him in nude bathing on their private beach.

'We have a few ghosts to put to rest.' Adam stood up as he saw the painful memories flickering in the bottle-green depths of her eyes.

'Not this way.' She shook her head, the memories too vivid to be denied.

'Exactly this way,' he nodded firmly, taking her in his arms. 'I should never have married you,' he murmured. 'Another man may have been more understanding about your shy inexperience, may have given you the confidence in yourself as a woman that I never could.'

She turned away. 'It wouldn't have made any difference,' she reminded gruffly.

'Sex isn't everything between a man and woman.'

'On their honeymoon it is!' she scorned.

He sighed. 'We're here to put those memories to rest, Leonie. Won't you let me try?'

She shook her head tearfully. 'I can't be seduced into forgetting that—that fiasco with champagne and a—a damned jacuzzi,' she told him sharply.

'I admit it would have been better if we could have returned to the villa, but I had enough difficulty getting you here without arousing your suspicions; the Bahamas would have been impossible!'

'Why should you want to try, Adam?' she sighed wearily.

'I want to replace the bad memories with good ones, erase the bitterness of the past——'

'And can you also erase your affair with Liz?' she scorned.

'There was no affair——'

'Your sleeping together, then,' she amended impatiently.

'No, I can't erase that,' he acknowledged heavily. 'But I would like to explain it one day, when you're prepared to listen. Not today,' he refused as she would have spoken. 'We'll erase one memory at a time, and today we're starting with our honeymoon.'

'I want to leave,' she said stubbornly.

'Without testing the jacuzzi first?' he teased.

'Without testing anything,' she looked at him coldly.

He shook his head. 'I can't let you do that.'

'You can't stop me,' she derided.

'And what's that starry-eyed receptionist going to think when you walk out after fifteen minutes?'

'That I did leave you,' she bit out. 'A year too late. If I'd had any sense at all I would have walked out after the honeymoon.'

'This is the honeymoon of our affair,' he told her huskily, not releasing her.

'Affairs don't have honeymoons,' she scoffed.

'This one does,' he insisted. 'It also has a ring.' He took a brown ring-box from his jacket pocket.

'A Woolworth's special, to convince the gullible?' she scorned.

'A Cartier special,' he drawled, flicking open the lid to the box, revealing a flat gold band studded with diamonds.

Leonie gasped at its delicate beauty. 'I can't take that, Adam,' she shook her head.

'Of course you can.' He lifted her resisting left

hand. 'I noticed you no longer wear the rings I bought you,' he pushed the diamond ring on to her third finger. 'I want you to wear this instead.'

She swallowed hard, the ring looking even more delicately beautiful on her slender hand. 'Why?' she choked.

'It's an Eternity ring,' he told her softly.

'Affairs are usually short-term, Adam,' she shook her head.

'Not this one,' he said with a return of arrogance. 'I want you to move in with me, stay with me.'

'We're getting a divorce, Adam,' she reminded exasperatedly.

'After the divorce then, if you think that living together might make that difficult. I think I can wait that long, if I can see you every night at my apartment or yours.'

'Adam, living together would be like being married!' she protested.

'It would be nothing like it,' his voice was harsh. 'You hated being married, remember?'

'Yes,' she shuddered at the memory of how much pain it had caused her. 'I did hate it,' she confirmed vehemently.

He nodded. 'But you've enjoyed the last few days we've been together, haven't you?'

She would be lying if she said she hadn't; it had been the first time she had felt really alive since she left him. 'Yes ...' she answered guardedly, knowing she was walking into a trap.

'Then wouldn't you like it to continue?'

'It couldn't,' she shook her head. 'Not indefinitely.'

'We could try,' he insisted.

'Adam, you and Liz——'

'I'm sick of feeling guilty about Liz and I!' His mouth was tight.

'But what would happen to us when she finally finds the courage to leave Nick?'

'Leave Nick?' Adam looked astounded. 'She isn't going to leave Nick!'

'Never?' Leonie frowned.

'Never,' he repeated firmly.

'But I thought——'

'I don't care what you thought,' he bit out. 'Liz is one of those women who make their marriage vows for a lifetime!'

Leonie looked at him sharply, wondering if she had imagined the rebuke behind the words; Adam's bland expression seemed to say she had. 'So I'll do as second-best, hm?' she said bitterly.

'You aren't second-best.' His voice was harsh. 'You never were, you never will be. What happened between Liz and I was already over when I met you. God, I've already admitted I should never have married you, but that doesn't mean we can't be together now. The other night was incredible, you can't deny that!'

'No . . .'

'And can you deny that you want me now?'

She knew she couldn't, knew he must be as aware of the pounding of her heart as she was. She did want him, the non-committal affair he was offering very enticing.

'Come on.' Adam sensed her weakening and took advantage of it, beginning to unbutton her blouse. 'Or the bath will be cold and the champagne flat,' he drawled as he slipped the blouse down her arms and moved to the fastening of her skirt. 'And we wouldn't enjoy it then—the way I intend us to enjoy it,' he added with relish as he stripped her naked.

Colour flooded her cheeks as reflections of herself appeared all over the room, looking very

pale next to Adam's dark colouring and the dark
suit he still wore. 'Are you sure this is a Bridal
Suite?' she asked irritably.

'Yes,' he laughed softly. 'But I think it's for the
more—experienced, bride and groom.'

'Shouldn't you undress too?' she suggested
awkwardly.

'Yes.' He looked at her pointedly.

She had had little experience with undressing
men, never taking such an initiative during their
marriage, their undressing the other night having
taken place in a darkened apartment, not broad
daylight, with images of them reflected everywhere! Her fingers fumbled a little at first, but
her confidence grew as she saw the effect she was
having on Adam, her hand trustingly in his as
they stepped down into the water together.

It was such a big bath that they could quite
easily have sat facing each other, but Adam had
other ideas, sitting down to pull her in front of
him, pulling her back to lean against his chest, his
arms around her waist.

He nuzzled against her throat. 'We forgot the
champagne,' he muttered, the ice-bucket and
glasses out of their reach.

'It isn't important.' She already felt intoxicated
just from his touch, gasping as his hands moved
up to cup the fullness of her breasts. 'Oh, Adam,
I——'

'No, don't move,' he instructed as she would
have turned in his arms. 'I haven't washed you
yet.' He took the soap in his hand and began to
lather her body.

By the time they had finished washing each
other the bath was filled with bubbles, all
inhibitions gone as they frolicked in the water,
Leonie facing him now, leaning against his chest

as she lay between his legs. 'Do you think we would drown if we made love in here?' The idea had been tantalising her the last few minutes, knowing Adam was as aroused as she was.

'It's too late even if we do,' he groaned as his mouth claimed hers.

They didn't drown, but the carpet around the bath did seem very wet when they stepped out on to it, not bothering to dress but wrapping towels around themselves as they carried the champagne through to the bedroom.

Adam dipped a finger in his champagne to trail it between the deep vee of her breasts.

'Oh, Adam . . .!' she groaned as he licked the wine from her heated flesh, turning in his arms, gasping her dismay as *all* the champagne from her glass tipped over Adam's stomach, dripping down on to the bed. 'Oh no,' she groaned. 'And I was doing so well too!'

'You were,' he agreed seductively.

She blushed. 'No, I meant——'

'I know what you meant,' he chuckled, making no effort to mop up the champagne with the towel he still had draped about his hips. 'Care to reciprocate?' he invited. 'Your clumsiness may be to my advantage this time.'

She knew what he meant, eagerly drinking the champagne from his body, tasting Adam at the same time, feeling the rush of need that engulfed them both as she removed his towel.

'We really should do something about ordering lunch,' Adam mumbled contentedly a long time later. 'I need to keep up my stamina if you're going to keep attacking me in this shameless way.'

'If I'm going to——!' She turned to look at him indignantly, only to find him watching her with one sleepy eye, his mouth quirked in amusement. She relaxed. 'Of course, if your age is going to slow you down,' she began mockingly. 'Maybe I should find myself a younger lover.'

There was a deep threatening rumble in his chest as he rolled over to trap her beneath him. 'Maybe *I* should just smack your bottom for you,' he growled. 'My age hasn't slowed me down so far, and—Leonie, did you mean what you just said?' he suddenly asked sharply.

She frowned at his sudden change of mood from lighthearted bantering to serious intensity. 'What did I just say?'

'That I'm your lover.'

She blushed. 'Well you are, aren't you?'

'You didn't seem to think so this morning.'

She shrugged. 'That was this morning.'

'And now?'

'We're in bed together,' she stated the obvious.

'And am I your lover?' he persisted, his hand cupping one side of her face preventing her turning away from him.

'Adam, what we just shared was very pleasant——'

'It was toe-curling,' he corrected emphatically.

'For you too?' she asked shyly. In her inexperience it had been very special to her, but surely to Adam, a man with many affairs behind him, it couldn't have meant the same thing.

'Especially for me.' His thumbtip moved across her slightly swollen lips. 'It was the way I always wanted it to be between us, before a marriage licence and a wedding ring fouled things up.'

She looked down at the eternity ring on her finger. 'I won't make any demands on you,' she told him huskily.

'You never did,' he said grimly. 'Not even sexual ones.'

Her mouth curved teasingly. 'Those weren't the demands I was promising not to make,' she drawled.

'Thank God for that!' He returned her smile.

She laughed throatily. 'Now that I've discovered the—delights of being in bed with you I may never want to get out!'

'Suits me,' he murmured as his mouth claimed hers again.

It was after four when they ordered lunch, Leonie groaning at the amount of food Adam had ordered. 'I'll get fat,' she grimaced.

'I hope so,' he nodded. 'I really meant it when I said I preferred you more—rounded.'

'You mean I really can start to eat again?'

'Please,' he said fervently.

They fed each other like starry-eyed lovers, and every time Leonie saw the diamond ring glitter on her finger she felt a warm glow. She wasn't altogether sure what the ring symbolised, they could hardly remain lovers indefinitely, but somehow the ring made her feel as if she really were Adam's lover, and not just a chattel that he took out for display every now and then. Because that was what being his wife had been like; surely being his lover had to be better than that. It *was* better!

'You like the ring?' Adam saw her glowing gaze on it.

'If it enables me to play the part of Mrs Smith, I love it!' she smiled across the table at him.

He laughed softly. 'You can play the part of Mrs Smith any time you want to, it's a two-way arrangement.'

'You mean if I want to spend another

afternoon like this I can just call you and you'll meet me here?'

'Well, not here,' he smiled. 'We can only play the newly married couple once, but I'll meet you anywhere else that you suggest.'

It sounded like heaven after the misery of their marriage. 'I think I'm going to like this arrangement,' she smiled her anticipation.

'Didn't I tell you that you would?'

'Now don't go and spoil it by saying I told you so,' she reprimanded. 'I love the ring, and I'll wear it proudly, but it gives you no rights over me other than the ones I choose to give you,' she warned.

'Right,' he nodded.

She eyed him suspiciously, never having known him be this agreeable in the past. 'I won't give up my job.'

'No.'

'And I won't move in with you.'

'Why not?' he frowned, although he made no objections.

She shook her head. 'It wouldn't work, Adam. When I lived with you before you swamped me, I became a nervous wreck, terrified of leaving the apartment in the end in case I did something wrong.'

'I didn't know that . . .'

'No,' she flushed. 'We didn't talk a lot in those days.'

'Then we'll make sure we talk now. Do I swamp you now?' he asked slowly, all laughter gone.

'Not while I have my own home to go to whenever I want to. I just couldn't live with you again, Adam.'

'Okay,' he shrugged. 'If that's the way you feel.'

'You—you don't mind?'

'No, because I'll move in with you,' he stated arrogantly.

'That isn't the idea, Adam,' she sighed. 'I knew this wouldn't work out,' she shook her head. 'I think we should just forget the idea, it was a stupid one, anyway.'

'If you want us to maintain separate households, then we will——'

'Oh, thank you, Adam,' she glowed. 'I would prefer it. I don't——'

'—for the time being,' he finished pointedly. 'Leonie, I can't keep going between two households when I reach sixty!' he said exasperatedly as she looked dismayed. 'The strain would probably kill me!'

'Sixty . . .?' she repeated dazedly. 'You expect us to still be together then?'

'Why not? Eternity is a hell of a lot longer than the twenty-one years it's going to take me to reach that age! At least, I hope it is,' he frowned.

'Adam, if you think an affair between us will last that long why did our marriage fail after only a year?' she reasoned. 'After all, I didn't know about Liz until that last day.'

'No, but I did,' he answered grimly. 'Our marriage never really started, Leonie. I rushed you into it, made all the rules and expected you to abide by them the way that my mother did. But that isn't a marriage, Leonie, it's just legalising the sexual act—and even that didn't work between us then.'

'Is that why you married me, for sex?'

'I married you because I wanted to be with you,' he rasped.

'Did you ever love me?' she asked dully.

'What difference does it make,' he dismissed. 'I couldn't make you happy.'

It was a bitter irony that they could now make each other happy, that they were now closer than they ever had been.

'I loved you,' she told him softly.

'I know,' he acknowledged harshly. 'And I hurt you. This way is much better, isn't it?'

She supposed it was—Of course it was! She just couldn't understand how they could make an affair work when their marriage had failed. Unless their expectations were lower, their demands less.

She had married Adam expecting forever, had thought him the man of her dreams, with no faults or blemishes. Hadn't finding that he couldn't banish all the problems of life for her, couldn't reach her physically when she put up a frightened barrier, made him less of a Knight in Shining Armour? She had forgotten she was married to a mere man, that he had needs and fears too, had thought only of herself when the marriage began so badly and continued on its downward slide. Adam wasn't responsible for what had gone wrong on their honeymoon, just as he wasn't solely responsible for the end of their marriage. She had taken his involvement with Liz as the easy way out, when in fact she should have realised she was the one he had married, the one he was trying to share his life with.

Poor Adam, no wonder the idea of marriage had been soured for him; the woman he had chosen for his wife just hadn't been woman enough to try to be his partner in life, to give him the same considerations he gave her.

But she was that woman now, could look back on their marriage with perspective, believed Adam when he said he hadn't slept with Liz after

their marriage. Yes, she believed him now, when
it was too late, when all he wanted was an affair.
But if that was all that could work between them
then it was what she wanted too, wanted Adam in
her life.

'Much better,' she assured him huskily,
standing up to take off the towel that was her
only clothing. 'Shall we go back to bed and see
just how much better,' she invited suggestively.

Adam needed no second invitation, his own
towel discarded long before they reached the
bedroom.

CHAPTER SEVEN

'No, Adam,' she said firmly.

After two more days together she had gained enough confidence in their relationship to say what she liked and disliked, and the idea of joining Adam's father for dinner that evening she disliked intensely!

'Why not?' came Adam's calm query over the telephone.

'You can ask me that?' she gasped. 'After the way he always treated me?'

'I was as much to blame for that as he was,' Adam reminded. 'I should have made sure he understood how things are between us.'

'And how are they?' she demanded tautly.

'If he wants to continue seeing me,' Adam told her softly, 'he'll accept you.'

Leonie was well aware of Charles Faulkner's love for his only child; she had often felt jealous of the closeness between them in the past. If Adam refused to visit his father because of her it would break the older man's heart.

'Adam, men don't introduce their lovers to their fathers,' she derided.

'This man does.'

She sighed at his stubbornness. 'And what are you going to tell him about us?'

'Nothing.'

'Nothing?' she frowned. 'Adam——'

'It's sufficient that we're together,' he explained arrogantly.

'Adam, I don't want to see your father again,'

she told him the simple truth behind her objection.

'I'm sure he feels the same way,' he sounded amused. 'He certainly sounded surprised when I told him you would be accompanying me.'

'Then why put either of us through what can only be an embarrassing experience?' She put her hand up in acknowledgement of the night security guard as he passed by on his rounds. She was working late tonight, felt as if she were the only person in the building; it felt good to know Mick was about.

'I thought you said you wouldn't stay hidden as a lover,' he reminded softly.

'And I haven't been!' She was angry with him for reminding her of that; the two of them hadn't exactly been keeping a low profile the last few days, Adam calling for her at the office for lunch, a rose, a real one now, continuing to arrive daily. She wasn't trying to hide their relationship, but neither was she willing to hypocritically sit down to dinner with Charles Faulkner; they both knew their dislike was mutual. 'I'm not going to have dinner with your father, Adam,' she repeated emphatically.

'He's expecting us.'

'Then you go on your own,' she snapped. 'You had no right accepting the invitation without first consulting me.'

'You would have said no,' he reasoned.

'Obviously,' she bit out. 'Now could we end this pointless conversation, I have work to do.'

'It's after seven,' he pointed out.

'And thanks to an insatiable man I know that kept me awake most of the night I didn't get to work until after ten this morning,' she reminded dryly, smiling at Mick as he passed by her open office door on his way back downstairs.

'Are you complaining?' Adam's voice had lowered sensuously.

'No.' She could still feel the warm glow whenever she remembered their nights together, magical nights when they couldn't get enough of each other, seeming intent on making up for the time they had wasted. 'But I am saying I have to work late tonight. I don't expect to be able to leave much before eight o'clock, and I am certainly not going to feel in the mood to cross swords with your father when I do!'

'I can tell that,' he drawled. 'Okay, I'll call him and change it to tomorrow.'

'Adam——'

'And I won't come to your apartment tonight so that you can get a good night's sleep and won't have to work late tomorrow,' he added huskily.

To say that she felt bereft at the thought of not seeing him tonight would be an understatement, the rest of the evening and night stretched before her like a long black tunnel. But she had a feeling Adam knew exactly how she felt, and she wouldn't give him the satisfaction of knowing how much she would miss him.

'That sounds like a good idea,' she agreed lightly. 'I can also get a few jobs done around the flat that I've neglected the last few days. And I'm sure Harvey would welcome my undivided attention for a few hours.'

'You sound as if you're looking forward to an evening without me.' Adam sounded annoyed.

She smiled to herself. She would spend a miserable evening without him, but it would be worth it to know that he didn't realise that. 'Well we did agree we would have a certain amount of freedom in this relationship, Adam,' she reminded brightly. 'And the idea of putting on an old robe, curling up on the sofa with a good book, sounds like heaven.'

'It sounds awful,' he rasped.

'Only because you don't have an old robe,' she mocked. 'And you never relax enough to read.'

'I prefer other methods of relaxation.'

She could just picture the scowl of his face, almost felt it was worth the night without him to have turned the tables so neatly on him. Almost. But she had become accustomed to curling up against him at night, and she knew she would sleep badly tonight. 'Take a hot bath and read for a while, Adam,' she advised mockingly. 'It's just as relaxing.'

'Like hell it is!' he exploded. 'Is that really what you would compare our lovemaking to, a hot bath and a read?' he demanded angrily.

'I didn't say it was as good,' she was enjoying baiting him. 'Only that it's as relaxing.'

'It's the same thing, damn it,' he snarled.

'Is it?' she asked with feigned vagueness, almost laughing out loud at his indignation. 'Adam, are we having our first lovers' argument?' She instilled disbelief into her voice.

'Yes,' he rasped coldly. 'I'll call you tomorrow.' He rang off abruptly.

Leonie put her own receiver down more slowly, knowing she had won that round, but at what price. She had denied herself a night with Adam, and the mood he was in now she couldn't even be sure he would call tomorrow. But she wouldn't go to him, had given in to him too much in the past to follow that pattern again. She looked at the ring on her finger; a long-lasting affair he had said. And she believed him. One little argument wouldn't spoil what they had now.

But that knowledge didn't cheer her up at all, and she had little enthusiasm for work now, her concentration level down to nil. She packed up after a few minutes, deciding she would be better off coming in early in the morning.

'Had enough for one day?' Mick sympathised as he unlocked the door for her to leave.

'More than enough,' she grimaced at the middle-aged man. 'I'll see you early in the morning,' she told him lightly, knowing he would still be on duty when she got to work at seven-thirty tomorrow. It must be a long boring night for him.

It was a long boring night for her too. Her bath was relaxing, so was Harvey's decision to spend the evening in with her for a change, but the book might as well have been written in Chinese for all she understood it, putting it down after several minutes; her favourite romance author deserved a more avid reader than she could provide this evening.

Had she fallen into the trap so quickly, wanting more from Adam than he wanted to give? There could be no doubting that they came together as equals now, but would marriage make so much difference to their relationship? Their approach to each other was different this time around, would a wedding ring and marriage licence really 'foul up' the relationship, as Adam had claimed it had last time. Couldn't he see that it wasn't those things that had ruined their marriage at all, that it had been their attitudes that were all wrong?

Was she saying she wanted to be married to him again? She knew she had changed since their separation, that she was more self-confident now, had independence in her career if not in her emotions, felt more able to meet Adam on an equal footing, both intellectually and emotionally, and certainly physically. God, how quickly she had changed her mind about being married to him, how she wished she didn't have to spend evenings apart from him like this! Could she accept just an affair now, when she knew she wanted so much more?

The insistent ringing of the doorbell woke her up, and with a bleary-eyed glance at the bedside clock she saw it was after three o'clock in the morning. She came instantly awake. She had told Adam that she was sure her obscene telephone caller wouldn't come here while she continued to take his calls, but suddenly she wasn't so sure. And she was very much alone here.

Should she call the police before answering the door, or try to find out the identity of her visitor first? The police certainly wouldn't be very thrilled with her if it turned out to be a false alarm. She decided to do the latter, moving warily to the locked and bolted door, knowing that if someone were really determined to get in that they could break the locks with one blow to the door.

'Who—who is it?' she demanded in a hushed voice, trembling from head to foot.

'Who the hell do you think it is?' rasped an all-too-familiar voice.

'Adam!' Her hands shook as she quickly unlocked the door, almost falling into his arms in her relief, barely noticing he wore casual denims and shirt, his jaw in need of a shave. 'Thank God it's you!' she groaned, her face buried against the warm column of his throat.

His arms tightened about her convulsively as

she continued to tremble. 'Who did you think—Oh no,' he groaned, holding her closer. 'You thought it was him, didn't you?' he realised, closing the door behind them.

'Yes,' she shuddered.

'I'm sorry, baby. God, I'm sorry,' he muttered over and over into her hair, holding her until the trembling stopped and she pulled out of his arms.

'Sorry!' she glared at him. 'You frighten me half to death and all you can say is you're *sorry*!' After the relief came her anger, and she was truly furious!

'I'm *very* sorry?' he said hopefully.

'That doesn't make up at all for the scare you gave me,' she snapped. 'Just what do you think you're doing here at three o'clock in the morning anyway?' she demanded to know.

He sighed, thrusting his hands into the back pockets of his already tight denims. 'I couldn't sleep——'

'Well you can take your damned insomnia somewhere else!' she told him angrily.

'You don't mean that.'

'Oh don't I?' she challenged recklessly. 'You just turn around and walk out that door. And if you want to see me again you can call at a reasonable time!'

'Have you been able to sleep?'

'Of course, why shouldn't I?' In fact it was because she had only eventually fallen asleep about an hour ago that was making her so bad-tempered, feeling nauseous with the suddenness of her wakening.

'Because you missed me,' he suggested huskily.

'Don't flatter yourself,' she said heatedly. 'I slept before you came into my life, and I'll sleep the times you aren't with me!'

His mouth tightened. 'You really want me to leave?'

'Yes!' She glared at him, still badly shaken from her imaginings of him being her obscene caller. 'What we have is a *relationship*, Adam. I'm not some available body you can take to help you fall asleep!'

He recoiled as if she had struck him. 'It wasn't like that——'

'Wasn't it?' she accused. 'Can you deny you came here to make love with me?'

'That was part of it——'

'I'm beginning to think that might be all of it,' she scorned. 'Now that I'm not such a non-event in bed you can't do without it, can you?'

A white line of fury ringed his mouth. 'You have improved in bed,' he bit out contemptuously. 'But I've had better,' he added woundingly. 'I thought this,' he twisted up her left hand with his eternity ring glittering on her finger, 'meant we had more than a physical relationship. I thought we had respect and liking, maybe even loving. But I was obviously wrong,' he thrust her hand away from him. 'I came here because I couldn't sleep until I'd apologised for the senseless argument we had earlier,' he ground out. 'But you obviously haven't been plagued by the same need. I will leave now, I'm sorry I troubled you!'

The colour had come and gone again in her face as they hurled the hurtful words at each other, knowing she had provoked this scene, a scene that could be the end of them. And suddenly the idea of Adam walking out of her life became too unbearable to contemplate.

'Adam!' She ran to him as he stopped at the door, her arms about his waist from behind as she rested her cheek against his back. 'I'm sorry,' she said breathlessly. 'I shouldn't have said those things.'

He didn't move. 'The point is, did you mean them?'

'No,' she sighed. 'I've just woken up after lying awake for hours aching for you,' she admitted gruffly. 'I'm a bad-tempered witch, and I'm sorry.'

The tension left his body in a ragged sigh. 'Can I stay?'

'Please,' she groaned her need.

He turned to take her in his arms, holding her tightly. 'Have you forgiven me for frightening you like that?'

'Of course.' She snuggled up against him.

'Has he called again?'

She shook her head. 'No, I told you, only Fridays at eleven-thirty.'

'I wonder why that is,' Adam frowned.

'Maybe that's his night out with the boys away from his wife,' she dismissed.

'You think he's married?' Adam's frown deepened.

'I try not to think about him at all,' she told him firmly. 'And I wish you wouldn't either. He's a sick man who vents his frustration on life by telling me dirty things.'

'If I ever find out who he is I'll kill him,' Adam ground out.

She smoothed the anger from his face. 'We'll probably never know, so let's forget him.'

'Yes.' He did so with effort. 'Shall we go to bed?'

She smiled up at him encouragingly. 'I thought you would never ask!'

Their lovemaking was different again tonight,

as enjoyable as it always was, but no more so than the closeness they shared afterwards as they lay in each other's arms. As she lay next to Adam Leonie knew that their relationship had transcended the physical, that even though she had no idea of Adam's feelings for her that she loved him, doubted she had ever stopped.

She could feel the tension rising within her as they neared Adam's father's house, wished with each passing minute that she had stuck to her decision not to go there with him for dinner. But her closeness to Adam that morning had compelled her to change her mind, sure at that time that she could survive the ordeal of meeting his father again.

She had changed her mind back again since then, had picked up the telephone a dozen times during the day to tell Adam to cancel the dinner, only to replace it again without speaking to him, sure he would find her cowardly behaviour less than attractive.

Getting herself ready had been a disaster, not realising her nail-polish wasn't dry, finding out that fact when her tights got stuck to it as she tried to get dressed. Then she had torn the hem of her dress with her evening shoe, having to change her make-up tones with the dress, realising at the last minute that she had grey shadow on one lid and green on the other!

By the time Adam arrived to pick her up at seven-thirty she was feeling hot and flustered, telling him she couldn't possibly go out, that she thought she might be going to come down with something. His method of persuasion had left her even more hot and flustered—but with a decided glow to her eyes.

The fact that they were now going to arrive very late didn't seem to bother Adam in the slightest, the intimate smiles he kept directing her way reassuring her that she had his support, that he wouldn't let her down as he had so much in the past.

The Faulkner staff must have been aware of the break-up of Adam's marriage, and yet the haughty butler didn't so much as bat an eyelid at Leonie accompanying Adam to dinner, his manner very correct as he took her jacket.

'Dad doesn't eat little girls for breakfast,' Adam teased her as she hesitated about entering the lounge where she knew the senior Mr Faulkner was waiting for them.

'That's only because he knows I'd give him indigestion!' she muttered ruefully.

Adam was still laughing when they entered the lounge, although Leonie sobered as she sensed the disapproval emanating from the rigid-backed man standing across the room from them. Charles Faulkner was an older version of Adam, still very good looking despite being over seventy, although the lines of harshness beside his nose and mouth weren't quite so noticeable in his son yet. And if Leonie had her way they never would be!

'You're late,' Charles Faulkner bit out critically without greeting.

'Are we?' Adam dismissed unconcernedly.

'You know you are,' his father said harshly, cold grey eyes turning to Leonie. 'What have you been up to now?' he scorned.

In the past she would have cowered away from such open contempt, but somehow tonight she knew Adam was on her side, and that gave her the confidence to steadily meet those critical grey eyes. 'Good evening, Charles,' she deliberately used the informality she had been too nervous to take while living in this house. 'I hope you're well,' she added politely.

The older man scowled. 'I'm as you see me.'

Her perusal of his rigidly held body was deliberate and slow. 'You're looking very well—considering your age.' Her expression remained deceptively innocent, although she could sense Adam was having difficulty containing his amusement.

'And what does age have to do with it?' Charles frowned heavily at the backhanded compliment.

'Well, I remember your once telling me you're just an old man who wants to see his son happily settled before you die,' she reminded him of the argument the two of them had had just before she left Adam; it had been one of many occasions when Charles Faulkner had verbally attacked her without Adam's knowledge. She didn't intend to bring those arguments to Adam's knowledge now, she just wanted to warn Charles Faulkner that she wouldn't stand for it a second time. From the look on the older man's face it was working.

'Oh?' Adam sounded suspicious.

'Don't worry, darling,' she gave him a bright reassuring smile, enjoying Charles Faulkner being the one to feel uncomfortable for a change; in the past she had never dared to mention his father's cruelty to Adam. 'I assured your father I only wanted the same thing.'

Adam looked across at the older man with narrowed eyes. 'It sounds an—interesting conversation.'

'Oh, your father and I had a lot of interesting

conversations,' she dismissed with feigned innocence. 'I've missed them the last few months.'

'I'll bet you have,' Adam sounded angry.

'Shall we go through to dinner?' his father
rasped. 'It's been ready almost an hour.'

'Then it should be nicely cooked, shouldn't it,'
his son dismissed hardly.

'Ruined more like,' his father muttered,
shooting resentful glances at Leonie, which she
promptly ignored.

'I've never known Mrs Simmonds to ruin a
meal,' Adam insisted.

'Always a first time,' his father bit out.

The meal was delicious, as they had all known
it would be. Emily Simmonds was as taciturn as
her employer, but her food melted in the mouth,
and it was always perfectly cooked, the Beef
Wellington, asparagus tips, and tiny new potatoes
that followed the home-made pâté better than
could be bought in any restaurant. But the food
didn't seem to have improved Charles Faulkner's
mood at all.

'You never did tell me why the two of you were
so late arriving,' he snapped as they were served
the chocolate meringue for dessert.

Delicate colour heightened Leonie's cheeks as
she left it to Adam to reply; after all, *he* was the
one who had delayed them. Even if she had
enjoyed it.

'I took Leonie to bed and made love to her,' he
stated calmly, continuing to eat his dessert in the
midst of the furore he had created.

'Adam!' Leonie gasped her dismay, not
expecting him to be quite so candid.

His father's mouth was tight. 'In my day a man
didn't discuss taking his wife to bed.'

'Only other women, hm?' his son mocked, the

elderly man spluttering his indignation. 'But Leonie is no longer my wife.' His hand clasped hers, his smile warm.

'You're back together,' his father pointed out abruptly.

'And we're staying that way,' Adam nodded. 'But not as husband and wife.'

'You—you mean you're just going to *live together*?' Charles made it sound decadent.

'Not even that yet,' his son replied happily. 'Not until Leonie is ready for it.'

'Leonie!' his father snorted. 'In my day a man didn't ask his wife's permission to do anything!'

'I know that,' Adam nodded. 'And for a while I followed your example. I walked all over Leonie as if she were a piece of the furniture, didn't ask her opinion on anything, didn't even care if she wanted to make love or not. I did, and that was good enough for me.'

'Adam . . .!' She looked at him pleadingly.

'No, Leonie, I have to make my father understand that things are different now.' He turned to the older man. 'Leonie is a person, with feelings and desires. It took me a long time to realise there was more to a marriage than putting a ring on some lucky woman's finger. Lucky!' he scorned. 'Leonie never knew a day's happiness after I married her. I was so busy being the strong man you had taught me to be that I killed the love Leonie had for me. I realise now that mother was just as unhappy with you as Leonie was with me.'

His father flushed with rage. 'Your mother wasn't unhappy! I gave her everything, cars, jewels, furs, this beautiful house, the servants, *you*!'

'You didn't give me to mother,' Adam contradicted impatiently. 'You created me together. And instead of giving things to mother you should have spent more time with her, talked, *laughed*.'

'I had a business to run,' his father scowled. 'I didn't have time for that.'

'Then you should have made time!'

The two men glared at each other, the similarity between them at that moment unmistakable.

'And I suppose that's what you intend doing, so that you can pander to this—to this——'

'To Leonie, yes,' Adam bit out.

'And the business will suffer because of it!'

'The business will do just fine,' Adam corrected. 'That's what delegation is all about.'

'I'm surprised you haven't decided to sell everything off,' his father scorned.

'I thought about it——'

'Adam!' Leonie gasped her shocked dismay.

'And decided against it,' he finished gently, squeezing her hand reassuringly. 'There would have been no point,' he shrugged. 'I would still have been the same selfish man, and a richer but unemployed one too. So I decided that it was *I* who had to change, not my life.'

'There's nothing wrong with you,' his father told him tautly. 'At least, nothing that can't be straightened out as soon as you're over this infatuation you suddenly have for your own wife!'

Adam shook his head, his smile sympathetic. 'There's nothing sudden about my feeling for Leonie, I was just too busy to express them before. Never show any sign of weakness, that's your motto, isn't it, Dad?'

'It's never failed me,' the older man ground out.

'Oh it's failed you,' Adam contradicted gently. 'Mother was never completely happy, never really sure of your love, and I've turned out to be made from your own image.'

'There's nothing wrong in that,' his father bit out. 'You're a successful man, well respected in the business world.'

'The respect of complete strangers doesn't mean a lot,' Adam told him impatiently.

'I suppose you're going to tell me next that all you want is Leonie,' his father derided coldly.

'Yes,' Adam answered quietly. 'That's exactly what I want. I also want *your* respect for her, and until you can give her that we won't be coming here again.'

'Adam.' She looked up at him pleadingly.

'It's all right, Leonie,' he assured her with a gentle smile, pulling her to her feet at his side. 'I'm sure my father knows I mean what I say.' The last was added challengingly.

'You're acting like an idiot, Adam,' his father rasped. 'Can't you see she's a little simpleton? Why, all she's been able to do for the last half hour is gasp your name in varying degrees of incredulity!' he added contemptuously.

'Good night, Father,' Adam told him flatly, guiding Leonie to the door.

'Adam!'

He turned slowly at the anguished cry. 'Yes?' he bit out coldly.

His father was standing too now, looking more disturbed than Leonie had ever seen him. 'Can't you see you're making a damned fool of yourself, and over a young slip of a girl who isn't worthy of you?'

Adam gave his father a pitying smile. 'If this is making a fool of myself I hope I never stop!' He opened the door for Leonie to precede him out of the room.

'Adam . . .!'

He ignored his father's second plea, his arm about Leonie's waist as they left the house together.

CHAPTER EIGHT

LEONIE sat quietly at his side as he drove them back to her flat, all of their nights spent there together, Harvey an integral part of her life now.

She was stunned by the evening with Charles Faulkner, had had no idea Adam meant to issue his father such a challenge because of her. She knew Adam had changed since their separation, but she hadn't realised just how much.

And he had done it for her, he had revealed tonight, that was what she found so incredible. He wanted her so much that he was willing to change his whole life for her. Surely that must mean he loved her? It was a word that remained conspicuously absent from their relationship.

But she loved him, more than ever after his defence of her in front of his father, knew that she had never really stopped loving him. And she believed him when he said Liz was out of his life for ever. But she wanted to be his wife again more than anything, wanted the children with him even a long-term affair couldn't give them. Maybe in time . . .

'Thank you, Adam,' she huskily broke the silence.

'For what?' He heaved a ragged sigh. 'For subjecting you to even more unpleasantness from my father?'

She put her hand on his thigh. 'I've known worse from him.'

'I'm sure you have,' he ground out. 'Just how often did he used to make those digs at you without my knowledge?'

'It's over now, Adam——'

'How often, Leonie?' he demanded stubbornly.

She sighed. 'Whenever he could,' she admitted. 'It was very demoralising.' She had no intention of widening the gulf between father and son by telling Adam how often his father had reduced her to tears.

'You should have told me what was going on,' he rasped.

Leonie shrugged. 'He never said anything that wasn't the truth. It really doesn't matter now,' she assured him.

'It matters to me,' Adam bit out. 'I was such a lousy husband I couldn't even see what a bastard my father was to you!'

'You were not a lousy husband,' she defended.

'Yes, I was,' he nodded grimly. 'God, I hope I'm a better lover than that!'

She felt any hope she may have had of persuading him to resume their marriage slipping away from her. It was obvious that Adam preferred things the way they were. 'Yes,' she told him softly. 'You're a better lover.'

She fed the cat when they got in, Adam watching her with brooding eyes as he sat on one of the armchairs. He still seemed very disturbed by the incident with his father, and she sat down on the carpeted floor in front of him as she turned to talk to him.

'He'll come around,' she said softly.

He looked startled. 'You mean Dad?' His brow cleared. 'Yes, he'll come around,' he acknowledged heavily. 'And I hope he's a wiser man for it.'

'But you weren't thinking about him, were you?' she probed.

'No,' he admitted flatly. 'I was just wondering

how you could have stayed with me as long as you did, and what damned arrogance made me assume I could just walk back into your life and get you to accept me as your lover!'

'But I did, didn't I?' She smiled up at him.

'Yes, you did.' He shook his head in amazement. 'I thought I had changed after you left me, you see I tried to do exactly that, but now I realise I'm still as arrogant, that I haven't changed in that respect at all. What right do I have to expect you to waste one day of your life on me after what you went through when you were married to me?'

'It isn't wasted,' she assured him huskily.

'And if I hurt you again?' he rasped.

She shook her head. 'You won't.'

'How can you be sure?'

'Why should I want to be?' she cajoled. 'One thing I've learnt from our marriage, Adam, is that the whole of life is a risk. You simply have to live it the way that is best for you.'

He pulled her up to sit on his knees. 'And this is best for us, isn't it, Leonie?' he said fiercely.

'Yes,' she said softly, hope completely gone. 'This is right for us.'

She met his kiss halfway, their emotions spiralling rapidly, standing up in unison to go to her bedroom, needing more than just caresses.

They had barely reached the bedroom when the telephone began to ring, Adam frowning heavily as he glanced down at his watch. 'Friday, eleven-thirty,' he muttered darkly. 'He's consistent, isn't he,' he ground out, turning to pick up the receiver.

'No, Adam, let me——'

He easily shrugged off her attempt to take the receiver from him, listening to the man in silence for several seconds. 'As I said before, it all sounds very interesting,' he finally cut in gratingly. 'But if you don't stop these calls I'm going to do some heavy breathing of my own—down your damned neck! Do I make myself clear?' He shrugged, putting down the receiver. 'He hung up.'

'Wouldn't you?' she teased, relieved that the call was over for another week.

Adam sighed. 'Leonie, he worries me. I know you say he's harmless, but——'

'He is,' she insisted. 'And maybe now that he realises I have an aggressive lover he'll stop calling.'

'Maybe ...' But Adam didn't sound convinced.

'Darling, let's not think about him now,' she moved sensuously against him. 'Can't you see this is exactly what he wants?' She sighed as she received no response. 'Adam, don't let one sick person ruin everything that we have.'

He looked down at her with pain-darkened eyes. 'If anything happened to you ...!' His arms came about her convulsively, carrying her over to the bed to make love to her until she begged for his possession, until neither of them had a lucid thought in their head other than pleasing each other.

Adam still lay next to her when she woke the next morning, and with a contented sigh she realised neither of them had to go to work this morning. She looked down at the man at her side, remembering the incredible night they had just spent together, a night when Adam seemed determined to possess her time and time again, and had.

'Adam ...?'

His lids opened instantly she spoke his name, almost as if her voice were all that were needed to wake him. A light glowed in his eyes as he saw the sensuality in her face. 'Again, Leonie?' he said huskily.

'Please,' she encouraged throatily.

It was after eleven when they woke the next time, Leonie resisting Adam's caressing as she insisted they needed food rather than more lovemaking. It was while they were eating the brunch Adam had prepared that she remembered she should have visited Liz and Nick that morning.

'What is it?' Adam was sensitive to her every mood, fully dressed as he sat across the table from her, although he had told her he intended bringing some of his clothes here the next time he came, sick of dressing in the same clothes he had worn the evening before. He did look rather out of place in the tailored black trousers and white evening shirt, although he had dispensed with the dinner jacket that completed the suit.

'Nothing,' she dismissed, not wanting to do or say anything that would dispel the harmony of the morning.

'Leonie?' he prompted reprovingly.

She shrugged narrow shoulders, wearing denims and a cream cotton top. 'I should have visited Liz and Nick this morning, but it isn't important. I can call them later.'

'There's still time——'

'I'd rather stay with you,' she said huskily.

'I have an appointment myself at twelve-thirty.' He sipped his coffee.

'Oh?' she frowned, had imagined they would spend the day together.

'Yes.' He didn't enlarge on the subject. 'And I have to go home and change first,' he added ruefully. 'So you can still go to Liz's if you want to.'

It seemed that she might as well when he put it like that. But she couldn't help feeling curious about who he was seeing at twelve-thirty; he wasn't exactly keeping it a secret, but he didn't seem anxious to talk about it either.

'Well, if you're sure,' she frowned.

'I am,' he nodded. 'I'll come back here around six, okay?'

'Okay.'

His sharp gaze narrowed on her. 'What's the matter?'

'Nothing,' she dismissed with a bright smile.

Adam smiled. 'I know you well enough to realise when you're sulking——'

'I do not *sulk*!' she claimed indignantly.

'Yes, you do,' he chuckled. 'Your bottom lip pouts—like that,' he touched the passion-swollen redness with the top of his thumb, 'and your eyes get stormy.' He looked into the glittering green depths. 'Like that. Yes, you're definitely sulking. What is it, Leonie?' he prompted softly.

She shrugged. 'I thought we were going to spend the day together, that's all,' she admitted moodily.

Pleasure glowed in his eyes. 'Tomorrow we won't even get out of bed,' he promised. 'But today we have our courtesy visits to make, you to Liz and Nick's, I to a business meeting.'

'On a Saturday?'

'Sometimes it's the only time that's convenient. But if you would rather I didn't go . . .?'

'Oh no,' she denied instantly, not wanting him to think she was acting shrewish, as he had once claimed a wife's possessiveness could be. 'I'll cook us dinner this evening.' That way they could spend more time alone together.

'It's about time *you* cooked me a meal.' He mocked the fact that he was the one who had once again done the cooking.

'You never used to like my cooking,' she reminded softly.

'That isn't true,' he sobered. 'You used to get yourself in such a state about it if something went wrong that I thought you would prefer to eat with my father. I couldn't have given a damn if some of the food was a bit burnt around the edges!'

'It was usually burnt all over,' she grimaced.

'Didn't you know that I didn't give a damn if it was charcoaled?' he rasped. 'I didn't even notice what I was eating, I was too busy looking at my wife!'

'Oh, Adam,' she choked. 'Tonight I'll cook you something really special,' she promised. 'It's just that I've been too exhausted the rest of the week to be able to crawl from my bed, let alone cook you dinner in the evenings,' she teased lightly.

'Tomorrow you won't have to bother,' he promised, standing up to pull on his jacket.

'I may starve,' she warned.

'You won't.' His gaze held hers before he bent to kiss her.

'Man—or woman—cannot live on love alone,' she told him.

'We can try,' he murmured throatily, shaking his head as he moved away from her. 'If I don't leave now, *I* may not have the strength to get out the door.' He gave her a quick kiss on the lips. 'I'll see you this evening, darling.'

Her flat seemed very empty once he had left, not even Harvey's presence as he jealously followed her from room to room helping to dispel the feeling of loneliness as he usually did. Accustomed to sleeping on the bottom of her bed at night he wasn't too happy about being relegated to the sofa in the lounge this last week.

To Leonie's dismay Nick was out when she arrived for her visit, feeling awkward at being alone with Liz, something she had pointedly avoided since the day she had seen her sister in Adam's arms. But she could hardly leave again just because her brother-in-law was out.

But she didn't know what to talk about to Liz, had felt uncomfortable with her sister since knowing she and Adam had been lovers. Luckily feeding Emma and putting her upstairs for her nap filled the first half an hour, although without the distraction of the baby Leonie felt even more awkward.

'That's a lovely ring.' Liz reached her hand across the kitchen table as they sat in there drinking coffee together, admiring the diamond-studded ring on Leonie's slender hand. 'It's new, isn't it?' she looked up enquiringly.

Leonie put the offending hand out of sight under the table. 'Yes, it's new,' she mumbled, wondering why on earth she hadn't thought to take it off before visiting her sister.

'It looks expensive,' Liz sipped her coffee.

'I—It probably is,' she acknowledged awkwardly.

Her sister's eyes widened. 'It was a gift?'

'Yes,' she admitted reluctantly.

'Well don't be so secretive, Leonie,' Liz laughed reprovingly. 'Who's the man?'

She shrugged. 'No one important.' She instantly felt disloyal for dismissing Adam in that way. 'That isn't true,' she said quietly, her head going back proudly. 'Adam gave me the ring.'

'You're back together?'

She wished she could tell more from her

sister's expression how she felt about the idea, but Liz was giving nothing away, her expression guarded. 'In a way,' she finally answered.

Liz frowned at the evasion. 'What does that mean?'

She moistened suddenly dry lips. 'We're together, but not *back* together if you know what I mean.'

'No, I don't,' Liz looked puzzled.

'Our marriage was a failure, being with Adam now is nothing like that.'

'But you are—together?' Liz persisted.

She drew in a deep breath, not wanting to hurt her sister as Liz had hurt her in the past, their roles somehow reversed now. 'Yes,' she confirmed abruptly.

Liz let out a long sigh of relief. 'You don't know how happy that makes me,' she said shakily.

Leonie frowned. 'Happy?' It was the last thing she had expected her sister to feel about her reconciliation with Adam. 'You realise I know of your involvement with Adam before we were married?'

'Yes,' Liz nodded. 'I always felt that it was partly that involvement that parted you and Adam.'

Partly! It was her sister's involvement with *her* husband that had ended the marriage!

'I'm so glad Adam has at last explained to you what really happened between us,' Liz said happily. 'He has, hasn't he?' she hesitated.

'I know about it,' she acknowledged curtly.

'Adam always said that knowing wouldn't make things any better between you, that you had other problems that couldn't be worked out.'

'Yes.' But they had worked those problems out now! So what was the secret behind Liz's involvement with Adam, how did her sister think Adam could ever condone their actions so that she could forgive them both?

'I couldn't imagine what they were,' Liz frowned. 'And it wasn't my business to ask. I know how kind Adam is, I couldn't think what could be wrong between you, but Adam insisted that knowing the truth about the two of us would serve no purpose, that things were over between you. I'm so glad he was wrong!'

Leonie had no intention of correcting her sister's assumption that Adam had explained everything to her, knowing that Liz was going to reveal it without realising she was doing so.

'Adam so deserves to find happiness, he was so kind to me. When Nick went through what I can only assume to be his mid-life crisis a couple of years back and had an affair with a young girl at his office I felt so—so humiliated, so—so unfeminine, so unattractive, that I just wanted to crawl away and hide.'

Nick's affair? This was getting more complicated than she had imagined! She made a non-committal noise in her throat, encouraging Liz to continue.

'Adam made me feel like a woman again, a beautiful woman,' she recalled emotionally.

'Wasn't going to bed with you a little drastic?' Harshness entered Leonie's voice. 'Offering you a shoulder to cry on might have been just as effective—and less complicated.'

'*I* was the one who instigated our lovemaking,' Liz admitted heavily. 'It could have been any man, I just wanted to prove, to myself, that I was still an attractive woman.'

'If it could have been any man why did you have to choose *Adam*!'

She shrugged. 'Because I knew he was too kind to rebuff me. He knew I couldn't take any more rejection, acted as if it were what he wanted too, but afterwards we both knew it was a mistake. I still wanted Nick, not Adam, and the only way to get Nick back was to fight for him, to show him how important he was to me, not have an affair myself.'

'You obviously won,' Leonie said dully, the involvement she had believed to be an affair not an affair at all. Then why hadn't Adam told her that! Because he didn't care enough about her to explain himself . . .? Somehow his actions now disproved that.

'Yes, although it wasn't easy,' Liz smiled tremulously. 'Knowing Nick had slept with another woman, was perhaps comparing me to her, was a difficult hurdle to cross.'

Leonie didn't need to be told about that torment, she had *lived* it!

'And I knew I could never tell Nick about the night I spent with Adam,' she sighed heavily.

'But he had an affair himself!'

'Yes,' Liz nodded. 'But to be told that I had spitefully slept with another man because he had betrayed me was something I knew he could never accept. Besides, Adam was married to you by this time.'

'All the more reason for the truth to come out, I would have thought!'

'And what was the truth?' Liz reasoned. 'That Adam had loaned me his body for a night so that I might feel a whole woman again? Why ruin five lives just to ease our consciences?' she shook her head.

Because Leonie had a feeling it was that guilty conscience that had ruined her own marriage,

Adam's guilty conscience that he had once gone to bed with her sister. 'You were never in love with Adam?' she probed.

'No,' Liz denied instantly. 'Or he with me. He took one look at my baby sister and fell like a ton of bricks,' she added ruefully. 'I'd always teased him that it would happen that way for him, and he had always scorned the idea. When I came back from my reconciliation holiday with Nick to be told the two of you were getting married I didn't know whether to be ecstatic for your sake or nervous of losing the happiness I had just refound with Nick.'

'*That's* why you were less than enthusiastic by our news.' She had thought it was for completely a different reason!

'Yes,' Liz grimaced. 'I should have known Adam would never break his promise to me. But when I knew I was expecting a baby it somehow seemed important that he reassure me Nick would never find out about that night I had spent with him. Adam assured me no one would hear of it from him.'

And she had walked in on that scene, had misread it completely. Could Liz be right, *had* Adam fallen deeply on love with her the first time they met? And if he had, did he love her still?

'He told me your marriage wasn't working out,' Liz looked sad. 'That he expected you to leave him any day. I couldn't understand it, the two of you had seemed so much in love. But Adam assured me my behaviour with him had done nothing to cause the rift.'

And he had lied. He had risked their happiness for the sake of her sister's! She knew it as surely as if Adam had told her so himself. But he never would. He *was* kind, had never deliberately hurt anyone in his life. Not even her, she realised now. Two years ago she had been too immature, too starry-eyed, to accept and understand what had prompted him to make love to Liz, a new maturity gave her the insight to realise he had been helping a friend cope with her pain. He couldn't have had any idea at the time that he would fall in love with Liz's young sister, that he would want to marry her even though he knew that, like Nick, she couldn't have taken the truth about him and Liz. When she had found out about the two of them she had acted predictably, hadn't cared that what she had thought to be their affair had taken place before their marriage, that Adam had been completely faithful to her since that time. All she had seen were the black and white facts; Adam had slept with her married sister!

But had he really sacrificed their happiness for Liz's sake? Eight months after their separation they were back together, happier than ever.

And suddenly she needed to tell him she understood the past, that she wanted a future with him, a permanent future, with a wedding ring. There would be no more evasions of the truth between them, she wanted to be his wife, and she intended telling him so.

'He was right.' She stood up to kiss her sister warmly on the cheek, seeing Liz's surprise to the first instantaneous show of affection she had given her in a long time. 'We had other, much more serious problems.' Such as not talking to each other about what was bothering them. She intended remedying that straight away!

'I'm so glad you're back together again,' Liz hugged her.

'So am I.' She gave a glowing smile.

'I hope it works out this time. Adam loves you very much, you know.'

Yes, she finally believed that he did. He had been brought up in a household where love was never expressed openly, found it difficult to show love himself as a consequence, even when he knew it was pushing them apart. While they had been separated he had set about changing a lifetime of emotional repression, of sharing his feelings and fears with another person. The despair he had shown last night when they got back from his father's because he thought he had failed was evidence of that.

It also made her question the affair between them now. What was it he had said the first night they had slept together since their separation, that the affair had been her suggestion? He believed it was what *she* wanted!

It was time they sorted out this mess, to tell each other of their true feelings, for the past and for each other. If an affair were really all he wanted then she would accept that, but she had a feeling they were both living a lie. God, she could hardly wait to see him again!

CHAPTER NINE

THE telephone was ringing as she entered the flat, and after falling over an awkwardly reclining Harvey as he lay in front of the doorway, she ran to pick up the receiver, sure it was Adam.

'Leonie?'

Her hand instantly tensed about the green-coloured receiver. 'Yes?' she sounded breathless.

'You sound as if you've just got out of bed.'

'I——'

'Is he still there, Leonie?' that taunting voice interrupted. 'Is your lover still in your bed?'

This couldn't be happening. This was Saturday, he never called on a Saturday!

'Leonie?' The man's voice had sharpened angrily as she remained silent.

'Yes! Yes, I'm still here,' she gasped, realising that something else was different about this call too. He was using her name! He had never done that before either

'Did your lover stay the night, Leonie?' he rasped.

'Look——'

'Is Faulkner still there with you?' he cut in furiously.

Leonie felt numb with shock. Not only did this man know *her* name, he also knew about Adam! She felt an uncomfortable tingling sensation down her neck, as if someone were watching her. How else could this man know so much about her and Adam? God, it made her feel sick—and frightened. It was a long time since she had felt physically threatened by this man's calls, but today was different, *he* was different, not talking about the sick things he would like to do to her as he usually did, sounding menacing as he questioned her.

'I said is he there, Leonie?' he grated again.

'I—er—Yes, he's here,' she invented desperately, suddenly feeling trapped, out of control of her own life.

'Liar!' the man gave an unpleasant laugh. 'He isn't there, is he, Leonie?'

'Of course he is,' she insisted. 'He—He's in the shower.'

'I saw him leave, Leonie.'

'You saw——!' She swallowed hard. 'Where are you?' Her voice rose shrilly.

'Wouldn't you like to know,' he taunted. 'Get rid of him from your life, Leonie. You're mine, do you understand? he growled. 'I stood by while that wimp Stevenson tried his luck with you, but Faulkner is a different matter. Get rid of him, Leonie, you won't like what will happen to him if you don't.'

'Wh-what?'

'I could love you much better than he ever could,' he told her softly.

'What will you do to Adam?' she repeated shrilly.

There was silence on the other end of the telephone, but she knew he was there, knew he hadn't rung off, could sense him there even though he didn't say a word.

'You're in love with him!' The man suddenly exploded.

'No!' she denied desperately. 'I just——'

'Yes, you are, damn you,' he rasped harshly. 'And I can't allow that, Leonie. I would have given you everything, everything,' his voice rose. 'But you weren't interested, were you? Oh no, you chose Stevenson over me, and now you're in love with Faulkner. You shouldn't have done that, Leonie. I'll never allow another man to have you. Never!' He slammed the receiver down with such force it hurt her eardrums.

She couldn't move, daren't move, felt frozen, her breathing constricted, her hunted gaze darting about the room like a cornered animal.

She had told Adam the man never threatened, but he had threatened just now. She had told Adam she didn't know the man, and yet she obviously did for him to know so much about her. But *who*, who could it be? Every man she had ever met came crowding into her mind, a jumble of male faces that suddenly all looked menacing.

And then she dismissed the majority of them as being too ridiculous; she hadn't seen most of them for years. But that still left so many friends, acquaintances. Two men she knew she could exclude from that list, Adam and David. It couldn't be Adam, she knew that without a doubt, and the man had been so scathing about David he couldn't possibly have been talking about himself.

But there was Tony, the boy she had been seeing casually before she met and married Adam so quickly, several friends of Adam's she had come to know, the man in the upper flat, and the man in the lower one, the men she worked with, the men she had worked for. God, the list was endless, and she couldn't begin to guess which one of them could be this sick.

But she did have to get out of the flat, couldn't stay here and just wait for him to arrive on her doorstep. She had to call Adam, that was what she had to do. It was almost three now, he would be coming to see her soon, and she couldn't possibly let him walk into a trap.

She let his telephone ring and ring, but received no reply, becoming more and more agitated as she didn't. Surely he couldn't still be at his business meeting?

She had to get out of here. She could wait for Adam at his apartment, didn't care how long she had to stand outside; she wasn't staying here.

She moved about the flat picking up her bag and jacket, pushing an unsuspecting Harvey, as he lay asleep on her bed, into his travelling basket; she didn't intend returning here, would have the rest of her things, and Moby Dick, moved to Adam's apartment as soon as she could.

She was just giving one last frantic look round to make sure she had switched everything off when the doorbell rang shrilly. Her breath stopped in her throat, and for a moment she couldn't move. Dear God, what was she going to do? What *could* she do!

She thought of pretending she wasn't here, but the sudden trip she made over the coffee-table, dropping an indignantly screeching Harvey, put lie to that idea. She righted Harvey's basket before moving cautiously to the door, pressing her ear against the white-painted wood. She couldn't hear anything—but what had she expected, heavy breathing!

The doorbell rang again. 'Leonie, are you in there?' called a familiar voice. 'I heard a thump, have you hurt yourself?'

Relief flooded through her as she ripped open the door. 'Gary!' she hugged him before quickly pulling him inside. 'Thank God you're here.' She felt like crying at the sight of a friendly face after her imaginings.

'I just thought I'd drop by for a coffee while Joan does her shopping,' he dismissed in a preoccupied voice, frowning at how pale she was. '*Did* you hurt yourself?'

She shook her head. 'Only Harvey's dignity when I dropped him.'

Gary looked down at the cat in the travelling basket. 'Are you going away?'

'Just to Adam's—Adam Faulkner,' she explained with a blush, although Gary must be as aware as the rest of the staff were at Stevenson Interiors that she was seeing Adam. 'You see, I've been having these calls, nasty calls,' she grimaced. 'I think I told you about them once . . .?'

'Yes,' he nodded.

'Well, I was sure he was harmless. But then he called just now, and he never calls on a Saturday, and I——'

'Hey, calm down,' Gary chided, his smile gentle. 'Why don't you sit down, let me make you a cup of coffee, and then you can tell me all about it.'

'No, we can't stay here.' She shook her head frantically. 'You see, when he called just now he was—threatening. I'm sure he's going to come here,' she shivered.

'With me here?' Gary soothed. 'I doubt it.'

He was a dear, but with his five-foot-eight-inch frame she didn't feel confident she could depend on him if it should come to violence with the obscene telephone caller. But she couldn't say that to him without hurting his feelings.

'I really don't think we should stay here, Gary,' she tried to sound calm. 'Look, why don't you come over to Adam's with me, he's sure to be back by the time we get there.'

'He isn't at home?'

'He had to go to a meeting, and he doesn't seem to be back yet.' She was speaking quickly in her agitation. Didn't he realise how dangerous this situation was! 'Please, Gary, we have to go,' she urged desparately.

'I don't think so.'

'But he could be here any minute! He——' her voice trailed off as she watched him walk over to the door, check that it was locked before putting the key into his pocket. 'What are you doing?' she asked—but she had a dreadful feeling she already knew!

He looked at her calmly. 'Stopping you from leaving.'

She swallowed hard. 'Gary, this isn't a time to play games. He could be here soon, and——'

'He's already here.'

She had guessed that as soon as he pocketed the key—and she had actually *let* him in here! Gary was the man who called her every Friday night, who whispered obscene things he wanted to do to her. She couldn't believe this nightmare, had always believed the two of them were friends.

'Why, Gary?' she asked faintly, feeling weak with nausea that it was him that said such disgusting things to her every week, that he had done so for the last six months, while still continuing to be so friendly at work. God, she had even told him about those calls!

'Why do you think?' he scorned, his eyes narrowed unpleasantly.

'I—I don't know.' She watched him warily, but he seemed to be making no move to cross the room to where she stood poised for flight.

'Because I want you, you little fool,' he derided mockingly. 'I always did, from the moment you came in to my office with David that first morning and promptly fell over the waste-paper basket. You made me feel protective, very much the man as I helped you to your feet. You looked so delicate and defenceless, and I wanted to take care of you.' There was a smile to his lips as he recalled the morning they had met. 'That month I worked so closely with you was the most enjoyable four weeks of my life,' he added flatly.

'I enjoyed it too,' she infused enthusiasm into her voice.

His eyes hardened angrily. 'You barely noticed me!' he rasped.

'You were married——'

'Yes,' he acknowledged harshly. 'But so were you.'

'I was separated from my husband.'

'I remember. I was jealous of any man who had had you and not had the sense to hold on to you. I hated your husband,' he stated coldly. 'I wanted you, no other man could have you.'

'No other man did,' she assured him quickly.

'David——'

'We've only ever been friends, nothing more.'

'Faulkner?'

She swallowed hard, paling even more, knowing after what he had just said about her husband that she daren't tell him Adam was the man she was married to. 'Adam and I are friends too,' she dismissed lightly.

'Very good ones from the amount of nights he's spent here with you,' Gary scorned.

'How did you—Have you been watching me?' she asked dully.

'I didn't need to,' he derided. 'Your face when

you came into work every morning this week has been enough to tell me just *how* friendly you and Faulkner have become.'

'Gary, you don't understand——'

'Oh, I understand,' he sneered. 'Like all women you need a man, any man, to make love to you and tell you how beautiful you are one hundred per cent of the time!'

'It isn't like that——'

'That's what Joan said when I found out about the little affair she had been having with a doctor at the hospital,' he cut in hardly. 'I'd been working hard, just wanted to sleep when I finally fell into bed at night, but the bitch couldn't understand that. Oh no, she had to go and find herself a lover to give her what I wasn't!'

She had met Gary's wife at the Christmas dinner, had found the other woman to be shallow and flirtatious, had been surprised to learn she was a nurse, the wine she had consumed with the meal making her silly and giggly, demanding kisses from all the men in the party, her willowy beauty making them all willing to comply.

'You could have left her,' she said softly.

'She would take Timmy with her.' He looked bleak as he spoke of his young son.

'Gary, can't you see that what you—what you're doing now is wrong?' she pleaded with his common sense—if he still had any!

'I haven't done anything—yet.'

She shivered in apprehension at the threat behind that last word. 'You made those calls,' she reminded.

'Not at first,' he shook his head.

She frowned. 'What do you mean?'

'I didn't make the first couple,' he sneered. 'And I wouldn't have made any of them if you hadn't started seeing David. You were really upset when you got the first call, remember, told me all about it. But it was David you let comfort you,' he added harshly. 'David who took you in his arms and told you everything would be all right. And for a couple of weeks the calls stopped, didn't they, Leonie?' he derided.

'And then *you* began making them,' she realised dully. She hadn't noticed a change in the voice, had been too disturbed by the first few calls to notice what it even sounded like!

'Yes,' he admitted with satisfaction. 'It felt strange at first, I didn't quite know what to say. But after a while it just came naturally,' he smiled his relish.

As he became more and more emotionally disturbed! It was his mentally disturbed state that made him so unpredictable now. She didn't quite know what to do next, or what *he* was going to do either!

'You always made such a joke about asking me out, Gary,' she tried to smile, although her face felt stiff. 'I didn't realise you were serious.'

'And if you had you would have accepted, hm?' he scoffed at her attempt to placate him.

'I may have done,' she answered sharply.

'You may have done,' he repeated derisively, his gaze mocking. 'Don't lie to me, Leonie.' His eyes hardened to blue pebbles. 'Joan is always lying to me.' His hands clenched into fists at his sides. 'And I don't like it!'

She could see that, swallowing hard at the anger emanating from him. 'I'm sure she loves you, Gary,' she encouraged. 'Every marriage has its problems, I'm sure Joan regrets her lapse with the doctor.'

'She stills see him.'

'Oh.' Leonie chewed on her bottom lip.

'Once a week,' he spoke almost to himself, not seeming to see Leonie at all at that moment. 'She tells me she's working at the hospital that night, but I've checked; she's seeing him.'

'Fridays,' Leonie realised weakly.

'Yes,' he bit out, focusing on her again.

'She can't really care for him, Gary, otherwise she would have left you to go to him,' she pointed out desparately.

'He's married too,' Gary scorned. 'This way they both have the best of both worlds!'

And Gary's jealousy and pain had acted like a sickness, growing, spreading, until he latched his unwanted love on to another woman—who also turned out not to want him.

'For a while I thought about killing both of them,' he continued matter-of-factly. 'But then I met you, and realised I could have the same arrangement Joan has. You should have gone out with me, Leonie, I would have been so good to you. Now all we'll have is this one night together.'

'Wh-what do you mean?'

'Well you know who I am now,' he shrugged.

'You—you're going to leave London?'

He seemed amused by the idea. 'No,' he drawled.

Leonie felt faint as his meaning became clear to her. She couldn't believe this were really happening—it happened on television, in films, *not* in real life!

'Gary, you're making a mistake,' she told him, breathlessly. 'I—I'll forget all about this if you—if you'll just leave,' she urged desperately.

He shook his head. 'As soon as I got out the door you would call the police.'

She would too, knew she would have to. Gary was a danger to other people as well as to himself. But by the sound of it she wasn't going to get the chance to call anyone.

'It would be your word against mine,' she reasoned.

'And Faulkner's,' he grated. 'It was him who answered the last two calls, wasn't it?'

She flushed her guilt. 'Gary——'

'We've talked enough,' he snarled. 'I didn't come here to talk!'

She knew exactly what he had come here for, and the thought of it terrified her. 'Gary, can't you see this is wrong?' she pleaded. 'Do you really want to make love to a woman who doesn't love you?'

'Why not?' he scorned. 'That's what I do at home!'

'But that's Joan, Gary,' she said softly. 'Things could be different between us. We——'

'Don't try the psychological approach, Leonie,' he scoffed. 'I've seen those bad films too!'

'I've always liked you, Gary,' she insisted.

'Then you're going to get the chance to prove it, aren't you?' he taunted. 'And for God's sake shut that cat up!' he rasped as Harvey scratched frantically at the basket to be let out.

Leonie weighed up the possibility of winning a fight against Gary, instantly knowing that she wouldn't, not even with desperation on her side. Gary may be short and stocky, but muscles bulged in his arms and legs. He could overpower her in a few minutes, possibly sooner.

She moistened dry lips. 'If I let him outside he'll stop,' she suggested desperately. 'He—He's likely to keep scratching if I leave him in the basket.'

Gary's mouth twisted. 'By all means throw the damned cat out. But don't try and scream,' he warned gratingly. 'You wouldn't like the way I silenced you,' he promised.

Leonie had a feeling *he* would enjoy it immensely, her hands shaking as she carried the wicker basket over to the window, all the time measuring the distance between herself and Gary, a plan formulating in her mind. He was too close, although as Harvey clambered thankfully out of the window the empty basket in her hand gave her an idea.

'Hey, Gary,' she called, at the same time launching the basket at him, knocking him momentarily off-balance, his language voluble as she climbed outside on to the ledge that Harvey used to get to the neighbouring buildings.

Only it wasn't as easy for her to balance there as it was for Harvey, the nine-inch-wide ledge that seemed more than adequate for his wiry frame suddenly seeming too narrow for her to negotiate with any degree of safety.

'What the hell do you think you're doing?' Gary's furious face appeared at the open window, his hand reaching out to clasp her ankle.

She had seen the move coming and scuttled a short distance along the ledge, sighing her relief as she realised she was out of his reach, leaning back against the rough brickwork of the wall behind her as she swayed giddily, the ground seeming a very long way down.

'You stupid bitch,' Gary's face was contorted with fury. 'Get back in here.'

'Are you joking?' she gave a shaky laugh, her eyes still closed as she fought back feelings of faintness. 'You *have* to be joking, Gary!'

'You'll fall and break your damned neck!'

She turned to look at him, breathing heavily in her anger. 'Surprisingly enough,' sarcasm sharpened her voice, 'I would find that infinitely more preferable to being attacked by you. Isn't that strange!' she bit out contemptuously.

Some of the bravado left him as he realised she was serious, taking on the look of a man who just didn't know what to do next. 'Leonie, please come back in here,' he encouraged softly.

'No!'

'I promise not to touch you, damn it!'

'You think I believe you?' she derided harshly. 'I wouldn't trust you—Oh!' she gasped as dizziness washed over her once again.

'Are you all right?' Gary sounded desperate. 'Leonie, for God's sake get back in here.'

'I can't,' she shook her head, pushing into the wall behind her, biting her lip as she became afraid to look anywhere but straight ahead.

'I won't hurt you,' he promised vehemently.

'Don't you understand,' she grated between clenched teeth. 'I can't move!'

'What is it? Is your foot stuck somewhere? Maybe if I——'

'No!' she cried her panic as she heard him attempting to climb out on to the ledge. 'Don't come near me,' she warned desperately.

'But if you're stuck——'

'I'm not,' she shuddered. 'I—I have vertigo!' Two floors up, and she was terrified! Heights had never bothered her before, although she did have to concede that the circumstance of her being out here on a nine-inch ledge may have contributed to the fact that she now couldn't move back into the window and couldn't attempt to reach the neighbouring building either! The thought of moving at all terrified her, frozen to the spot.

'The let me help you——'

'Don't come near me,' she warned as Gary would have joined her out on the ledge. 'If you come out here I—I swear I'll jump!'

'But you can't stay there!'

'Why can't I?' she was near to hysteria.

'Leonie, you have to come in some time,' he encouraged.

'And face a raving sex-maniac?' she shook her head vehemently. 'No, thank you!'

'It was only a game——'

'Remember, Gary,' she bit out grimly, 'I watched the same bad films.'

'You would rather stay out there, possibly fall, than come back in here with me?' he sounded exasperated.

'In one word, *yes!*'

'You stupid——'

'Bitch,' she finished curtly. 'I've noticed that seems to be your favourite word for a woman who won't do things your way,' she scorned. 'No wonder Joan found herself another man!'

'You know nothing of my marriage to Joan,' he snarled.

'I know that the failure of it has involved me,' she bit out. 'And I——' she broke off as the telephone in her flat began to ring. 'It's Adam,' she breathed. 'It has to be Adam. If I don't answer that Gary, he'll know there's something wrong.'

'Why should he?' he dismissed logically. 'He'll just think you're still out.'

He was right, of course, but she had to try. 'No,' she insisted. 'He said he would call me. If I—if I don't answer he'll think something has happened to me.'

'Then come in and answer it,' Gary invited softly.

God, the phone would stop ringing in a minute, with the caller—*possibly* Adam, thinking she just wasn't at home!

'I didn't think you would,' Gary said smugly.

'You—you're insane!' She told him angrily as the telephone stopped ringing, the silence it left unnerving.

'I thought you had already concluded that,' he dismissed. 'I'll be waiting inside if you should change your mind about coming in,' he told her conversationally.

When she finally dared to turn her head it was to find him gone from the open window. 'Gary,' she called sharply. 'Gary?'

There was no answer. Was he playing a game with her, waiting for her in silence inside her flat? If he thought she was lying about the vertigo, that believing him gone, she would climb back inside, he was wrong. She really couldn't move!

'Gary,' she called again. 'Gary, please answer me.'

He had gone, she was sure of it. God, what could the time be, about three o'clock? That meant she had another three hours before Adam was due to arrive. She wasn't sure she could balance on this ledge for that amount of time. But if she couldn't, that left only one way off it, and that was down!

CHAPTER TEN

IT was amazing how traffic could pass by and not even realise there was a young woman balancing precariously on a second-floor ledge above them! It was a street that had little or no pedestrians, and the people in their cars were too engrossed in their own lives to look up and see Leonie.

One really bad moment came when Harvey decided to make his way back along the ledge, rubbing against her legs in greeting, not understanding when she wouldn't move out of his way and allow him into his home. He became quite agitated by her refusal to move, and with his usual stubbornness refused to go back the way he had come. Leonie vehemently decided that his wandering days were over if she ever got off this ledge.

And so were someone else's if she survived this! Her fury turned to Adam. If they had been living together as husband and wife instead of conducting this ridiculous affair this wouldn't have happened to her. And if an affair were all he wanted he could find some other woman to have it with, she would be his wife or nothing!

What time was it now? She felt as if she had been in this ledge for hours. Surely it must be almost six by now? She was too afraid to even raise her arm and look at her wrist watch! But as if in answer to her question she could hear a clock striking the hour, one, two, three, four, five—she waited for the sixth bell—nothing happened. Five o'clock, it was only five o'clock!

She wasn't sure she could stay balanced here for another hour.

Suddenly she heard a noise in the flat behind her, freezing, almost afraid to breathe. Gary had been playing a game with her all along, he was still in there waiting for her.

'What the——! What the hell are you doing out there?'

She turned sharply at the sound of that voice, regaining her balance with effort, feeling shaken as the world swayed up to meet her.

'Be careful, damn it,' Adam rasped. 'You almost fell then.'

'You don't say,' she scorned shakily. 'You aren't supposed to be here for another hour,' she accused.

'What?' he frowned his disbelief, in the act of climbing out of the window.

'It's only five, you said you wouldn't be here until six,' she stupidly reminded. Had she lost her mind? What did it matter what the time was, he was *here*!

'Well if that's the way you feel about being rescued,' he ground out, climbing back down. 'I'll come back in an hour!'

'Adam!' she screamed her fear that he would really leave her alone again out here. 'Oh, Adam,' her voice broke on a sob. 'Don't leave me. Please, don't leave me!'

'It's all right, Leonie,' he soothed, sounded closer now. 'I'll be with you in a second, and we'll go in together.'

'We might fall,' she cried.

'We won't,' he told her calmly.

She felt his fingers on her arm, clasping her hand now as she clung to him, feeling his strength flow into her. 'Adam,' she sobbed, still not turning. 'Oh, Adam!' Sobs wracked her body.

'That bastard!' he grated feelingly. 'He didn't tell us he had left you out here.'

'Gary? You mean Gary?' she prompted. 'Did you get him?'

'We got him——'

'How?' she breathed raggedly. 'I had no idea it was him, I even invited him in thinking he could help protect me after the man called again. Oh God, Adam, I've never been so scared in my life!'

'I can imagine,' he cut in harshly. 'And once I have you safely inside you can tell me exactly what happened here this afternoon. But right now I have to get you inside.'

'I can't move,' she shook her head.

'Of course you can,' he soothed.

'No.'

'Leonie, you will move,' he instructed coldly. 'Do you understand me?'

Her bottom lip quivered emotionally. 'There's no need to shout at me.'

'I'll shout at you a lot more than this if you don't soon get yourself moving,' he rasped. 'It's damned windy out here.'

She turned to glare at him. 'Do you think I don't know that?' she snapped furiously. It may have been a warm day but the wind had started to blow about an hour ago, increasing in intensity the last ten minutes or so. 'I've been stuck out here for hours,' she told him angrily. 'I've probably caught pneumonia.'

'You probably deserve to,' Adam said callously. 'No one in their right mind balances on a ledge like this one for hours!'

'That's just the sort of remark I should have expected from you,' Leonie eased along the ledge behind him, glaring at him as she allowed him to catch her under the arms and lift her inside. 'You don't—Oh!' Her legs gave way as she realised where she was, Adam catching her deftly before she fell.

'It's all right now, Leonie,' he soothed, smoothing her hair as he held her. 'I have you safe.'

She shuddered as she realised she was at last off the ledge. 'You deliberately made me so angry that I didn't know what I was doing,' she accused between her tears.

'As long as it worked I don't care what I did,' Adam was trembling. 'I've never been so scared in my life as when I came in and saw your open window and realised you were out there.'

'I tried to use psychology with Gary,' she remembered with a quiver. 'It didn't work.'

Adam's arms tightened about her. 'He's safely in police custody now.'

'When? How?' she frowned.

Adam led her over to the sofa, sitting her down before pouring her a drink, standing over her while she drank the brandy. He took the empty glass from her fingers, sitting down beside her to pull her into his arms. 'Did he hurt you?' he asked gruffly.

She knew exactly what he was asking. 'No,' she assured him softly. 'Now tell me how you knew it was Gary? Is he really in police custody?'

'Yes,' Adam sighed his relief. 'The police arrested him when he arrived home two hours ago. I was with them, and when they knocked on the door he just crumpled. He told them everything when they took him to the police station. But he didn't tell us he had left you perched out on a ledge,' he frowned his anger.

'It's over now, Adam,' she touched his thigh.

'Thank God,' he breathed. 'Having you followed told us nothing——'

'You're still looking for the grounds to divorce me?' she pulled away from him, her expression pained. 'I hope your detective told you that you're my only visitor! Can you be named in your own divorce?' her voice rose shrilly.

'Leonie——'

'I don't think you can, Adam.' She stood up, moving away from him. 'So we had better stop our affair so that I can find a lover you *can* name. Maybe I should have just let Gary do what he wanted to do after all,' her voice broke. 'Then you could have named *him*.'

'Leonie——'

'Silly me thought that climbing out on that ledge was better than being violated,' she said self-derisively. 'If I had just let him go ahead I could have saved us all a lot of trouble. You really should have told me——'

'Leonie, if you say one more word, *one more word*,' he repeated icily, 'I'll put you over my knee and beat the living daylights out of you.'

'I wonder why I never realised how gallant you are.' Her eyes flashed. 'I've just escaped attack by a sex-maniac by balancing on a ledge for more than two hours and you intend to beat me!' She gave a choked laugh. 'And to think I'd decided, if I ever got off that ledge, that I was going to talk to you about what went wrong in our marriage. It looks as if I needn't bother. Although you'll have to provide the evidence for the divorce, the thought of taking a lover nauseates me!'

'Leonie . . .?'

'Although I know it won't be Liz,' she looked at him accusingly. 'All this time you've let me believe the two of you were lovers, and you were lying! Liz told me the truth today.'

'If she said we didn't sleep together then *she* lied,' he bit out.

'I know you went to bed together, before we were married. I also know now that it only happened the once. And Liz told me it wasn't done out of love on either of your parts.'

'I still slept with your sister,' Adam told her flatly.

'You helped a friend when she needed it,' Leonie amended abruptly.

'By making love to her!'

'Do you want a whip to beat yourself with?' Leonie scorned. 'What you did wasn't wrong.' She shook her head. 'Misguided, perhaps, but not wrong. I've believed all this time that you were in love with Liz.'

'I never was,' he denied softly.

'I know that now!'

He sighed. 'The night I made love to her should never have happened, I knew that. Never more so than when I met you,' he rasped. 'I think I fell in love with you on sight, and yet my guilt about Liz stood between us.'

Leonie moistened suddenly dry lips. 'You *did* love me?'

'Yes.'

'You never once told me that.'

He frowned. 'Didn't I? But surely it must have been obvious,' he dismissed impatiently.

His emotionally repressed childhood again! 'I ought to hit you over the head with something!' she snapped.

'Why?' he looked dazed.

'Because I loved you from the moment we met too,' she glared at him. 'But my inexperience, my clumsiness, my naiveté, seemed to be driving you away!'

He shook his head. 'Your inexperience enchanted me, your clumsiness amused me, and your naiveté enthralled me!'

'Then why couldn't you bear to be near me!'

'Because of Liz,' he admitted heavily. 'I was terrified that one day you would find out about that night I spent with her, and that you would hate me for it.'

'Why couldn't you have just told me about it before we were married?' she sighed.

'I'd promised Liz. Although, believe me, if I had thought you could accept what happened I would have broken that promise,' he added grimly.

'You thought me too immature to understand,' she nodded. 'I believe I was,' she acknowledged heavily. 'But I understand now.'

His eyes were narrowed. 'You do?'

She gave a ragged sigh. 'Liz told me about Nick, his affair, how you tried to help her through it.'

His mouth twisted. 'I'd like to say it was all a question of helping Liz, but it wasn't. I couldn't have made love to her if I hadn't desired her.'

'I understand that too,' Leonie nodded. 'But you didn't love her, or want to marry her.'

'God, no.'

'I thought you did, you see. That day I saw you together at your office, I thought you had married me because Liz had decided on a reconciliation with Nick rather than marriage to you, that you both now realised your mistake, but that it was too late for you to be together, because Liz was expecting Nick's child. I believed I was a

very second, second-best,' she admitted miserably.

'You were never that.' Adam shook his head.
'The night I met you I was driving past Liz's
house and saw the lights on. My first thought was
that it was burglars. Then you opened the door!'
He gave a tight smile. 'I fell, God how I fell. And
yet Liz stood between us. I rushed you into
marriage before I could talk myself out of it,
knew I had to have you even if I lost you later.
But our problems began straight away.'

'I was a failure in bed,' she sighed.

'You weren't a failure,' he rasped angrily. 'You
were a very young girl with a problem you were
too embarrassed to even talk about. And by the
time we had dispensed with that problem your
barriers were well and truly up, you were self-
conscious about lovemaking to the point where
you didn't even like me to touch you. You can't
know what that did to me! But my own guilt
about Liz made it impossible for me to reach you.
I knew I was driving you further and further
away from me, but I didn't know how to stop it.
When you decided to end the marriage I knew I
couldn't stop you.'

'And now?'

'Now I'm giving you what you want,' he
shrugged. 'An affair.'

'While you divorce me,' she said bitterly.

'For God's sake, I wasn't having you followed
so that I can divorce you!' Adam grated. 'I was
protecting you, because of those telephone
calls.'

'A lot of good that did me,' she scorned, not
believing him.

Adam flushed at the rebuke. 'There was a flaw
in the plan. On Saturdays I met with the

detective to get his report. We met at twelve-thirty today for lunch.'

'So that was who you were meeting?' she realised.

'Yes,' he bit out. 'And while he was telling me that he had followed through investigations into the two men that live here, into the people I work with, and the people you work with, coming up with Gary Kingsfield as the caller, *he* was here threatening you! No one was here watching you, damn it,' he admitted tersely.

Leonie could see the humour in the situation now that she knew Adam wasn't trying to divorce her. 'That was the flaw?' she couldn't hold back her smile any longer.

'It isn't funny,' Adam growled. 'He could have—could have——'

'But he didn't,' she soothed. 'And unless I'm mistaken, he's done me a favour.'

'I can't think what,' Adam scowled.

She walked into her bedroom without answering, coming back seconds later, opening her hand in front of him to reveal a thin gold band, and another ring with the stone of an emerald. 'Will you marry me?' she invited softly.

His startled gaze was raised to hers. 'The affair . . .?'

'Is not what I want,' she said with emphasis. 'I only said that in the heat of the moment, because I was hurt. I'll grant you the last couple of weeks have been exciting, that first night, the afternoon at the hotel, the rose every day. But can't we still have that and be married?'

Adam looked confused. 'I don't understand.'

'Do you still love me?'

'Yes,' came his emphatic answer.

She felt the glow begin inside her. 'And is an

affair really all you want?'

He flushed. 'I thought after an appropriate time, when you'd got used to my being around all the time, that I would ask you to be my wife again.'

That's what she had thought, had finally come to know the workings of her husband's devious mind. 'I want to be your wife now,' she told him softly. 'And I want you to be my husband.'

'Are you sure?'

'As sure as I was when you first asked me to marry you,' she smiled. 'We've made mistakes, Adam, terrible, destructive mistakes, but we still have so much, still love each other so much. Don't you agree?' she looked at him anxiously.

'Gary Kingsfield will never hurt you again, you know. He should go to prison for some time once the police know how he threatened you today.'

'I don't care about Gary,' she dismissed impatiently. 'I'm talking about us. *Will* you marry me?'

'Give yourself time to get over the shock of this afternoon——'

'That does it!' she glared at him, pushing the two rings on to her finger next to the eternity ring herself. 'Now we are officially married again,' she told him crossly. 'And you will be a good, and always *truthful*, husband,' she warned.

He raised dark brows. 'I will?'

'You will,' she told him firmly. 'I'll continue to work, we'll lunch together when we can, you'll come home to me at five-thirty every evening, and we'll live together at your apartment. Your new one, I mean. I don't think we would be welcome at your father's again,' she grimaced.

'He called this afternoon and invited us over for dinner next week,' Adam put in softly.

Leonie became still. 'Did you accept?'

'I thought I'd ask you first——'

He was learning, this arrogant husband of hers! 'Then accept,' she instructed. 'I hadn't finished with the outline of our future,' she reproved sternly.

'Sorry,' he said, but there was a devilish glint in his eyes.

'Apology accepted,' she said primly. 'Now I will decorate your apartment as you once suggested I should, and one of those rooms will be a nursery——'

'Children,' he said softly. 'Are we going to have children?'

'Three,' she nodded.

'Why three?' he frowned at the odd number.

'Why not?' she frowned.

Adam shrugged. 'Why not? And when do you plan to have the first of these offspring?'

'Well I thought I needed a bit more practise at the basics first,' she told him thoughtfully.

'Believe me,' he drawled, 'you don't need any more practise.'

She smiled. 'But it might be fun, don't you think?'

'I'm sure it will,' he nodded, taking her into his arms. 'Oh, Leonie, I do love you,' he groaned. 'I'm sorry I was such an idiot when we were together last time.'

'And I'm sorry I was so stupid and left you,' she sighed.

'I'm not,' he shook his head. 'We needed the separation,' he explained at her frown. 'Otherwise we might never have realised how much we love each other.'

She rested her head against his chest as they

held each other silently for a very long time, each cherishing the fact that they had at last managed to find happiness together.

'Oh, Adam,' Leonie greeted him at the door, her face glowing. 'It's triplets!'

The briefcase slipped out of his hand, his face paling. 'Are you sure?'

'Of course I'm sure,' she said impatiently, pulling him into the house they had shared with his father for the last four months, since Leonie had become pregnant and Charles Faulkner had humbly asked them to. 'I've seen them.'

Adam swallowed hard. 'You have?'

'Yes,' she laughed exultantly. 'Your father is delighted.'

'He is?'

'I must say, you seem less than pleased,' she told him crossly.

He looked dazed. 'I just never thought—One seemed enough to start with,' he finished lamely.

'One?' she frowned. 'I don't think that's very usual, they usually come in four or fives.'

Adam frowned. 'Leonie, what are you talking about?' he sounded puzzled.

'Suki has had her kittens,' she sighed her impatience with him. 'Harvey is proudly sitting next to the basket, as if he did it all himself, and your father gave a cigar to Chambers.' She giggled as she remembered the look on the butler's face when Charles Faulkner pushed the cigar in his breast pocket.

'Dad is excited about his prize Siamese giving birth to Harvey's kittens?' Adam sounded disbelieving.

She nodded. 'He says he's going to keep one of them,' she announced triumphantly. 'Adam,' she frowned. 'Just what did you think I was talking about when you came in?'

He looked down at her slightly rounded stomach. 'Well . . .'

'Adam!' she gave a shocked laugh. 'I've had a scan, there's only one in there.'

He took her into his arms. 'One can never tell with you,' he nuzzled into her hair. 'That one came as a complete surprise.'

'I think we practised too much,' she mocked.

'What shall we call it now?' he said as he led her up the stairs to their bedroom.

'Well, we can't allow all that expertise to go to waste,' she teased as she began to undress him.

'No,' he agreed as he undressed her.

'So we'll just say we're practising for the next one,' she murmured as they sank down on the bed together.

'By the time we're ninety we should be perfect,' Adam groaned.

Leonie giggled. 'We're perfect now, but so what . . .'

Everything was perfect, their love for each other, the fact that Charles Faulkner seemed to have accepted her as a member of his family since she was carrying his grandchild.

'By the way,' she caressed his chest. 'I've booked Mr and Mrs Smith a room at The Savoy tomorrow afternoon.'

Adam gave a throaty chuckle. 'I think we're going to have to stop being afternoon lovers soon.' He looked down at her with tender eyes, one hand lightly cupping her rounded stomach. 'As it is our baby was conceived in a hotel room.'

'I remember,' she smiled. 'I remember every minute we spend together.'

'So do I,' he told her gruffly. 'So do I—and I thank God for all of them! I'm so proud to have you for my wife, darling.'

And his pride and love for her were all that mattered.

Next month's Romances

Each month, you can choose from a world of variety in romance with Mills & Boon. These are the new titles to look out for next month.

TEMPESTUOUS REUNION Lynne Graham

A CURE FOR LOVE Penny Jordan

UNDERCOVER AFFAIR Lilian Peake

GHOST OF THE PAST Sally Wentworth

ISTANBUL AFFAIR Joanna Mansell

ROARKE'S KINGDOM Sandra Marton

WHEN LOVE RETURNS Vanessa Grant

DANGEROUS INFATUATION Stephanie Howard

LETHAL ATTRACTION Rebecca King

STORMY RELATIONSHIP Margaret Mayo

HONG KONG HONEYMOON Lee Wilkinson

CONTRACT TO LOVE Kate Proctor

WINTER DESTINY Grace Green

AFRICAN ASSIGNMENT Carol Gregor

THE CHALK LINE Kate Walker

STARSIGN

HUNTED HEART Kristy McCallum

Available from Boots, Martins, John Menzies, W.H. Smith and other paperback stockists.

Also available from Mills and Boon Reader Service, P.O. Box 236, Thornton Road, Croydon, Surrey CR9 3RU.